IMPERFECTION

RAY CLARK

IMPERFECTION

urbanepublications.com

First published in Great Britain in 2017
by Urbane Publications Ltd
Suite 3, Brown Europe House, 33/34 Gleaming Wood Drive,
Chatham, Kent ME5 8RZ
Copyright © Ray Clark, 2017

A CIP catalogue record for this book is available
from the British Library.

ISBN 978-1-911331-24-7
MOBI 978-1-911331-26-1
EPUB 978-1-911331-25-4

Design and Typeset by Michelle Morgan

Cover by Michelle Morgan

Printed and bound by CPI Group (UK) Ltd, Croydon, CR0 4YY

urbanepublications.com

Imperfection.

1. Being imperfect.

2. A fault, a blemish.

IMPERFECTION

CHAPTER 1

Man, by the very fact of being man,
by possessing consciousness, is, in
comparison with the ass or the crab,
a diseased animal. Consciousness is
a disease.

[The Tragic Sense Of Life.]
Unamuno, Miguel de (1864 - 1937)

Detective Inspector Stewart Gardener ran across New Briggate before mounting the steps leading to the Grand Theatre two at a time. At the top he banged on the glass doors with his right hand whilst displaying his warrant card with his left.

They were quickly opened by a man as tall and gangly as a stork whose eyes were so intense that Gardener thought he was staring into a double-barrelled shotgun.

"D I Gardener..."

"Good grief, that was quick! I only rang a few minutes ago." The man extended his neck past the entrance and asked where Gardener's car was.

Gardener glanced behind him. Two constables pulled up and parked in the loading bay. The town centre was pretty quiet: too late for shoppers, too early for the club crowd, and the theatre-goers were already inside.

Gardener waved them up the steps and all three men entered the building. "Can you close and lock the door, please?" The SIO ordered the man holding it. "And then tell me who you are?"

"Paul Price, theatre manager. Where are the others?"

"On their way..." He glanced around the foyer. Members of staff huddled together: some on the ground floor – others on the stairs leading to the circles, all with desperate expressions. The whispering stopped when he entered. All eyes turned toward him.

Gardener addressed the young constables, pointing to one of them. "I'd like you to stay here and guard the entrance." To the other, he said: "You walk all way around the outside of the building, take a note of all the exits, including the windows."

"How did you get here so quickly?" asked Price.

The manager had a habit of interrupting Gardener, something he didn't appreciate. He was annoyed enough already.

"Let's stick to what's important, Mr. Price. I need to see the crime scene. It has to be secured and I can't do that standing here."

Price turned tail and did as he was told, but his expression told Gardener that he was used to giving orders, not taking them.

Gardener was escorted down a long narrow corridor with cream coloured walls that smelled of disinfectant and polish. On his right were the dressing rooms; each door was closed. On his left, a notice board contained information of performance times, future productions, safety regulations and very probably everything else anyone needed to know. To the right of the board was a set of double wooden doors leading to the stage. Behind them, Gardener could hear the frenzy of panicked voices.

As he entered he was greeted with a mixture of smells: antique leather; make up, sweat. On his left was a man with a pale complexion standing next to a mixing desk. From his right a powerful breeze blew into his face. The huge roller shutter door at the back of the building was open. He wasn't pleased.

"Close that," Gardener told Price.

He then surveyed the scene before him: the safety curtain had been lowered. Stage left was an old two-seater leather settee with a narrow rug placed in front of it. On top of the table next to it was a decanter of wine with glasses. Two small tables elsewhere on the stage had brassware and candlesticks, all of which had been neatly coated with cobweb spray.

He glanced upwards. The backdrop was an oak panelled library, displaying shelves crammed with a selection of leather-bound, dusty tomes. Hung at strategic intervals, posters advertised films in which tonight's guest actor, Leonard White, had had starring roles. A log-effect fire created a comforting ambience.

The whole thing reminded him of the old Universal horror films of Boris Karloff and Bela Lugosi.

Especially the corpse at the end of a rope.

CHAPTER 2

"Has anyone touched the body so far?" Gardener asked Price.

"No."

"So no one's checked to see if he's dead?"

"Looks pretty dead to me," said Price.

Gardener had to agree with him. "How long has he been there?"

Price checked his watch. "About fifteen minutes."

Gardener removed his shoes, left them by the stage doors. From an inside pocket he produced a pair of gloves and paper shoes. Slipping them on he walked towards the body. He checked for a pulse. There wasn't one. The corpse was dressed in a black evening suit, white shirt and a black bow tie: he also wore a black waistcoat. His complexion was ghostly white: anaemic; not that he expected a dead body to appear as a picture of health.

Glancing beyond the body, Gardener noticed a scenery board with an open door frame: two more people had arrived. Staring upwards he peered into the recess. He saw the ceiling, the rafters, a beam with the rope attached – but no people. He glanced over at the roller shutter door that had now been closed by Paul Price. He doubted very much the killer was still on the premises.

IMPERFECTION

He scrutinised the whole area before shouting: "I want everyone to stay exactly where they are. Do not wander around and do not come on to the stage."

He needed Scenes of Crime as quickly as possible.

Walking back to meet Price he produced his mobile and called Steve Fenton, the Crime Scene Manager, explaining that he wanted him to run an ESLA.

Price piped up. "Excuse me, this is my theatre. What's an ESLA?"

Gardener faced him. "You're wrong, Mr. Price. It's a crime scene, so now it's my theatre. And you wouldn't understand."

"Don't patronise me. I do watch the crime shows on the TV."

Gardener smiled. "Very well: ESLA is the Electro Static Lifting Apparatus. It looks like a sheet of tin foil. Once we've rolled it over the stage we'll attach wires to either end where a machine will then pass a charge through it. That will lift all the dust exactly as it's laid out on the floor. We can then take it away for examination, which will give us very precise details of foot marks, which can then be compared against any suspect's shoes we might recover at a later date."

Price glanced at his own feet and then to Gardener.

Judging by his expression, Gardener thought the theatre manager's heart had stopped. "Well, I've never seen that on Midsommer."

"My point exactly," replied Gardener. "Now can we get back to business? What happened?"

"When?"

The SIO wasn't sure whether or not his temper was shorter than usual or if everyone he'd met so far was stupid.

"Can you take me through what happened from the beginning of the show?"

"Oh," replied Price. "Well, not much. The place was full, the lights dimmed and then a voice came over the PA system..."

"Live? Or recorded?" interrupted Gardener.

"Does it matter?"

"Live or recorded," he repeated.

"I'm really not sure. I suppose it sounded live now I come to think of it."

"Did you recognise the voice?"

"No, but it could have been any one of my staff."

"And it might not have been. Was it in the script?"

"I never saw the script. I have no idea what was planned."

"Was the show being recorded?"

"No."

"Where were *you* when it happened?" asked Gardener.

"Sitting with your father," replied Price. "The first box in the dress circle to the left of the stage."

Gardener suddenly remembered his father's presence. The reason he had made it to the theatre so quickly was because he was sitting in a coffee bar around the corner, intending to pick his father up after the show. "How is he?"

"Shocked, like the rest of us."

Gardener wanted to see his father, Malcolm, but at the moment his professional capacity wouldn't allow that. "Carry on."

"Well, after the voice – before the curtain was raised – we saw fog creeping out from underneath. The curtain rose but Leonard White was nowhere to be seen."

"Where should he have been?" asked Gardener.

"On the settee I assume, but as I've said, I never saw the script. Suddenly, there were a couple of explosions and lots of lighting before a voice screamed out something I didn't catch ... and then ... the body simply dropped ... and just sort of dangled there."

"Did you come on stage immediately?"

"I think so."

"Think isn't good enough, I need to know," replied Gardener.

"Well ... not straight away. I left my box and came down the stairs and telephoned the police first."

"So, when you entered the stage, did you see anyone?"

"Only my stage manager, Steve Rogers."

"Where is he now?"

"I think he went in the direction of the roller shutter door."

"Was it open?"

"Yes."

As if to back up Price's story, a door to the side of the steel shutter opened and a man wearing jeans and a plain black T-shirt came through it.

"Are you Steve Rogers?" asked Gardener.

"Yes."

"Stay there, please. Where have you been?"

"I stepped outside for a bit of fresh air." He glanced at the corpse. "It's not every day you see one of those."

"Did you see what happened?"

"Not really," replied Rogers.

Not really: what did that mean?

Gardener heard the voices on the other side of the safety curtain. Judging by their impatient comments he would have to say something.

"Can you get me a microphone?" he asked Price. "When I've finished talking to the audience I'd like a word with your stage manager."

The instrument was only a matter of feet from Gardener. The man behind the mixing desk passed it over.

Gardener stepped around the side of the curtain and walked to the middle of the stage. A hushed tone returned. He stood in the centre, unsure what to say. He realised that although every one of these people was a possible witness, they were also suspects.

From the stage the theatre was different, particularly as the house lights were on. It was cavernous, and as he gazed upwards, much higher and more daunting than he had ever noticed before. He couldn't imagine what it took to tread the boards night after night, performing in front of others. He glanced toward the box where he understood his father to be sitting, and nodded.

He focused himself, addressed a restless crowd. "Ladies and gentlemen, I am Detective Inspector Stewart Gardener." He flashed his warrant card: aware that no one could actually tell whether or not it was genuine. "I realise how inconvenient all this is going to be but I have to ask that every one of you remain in your seats until you are told otherwise. I'm afraid there will be no show tonight as planned. I'm sure that most of you will have guessed what you've seen to be real. It was, and the whole building is now a crime scene. In due course each and every one of you will be asked your name and a few other details. So, please do not try to leave the theatre before we have spoken to you."

He couldn't help but notice the concerned expressions: whether it was for themselves, or the death of the actor he wasn't sure, but knowing the depth of human nature he could guess.

As he turned to leave, the people seated in the front row tried to engage him in conversation. He ignored their questions and returned backstage, thankful of the approaching sirens.

He glanced at Paul Price. "Can you confirm for me that the dead man is Leonard White?"

Price simply nodded.

CHAPTER 3

Back on stage, Gardener switched off the microphone and handed it back to the sound technician. He found Steve Rogers where he'd left him, near the roller shutter door. The fact that it was open when he'd arrived had really bothered him. If the murderer had used it as a means of escape he could be anywhere by now.

"What time did you start work?"

"About two o' clock this afternoon." Rogers glanced at his watch.

Gardener wondered why people did that when you asked them a question relating to time.

"I know we're in a theatre and people come and go, but have you seen anyone suspicious lurking around the place, anyone who is not connected to the production?"

Steve Rogers shrugged his shoulders. "No one I can think of. I mean, it's only a one man show, we don't need much in the way of staff."

"When was the last time you saw Leonard White?"

"The dead man, you mean?"

"Is there anyone else called Leonard White around here?"

"No ... sorry ... er ... when I came in, just after two."

"Where was he?" asked Gardener.

"In his dressing room."

"And?" pressed Gardener.

"I was on my way to see Mr Price, but I knocked on his door and introduced myself, he had his back to me, facing his mirror."

The stage manager had stopped, as if that was the end of the sentence. Like a wind-up toy he suddenly started again. "He ... er, just nodded and said something, but I didn't catch what it was."

The technician was provoking Gardener. It wasn't that he was slow, but he didn't seem to realise how important his information may be. Even more annoying was his habit of protruding his bottom lip and blowing upwards to clear a lock of hair, which kept falling across one eye: the option of having his haircut had obviously escaped his attention.

"Did you see him after that?"

"No. I passed by his dressing room at around four but the door was closed."

Gardener thought back. That was when his father must have been there. He'd called to collect Malcolm and remembered having to knock on the door. He had nodded and exchanged pleasantries with the aged thespian and then both men had left. On the journey home he also recollected his father mentioning Leonard White's mood: the actor had seemed subdued, not his usual self; but no further reference had been made.

"Do you know Leonard White?" asked Gardener.

"Not really."

There was that phrase again. You either knew the man, or you didn't.

Gardener and Steve Rogers were disturbed by the arrival of his partner, DS Sean Reilly: the Home Office pathologist, Dr George

Fitzgerald: the DCI, Alan Briggs, and a team of SOCO's. A number of constables remained by the stage doors, each craning their necks to see what had happened. All his team had already donned the protective white paper suits so as not to contaminate the scene.

Gardener quickly took Briggs through what he'd found. The DCI listened without interfering.

A sharp rapping on the roller shutter door attracted their attention.

"I imagine that's Steve Fenton with the ESLA gear," said Gardener.

Briggs shouted over to Steve Rogers: "You, open the door and let him in."

The DCI, a physical bear of a man originating from Liverpool had held the position for a little over a year, having taken it shortly after the death of Gardener's wife. In the early days, neither he nor Gardener had seen eye to eye. Time had settled their differences and both officers now held a great deal of respect for each other.

Briggs had a huge barrel chest. Little could be seen of his face due to a thick black beard and moustache. A few inches shorter than Gardener he carried his authority well. In Gardener's opinion, Briggs' only failing was his short temper: during those outbursts he spoke extremely fast, never fluffed his words, and grew in confidence with each one spoken.

As the senior officer, Briggs allocated the tasks. He asked Gardener's second in command, D.S. Reilly to interview the two stagehands on the other side of the auditorium – both of which were still staring into space.

Briggs stepped outside the stage area, calling Colin Sharp over.

"Colin, take a number of uniformed officers and cover all the exits. Go to the entrance and set up tables. Sort out a couple of digital cameras for the officers, mouth swab kits and personal description forms. I want names, addresses and any available ID. After that send them to a table for a DNA mouth swab and get the officers to write down all details including what they're wearing."

Sharp sighed. "Looks like we're in for a long night, sir. Are we allowed to take their DNA?"

"Not by law," replied Briggs. "You'll need to ask their permission, sign a form. Explain to them it's only for this investigation. After that we'll destroy it. If anyone gives you any trouble, call me and I'll come and sort it."

Sharp nodded before leaving.

Finally, Briggs organised a roof search with the use of a helicopter.

Back on stage, Briggs asked. "Who found the body, other than the entire audience?"

"Still trying to determine whether the first person on the stage was Paul Price or his stage manager, Steve Rogers," replied Gardener. "As soon as I got here I checked that Leonard White was dead and then went out and spoke to the audience."

"Where have you been since then?"

"Over there to talk to him," pointed Gardener.

"In that case," said Briggs, "You stay here with Fitz until he's completed his examination and the body is removed. I'll interview Steve Rogers."

Gardener and Fitz had to wait for the SOCO's to finish the ESLA before approaching the corpse. During that time, Gardener asked the sound technician to check all of the equipment to see if it had been tampered with. He requested any or all tapes – whether they belonged to the theatre or not – to be taken away for analysis.

Fitz eventually donned a pair of surgical gloves. "So, what happened?"

Gardener repeated what Paul Price had told him.

"Was this how you found him when you came backstage?" asked Fitz, checking each of the man's joints.

"Yes."

"Let's cut him down, then."

Gardener ordered a couple of uniforms to cut the rope from the beam but save the knot. He also wanted photos before they made the cut.

The pathologist inspected the skin around the neck "The rope marks on the neck don't bear the inflamed edge of a vital reaction."

"Meaning?" inquired Gardener.

Fitz sighed, clicked his tongue. "There are no signs of a struggle, which suggests it wasn't suicide."

When the body was finally on the floor, Gardener leaned nearer. "I know he's dead but why is he so pale?"

Fitz produced a thermometer from his surgical case, removed the actor's trousers and underpants and placed it inside his rectum. After a short period of time he removed it, noting the reading, before reaching into the bag for a razor blade.

Gardener felt hollow inside, not only for the fact that he'd seen the man earlier in the day, but how was he going to break the news to his father? Leonard White had been a close friend.

"I can't believe all this has happened in ... what..." he checked his watch. "...Four or five hours."

"It hasn't," replied Fitz, slicing the right thigh of the corpse.

"It must have done," protested Gardener. "I came to pick my father up at four o' clock. We exchanged a few words."

"Not with him you didn't." Fitz pointed to the thigh. "Leonard White's body is stone cold. The reason he's so pale is because he has no blood. At a guess – and that's all it is for now – I'd say Leonard White has been dead since yesterday."

CHAPTER 4

Once the body had been removed, Gardener and Reilly decided to interview Paul Price.

The SIO glanced curiously around the manager's office. It was small, sparsely furnished and disorganised: a desk had been placed in the middle of the room without a moment's thought to the symmetry. Along the left wall Paul Price's computer was perched incongruously on another small desk that could barely be seen due to a mountain of paperwork. A couple of wall-mounted shelves on the right contained an assortment of files without labels. The decor consisted of a carpet that had probably been left over from a production when the theatre had first opened. A pale green emulsion covered the walls.

It was extremely warm but despite appearances smelled fresh: lavender, and something he couldn't put his finger on.

Sean Reilly was sitting in the only chair available. He had a notebook and pen in his hand.

Paul Price leaned forward and removed a bottle of whiskey and three glasses from one of the desk drawers.

"For emergencies, you understand," he offered, as if excusing himself. "Would either of you two officers like a drink?"

"No, thank you, Mr Price," said Gardener. "We're on duty."

The manager poured himself one before very quickly draining the glass. He then poured another, placing the bottle back in the drawer, along with the two unused glasses. Sitting back in his chair he sighed very loudly.

Gardener closed the office door, leaned back against it: his arms folded.

"Has a murder ever occurred in your theatre before?"

Price sipped his whiskey, clasping the glass with both hands. He was dressed in a pale blue suit, white shirt and blue tie. He had a large head with a round face, dark blue eyes, and a thin pencil line moustache. What hair remained – around the sides – was still black.

Gardener suspected his nose had been broken and reset ... and then broken again. On the bridge of his nose, a line suggested glasses were any everyday item but he had chosen not to wear them. His frame was abnormally thin and emaciated and the white spots on his teeth and fingernails indicated a lack of calcium within his diet.

"Not to my knowledge."

"How long have you worked here?"

"Over thirty years. In its one hundred and twenty seven year history, the theatre has only had five managers. I took over from the late John Beaumont in 1974, who'd taken the position in 1933 after his father had vacated."

"You did say, *late*," interrupted Reilly.

"Yes."

"Be no good calling him, then."

Price didn't reply. He merely continued to sip the whiskey.

"What are you actually responsible for, Mr Price? What do you do?" asked Gardener.

"I'm pretty much a one man band. I look after the general running of the theatre. I book all the shows, take care of the marketing, supervise the team that work for us, oversee the finances, and I cover all the health and safety as well. It's a very demanding position."

Price let out another heavy sigh before draining the contents of his second tumbler of whiskey.

Gardener wondered what all the sighing was about, and how many whiskies he was going to drink before the night was out; in fact, before the interview was concluded.

"I take it then that you booked Leonard White?"

"Yes. I had the details of his nationwide tour. His films were good so I thought it would be interesting to hear him talk about his life."

"Did you book him through an agency?"

"PFA Promotions in Manchester."

"Did you actually know him as a person?"

"No."

"Do you know if he was married?"

"I think he was, but I'm sure the agency will be able to supply that sort of information."

"How much have you seen of him today?"

"Not at all."

"Pardon."

"I haven't been here. I've had meetings all day, didn't get in until about five o' clock."

"And you didn't see him, then? Didn't think to go and introduce yourself?"

"Well as a matter of fact I wanted to, but as soon as I arrived I had a number of phone calls to make and that took me well past six o' clock. There was little point after that. But I'm sure my staff looked after him in my absence."

Gardener changed topics. "Who owns the theatre, Mr Price?"

"A consortium. There are four of us who have an equal share of twenty five percent."

"Any financial problems?" asked Sean Reilly.

"I don't think that's any of your business but since you ask, none whatsoever."

Price sounded appalled by the last question, though Gardener couldn't think why.

"It is our business and we're curious," said Reilly. "Get a few money problems you never know what folks will do."

Price jumped out of his chair. "I hope you're not suggesting one of my partners would be involved in something like murder."

"You know them better than we do."

"We're not suggesting anything, Mr Price. We're merely conducting an investigation and we have to explore every avenue." Gardener paused. "Now, back to the questions. No financial problems. Has anyone approached you wanting to buy the theatre? Perhaps someone who wants to demolish it and build a supermarket?"

Price resumed a seated position, poured himself another whiskey.

Gardener was pleased to see that he didn't drink any.

"No." Sentence over, he sighed again.

"What kind of a staff turnover do you have?"

"Very small. Despite the fact that it's a consortium, we're actually family run. All the owners are related to each other, which is why I took exception to your earlier comment."

"You can't think of any disgruntled ex-staff member with a grudge to bear?"

Price stared hard at both detectives. "This is not an inside job, if that's what you're thinking. Nearly all of the people who work for the theatre retire. As I've said, we're all happy to work here."

Gardener doubted that very much. "If you say so."

The D.I. changed topics again. "Let's talk about the general public. We all know that it can't be easy dealing with them. People tend to complain about all sorts of things. The price of tickets – seating availability, have you experienced anything of the sort recently? Received any intimidating letters? Complaints about the standard of shows, for example?"

The manager snorted and then laughed. "You really do watch too much Agatha Christie. Do you honestly think someone is going to murder for the price of a ticket?"

Gardener had had enough of Price's demeaning manner.

"You'd be surprised why one person decides to murder another. But it doesn't really matter what I think. The information I extract from others is far more important."

Gardener moved away from the door, leaning over Paul Price's desk. He spoke slowly and methodically, his anger having reached a peak.

"Now, as I've already said. We're conducting a murder investigation. I don't think you realise how important it is. So, when I ask you a question I would like a straightforward answer, not some snotty nosed, derogatory remark filled with sarcasm: or, for that matter, your opinions. That way, we'll all be through a lot faster and still be friends."

Price's expression would have stopped electricity travelling through cables.

Gardener continued. "And where tickets are concerned I'd like to see your bookings for the whole of this year." He then added. "Last year as well."

"Why?"

"So that we can check any last minute cancellations, advanced bookings made at the start of the season for a reduced rate; see if a new customer has suddenly started appearing at Saturday afternoon matinees when he normally attends evening performances.

"You see, Mr Price, whoever killed Leonard White knows this theatre like the back of his hand. He managed to not only get *himself* in here but a dead body as well, not to mention concealing it somewhere while he carried on with whatever he wanted to do. He's fooled all your staff into thinking he has a connection with the theatre and is very probably - in my opinion – pretty good at disguising himself.

"I want to know everything about this place: attempted break-ins, trespassers, threatening or strange phone calls, obsessive fans, mysterious events at previous performances by earlier theatre groups – everything! Whatever you know about this theatre, I want to know."

Gardener stood back, folding his arms. "And for that matter, I'm going to make it my job to find out everything you don't know."

A resounding knock on the door broke the tension. Reilly stood up but Gardener opened it and was met by his colleague, DC Colin Sharp.

"Sir," said Sharp. "We need you on the stage."

"I'll be down in a minute."

He turned back to the theatre manager. "Well I think I've outlined everything I want Mr Price. I'll leave one of my officers on hand to collect the information as soon as you have it."

"Just hold on, I can't do all that by myself."

"Why not?" Gardener replied. "You seem to manage everything else."

Gardener opened the door to leave and then turned back. "Two more things, the theatre will be closed until further notice. Secondly, I'd like a list of all your meetings for today, names and contact numbers."

"I'm a suspect now, am I?" asked Paul Price.

Both detectives left without answering.

CHAPTER 5

Albert Fettle was a small stump of a man with a rotund belly that stretched a pair of brown braces almost to breaking point. His legs were too small, his shoes too big. He was bald, had blue eyes, and wore a pair of wire-rimmed glasses, which he kept pushing back up his nose. His mouth was cavernous because his teeth were small and stumpy like him.

He walked with a limp, his voice was high pitched and his accent broad West Riding. He was dressed in a checked blue and red lumberjack shirt with rolled up sleeves and brown pleated trousers.

"Detective Inspector Stewart Gardener and Detective Sergeant Sean Reilly, Mr Fettle."

Both men showed their warrant cards. They were standing in the corridor leading to the stage. Three of the dressing room doors were open and now being searched by SOCO.

"Aye, I remember you, Stewart Gardener. You won't remember me, though. Caught you and your mate one time nicking tree trunks from round back of my shed."

Fettle pointed at Gardener but chose to stare at Reilly. "He were bloody selling 'em by the bagful. Took me ages to find out who it was." The old man smiled and turned back to Gardener. "You made good on yourself, though."

Gardener vaguely recalled the incident and smiled. "I'm sure you must be mistaken."

"Like hell," replied Fettle.

"So, what have you got for us, Mr Fettle?"

From further down the corridor, DC Sharp called to his superior officer. "Sir, we're having trouble with this door. It's locked."

Reilly glanced over. "Whose dressing room is it?"

"Leonard White's."

"Go and find a spare key, somebody must have one!"

Fettle piped up again. "Well, do you want to know, or don't you?"

"Know what?" asked Gardener.

"Christ, Gardener, how the hell did you make a copper if you can't concentrate on the job in hand?"

"There is rather a lot going on at the moment."

"I saw Leonard White walk out the building. He left the theatre through the stage door."

"When?"

"Just after half past seven. I'd been for a leak. I wondered what the hell were going on. Then I heard a lot of noise from the theatre. Only it can't have been Leonard White, can it? He were dead by then, so it must have been your killer." Fettle snorted. "Bloody perfect disguise, I can tell you."

Gardener was about to ask another question.

"Jesus Christ!" shouted Sharp, as the dressing room door opened.

Gardener glanced in his direction.

Reilly immediately made his way to the room.

"Boss, you'd better come and see."

"There's never a dull moment." Gardener turned to Albert Fettle. "Stay here, I need to ask you some more questions?"

Gardener brushed passed Sharp. Already crammed into the small dressing room were Fitz, Reilly and Alan Briggs. The tension increased, though no one spoke.

At the back of the room stood a table: above that, a mirror had been fixed to the wall. Perched on the table were eight one-pint glasses. Each one was full with a substance resembling raw liver: the bottom section of the glass however, was a clear serum.

"What's going on?" asked Gardener.

"At a guess I'd say we've found Leonard White's blood," replied Fitz.

Gardener stared at the glasses, horrified. "It doesn't look like blood."

"That's because it's clotted. It's been in those jars quite a while. Like I said on the stage, I think the victim was killed yesterday. And that's not all," said Fitz. He pointed to the wall above the mirror.

The colour of the scrawl was slightly lighter than the congealed blood, but Gardener suspected that's what had been used:

FOR LONG WEARY MONTHS I HAVE AWAITED THIS HOUR.

CHAPTER 6

Gardener was standing in the garage, staring at the stripped Bonneville.

The place was a tip as usual, with spare parts all over. A variety of engine parts were in one cardboard box, transmission parts in another: at least he hoped they were, and not mixed up. Two wheel rims leaned against one wall, ready for cleaning. Almost every other part on the bike was in a random location he was yet to discover. There were photocopied pages of the service manual tacked to every wall. He was pleased that he'd eventually sent the frame to Jeff Harrison – the enthusiast he'd met in Rawston – to have it professionally cleaned and protected.

His CD player was blaring out *Holding On For A Hero* by Bonnie Tyler, the excessive drum rolls reverberating around the small enclosure, rattling the door and anything else that was loose. He could feel the beat on the floor under his feet.

He allowed himself a brief moment to think about Sarah and that fateful night in Leeds. She had been holding out for a hero – her husband, but he couldn't find the necessary superpowers to save her. He hadn't felt like a hero then and he didn't now.

The track changed to *Cold As Ice* by Foreigner, which led him into thinking about the case.

It had been a long night. Technically speaking he was still on duty: he'd only come home to grab a shower and a fresh change of clothes. He was tired and his bed would have been a better option but he didn't have that kind of a job.

Everyone had finally left the theatre at four o' clock in the morning. Gardener and Reilly had returned to the station to set up the incident room. He'd called Mike Sanderson and asked for HOLMES to set up their equipment ready to compare the first of the witness statements. The building had been sealed and closed and a search team put in place. He had kicked off the ANACAPA chart by placing Leonard White's name in the centre.

He glanced at his watch: 7:30. He was hoping to return there shortly when they would hopefully have all the photographs on the board.

Gardener had been disturbed by what he'd seen: a body at the end of a rope was natural enough in his line of work. The lack of blood was the real problem, and he'd been distracted by that fact when trying to interview Paul Price.

The music changed and Cher's *Love And Understanding* permeated the airwaves. Gardener turned the volume down. The time for loud music and a clearing of his head had finished. What he needed now was logic.

Until he'd found the blood the first thing that had run through his mind was – why? Without the correct certificates the value of the blood even on the black market was not worth killing someone over. If not for sale, what would the killer have wanted with it? A fleeting thought of Jack The Ripper came to mind when he tried to write letters to the police using the victim's blood. He'd failed because it had hardened in the fountain pen.

His thoughts changed when they found it in eight one-pint glass jars in the dressing room. Gardener then suspected that it was all a part of some perverse game, especially with the quote on the wall.

Then came the startling revelation that someone who closely resembled Leonard White had calmly walked out of the theatre as all the commotion was unfolding. In fact, resemblance was probably far too weak a word. By all accounts the disguise was that good that it had fooled people. He wondered how many had actually seen him: so far, only Albert Fettle. Surely to God, no one could be that good!

The connecting door to the kitchen opened and Gardener immediately caught the mouth-watering aroma of grilled bacon. His taste buds tingled. He would normally prefer a healthy option but he hadn't eaten for something like fourteen hours, so anything was better than nothing.

His father appeared in the doorway. "You okay, son?"

Gardener turned off the CD player, glancing at the old man. His complexion was still ashen. He was wearing the same clothes as he'd worn for his night out so he obviously hadn't slept either. Malcolm's posture was stooped. Gardener realised his father was no spring chicken. The bad news must have hit him hard. We all take our parents for granted: we think they will be with us forever.

He said he was fine and they both walked into the kitchen. Chris, his son, was grilling the bacon. Mugs of tea were already on the table, as were placemats and plates. The room was warmer than the garage and the music somewhat different as he heard BBC Radio 2. Spook was sitting in the corner wolfing down some scraps of bacon fat – paying little or no attention to anyone or anything apart from the snack.

"Come on, Dad," said Chris. "You have to eat."

Chris backed up his statement by serving his father first.

Gardener smiled. No matter how good, bad, or indifferent times were, family meant everything.

The telephone shrilled. Before he did anything else Gardener answered it. Colin Sharp informed him the photos were back and they were waiting to set up the incident room.

He said he would be there shortly.

CHAPTER 7

Every muscle in Janine Harper's body ached, or at least it felt that way. Although her headache had subdued to a mild pounding sensation, her arms and legs felt heavy and the stomach cramps were becoming unbearable. It was a symptom she recognised all too well: the first full day of her period always started – and finished – the same way.

Adding to her explosive mood was the fact that she had had a violent row with her boyfriend, Carl, last night. He was immature and had kicked off about the fact that she didn't want sex because of how she was feeling. But he didn't care about her feelings, or her moods: a typical male. He'd said he thought sex was better at that time of the month. The actual words he'd used had made her feel sick – still did.

She sighed and glanced around the room, holding the clipboard in her left hand, the pen in her right. Stocktaking was a job she disliked at the best of times. The room was clean and tidy. The decor easy on the eyes: plaster finished walls in two different colours with a border separating them. She worked in a retail outlet for theatrical supplies. A lot of the products they stocked were small: consumed a lot of space, took an age to count.

The strong parquet floor supported at least a dozen racks of Dexion, which contained everything from bottles of acetone, aluminium powder, collodion and spirit gum, to flexible plastic skin, curling irons, eyebrow pencils and foam rubber. Even obscure products like fishskin, a thin, tough transparent material made from the stomach lining of animals for building up layers of skin on the face or body, used mainly in olden day theatre.

Janine made it to the top of the ladder when the doorbell suddenly chimed. She grimaced, slamming the clipboard on the shelving. The pen bounced upwards before finally landing somewhere behind the cabinet.

Brilliant, thought Janine, glancing at her watch. And it's only nine o' clock!

She descended the ladder two steps at a time and wished she hadn't. Janine lost her footing, slid the rest of the way. At floor level her left foot gave way: she keeled over and hit the Dexion before hitting the ground. Her ankle hurt from the collision, her hands burned from the ladder slide, and her back felt as if it had now been broken.

Janine picked herself up, dusted down her clothes and set off towards the shop faster than she meant to, which left her feeling a little nauseous.

She really didn't need today.

Furthermore, on reaching the entrance leading into the shop, she saw something else she didn't need.

The creep.

Standing with her back to the wall, Janine wanted to cry. She felt as if she was in a cupboard where the walls constantly closed in.

Why of all days was she going to have to put up with William Henry Corndell today? He was such a pompous bastard. He barely spoke and when he did it was always that soft nasal drawl. William was very condescending, had the ability to make her skin crawl simply by staring at her. He had a face that only a mother could love, one she wanted to punch, continuously.

Janine summoned up the courage, stepped through the doorway.

"Morning." Her greeting was forced.

He of course made no reply but simply continued to gaze in her direction.

Janine wondered if he ever slept. The bags under his eyes were more like suitcases. His skin resembled an elephant's hide. The wrinkles in his forehead were deeper than first-world-war trenches. His long drooping nose came out so far that it entered the shop two minutes before he did. He had a long scraggy beard and bushy eyebrows and he desperately reminded her of someone.

William was dressed entirely in black: fedora, shirt, jacket, trousers, socks – from what she could see, as well as a pair of the most expensive shoes she had ever laid eyes on. In fact, despite his appearance, Janine would say that none of his clothes were cheap. They all appeared to have been cut from the finest cloth. She simply couldn't understand why anyone chose to make such a fashion statement. But that was actors for you, an eccentric bunch if there was one.

"My order is on the counter," were his only words.

He continued to glance around the shop as though he was bored, occasionally lifting an item from the shelves, clicking his tongue if it didn't meet with his approval.

He ran his finger along the ledges, rolling his eyes upwards. The cheeky bastard was checking for dust. He leered toward Janine as if he'd found some.

She started to pick at her fingernails, wishing him in hell.

Ignoring his glare she searched underneath the counter for a pair of scissors. It was time she trimmed them. A complete makeover with a wild night out on the town was what she really needed. Having found them she walked across the shop behind the counter, dragging a bin over to where she was standing.

She was about to make the first cut when William stood stock-still and shot her a glance. It was perhaps the most disturbing expression she had ever seen. The depth of his eyes was limitless.

Janine suddenly thought of a saying her grandmother often used, about a person having an evil eye. She believed such a person could inflict disease or death simply by a glance.

Her fear increased and her stomach contracted. She suspected it had nothing to do with her period. She'd always known that the man called William was strange but he'd never frightened her to that degree. Janine even wondered if the heating in the shop had stopped working.

She noticed a nervous tick in his left eye before his mood changed, as if he'd meant to terrify her and had realised his achievement.

"What on Earth are you doing, girl?" He dragged the sentence out as if his life depended on it.

Janine lowered her head, noticed she was at the point of cutting the nail on her forefinger. The scissors were open, at the ready. For a reason she couldn't explain she felt ashamed. Perhaps it was the tone in the creep's voice: the demeaning manner in which he'd addressed her, as if he'd caught her masturbating.

Another stomach spasm resulted in her mood flipping as quickly as his.

"What's it to you?"

William lifted his head to the point where he must have struggled to peer down his nose, but he persisted.

"Young lady, how you pass your time is of no consequence to me, but there is a certain etiquette one should follow."

"What the hell are you talking about?"

And with that, she cut the nail. A quick snip and it fell into the bin.

"Oh my good God," exclaimed William, gripping his walking stick a little tighter. "She's done it," as if he wasn't actually talking to her.

Janine snipped another, wondering if they had started a game, clearly delighted at having unsettled him for a change.

"Stop it at once, you stupid girl," barked William. "Don't you realise what you're doing?"

"I'm cutting my nails for Christ's sake..."

"Never on a Friday!"

Janine stopped mid-cut.

William had managed it again. His expression and the tone of his voice had made her feel inadequate.

"What are you talking about?" asked Janine, a little more placidly.

"Don't you know anything about fingernails, young lady?"

"Not as much as you, evidently," she replied, wishing she hadn't.

"White specs on the nails of the left hand, signify gifts on the thumb; friends on the first finger; foes on the second; lovers on the third and a journey to be taken on the fourth."

William reached out and placed her left hand in his. His touch was so cold, Janine wanted to retract but didn't for fear of sending him over the edge.

He stared intently. "Second and fourth, foes and a journey. To have yellow speckles is a great sign of death." William held her gaze. "You must never cut the nails of a child under a year old. The mother should bite them off or the child will grow up to be a thief..."

William stroked her left hand with his right.

Janine felt repulsed by his attention but had neither the power nor the nerve to withdraw. There was something distinctly unbalanced about him.

"Cut them on Monday, you cut them for health. Cut them on Tuesday, you cut them for wealth. Cut them on Wednesday, you cut them for news: on Thursday, a new pair of shoes. Cut them on a Friday..." His eyes met hers and he lowered his voice yet further, deliberately – in her opinion – speaking even slower. "...You cut them for sorrow. Cut them on a Saturday, you see your true love tomorrow."

William then whispered, which she found even more disconcerting. "Cut them on a Sunday, the devil will be with you all of the week."

Janine flinched. The man was seriously fucked in the head. What the hell was he talking about, cutting your nails on different days of the week? She wished the manager, Mr Cuthbertson, were here. But he was more of a creep than William. He would revel in what was happening.

She had to think of a way to persuade William to leave. He had suddenly grown very quiet, but he was still staring at her, still holding her hand, and still stroking it for God's sake.

Janine pulled away quickly, the draft whizzing past the list he'd left on the counter, blowing it to the edge.

William continued to stare at Janine for what she thought was a long time but probably wasn't. He didn't appear to be gazing at her, more *inside* her.

She felt her breathing increase both in speed and depth. Her heart pounded against the inside of her chest. Her muscles weakened and she became aware of how full her bladder was. When he finally spoke to her, the tone of his voice was soft and menacing.

"You smell unwell, Janine."

Oh fuck! A warm spurt of urine created a damp patch between her legs. She was embarrassed and terrified and warm and cold all at once.

How did the man have the power to create so many emotions?

She found the nerve to speak but the voice didn't sound like hers.

"How do you know my name?"

He didn't answer.

Her entire body felt as if it had been enveloped in ice. Her skin started to itch and her vision had dark shadows around the edges. What did he mean, she smelled unwell? Surely it wasn't because it was that time of the month? She'd taken every precaution. Always had.

"Fear, Janine," said William, as if he'd seen inside her head. "I can smell fear. Are you frightened of me?"

She saw William's lips part, but it wasn't a smile.

"No," she managed to lie.

He let go of her hand. Smirking he turned to leave the shop. "If you say so."

CHAPTER 8

Gardener and Reilly met outside the mortuary.

For a Sunday morning in late March the weather was acceptable: blue sky with a little cloud; the sun was low but the breeze took away any warmth.

Reilly glanced upwards. "You got it, then?"

Gardener smiled. After a shower he'd changed into a new pair of designer jeans and Ben Sherman shirt, finished off with a pale grey suit jacket. It was what all the teenagers were wearing these days, Chris had assured him. He'd wanted his Dad to change his image, bring himself more up to date. Gardener had readily agreed, feeling that the time was right, considering he'd had his hat repaired: the bullet hole filled in. He'd collected it yesterday afternoon after picking his father up from the theatre.

His partner stared a little more intently. "Done a great job: can't even tell."

"I thought so as well," said Gardener, removing the hat, admiring the repair.

"How much?" asked the Irishman.

"More than I should have spent. But it was well worth it."

"Like the new image as well."

"Not really my idea, you can blame Chris for that one."

"A young man with taste."

"Maybe he can start on you next."

The pair of them laughed. Gardener replaced his hat. It was time to work.

"So, what are we dealing with, boss? Why hang a bloke after you've killed him?"

"Maybe he's trying to prove a point."

"What point? The man was already dead."

"He's trying to tell us something, Sean. There's a reason to what he's doing, as far as he's concerned anyway. He's drained the blood for a reason. He's very obviously killed the man for a reason. We just have to find out what it is."

Reilly shook his head. "I've been thinking about what he might have done leading up to that. Did he leave him alive and let him watch his life drain away? But once he'd done him, he packed him up, moved him, hung him in front of an audience, and then calmly walked out of the place dressed as the man he'd killed. Why? It was a hell of a risk."

"Impact, Sean. Everything he's doing is meant to shock. The first is for the audience. They have no idea anything has happened, consequently, they think they're watching an execution, which – to all intent and purpose – is part of the show. The second is for us. We have a corpse with no blood. The next is for anyone who sees him walk out. And the final shock is ours again, we get the blood back."

"A control freak?" asked Reilly. "Is he doing it all because he can? It's a great way to cover your tracks, so it is."

"That's all part of it, isn't it?" said Gardener, "He can do anything he wants if we don't know who he is. If he's so good at disguising himself, how the hell are we going to stop him?"

"The same way we usually do: we wait for him to make a mistake."

"Only one problem, Sean," Gardener glanced around. The city was busy with people and traffic. The cafés had plenty of business with customers sitting outside, taking advantage of a break in the weather. "How many is he going to take out before he does?"

The pair of them entered the building, walking down the corridor leading to Fitz's workroom, the resonant sound of their heels bouncing off the walls.

Gardener nodded to the receptionist as they passed.

"You know, I can't believe that someone could be so good with make up that he could fool everyone around him."

"Wouldn't take much if you didn't really know who he was supposed to be," replied Reilly.

"My dad did."

"What do you mean?"

Gardener turned to face his partner. "My dad went to see Leonard White at the Grand Theatre yesterday afternoon. He spent an hour with him."

"And he didn't notice anything?"

"I haven't spoken to him, yet. I've only had an hour at home and that was before I came here. It doesn't look to me like he's had any sleep. I thought maybe we could both talk to him later."

"Has he not said *anything*?"

"No. The only time we spoke was when I picked him up from the theatre. He was really quiet so I asked him what was wrong and he said he didn't know. He told me that Leonard wasn't himself, he was very subdued."

"Did your *dad* ask him what was wrong?"

"He did, but he said his friend wasn't very talkative, which was unusual in itself. But he also said that Leonard seemed worried about his wife ... and how she was going to take the news."

"What news?" Reilly asked.

"That's just it, he didn't say, even though my dad tried to get it out of him. He said he seemed depressed. My dad had the feeling something awful had happened and his friend couldn't bring himself to discuss it."

Reilly seemed deep in thought before speaking. "Still, it doesn't really matter now, does it? We already know that your dad *wasn't* talking to his lifelong friend."

"Frightening thought, that one."

Both men turned and continued toward the steel silver door at the end of the corridor. Reilly opened it, allowing Gardener to walk in first. Theatre No1 was a narrow building, long and low with strip lighting, accommodating four steel gurneys. Only one was occupied.

Fitz stood behind it, facing Gardener, talking to DCI Alan Briggs. The pathologist wore gloves and a green surgical gown. His mask had been lowered. A microphone hung above his head.

The smell of formaldehyde was overpowering. Gardener had never become accustomed to it.

"Morning," said Fitz. "You're just in time."

Before Gardener had a chance to reply, four wall-mounted speakers powered out the opening bars of Puccini's Tosca, which was quite possibly the only opera that Gardener knew. After the loud opening, the volume dropped to a more acceptable level.

"For what?" he asked.

"The next piece of the puzzle," said Briggs, nodding to Fitz.

"I'd like you to take a look at this."

Fitz had obviously been at work some time, the bottom half of Leonard White's body was already naked. The pathologist pointed to the bruising on the inside of the dead man's left thigh.

"The killer has pumped the blood out through the femoral artery. While he shows a small amount of medical knowledge, he's not as good as he'd like us to believe. If you look here..." Fitz pointed. "There's extensive bruising where he's probably jabbed away with the syringe until he's found the artery."

"Looks like he's had a game of darts," added Reilly.

"The blood in the pint glasses: was it Leonard White's?" asked Gardener.

"I've taken samples for analysis. I think it's safe to assume it was." Fitz paused before continuing. "I can't see where all this is leading. He's drained the man's blood and then given it back to us. There are no broken bones. If you look at the hands, all the fingernails are intact, which suggests no sign of torture. There seems to be a sense of purpose to what he's done, but it's not obvious."

"A ritual?" asked Reilly.

"That's more your territory, Sean," said Briggs. "You ever come across anything like this?"

"No."

"I don't think it's a ritual," added Gardener. "If he'd kept the blood, maybe..."

"Was the blood drained while he was still alive?" asked Briggs. "I saw a film like that once."

"It's possible," said Fitz. "I know the film you're thinking of: *The Abominable Doctor Phibes* with Vincent Price."

"Sounds about right," said Briggs. "But that was just a film, is it possible to do that in real life?"

"Nothing surprises me with the criminal mind," replied the pathologist. "You can do anything if you're so determined."

"Interesting comment," said Gardener to Briggs. "If the killer is a master of disguise, maybe the film world is somewhere we should start looking for clues."

Briggs was about to speak when Fitz interrupted.

"There's something on his chest," he said, with a sense of urgency.

Fitz had removed Leonard White's evening jacket, revealing a starched white shirt. Allowing time for photographs he then quickly took away the aged actor's final item of clothing. He lowered the microphone ready for his report.

"We have a message on his chest," said Fitz, examining more closely. "It hasn't been written on top of the skin but burned into it – and very possibly while was still alive if the blisters were anything to go by."

Gardener leaned forward, reading:

Man cannot hide from his sin

As the past will always reveal

One has paid while others remain

But be warned, a deal is a deal.

CHAPTER 9

Briggs finally broke the silence.

"I can't work out whether he's a psychopath or a genius. If you're nuts, you don't leave puzzles that have been very cleverly put together with an obvious meaning."

"The puzzles are inconsistent," said Gardener, stepping back from the body. "The verse on the body is something he's made up. The writing on the wall in the dressing room read more like a quote to me."

"From anything you recognise?" asked Briggs.

"No," replied Gardener. "But let's be honest, it could be anything."

"What's he trying to tell us?" Briggs asked.

"The fact that he's harboured a grudge for a long time?" questioned Gardener.

"Maybe," said Briggs. "And he'll make us work to prove his point. The key to the investigation hinges on the clues he's offering."

Each man stepped outside the room, leaving the pathologist to finish his job. The quicker he did that the quicker they would have their report.

"You see that's where he shows his intelligence," offered Reilly. "That verse on the old guy's chest was something he created. He knows what he's doing and it's been well planned. He knew who he wanted and where to find him. What he's doing now is making us play his game. It's cat and mouse: are we clever enough to catch him?"

"If he killed Leonard White the day before," said Gardener, "He must have known about the tour and where he was staying. He probably picked him up. So we need to find out where he was staying. After he'd killed him, he went to a lot of trouble to impersonate him and then make a public spectacle of the whole thing, before quietly and confidently walking out of the theatre."

"How did he get him into the place and do what he did without being noticed?" asked Reilly.

"I think it's an inside job," said Briggs. "Let's face it, he managed to blend in, and he must have known his way around the theatre, particularly that one."

"Paul Price seems to think not," replied Gardener.

"Doesn't matter what he thinks," said Briggs. "He doesn't *want* it to be an inside job because it looks bad on him and his theatre. What's your opinion on Price? Is he capable of murder?"

"Anyone's capable of murder," replied Gardener. "I think he's hiding something. The only thing he was bothered about was upsetting the smooth running of the place. Never mind that some bloke's just been killed on his stage in full view of everyone. But my gut instinct tells me he's not involved."

"All the same, we'll have him investigated," said Briggs. "And the rest of them that run it. If word gets round, no one'll work there."

"I'm not sure about that. I don't think anyone is trying to bring the theatre into disrepute," pursued Gardener. "I think it's personal. Leonard White – and others, according to the verse on his chest –

has upset someone. He's out for revenge. Here's one to think about. Leonard White was in his seventies. The others probably will be, so how old is the guy we're looking for? I can't imagine someone that old being able to do everything he's done single handed."

"Well, from what we've seen, boss, I think he works alone but because he appears as one of them." Reilly held his fingers up at the side of his head as if they were quotation marks, "Showbiz people – he's able to blend in and get others to help him without them knowing. Even if he is as old as them, the real problem is still identifying him. If he's a make up specialist, where the hell do we start? For all we know, he could have crept back into the theatre last night, watched us. We might have even interviewed him."

"We'll have to go through White's past with a fine tooth-comb and that won't be easy," said Briggs. "He's been around a long time, spent a lot of his life in different parts of the country. His wife will be able to help us there. She rang me just before I went in to see Fitz to say she was at The Queens Hotel."

"Sean and I are going to talk to my dad," said Gardener. "He and White were friends, have been for quite a number of years. He's also a big film buff, never away from the cinema. Maybe he'll remember something that will help."

"That's interesting," replied Briggs. "If that quote on the dressing room wall is from a film, your dad might recognise it."

"Bit of a long shot, there, sir," said Reilly.

"I don't doubt it, but every now and again the long shot pays off."

"We'll certainly give it a go. But it's been a hell of a shock to him, I don't want to put him under too much pressure."

"Okay. Well if you need any help, if you're uncomfortable, you only have to ask."

"Thanks."

"Right," said Briggs. "You go and speak to your Dad and then get to The Queens to see Val White. I'll get one of the lads to organise the incident room and the rest of them on the statements."

CHAPTER 10

Gardener had made two coffees and one herbal tea while Reilly sat with Malcolm at the kitchen table. The room was long and wide and had fully fitted Scandinavian pine units running its entire length; with concealed strip lighting. The walls and the floor were tiled to match the units.

For Gardener, the kitchen was a room with pleasant reminders of Sarah. Everywhere he glanced he saw something on which he could reflect: several small clay-figure animals she had made herself; an oil painting of her parents' cottage – her first and last attempt. A wall clock in the shape of a tulip reminded him of their romantic weekend in Amsterdam.

He placed the coffees on the table, sitting opposite his father.

"Look dad, I appreciate there's never a good time, and I know it's been a terrible shock, but we have to talk to you about Leonard White."

The expression on Malcolm's face softened. "Of course. I'm sorry about yesterday, son."

"You don't have to apologise. What happened at the theatre was pretty horrific by anyone's standards. If it wasn't for the fact that we have an investigation to run, I'd respect your privacy to grieve a little longer."

"Thank you. You can ask me anything you want but I don't know how much use I'll be."

"You'd be surprised how many people say that, Malcolm," said Reilly.

"How well did you know him, dad?"

"Perhaps not as well as you might think. We didn't meet properly until the mid seventies. Pretty much after his days at Hammer Studios."

"And you'd never met before then?"

"No. I'd seen his films. You know me, Stewart, I've always loved films. Deep down, I'd have given anything to be an actor."

Gardener didn't need reminding of his dad's love of the cinema. He had managed to take Chris once a week for as long as he could remember.

"So, when and why did your paths cross?" asked Gardener.

Malcolm pursed his lips. "I think it would be late 76. He formed part of the local watch committee."

"What's a watch committee, Malcolm?" asked Reilly.

"Every town has one – or used to, anyway. When you make a film, after its final edit you send it to the British Board of Film Classification. They issue a certificate. Once it's distributed, the local watch committee for the area then vet the film. They have the power to make further cuts and even issue another certificate. Well, that's what we did, watched the films and either approved or disapproved."

"How many made up the committee?" asked Gardener.

"Four."

"Can you remember the other two?"

Malcolm thought long and hard. "Sorry, Stewart, it's a long time ago."

"I realise that, dad, but you'll have to try to remember. It's a possible link. A long shot, maybe, but we have to investigate everything."

Malcolm took another sip of coffee. "I'm pretty sure one of them died a few years ago, in a car crash. I will try, Stewart, it's just, with everything that's happened."

"It's okay, dad, take your time." Gardener changed topics. "What about his wife, did you ever meet her?"

"Occasionally, social functions, town hall duty, that sort of thing. Val, I think her name was."

"How did she strike you?"

"Full of her own importance, didn't seem to care about anyone but herself. I always got the impression that she thought she was above us all. To be honest, I don't think she had two farthings to rub together when she met Leonard. I never thought it would work: they were like chalk and cheese. I think she married him for his money, I certainly can't think of another reason. She always made me feel uncomfortable."

"But you wouldn't take her for a murderer?" asked Reilly.

"No ... well ... you never really know, do you? I can't say I liked her, but I wouldn't speak ill."

Gardener thought his father had handled the question well. "Where did they live?"

"Horsforth. Big house, it had a name but I can't remember it, something Manor, I'm not sure what?"

"Can you think of anything that happened during those years? Anything scandalous, a serious incident that someone might want to brush under the carpet?" asked Gardener.

"Stewart, Leonard White was as straight as a die. He worked for Hammer studios for years, alongside all the big names: Peter Cushing, Christopher Lee. He told me himself that he'd wanted to leave Hammer for a long time. He'd been concerned about their policies. They went through a period of making vampire films, full of nudity and lesbianism. He wanted out." Malcolm took a mouthful of coffee and asked, "Why the question about a scandal?"

"What we've learned so far points to revenge. Leonard White appears to have been killed because of something that happened in his past. Now that could be anything at any time, it's a big playing field out there. I just thought, if you knew something, however insignificant you might think it is, it could help."

"What about his wife, any scandal involving her?" Reilly asked.

"I'm sorry, I don't know her well enough."

Gardener wondered how his father was really coping with the kind of pressure they were putting him under. He felt guilty. He didn't like what they were doing but they had a job to do. At least they were conducting the interview in the comfort of their own home and not the station, with tape recorders.

"The thing is, Malcolm, someone's playing games with us," said Reilly.

"Why? What's he doing?"

"We shouldn't be telling you this, dad, but he's leaving messages. When we managed to get into Leonard's dressing room the other night there was a message on the wall. I think it's a quote but I don't know where from."

"What did it say?" asked Malcolm.

Reilly took out his notebook. "For long weary months I have awaited this hour."

"Certainly sounds like a quote," offered Malcolm.

"Do you recognise it?" pressed Gardener.

"No. Could be anything."

"We were also left a verse, a puzzle perhaps. He's taunting us: leading us to believe there'll be more." Gardener paused. "Let's come back to something you said yesterday afternoon. After I picked you up from the theatre you were pretty quiet. You said that Leonard White wasn't himself. He seemed worried about what his wife was going to think. Did he elaborate? What was it that would concern his wife?"

Before his father replied, Gardener studied the once solid features he had come to depend on. He was seventy-five years old but his normal healthy pallor carried a haunted, defeated expression. The lines in his face were deeper, the eyes darker, lifeless.

"I don't know, son."

"Can you remember the exact words he used?"

"Not the exact words, no. He kept saying Val wasn't going to like it. She wouldn't forgive him. I had no idea what he was talking about and he wouldn't tell me. He was obviously in some sort of trouble, but I don't know why. Maybe it was something he couldn't forgive himself for. Therefore, *she* wouldn't forgive him."

"And you didn't pick up on anything in the conversation?" asked Reilly.

"No," replied Malcolm. "I mean, at his age I didn't think it was another woman. I couldn't imagine him having money problems so I couldn't think what else it could be."

"You don't think someone was blackmailing him?"

"It's possible, but if they were, he wasn't letting on. Maybe that was it," said Malcolm.

"But he never gave you an inkling? Not one bit of evidence about how much trouble he was in?"

"No, nothing. He didn't really say very much. As I told you, he was quiet, subdued, not himself." Malcolm waved his finger in the air. "I'll tell you what *was* strange. When I got there, Leonard ordered tea for us both. When it arrived, he never touched his, just left it on the tray. He never touched a drop."

"What's so unusual about that?" asked Reilly.

"He was legendary for halting productions just so as he could have his cup of tea. It was like a ritual."

Gardener and Reilly stared at each other.

"Is there something you're not telling me?"

Gardener sighed. "Did you ever consider – at any point – that you were talking to someone else other than your friend?"

Malcolm lowered his cup to the table. "What are trying to say?"

"Are you *certain* you were talking to Leonard White?"

"Of course I was. Who else could it have been?"

"That's what we'd like to know."

Malcolm's grave expression disturbed Gardener. "Are you trying to tell me that someone was impersonating Leonard White and I couldn't tell?"

Gardener took his time answering, unsure how his father would take the news. "It looks that way, dad."

"Surely to God no one could be that good, son."

"That's what we thought. But we've had it confirmed that Leonard White had been dead somewhere in the region of twelve to twenty-four hours when he hit that stage. I'm sorry, dad, really I am."

Malcolm left the table without saying anything else.

CHAPTER 11

The room at The Queen's was large and airy, well lit – with adequate heating. The beige carpet matched the drapes and the bed linen. The antique furniture added an air of elegance.

With her bleached blond hair tied up, too much face paint and an excess of fine jewellery – none of which complimented her leopard skin top – Val White was exactly what he'd been led to believe: common, and unsuited to the luxury that life – or more to the point, her late husband – had provided for her. His only complimentary thought was that she carried her age well.

No sooner had Gardener and Reilly displayed warrant cards, she had called for room service. When the refreshments arrived she told them to help themselves – and do the honour of pouring her a cup of tea – while she continued to smoke a cigarette through an eight-inch filter tipped holder. She never once asked them anything about her late husband.

Gardener was surprised. The woman must have been as hard as granite. His heart went out to the aged actor. It was sad for someone to have achieved his level of status for it all to go unrecognised by the one person he'd chosen to share his life. She didn't – and probably hadn't – reciprocated the emotion when he'd been alive.

Eager to press on and satisfy his curiosity, Gardener opened the conversation.

"Would you like to tell us about your late husband, please, Mrs White?"

"Not much to tell really, cock."

"I doubt that. He was a fine actor, travelled extensively and led such a full life, probably seen more than most people could even dream about. There must be something to say."

"I'll not argue with that summary," she replied.

If her expression was anything to go by she must have left her enthusiasm back home in the Lake District. Her answers were blunt, emotionless.

"But you're talking from a personal point of view," she continued. "I were the one that shared his home. Your view is from the public eye. As you say, a fine actor, well liked on the silver screen. Off screen, not the husband I'd hoped for."

Gardener thought back to what his father had said. Val White certainly had a talent for making people feel uncomfortable. Despite the heating there was a distinct chill in the atmosphere.

"If that was the case why stay together?" asked Reilly.

"I had my reasons."

"Money being one of them, I shouldn't wonder," said Sean Reilly, cutting to the chase.

Val White stared at Reilly. His comment had hit a nerve. "Maybe." She maintained her self-control. "You're entitled to your opinion, cock, it's a free country. Not everyone's relationship runs to what's expected."

Gardener sensed a real difference of opinion building, not to mention an instant dislike between Val White and his partner

Sean Reilly. That was nothing new – most people didn't like his abrupt manner. He had an unerring ability to see through people. He had an excellent technique for ruffling feathers and obtaining the information he wanted when interviewing.

"So there is something you can tell us," continued Gardener. "Why wasn't he the husband you wanted?"

"My home life were what I made it. He were never there. When he were he might as well not have been. We hardly ever talked, rarely went out as a couple unless it were a social function of some standing. Quite frankly I played second fiddle to everything, especially his life on screen. The film industry was his mistress."

I wonder why, thought Gardener.

"Let's start at the beginning," said Gardener, eager to maintain a better balance. "Tell me how you met, where you went from there. I need to build up a picture. Someone didn't just kill him, they went to great lengths to make a public spectacle out of an extremely gruesome murder, which suggests an enemy – and a very personal one at that."

"Doesn't surprise me."

"Why?" Gardener asked.

"He were pompous. I've known people stop him in the street for an autograph and he'd turn 'em down flat. Nothing and no one ever seemed good enough for him."

That wasn't the impression his father had given him, but then again, he wasn't married to the man. You have to be much closer than a friend to claim you really know someone.

"It would take more than a down-trodden autograph hunter to do what was done to your husband."

Val White finished her tea and poured another without offering Gardener or Reilly. If she had been a party to all the gruesome details she was not letting on.

"I dare say. He were born in Blackpool in 1940. He had three sisters and one brother. They're all dead! He left school at sixteen and joined the RAF. After leaving the services he landed a job in the theatre. A talent scout spotted him in 1959 and he went down to work London's West End. He were there until 1964, then he landed a small part in a film."

"All sounds very condensed."

"It's short and sweet because I don't know a great deal about his life before we met."

"Where and when did you two meet?"

"I think it were the late sixties because by then he'd settled into films at Hammer Studios. But he'd taken a part in a play back in the West End. The whole thing went on tour and we met here, in Leeds. I went to see the play with a friend. She had backstage passes and Leonard and I met at the party thrown afterwards. It were the last night, you see."

"What first attracted you to him?"

"He were very confident, knew what he wanted out of life, outspoken ... and he had money." As Val White had made her last comment, she smiled at Reilly. "Six months later we were married and bought our first home."

"Where?"

"Horsforth, on the A65 going out towards Rawdon. You can't miss it, big grey house set back from the road, black and gold wrought iron gates guard the arched entrance, grounds full of poplar trees."

"My father mentioned that but he couldn't remember the name. Can you remember who you bought it from?"

"Not really, although the name Ashington rings a bell, I think that's what it were called, Ashington Manor."

"It's not that important, I suppose I'm clutching at straws, trying to find a link where there isn't one. What happened next?"

"We stayed up here in the house for a couple of years but then the film bug got him again. He went back to Hammer sometime around 1966 to work with Christopher Lee in one of his Dracula films. And he stayed there for the next ten years. I hardly saw owt of him."

"Any family?"

Val White took a sip of tea and lit a fresh cigarette. "No." Her expression softened. "I would've liked a couple of kids."

"Judging by the circumstances in which he died, he must have made an enemy for himself. You said it didn't surprise you, can you elaborate?"

"I'm not sure I can, cock. I've no idea who he saw and what he were up to in the ten years he were at Hammer. I'm basing my comments on his attitude."

"Did your husband ever conduct any private business deals, either in or out of the film world?"

Val White was obviously thinking about the questions as she inhaled deeply on her cigarette and blew out smoke rings.

"None that I'm aware of."

"There's nothing in his past that you can think would generate such a callous act of revenge?" pressed Gardener.

"We've all got skeletons, Mr Gardener. Just because I can't think of anything doesn't mean they're not there."

There really was very little to go on. Gardener had a conflicting picture. According to his father, Leonard White was an icon, a straight man with whom you could trust your life. He felt the same way about his father. Whatever the old man had told him, Gardener had no reason to distrust: but then, had he really known Leonard White?

As for his wife, she couldn't abide to be in the same room. Why was that? What was she hiding? What had Leonard White done that had so turned her against him? He needed to find the root of the problem.

"So what happened after Hammer?"

"He sort of retired. We had enough money for him not to work again."

"But he did, work again, that is?"

"Oh, aye. He couldn't help himself. He formed part of a local watch committee here in Leeds."

"I wondered when you'd come to that."

"You already know about it?"

"I know quite a lot about your late husband, Mrs White. My father was on the same watch committee."

"Really? What were his name?"

"Malcolm Gardener."

"My God! Are you, Stewart? You always were a good looker."

Gardener blushed, but the name drop may prove effective. Maybe now she would open up – say what was really on her mind.

"What a small world. Well, I'm pleased to see you've made something of yourself."

Eager to continue, Gardener repeated his point. "The watch committee, what can you tell me about it?"

"Not a lot." Her attitude had softened. "I were never that involved."

"Did you meet the other members?"

"I did. There were your dad, a bloke called Fletcher, I think he were a writer. No idea where he is now. And then there were Jack Harper, don't know what he did, a historian, something like that. I don't know where Fletcher is, but Jack Harper were killed in a car crash a few years back."

"Yes, my dad mentioned that, he just couldn't remember their names."

"Oh well, there you are, then, something's come out of this morning."

"There was nothing involving the other members of the committee that may have caused ill feelings towards your husband? No scandals? No major disagreements?"

"None I can think of, but I'm sure if there were your dad would remember."

Gardener was beginning to feel frustrated. Despite the fact that Val White hadn't liked her husband she had still not provided any real evidence, or a reason to kill him.

"What about the years after the watch committee?"

"We sold the house in about 1979 and moved to the Lake District, where I live now. Leonard continued working theatre until 1995 when he officially retired."

"Who did you sell the house to? Can you remember?"

"I certainly can. It were one of his friends in the film business: a director, Corndell, his name were."

"Do you know if he still lives there?"

"No, he doesn't. We had a letter from his wife, apparently he died four months after buying the house."

"So *she* might still live there?"

"It's possible, she'd be getting on a bit now, though."

Gardener glanced at Reilly. "It's worth a visit."

"I take it then that your husband came out of retirement again."

"A couple of years back; playing small parts in small theatres. Earlier this year he was persuaded to go on a national tour to talk about his life in films."

"Who persuaded him?"

"His agents, a company in Manchester called PMA."

"How did he feel about that?" asked Gardener.

"He loved it."

"So, it wasn't something he was forced into doing because he needed the money?"

"You must be kidding, cock. Leonard were worth a fortune. Money were the last thing on his mind. He did it because he loved it."

"Where was he staying for the Leeds gig?"

"Same place he always stayed while he were here, The Manor House in Skipton. Big luxurious place on the road going out to Keighley."

"Same place? Was he a man of routine?"

"I wouldn't say so. He liked to do certain things in certain ways."

"Such as?"

"Well, it were more when he went on stage really. He were very superstitious. Most thespians are. He would never have live flowers on a stage, something to do with flowers having a short life and it would reflect on the performance. He didn't like whistling on stage. That were to do with the early days of theatre, when dock workers were often scenery change men and whistle calls went wrong. But other than that, no."

"So, he never had a cup of tea at the same time every day, or did anything else at a certain time in a certain way because that's the way it should be done?"

Val White thought about the question. "Not that I can recall."

"When my father came to see him last week, he said that Leonard wasn't himself. He seemed worried about something, and that you wouldn't understand. Any ideas what that might be?"

"Like I said, we didn't get on very well, we didn't talk much. If he did have a problem, he never told me about it."

"You obviously knew him pretty well, you'd been married a long time. Despite not getting on, any reason to think he'd been acting strange lately?"

"No."

She'd answered a little too fast for Gardener's liking.

"Who checked his post while he was on tour?"

"Well I did, of course."

"Nothing unusual there? No threatening letters, or phone calls?"

"No. His post were mainly fans wanting signed photos. Asking the usual questions: would he ever go back into films? Was his stage show coming to their area? We had the odd bill, but there were nothing that carried any warnings about him being killed, or blackmailed, or anything else."

Reilly gave her time to sip her tea and take a drag on the cigarette before *his* next question.

"Where were you last Thursday night, Mrs White?"

"Come again?"

Judging by her expression, Gardener suspected she was puzzled by the question, as if Reilly had no right to ask her about her private life.

"It's a simple enough question," retorted Reilly. "Where were you on the night your husband was murdered?"

"Back home in Kendall."

"By yourself?"

"No."

"Who were you with?" Reilly persisted.

"I don't think that's any of your business."

"We would like to establish your whereabouts," said Gardener. "Do you have an alibi?"

"You think I murdered him?"

"No, we don't think that," retorted Gardener. "But unless we can eliminate you from the list of suspects..."

"Why the hell would I murder him?" demanded Val White.

"He *was* worth a fortune," said Reilly.

"And it were all mine, alive or dead." Val White stubbed out one cigarette and then immediately lit another.

"But we don't know that, do we? For all we know you arranged to have him murdered because he wasn't prepared to leave you all his money. You made it plain that you didn't get on."

Gardener noticed her mood switch very quickly.

"That's as maybe, but I'm not a murderer. I were at home in Kendall, all night."

"All night?" asked Gardener.

"Yes."

"But not alone?" questioned Reilly.

"No. I was with a man called Anthony Thompson, if you must know. He's been my lover for at least ten years." Val White smiled. "Well, seeing as you want to know everything, your perfect Mr White wasn't very good in that department."

CHAPTER 12

It was late. Gardener was tired and hungry and had had more than enough for one day: he'd only had about an hour away from the investigation in the last twenty-four – which was when he'd last eaten.

The full team was here – not to mention a number of local PC's for support. They'd all pulled together, done an excellent job preparing the incident room. The bulletin board was littered with crime scene photographs. Chairs were scattered all over in no particular order. A table contained items of evidence in clear sealed bags. The atmosphere however, was stilted.

Briggs opened the meeting.

"Right, let's have some order. I know it's been a long day and we're all tired but we have quite a few things to talk about. Stewart will take over, he'll tell you what little we know and what actions need attention."

Gardener stood up. Dispensing with formalities, he went straight in. "Leonard White's death is a bit of a mystery. We think he was alive and well on Friday. He was not due on stage at the Grand Theatre until Saturday, but we suspect he was picked up early from his hotel and taken somewhere secluded, given a sedative and his blood drained. The next time anyone saw the actor, he was dangling from a rope in front of his audience – despite already being dead. In his dressing room we found eight glass jars of what looked like raw liver. Although Fitz is still waiting for the results there's no reason to think it wasn't White's blood."

Gardener paused to take a drink of water.

"Sean and I interviewed his wife, Val, this morning. She gave us almost nothing to go on. By all accounts, Leonard White was the conscientious type who went to work, did his job, came home, put his money in the bank and enjoyed what he did without creating enemies ... or so she says.

"She can't think of anyone who would want to kill him. She knows of nothing in his past to suggest otherwise. Checking his career will be a big job because he's travelled all over the UK, if not the world. We need to ferret out his friends – if he had any locally. Check his bank accounts, insurance policies, see if anyone stood to gain anything from his death aside from her. What Val White knows may be open to question because her husband spent so much time away from home."

"Include her in the search. I want to know where she goes, what she does, who she sees. Despite the fact that Sean and I don't like her, neither of us suspects she actually murdered him; or for that matter, *had* him murdered."

Thinking about the interview, Gardener was unhappy. He wasn't sure who or what to believe. The fact that she disliked her husband was obvious. Why, was another matter? Whilst she was probably innocent – having said everything he had was hers, dead or alive – she was still a suspect. Though he had no doubt her alibi would check out. She had given no indication of bad business deals: people crossed, or enemies made; but something in the man's past must have triggered that attack.

Malcolm had painted a different picture, and he was quick to realise that it could affect his father, and the remaining member of the watch committee should that eventually prove to be the connection.

"Before we spoke to her this morning I had a rough idea where the couple had lived when they were here but little in the way of details. Val White thinks the house was called Ashington Manor. Might have a different name now. It's out on the Horsforth Road towards Rawdon, big grey house set back from the road. Black and gold wrought iron gates guard the arched entrance, grounds full of poplar trees. Someone please check that out. Find out when White bought it, who from and how it was paid for. And who lives there now."

Gardener glanced around the room. He hadn't aimed his speech or given actions to anyone in particular.

Prior to the meeting, both he and Reilly had trawled through at least half of the witness statements, which had revealed nothing. After all, everyone was inside the theatre, seated and waiting.

Gardener updated the ANACAPA chart as he went along. The white board was full of straight lines and arrows pointing all over the place: it resembled a map of the London Underground already.

"So, there we have it, just because his wife doesn't know about any misdemeanours – or claims not to know – someone does. One thing we have picked up is that he formed part of a watch committee between 1976 and 1979: a group of people who vet films and decide on the certificate before they're shown locally. It's an area worth concentrating on. The only other surviving member apart from my dad is someone called Harry Fletcher: at the time, a local writer. He shouldn't be too hard to find. Look close: dig deep. I can't help wondering if there was an incident connecting the watch committee."

"Has your Dad said anything, Stewart?" asked Briggs.

"Nothing that helps us with the investigation. It's all been a bit of a shock."

"And he can't remember anything involving the watch committee?"

"No. He couldn't even remember the names of the other two. But, as I said, I don't think he's on top form."

"Okay, so let someone else take a statement from him when he's calmed down a little: one of our lovely WPC's, maybe? I'm sure he'd like that."

Gardener nodded and continued. "Val White gave us another lead. Her husband always stayed at a hotel called The Manor House in Skipton. Sean and I will be going there tomorrow. I'd be surprised if we didn't have a few leads to follow after that."

The SIO glanced around the room. "Does anyone have any questions?"

"You seem to have ruled Val White out," said Thornton. "She obviously has an alibi."

"Yes," said Gardener.

"And her lover will no doubt back it up," said Reilly.

There were a few nods and glances but no-one offered anything further on that score.

"Is there any particular reason for hanging the man after he was dead?" asked DC Sharp.

"None that I know," replied Gardener. "Other than to cause a stir or make an impact of some sort. I want someone to take the rope and find out everything you can. Is there anything special about it? What was it made from? What type of a knot is it?"

"Do you think there's any real relevance to the rope and the knot?" asked Bob Anderson, Thornton's partner.

"Could be," replied Gardener. "We can't rule out anything. I think we're going to have a lot of problems with this one. The killer's obviously very intelligent, and from the knowledge we've so far gathered we think he's an expert in the art of disguise. He fooled my father who had been a friend of Leonard White's for a number of years. He fooled the theatre staff because he somehow managed not only to get himself into the building but the corpse of the aged actor as well. So it seems he's someone who knows the background, has very probably worked in theatre, perhaps even The Grand. Maybe he's worked with Leonard White himself."

Gardener turned to Steve Fenton, the Crime Scene manager.

"Steve, it says in your report you found traces of aluminium powder in the dressing room. Any idea what it is?"

Steve Fenton's physical features were similar to his superior officer's: short black hair, slim build. Gardener had long since become accustomed to Fenton's eyes, which differed in colour from day to day. At first, the contact lenses had confused him.

"Yeah, we found hairs on the table in front of the mirror. It was used in olden day theatre apparently, to whiten or grey the hair. From what I've found out it's bloody hard to wash out, and if you got it on your face it would darken the make up and still wouldn't wash out."

"Another reason to support our man's theatre background," said Gardener. "If he's using material from the olden days, is he as old as Leonard White? If so, how could he manage to do all he's done by himself? Does he have an accomplice?"

Briggs stood up. "Anyone picked anything up from the witness statements?"

There was a buzz of conversation but the general answer was negative. It was far too early.

"I issued a press statement before coming in here. I couldn't tell them anything, so I just appealed for witnesses to come forward. I suggest some of you carry on checking into that. Speak to the HOLMES lads as well, see if any of their information has thrown up a lead worth following."

Gardener turned to Fenton. "Fingerprints?"

"None."

"He was probably wearing gloves," said Reilly.

"Either that, or because of his theatrical background he's developed something to hide his prints," said Fenton.

Gardener continued. "I need a couple of you to check out any shops in the city that specifically sell theatre and stage make up. You could broaden your search by using the Internet. Whoever is doing this may not necessarily buy it locally, may not even live locally.

"And then we have the puzzles." Gardener pointed to the board. There were a number of photographs, many of them contained the same picture but taken from different angles. The verses were also highlighted in large print.

"The one found on the dressing room wall reads like a quote."

He walked closer and read it out aloud. "For long weary months I have awaited this hour."

He turned and addressed his officers. "Any ideas?"

"Judging by those words," said Thornton, "Someone has a serious grudge."

"I didn't mean that so much, I was thinking more about the overall context. A needle in a haystack maybe, but we need someone to follow it up. Is it from a film, a play, a book, or has our intelligent psychopath made it up? Can you all honestly say you've never come across those words before?"

The only feedback was a couple of wisecracks.

"Okay, you two at the back," said Briggs. "Smith & Wesson or whatever your names are, it'll be a good education for you. Visit the local libraries, the historians, the film museums and wherever else you can think of, see if you can shed any light."

Gardener turned back to the board. "The second one we came across had been burned into Leonard White's chest, while he was alive judging by the blisters on the skin. Fitz suggested a caustic pencil was used, which would have been extremely painful. Sean and I are of the opinion that it's not a quote but a taunt. Whilst we haven't unearthed any evidence of a disagreement between Leonard White and anyone connected to him so far, there obviously has been one.

"'Man cannot hide from his sin, as the past will always reveal'. It's obvious our aged actor has done something he shouldn't. I think you're right, Frank, someone definitely bears a grudge. And it's not just against Leonard White. According to the message, there are others. 'One has paid while others remain, but be warned, a deal is a deal'.

Gardener allowed time for more questions but his officers were tired, so he quickly brought things to a halt. He raised his hand to the board. "Actions for tomorrow. I want answers on the rope, any shop in the city that stocks theatrical products, and any information anyone can find on the quote on the dressing room wall. I also want someone checking out Paul Price and his theatre. Again, there was nothing to suggest he was directly involved but you never know. I want someone listening to the tapes we pulled from backstage. Something might come to light. And we also need the results of the ESLA.

"We need to pull out all the stops if we're going to prevent another death. So, we have a few things to be going on with, but by no means everything. Sean and I will be in Skipton tomorrow. Hopefully, we'll have something more to add."

CHAPTER 13

The room resembled a dungeon. The walls were painted matt black, the ceiling grey. In each of the corners running the length of the walls, were huge cobwebs, artificially created, by him, despite his loathing of the creatures that spun them.

His mind was instantly cast back to a particular morning. The big black spider was half way down the wall when he discovered it. Judging by the direction in which it was heading, he suspected the only place it could have come from was behind the wardrobe.

He'd felt tense, uncomfortable. His whole body had shivered, his breathing grew heavier and within seconds he was sweating.

Where had it come from? More to the point, where the hell was it going?

He and spiders didn't mix. The thought that the monster had been hiding behind his furniture generated absolute revulsion within him.

He'd hated spiders for as long as he could remember: all too aware of commonly held beliefs about them being carriers of disease. But he knew other things about them as well – like the fact that it was unlucky to kill a spider. If you were sweeping and came across a web, you should not destroy it till the spider is safe, when you may sweep away the web; but if you kill the spider, it will surely bring poverty to your house.

Thereby creating another problem.

To ensure the safety of the spider meant he had to leave it. So it was still in the room. He couldn't sleep knowing it was permanently at large. If he did manage to drop off it might creep out and watch him: run all over the bastard place.

Across his face: couldn't have that!

Then again, he knew there would always be a spider in the room if he grew ill. A long-standing cure for ague or a fever was to imprison a spider in a nutshell and then wear it as an amulet. Question is, how would you imprison it in a nutshell if you didn't like them in the first place?

He shuddered again before continuing with his inspection.

Bare boards lined the floor, treated, and stained light green. But it was not dirty! The display was merely for effect. It was in fact spotless and smelled of lavender.

Lining each of the walls – either side of a collection of mannequins – were posters of Lon Chaney, his favourite film star, in a variety of different disguises. The Phantom. The Hunchback. The Ape Man, from the film *A Blind Bargain*. The Vampire, from *London After Midnight*, his own particular favourite, now sadly out of print: a lost film, no copy in existence save his own. Littering his worktops and shelves were a whole selection of make up effects.

Standing in the corner was a full-length mirror with a light attached to the top. He was – at present – admiring his finest creation, from that favourite film. He was dressed in a black beaver hat and a black Inverness coat. His face had the pallor of death. His hair was long and straggly and came down to his shoulders. The eyes terrified even him. He had darkened his eyebrows and fixed a wire ring – like a monocle – allowing a hollowed-eye expression. The teeth had taken him an age, but had been worth the effort. Both upper and lower sets were sharp and pointed – and were as real as he could make them. His grin was fixed and further emphasised by shading in the upper corners of his mouth.

He was a genius, of which there was no doubt. Perhaps not quite in the league of his idol. But then, who had been? In his opinion however, it was more than good enough. It would allow him into places undetected. Carry out the most heinous of crimes without being caught. Grant him permission to continue his work to the full.

Eyewitness reports would be considered inadmissible and would therefore do him no harm. They did not give up his true identity. Only he knew that. And once he had completed his mission – without being caught – he would disappear into the night.

He was not a serial killer. He was not disposing of people without reason. And the killing spree would not continue when he'd done what he needed to do. He did not have an insatiable appetite to wipe out and destroy as many people as possible. What he was doing could not be tied to religion, nor did he belong to any satanic cult. His plan was not to go down in history alongside the likes of Jack The Ripper or The Boston Strangler or Dennis Neilson or Harold Shipman.

He was extracting revenge on people who deserved it. People who had wronged him in the past. It was plain and simple and would be short and sweet. There were only four. It wouldn't take long. And that was why the police wouldn't catch him. They had no idea now, after victim number one. And they would have no idea by the time they discovered victim number four.

Why?

Simple! They didn't know who he was. And they were not going to find out!

Nor would anyone else, even after the next victim, whose demise was going to be very different. Victim number two should eradicate any pattern and perhaps lead them in the wrong direction.

And at the moment, that was all that mattered.

CHAPTER 14

Skipton's Manor House hotel was a two-storey greystone building, sitting in acres of luscious green woodland, enhanced by dark wood, leaded windows, a traditional grey slate roof and Creeping Ivy covering the exterior. Each window adorned an intricately hand crafted window box containing a colourful array of plants. The gravel drive leading to the hotel encompassed a circular fountain and ornately carved bushes.

Gardener admired the view and could only find one word to describe it: elegant, the sort of place he would expect an old country gentleman – or perhaps retired actor – to have stayed. The building spoke of money. Set against the background of a clear blue sky in a late March Monday morning the view was picture postcard.

Gardener stepped out of the car and recalled what he knew of the market town: originally a village settled by Anglican sheep farmers in the 7th century before becoming – in the 12th century – a Norman castle town under the de-Romilles who built their fortress on a rock above the Eller Beck Gorge.

There were weekly markets concentrating on perishable goods, and fairs dealing with bigger quantities of different commodities such as wool, fabrics, metals, leather, salt and wine. Many of the high street properties were rebuilt in the second half of the 17th century, and in the 1720's weavers and wool-combers built houses at the bottom end of the town.

Nestled into what was left of the high street shops were tunnel-like openings leading to narrow alleys, home to family run café's using traditional country recipes; along with small specialist shops selling local crafts, which had eventually led to prosperity, and the town becoming almost self supportive.

Reilly left the car and stood beside him. "You're in a good mood, boss, for a Monday morning with the case from hell."

Gardener turned to his partner. "My Christmas present was delivered this morning. I was just leaving the house."

"The King and Queen seat?"

"Chris and my Dad had the box ripped apart before I knew what day it was."

"Was it worth the money?"

"I'd say so. I've never seen anything like it." Gardener widened his arms to indicate the size. "It's really deep and finished in black leather with big round buttons. It's the first new part for the bike."

Gardener's eyes glazed. "And my dad had the foresight to have mine and Sarah's name stenciled into the sides. It's brilliant."

"Can't wait for a wee demo on this bike of yours," said Reilly, rubbing his hands together.

"You'll probably have to fight my dad for the first test drive."

"Shouldn't be a problem," said his partner. "Time you've finished it your dad will have his own set of wheels, so he will, with its own seat, and handles, for you to push."

Gardener laughed. The Irishman was probably right.

"Anyway, let's get back to the case from hell."

The Manor House entrance hall was a mixture of marble and a

highly polished wood veneer, with the fresh smell of pot-pourri, no doubt well hidden. The oil paintings were expensive, almost certainly originals.

As was the receptionist.

"Detective Inspector Stewart Gardener and Detective Sergeant Sean Reilly." They flashed their warrant cards.

Gardener tipped his hat. "We'd like to ask you a few questions if we may?"

"Oh my God, not another."

"Another?" asked Reilly.

"Yes, another!" His reply was terse. "I know you people have a job to do but so have we. I have a hotel to run and when you keep swarming in and closing down rooms. Well, I'm sorry, but it's simply not good for business."

"Neither is murder," said Reilly.

Gardener studied the man. With his smooth complexion and neatly combed, dark hair, he estimated an age of late twenties. He was very slim, wore a pale blue suit with a shirt and tie to match. The man had exceptionally white teeth, manicured hands – and eyes to compliment his attire. Given the way he spoke and fluttered his eyelashes, not to mention excessive hand gestures, Gardener suspected the man definitely did not have an eye for the ladies.

"Can you clarify that statement, Mr. Sparrow?" asked Gardener.

Sparrow glanced down his nose at the name badge on his jacket, wishing it in hell judging by his expression. He seemed dissatisfied with the familiarity it caused.

At the same time he also gave Gardener the once over. The SIO felt a little conspicuous, especially after his image change. Today's attire was a Racing Green authentic sportswear purple and white striped shirt and a pair of St. Vdio black slacks with a Jeff Banks tailored jacket, all of which were picked up at the local meanswear outlet in Leeds for a fraction of the price they would normally have cost – otherwise he wouldn't be wearing them. He was really taking to his new image and felt it brought him closer to his son – though at the moment, Sparrow appreciated the view even more.

"Yes, Mr. Gardener, I can and I will. We have already had a visit from the police regarding the unfortunate death of Mr. White. He was by himself and spent approximately two hours in the room. Alone."

Sparrow spoke as if he severely resented the police and their business, whilst continually moving his hands and arms as if to express those feelings.

"And then told us we were not allowed to rent the room out to anyone until the investigation had been closed. And furthermore, he covered the bloody door with Scenes of Crimes tape, so as everyone else staying here would know."

"Did he ask you for a current guest list?"

"No. Should he have done?"

Gardener glanced around. "Is there somewhere we can talk?"

"Well I am rather busy at the moment."

"So are we Mr. Sparrow. And *we* are *real* police officers and we *would* like a current guest list. I also want someone to take over the reception desk while you tell us everything you know: what he looked like, his name, where he went, where he said he was from..."

Sparrow's expression became grave. To his credit he arranged for Gardener's requests to be carried out immediately. Two minutes later they were sitting in the hotel bar, which was equally as quaint but with an interior design slightly different to the rest of the building. Wooden ceiling beams, red velvet curtains and carpet. Classical music played low in the background.

"What was his name?" asked Gardener, seated comfortably in a leather Chesterfield chair.

"Inspector Burke."

Gardener glanced at Reilly, who simply shrugged.

"What's wrong?" asked Sparrow.

"Can you give us a description?"

"He was tall, well built: stocky, but not fat. His hair was gray, combed back, and he had long sideburns. He had quite big ears, and the most appallingly wrinkled skin. The man had clearly never seen a tub of moisturizer. He was dressed in a suit that was almost as wrinkled as his face, probably came from an Oxfam shop. There's enough of them in the town."

Sparrow sighed more than necessary, glanced at his manicured hands frequently before making comment.

"His nails were disgusting, bitten to the quick. To be perfectly honest, he reminded me of a 1930's film star."

How interesting, thought Gardener, that Sparrow's comment should be linked to the film world.

Gardener was beginning to feel the killer had not only left them a bunch of puzzles and clues to follow, but he was clever enough to stay a step ahead of them.

"We will need to see the room," said Gardener. "But for now, let's concentrate on Leonard White. Who picked him up last Friday?"

"Well now, he *was* something. Very smart chauffeur, peaked cap, blond hair, good looking, slim, *he* should have been in films."

Gardener realised Sparrow had a weakness for men in uniform – good job he wasn't a PC.

"Did he say where he was from?"

"I think the company was called Executive Cars."

"Did he give you a card?"

"No. Now there's the strange thing, you see. It wasn't Leonard's usual choice of limousine. Different company altogether."

Gardener noticed the first name terms, and the fact that

Sparrow's attitude had changed somewhat.

"Who *were* the usual company?"

"Star Limousine's in Leeds."

"Did he offer an explanation for the change of companies?"

"He most certainly did, Mr. Gardener," said Sparrow. "After I phoned his room, Leonard came down. He was quite confused at being picked up a day early. With no engagement on the Thursday night all he wanted to do on Friday was relax in the hotel and go for short walks in the countryside. The driver told him that his wife had had a serious accident and the car had been laid on to take him all the way back to a hospital in the Lake District. Despite the driver being quite calm there was an edge to his manner." Sparrow paused, and then added. "Lovely fingernails I have to say.

"Which hospital?"

"I don't believe it was mentioned."

"Did you notice the registration of the car?" asked Gardener.

"I'm afraid I didn't, but at that point I didn't suspect anything."

"So what happened next?"

"Well, Leonard seemed quite concerned. He wanted to go back to his room to use the phone and to pack. The driver said there wasn't enough time. The old man was beside himself with worry. I told him to keep calm, when I had the time I would pack his things and send them on. Leonard is a regular of ours, you see."

"And have you?" asked Reilly.

"Not yet. Inspector Burke arrived first thing yesterday morning and told me not to disturb the room. And I had to leave it exactly as it was, after *he'd* left."

"So off they went, just like that, Leonard and the chauffeur?" questioned Reilly.

"Yes. The driver said Leonard could use the phone in the car to check on his wife's condition."

"Did *you* think to phone anyone?" asked Reilly. "The limo company: any of the hospitals? Leonard White's agent?"

"I'm afraid I didn't. I do have a hotel to run."

"So you just let them go without asking for identification? Afterwards, you did no checking?" pushed Reilly. "If he was such a regular customer I would have expected a little more courtesy towards him. Surprising, really?"

"What is?" asked Sparrow.

"The fact that you didn't," said Reilly. "You don't seem to have missed much else Mr. Sparrow."

The receptionist didn't answer, preferring instead to study his nails.

"Let's see the room," said Gardener.

"Of course."

The three of them left the bar and walked up a wide, sprawling staircase with a well polished banister and a luxurious wool carpet. A door opened into a small square lobby, the entrance to three of their rooms.

Gardener took a pair of gloves from his jacket pocket and removed the scene tape. He opened the door. An entrance hall led to the bathroom on the right. The main room – beyond glass doors – was enormous, possibly the largest Gardener had ever seen for a hotel.

"Jesus Christ!" said Reilly. Obviously the biggest he'd seen as well.

It must have been forty feet long and the window on the far side took almost the entire section of wall, affording a panoramic view of the sprawling gardens and the breathtaking valley that lay beyond. He saw smoke from a steam train – probably the Keighley and Worth Valley Railway. Everything was to hand. A TV, VCR, and DVD; stereo, a bed that was even bigger than king size. A trouser press, tea and coffee facilities. Everything you could want, and probably everything you were unlikely to need.

But the room was spotless. Clean – nothing out of place.

Gardener and Reilly immediately began checking wardrobes and drawers, which were all empty.

"I don't understand," said Sparrow.

"I do," said Gardener.

"No one has been in the room since Inspector Burke."

Gardener turned to stare at Sparrow. "There is no Inspector Burke."

"He was probably the feckin' limo driver as well," added Reilly.

"Who was?" asked Sparrow, agitated.

Gardener turned and stood in the centre of the room, before walking over and staring out of the window, across the valley.

"What are we missing, Sean?"

"A message?"

"So where is it?"

"Would you gentlemen mind telling me what this is all about?" pleaded Sparrow.

Gardener faced him. "You've been taken in, Mr. Sparrow. Inspector Burke does not exist, neither does the limo driver or – for that matter – Executive Cars. It's all been an elaborate set up."

Gardener glanced at Reilly with an expression of bewilderment.

"Where would you put the message, Sean, if you were him?"

"I reckon he's going to make it more of a challenge. He'll leave puzzles but we'll have to dig for them."

Gardener glanced beyond his partner. "Step to your left, will you, Sean?"

As he did so, Gardener stared at the TV. He kneeled down, noticing that the VCR power light was still lit.

He switched on the TV, and pressed the play button on the

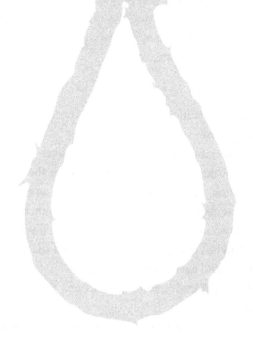

VCR. The machine whirred into life and the screen was filled with their first image of the man they were searching for.

"That's Inspector Burke!" shouted Sparrow.

The officer was exactly as Sparrow had described.

Gardener peered beyond the actor on the screen but was unable to make out anything in the background.

Burke spoke. Whether the voice was his own or dubbed was anyone's guess, but the message was loud and clear.

"Now you've allowed the dust to settle, best pay a visit to Albert Fettle."

CHAPTER 15

Later in the day, Gardener and Reilly entered the theatre through a stage door located in a small side street off New Briggate. The steps leading down took them to the room where Albert Fettle kept himself hidden for most of the day. The silence in the building was haunting. Every sound they made had a resonant echo.

"Now then," said Fettle, from an area that neither detective could pinpoint.

Gardener glanced around Fettle's makeshift home.

The decor had been neglected. The walls were covered with a heavily smoke-stained, flowered wallpaper, which had been out of fashion for so long it was almost in again. A table stood in the middle of the room, covered with magazines relating to the entertainment world, and an empty butter container that now doubled as a lunchbox. Other than that there were two cupboards: on top of one were tea making facilities: at the side of the other, a waste paper basket.

Fettle suddenly materialised from a hidden corner, a partially eaten sandwich in one hand and a mug of tea in the other. His rotund belly was still adding pressure to the brown braces. His bald head currently had a black mark running right down the centre and today's attire was a checked, black and red lumberjack shirt with the same brown pleated trousers and black brogues.

"Not much for me to do round here these days, apart from the odd spot of cleaning."

And the odd spot was all it seemed to be, thought Gardener.

"Won't be for much longer now, Mr. Fettle."

"Caught him, have you?"

"We're still making inquiries."

"You haven't, then. You'll never catch him if he's that good wi' a brush and paste."

"Perhaps you should have a go," said Reilly.

"Just stating facts, son. Anyway, don't stand out there, get yourselves in here and have a pot of tea, I could do wi' a fresh one now. I dare say you've come to ask a few questions, see if I can remember owt?"

"You could say that. How are things here at the moment?"

"Bloody awful!" he replied, switching on the kettle and digging out a couple of clean mugs from the cupboard, without actually finding out whether or not they wanted a drink. "Like I said, there's nowt to do."

"Should give you plenty of time to remember things, then," said Reilly. "Mine's two sugars."

"You've a sharp tongue, for a leprechaun."

Gardener and Reilly chuckled at the comment and the good faith in which it had been delivered.

"How long have you worked here?" Gardener asked.

"A good forty year," he replied.

With the kettle having come to the boil, Fettle poured the tea and brought it across to them. He then brought over the tray containing milk and sugar.

"Help yourselves lads."

"How would you describe the atmosphere?"

"Good, or else I wouldn't have stayed. I've enjoyed meself, I've no intention of retiring and Mr. Price is happy to keep me as long I want to be here."

"How do you get on with him?"

"Fine. He can be a bit temperamental but can't we all? So long as we do us job we have no problems from him."

At last, thought Gardener: two people who agreed with each other. But it didn't help the investigation.

"So, you've known him as long as anyone else, how would you describe him?"

"How do you mean?" asked Fettle.

"What's he like to work for? What he's like outside work? The usual stuff."

"He's not a murderer, if that's what you're hinting at. He's a good bloke. Pays us wages on time, doesn't grumble if you have a day off sick. He often pops down to see how I'm doing. No, if you're looking for a scapegoat, Gardener, he's not your man."

"Pleased to hear it," said Gardener, moving on. "Let's go back to last Saturday. What time did you start work?"

"I were here early that day, I wanted to have a chat wi' Leonard White. Started work about eight in the morning."

Fettle finally finished his sandwich and scooped up the last one from the lunch-box.

"Anyone else around at that time?"

"Cleaners."

"No one else?" inquired Gardener.

"I don't think so, box office staff, maybe."

"Anything strange happened around here recently? You've not received any odd phone calls, threatening letters from anyone?"

"Well if we had I wouldn't know about 'em. I don't get involved in that side of it. It's my job to greet the people who come through that door and down the stairs." Fettle gestured with his eyes.

"So you were here when Leonard White arrived?" asked Gardener.

"Aye, I was that."

"Which was what time?"

"After his mysterious trunk had been delivered."

Gardener's senses went on full alert. "What trunk?"

"Bloody great big thing it were: van were outside the roller shutter door at the back of the stage. Bloke had dropped tailgate on the stage and slid trunk out afore asking me to sign."

"Any slogans on the van," Reilly asked, "any advertising?"

"There were nowt. It were just a white one."

"What did the driver look like?"

"He were wearing a black cap. Had a cig in his mouth but it wasn't lit. He were quite big, around six foot I'd say, same build as your mate here. He wore a pair o' dark brown overalls and he walked wi' a limp, 'cause I wondered how the bloody hell he'd managed to move the trunk, but it were in front o' me almost afore I'd signed."

"Did he say where he was from?" asked Gardener.

"No, in fact he didn't say much, apart from, sign here."

"Did he say where the trunk had come from, or who'd given him instructions to deliver it here?"

"No. Trunk were big and black, quite old, had Leonard White's name on the side of it."

"What happened after you'd signed?"

"He jumped back in the van and took off."

"Did you notice the registration?" asked Reilly.

"No. I don't normally take deliveries."

Fettle took a bite of his sandwich and a slurp of tea.

"Who does?"

"Stage-hands mostly."

"So how did you find out about the delivery?"

"Van pulled up outside here first." Fettle pointed to the grimy, frosted window that formed part of his room.

"Then the door at the top of the stairs opened and someone shouted 'delivery for Leonard White', and that were it. He were back in van and driving down the bottom afore I could say owt else."

"So, by the time you arrived on the stage, everything had more or less been done?"

"Aye, I signed and he took off."

"Was the tailgate still down, or had he lifted it back up?"

"Back up."

"Did you inspect the trunk, open it up to see what was inside?"

"No, but it were locked anyway, bloody great padlock."

"Was it heavy? Did you try to move it?"

"No, just left it."

Gardener had wondered how the killer had managed to smuggle Leonard White's body into the theatre: it was pretty obvious now.

"How soon after did Leonard White arrive?"

"A couple of hours, maybe"

"Did he ask about the trunk, or did you tell him?"

Fettle chewed another bit of his sandwich and swallowed before answering. "I told him. Nice pot o' tea, this." He took another mouthful.

Gardener noticed Reilly was half way down his cup. He tasted his own – wasn't bad.

"Did White seem surprised?" Reilly asked.

"No, just pleased that it were here."

"Did you offer to go backstage and help him with it?"

"Aye, as a matter of fact, I did. But he said it were okay, he wouldn't need it straight away, but he'd give me a shout when he needed some help."

"Did his voice sound like Leonard White?"

"Can't say as I noticed. I think so."

"What happened next?"

"Well I carried on in here. A couple of hours had passed and I went backstage to see if he needed that hand and it were all clear. There were no trunk and no Leonard White. I gave him a shout but no one answered. I went back to his dressing room and knocked on the door but he never answered that either."

"Did you check anywhere else?"

"Only to see if he were with Mr. Price, and he wasn't. But it's not unusual for actors and actresses to take a break. Sometimes they go outside for a smoke, or a walk. They don't always leave out the stage door."

"Was he alone when he arrived?"

"Aye, he was."

"Did he seem okay to you? Not out of breath, or looking worried about anything?"

"No, he were fine. Didn't say much, which I thought were unusual, 'cause I've met him afore and I knew him to be a bit of a talker. And I'll tell you what else were unusual, shall I? I thought the trunk were a bit too much for a man who'd had hip replacement, which is why I went to offer my help. Not that I'd be much use to him anyway, 'cause I'm getting on a bit now. I were still younger than him, though."

"So you have no idea what happened to the trunk?"

"Come to think of it, no. It were too big to just hide in a corner but I never saw it anywhere afterwards."

Gardener glanced at Reilly, who in turn nodded. "Where is it?"

Reilly glanced at Fettle. "Could it still *be* here?"

"Probably, no one came to pick it up."

"Any idea where?"

Fettle chewed on his sandwich, gulped more tea. "Could be anywhere."

"Where do you store the props and the scenery you're not using?" asked Gardener.

"We have a couple o' different rooms."

"The sort of place that someone would only know if they had worked here?" pressed Gardener.

"I suppose so. As I've said. I've been here forty year. Whoever this bloke was I didn't recognise him."

"Well you wouldn't, would you?" said Reilly. "He was disguised."

"But no one's that good. I don't care how good you are, you can't imitate someone so perfectly. You'd have to slip up somewhere."

"I think you'll find you're wrong," said Gardener. "We might all be in for a surprise with this one. Can you show us the rooms?"

"If you think it'll help."

The detectives followed Fettle into the labyrinths of the theatre. For a man with a limp he could walk at a fair pace.

The two storage rooms he showed them were located either side of the stage, down a flight of steps. Though the rooms were full of dust encrusted furniture, neither one contained the trunk they wanted.

"Are there any more?" asked Gardener.

Fettle stood and thought. "Well there is, but they're way down in the basements, I don't think anyone's been down there in ages."

"I'll bet you're wrong about that as well," replied Reilly.

Each man trooped down to the very bottom of the theatre. It was cold and Gardener could see his own breath.

The first room they came across was at the end of a corridor. There were no physical signs that it had been used recently,

Fettle pulled a bunch of keys from his pocket and tried a few before selecting the correct one. The door opened with a loud crack and a dank smell penetrated their nostrils. The room was small and other than posters from previous productions there was nothing of any interest.

Fettle locked the door and took them back down one corridor and into another. He reached the door, produced the keys and tried all of them. He stood back and scratched his head, puzzled.

"Surely one of the keys has to be here."

"Maybe it's not locked," said Reilly.

He used a pair of gloves and tried the handle.

To Fettle's amazement but not Gardener's, the door opened. Standing in the middle of the room was the big black trunk. Leonard White's name was stencilled on the side – no padlock.

Gardener also produced gloves from his pocket, lifting the lid. In the bottom of the trunk was a long coil of rope. On the inside of the lid a piece of paper had been attached. Judging by the texture it was a little thicker than normal paper and had an elaborately designed scroll top and bottom. The outer edges of the paper were blue but the scroll was beige and flecked with brown spots, the finish resembling a cup of cappuccino.

As Gardener had figured, a message had been left:

I imagine you're used to this now
And you're probably wondering, just how?
Perhaps you should focus in order to be true
And more to the point, ask who?

I've invited you in, but beware, my world is big

Not long now, before the next gig.

You should study your city and seek out a shop,

The next of my chosen will be a big shock.

I'm enjoying myself, playing this game,

And it would be all too easy to give you a name.

It's time to detect, and study the clues,

Be sure to keep up, otherwise you'll lose.

"He's a crafty bugger is this one," said Fettle. "You'll have a job an half if you don't know what he looks like."

Gardener sighed, frustrated. "Give forensics a call, Sean. Let's have them check this out."

"Do you recognise the rope, Mr Fettle?" asked Gardener.

The old man was about to reach inside but Gardener stopped him.

"Looks like one of ours."

Gardener picked it up. One end had been cut. It didn't take a genius to realise that the other section had to be the one used to hang Leonard White.

He had evidence bags in the car. He dropped the rope, left the lid open and turned to walk back out of the room. Before doing so he glanced at Fettle.

"One more question, Mr. Fettle, have you ever heard of an Inspector Burke?"

Fettle appeared deep in thought.

"Inspector Burke," he repeated. "Can't say as I have. What makes you ask?"

"Just curious," said Gardener.

CHAPTER 16

Early evening back at the incident room, Gardener was still shocked by the apparent ease with which the killer had carried out his actions against Leonard White. The man had oozed confidence, as if being caught was completely unheard of. Or equally as bad, the prospect of capture didn't bother him.

Perhaps it was a mission. Maybe when it was over he would do one of two things, disappear forever, or hand himself in.

Little or no evidence was frustrating, and it was beginning to feel like a conspiracy that no one ever noticed anything: vans, registration plate's ... logos.

Gardener's only consolation was the items of evidence he and Reilly had managed to collect. The video of Inspector Burke: the new puzzle, and the rest of the rope. He was well aware of the mounting pressure to find answers ... not to mention the person responsible.

Gardener addressed his team. "Sean and I have uncovered some disturbing evidence relating to the case. If and when the press get hold of it we're going to come under intense scrutiny from the public, particularly if he kills again. We know that whoever the killer is, he's a master of disguise. The receptionist at The Manor House near Skipton said Leonard White was picked up on Friday by a chauffeur from Executive Cars, who had used the excuse that his wife had been taken ill and the car had been laid on for him. We've checked and there is no such company. So where the did the car come from? And where is it now?"

"What make of car was it?"

"The receptionist doesn't know," replied Gardener. "The hotel doesn't have CCTV, they don't feel the need. We have a guest list so I'd like a couple of you to follow it up, see if anyone can help."

Gardener continued with the briefing. "The following morning – yesterday – the staff at The Manor House had a visit from the police."

He let the remark sink in while glancing around the room, studying the expressions of his team.

"I know what you're thinking, you're trying to work out if anyone else has been there apart from us. Well it wasn't any of you. It was in fact an Inspector Burke."

"Inspector Burke?" repeated Briggs.

"Sean." Gardener glanced at his colleague and passed over the video. "Will you do the honours?"

As the tape played, Gardener was amazed that he hadn't realised the small segment of film had actually been recorded in black and white. Further proof of the killer's love of the movie world, particularly old ones; the clues were there, if only they opened their eyes.

"Is that him?" said Briggs.

"Looks like it," replied Reilly.

"He looks familiar."

"The actor, you mean?" asked Gardener, wondering what Briggs was thinking.

"Yes." But his superior didn't elaborate. "He must be bloody confident to play tricks like this. And he's thought it out as well. Any idea where that is?"

"No," said Gardener. "If you look closely, the background is out of focus. Maybe our lads can clean it up a little bit. Even if they do I don't think it will show us much."

"What did Fettle have to say?" asked Briggs.

Gardener told them and then held up the two clear plastic bags. One had a rope, the other contained the latest puzzle, which he'd now copied and pasted to the ANACAPA chart.

"I want that trunk back here," said Briggs. "He's taking the piss! All right you lot, let's have some answers. This bloke's far too confident and he's gonna make mugs out of us if we're not careful. And what's that supposed to mean? 'Perhaps you should focus in order to be true'"

Gardener made his suggestion. "He's very well organised. Everything's been planned down to the finest detail. He's suggesting we do the same."

Gardener turned, directing a question to a junior officer, Patrick Edwards. "Have you looked at ritual killings and murders involving draining the blood?"

"I have, sir, but I haven't learned much. I've studied books in the library, and the Internet. I've done a small report for you." Edwards placed it on a table in front of Gardener. "I don't really think it will help us."

"Keep digging. Don't rule anything out," said Gardener, suddenly turning his attention to another member of the team. "Colin, what do you have on Leonard White?"

"I'm waiting for copies of his legal documents but nothing seems untoward. His solicitor confirmed that in the event of his death everything he owned would be left to his wife. As for her, she seems pretty straightforward on the face of it but I haven't been looking long enough, yet."

"Okay. Thornton, Anderson, what about the rope?"

"There's nothing special about it..."

Gardener held the evidence bag aloft. "I think we'll find it's the other half of the one in this bag. We'll get forensics to check it out for prints."

"But the knot threw up something interesting," replied Anderson. "It's known as a sailor's eye splice. Not too complicated to form but pretty effective at holding something in place."

"Which takes us in another direction," said Gardener. "Has our killer spent some time in the Navy?"

"Or is it a red herring?" said Briggs. "If you'll pardon the pun. Has he just studied ropes and knots in order to have us running all over the place?"

A silence descended and Gardener realised they were going nowhere fast.

"What about witness statements?" Briggs asked.

A young PC brought in as support put his hand up. "I'm following up on a woman who thought she saw Leonard White getting out of a taxi outside the theatre on the Saturday afternoon. I've telephoned twice to make an appointment but I've had no answer."

"Go round tonight, then" said Briggs. "We want the registration of the taxi, the name of the firm, the driver, where he picked him up, everything. I want someone back at the theatre to see Paul Price. We need a list of everyone who's worked there in the last thirty years. Add the hotel guest list to your witnesses and see if anyone's on both lists: or if any of them noticed the vehicle from Executive Cars. Somebody must have seen something. This bloke's luck has to give out sometime."

"You also have a white van to add to your list," added Gardener. "Seen in the city centre on Saturday afternoon. I know there must be hundreds of white vans a week in the centre of Leeds. Get as many registration plates as possible and then check them out. Go back to The Grand and once again check out the CCTV."

Gardener glanced at the ANACAPA chart before turning to face them all. "Harry Fletcher was a name that came up last time, has anyone found him?"

Dave Rawson stepped forward, a man with the build of a rugby centre forward. He had short black hair, a small beard and moustache, neatly trimmed, and strong square teeth that could probably chew bricks without a problem.

"I'm taking care of that one, sir. Back in the 1960's he was a writer, mainly detective fiction. Turned them out pretty fast by all accounts. Then he disappeared for a while. Next thing he was working for the watch committee in the seventies. After that he seems to have gone to ground again. Popped up again in the nineties as a commissioning editor for The Playhouse, before disappearing again."

"Has he now?" said Briggs. "What do you think, Stewart?"

"He could be our man," replied Gardener. "We need to speak to him if only to eliminate him, but more importantly, if he's not our man he may know something that will lead us in the right direction."

Briggs glanced at the board again. "It's a bit coincidental that we have a writer of crime fiction from the 60's popping in and out of the world when he feels like it, and a poet who likes killing people and leaving puzzles. What do you think the second verse means?"

"*I* think it's obvious we're looking for an actor," replied Gardener. "Certainly someone connected with the theatre, and possibly films from a forgotten era. Maybe there's someone he admires. So we need someone checking the film world. Who was big in the years gone by? Who was good with make up? Whether or not there's a connection to an Inspector Burke."

"Maybe he's a failed actor with a grudge," said Reilly.

"Possible." Gardener continued. "He's directing us as well: a shop, where the next of the chosen will be a big shock. Any luck with that one?"

"There is one in the city, specialises in theatre supplies, called ... wait for it ... *Let's Make Up*."

"You're joking?" said Reilly.

"No, I'm serious," said Dave Rawson.

"Where is it?" asked Gardener.

"One of the arcades running off New Briggate: run by an old guy and his assistant. They call him Cuthbertson. He's been there about thirty years, knows all there is to know about theatre and stage, and just about everybody who goes in there."

"Anyone bought any Aluminium Powder recently?"

"Quite a lot of people. I've made a list so we can start following them up."

Gardener nodded. "You said he knows everyone who goes in there. He hasn't had any strangers in recently, asking for oddball stuff?"

"Not that he knows of. I asked his assistant, Janine Harper, but she didn't seem as if she was on the same planet."

"It could be him," said Reilly. "He runs a shop so he'd have no trouble getting the stuff. Knows all there is to know about make up, chances are he could apply it professionally."

"Did he have an alibi for the night of Leonard White's death?" asked Gardener.

"He claims he was at home, by himself. No wife, no kids."

"And no alibi," said Reilly.

"So he could be our man," said Gardener. "Then again, he could be next. The riddle says, 'the next of my chosen will be a big shock'. Maybe it's nothing to do with the local watch committee. We need to check him out further, Dave."

Gardener addressed Briggs. "Do you think it's worth tailing him for a couple of days?"

"I suppose we could spare someone to watch his movements," replied Briggs. "Let me see what I can do."

Gardener addressed the team again. "The end of the riddle. 'It's time to detect, and study the clues'. Despite being cocky, he's right. And so is DCI Briggs. He's taking us for mugs, especially if he gets away with another murder. We have to try to prevent it. Sean and I are going to pay a visit to Leonard White's former home. Apparently it was a colleague of White's who bought it. Although he's dead, it's possible his wife is still there."

"Okay, let's *be* more focused." shouted Briggs. "It doesn't sound like we have much time but you're going to have to do your best. Otherwise, the press will do their worst. The way I see it there are three suspects."

Briggs held up one hand and counted with his fingers on the other.

"Val White. She had the motive and the ability but she has an alibi. Dig deep, someone. Harry Fletcher. We don't know enough about him either way. We can't put him in the frame and we can't rule him out so we need to find him. Cuthbertson, who runs the stage make up shop. He's a possible suspect, but he may also be the next victim. Someone tail him for a couple of days. We have to be seen to be doing something, despite the fact that we're getting nowhere."

Gardener glanced at the chart again, ticking off the subjects he'd covered, stopping when he reached the word ESLA.

He addressed Steve Fenton: "Anything?"

"Yes. We've got the results in. We need everyone back at the theatre with their shoes so we can check them off."

"Good. Go and ring Paul Price now and tell him I'd like everyone there tomorrow, with the shoes they were wearing on Saturday night. I'd also like to see the results at the next incident room meeting."

He glanced at them all as a group. "That just leaves the sound problem. The word that Paul Price heard spoken before Leonard White was hung."

"I know about that one, sir," said Colin Sharp, producing a notebook. "It was on a cassette tape. Once we'd identified which one I popped over to the theatre to speak to the sound technician."

Gardener glanced over the evidence bags, spotting a tape. "What did he have to say?"

"The sound tech identified it as the tape he'd been given by Leonard White about ten minutes before he went on, with the instructions that he should play it after the safety curtain had been raised."

"Where did White go then?" asked Gardener.

"To the other side of the stage to wait in the wings, only, our sound technician couldn't see him. Once the curtain was up, he played the tape. At first he thought it was blank, the wrong one, maybe. The he heard something screamed out, which was a bloody sight louder than he'd anticipated. When he searched the desk for the volume level it was too late. There was nothing else on the tape and the body was in front of the audience."

"Did he see White at all after that?"

"No, but to be honest I think he was in shock. He said he just stood staring at the body until Price came barging through the stage door."

IMPERFECTION

"Did he recognise the word on the tape?"

"No."

"Do you?"

"The sound lads have been playing with this for ages. The recording is pretty loud, which means it's distorted," said Sharp. "But they have managed to clean it up and they think it's two words, even though it's said quite fast. Someone shouts 'look out', and that's it."

Gardener glanced at the ceiling, defeated. It would be nigh on impossible to identify that but he had to try.

"Any ideas?"

Sharp spoke up again. "The sound lads think it comes from an old film. There's lots of crackling and a definite hiss, so it hasn't been recorded live. Whoever did it might have used the latest technology but the soundtrack is very old."

"Okay," said Gardener. "Everyone take a copy of that tape. I'll have one for my Dad. Any of you talking to the film historians, play it to them, see if they recognise it. I'm not expecting miracles but you never know."

Gardener updated the board and added the word 'video', intending to follow up on the Inspector Burke clip.

Briggs stood up. "Before you all go, the Chief Super's been talking to a retired profiler who's offering his services for free."

"Do we need one?" asked Reilly.

"It won't hurt," replied Briggs. "And it isn't going to cost us anything. He's got a lot of experience dealing with these people. He worked on the Yorkshire Ripper case..."

"That's reassuring," retorted Reilly. "They never actually caught that bastard in connection with his crimes."

"We should have had the bloke who caught him working for us," shouted Thornton. "At least he clocked number plates."

The comment raised a laugh and Gardener did his best to bring the meeting back to order. "What's his name?"

"Trevor Thorpe."

"Can't say I've heard of him."

"Well all this is irrelevant," said Briggs. "He's offered to help, the Chief Super's accepted, so he's coming in during the next day or so to study everything we have. So the next time we meet in this room we'll have a guest. Can we show him some respect?"

The officer's dispersed without a word. Gardener wasn't particularly happy about it, and judging by the expressions of his team as they were leaving, neither were they.

CHAPTER 17

Martin Brown leaned forward and stared at the documents on his desk.

Running the fingers of his right hand around the inside of his collar, he realised the office was too warm. The general mess – which resembled the aftermath of a nuclear fallout – was also adding to his discomfort. The cupboard to his right was crammed full of magazines and journals. The shelves on the walls were at the point of collapse. Paper was strewn everywhere. On window-ledges, pinned to the walls, left on chairs – mostly information or posters of forthcoming productions.

But they *were* students, what could he expect?

And they were so bloody noisy. He could hear them now in the corridor, shouting at each other all the time, even though they were standing together.

"Hold on a second, Dave." Martin rose from his seat and closed the door. He came back to the desk and picked up the phone to continue the conversation.

"Are you sure?"

"Of course I'm sure, Martin. I've worked for BT for about thirty years. I've checked it out three times."

Martin struggled with the information he'd been given.

"But this is William Henry Corndell we're talking about."

"So you keep saying. But who the hell is William Henry Corndell?"

"Probably one of the greatest actors of our time," replied Martin, growing more frustrated.

"Well I've never seen any of his films."

"He's not really in films, Dave," said Martin. "He's more a classical actor who works in the theatre."

"So where have you seen him?"

"London."

"When?" Dave asked.

"Oh, God, years ago."

"What in?"

"When I saw him he was in rehearsals for *Phantom of the Opera*."

"Good, was he?" asked Dave.

Martin wasn't keen on his friend's tone. "The best, from what I saw."

"So why didn't *he* get the part instead of Michael Crawford? And did you actually see the play itself?"

"No. I missed the opening night. Apparently, William had a major accident. Fell off a piece of scenery and broke his leg."

"And after that?"

"I left London shortly afterwards. I'm not so sure what happened to him. But I'm telling you, a man of his acting prowess must have been working constantly. Which is why I'm asking, are you sure it's the same William Henry Corndell?"

"Are you?"

"I just can't believe a man of his talent isn't in constant demand.

You're positive he's never had a single phone call to his landline in what ... ten, fifteen years? And he's never made a call?"

"He hasn't taken a call." Dave sounded as if he was tiring of the game.

"What about a mobile?"

"He doesn't have one. I've done the most comprehensive search with the most up to date technology. Anyone who's anybody who has a mobile phone, I know their number: Cliff Richard, Tom Jones: Paul McCartney. All your top actors, John Hurt, Ben Affleck, I can get you just about anyone's number. Posh and Beck's if you want. But I can't get one for William Henry Corndell because he doesn't have one!"

"Is it legal, this program of yours?"

"Of course it isn't legal. And I don't want anyone knowing about it, either."

The conversation ceased while Martin swallowed a mouthful of coffee.

"I can't believe it, Dave. I really can't."

"Why do you want this bloke, Martin?"

"If you'd seen him you'd know."

Martin recalled the time he'd been in London when Corndell had been rehearsing at Her Majesty's Theatre for the lead role. The emotion, the feeling, the way he'd delivered his lines and the expressions he'd used were as good as anyone he'd ever seen.

"What about the bill? Is it paid regularly?" asked Martin.

"Like clockwork."

Martin blew out a sigh. "I don't know what to say."

"You're going to have to call him, Martin. See if he is your man, which I'm pretty sure he is. Maybe he'll tell you what he's been doing all these years. Maybe he's dropped out of show business. He's probably a recluse. You know what it's like, most of them can't handle the pressure."

"Not Corndell. If you'd seen him, you'd know."

"So you keep saying. But I haven't, and I'm not likely to now, if he's a recluse. Nor are you by the sound of it. Listen, have you tried a round of the agents?"

"Yes, but he doesn't seem to have one of those, either. You're right, Dave, I'll have to give him a ring, see what he's up to and whether or not he'll do it."

"Might be too rich for university blood. You know what penny-pinching students are like."

"I'll ignore that. Anyway, thanks for what you've done, you've been a great help."

"No problem. Let me know how you get on."

"Okay, mate."

Martin put the phone down, sighing. Staring at the back wall he allowed his thoughts to drift.

Martin knew a natural when he saw one. Born and bred in Borehamwood, he'd lived there until he was twenty-five. Most if not all of his childhood had been spent at Elstree Studios. He went on to train at RADA before lecturing in dramatic arts. His fascination with the film industry and the entertainment world were second to none, or so he thought. Eventually he moved to Leeds with his wife and two children to take a post at The University. His children, now in their late teens, were about to attend.

He'd seen and studied William on and off over the years. He'd met William's father, himself a fine actor who had spent many years on the stage before turning his hand to direction where he made a multitude of films for Ealing Studios. William's father had died in the nineteen-eighties and he was pretty sure that William had moved up to Yorkshire to reside in the Corndell mansion in Horsforth.

But where had he been since then?

There's only one way to find out.

Martin picked up the receiver and listened to the dialling tone, hoping to find a little extra courage. He felt apprehensive. He realised he'd obtained an ex-directory number the only way you could, illegally.

He dialled, listening for an age before the phone at the other end was eventually picked up.

"Hello?" the voice sounded far more nervous than Martin.

"Am I speaking to William Henry Corndell?"

"Who is this and how did you get the number?"

Bad start, thought Martin.

"Mr. Corndell, I'm sorry to bother you, my name is Martin Brown and I work for The University of Leeds."

"That's one question answered."

"Am I talking to the same William Henry Corndell who once played the lead role of *The Phantom* in the West End?"

"Good grief, young man, you have done your homework."

Martin Brown almost laughed at the change in tone of William's voice. He sounded like an eccentric country squire.

"So it is you, then?"

"It most certainly is. But I'd still like to know how you got this number and what you're after."

"I'm sorry Mr Corndell, but I've seen and admired your work. I've even seen a copy of the film you produced which your father directed. Ahead of its time is all I can say."

"You flatter me Mr Brown, but don't stop, I could get to like it. However, you still haven't answered my question. What do you want of me?"

"I'd like to book you Mr Corndell."

"Pardon?"

Corndell sounded shocked, as if what Martin was asking was not an everyday occurrence.

"I'm in charge of the entertainment at The University of Leeds and one of the students suggested we have a night of culture. They wanted me to find a classical actor of your ability to put on a one-man show here. I was really hoping that you were still involved and wondered whether or not you'd be interested."

"You have my undivided attention. I'm flattered you know so much about me. But there are two things I must ask. Firstly, when is it? Second, and perhaps equally as important, do you have the necessary funding?"

"I'm sure we could negotiate the price."

"Don't count on it, Mr Brown."

Martin's heart sank a little. He might be stepping out of his league and he was beginning to think it was a bad idea. But at least he'd managed to avoid answering how he'd obtained the number.

"I wondered if you would consider April 1st."

The pause on the end of the line went on forever.

"I'm impressed, young man. But I have to say I'm extremely busy with Hollywood at the moment, negotiating for my latest manuscript, which, of course, must take precedence. But you've obviously gone to a lot of trouble to track me down and ask me to entertain your students. And furthermore, you're asking if I'll do it on my birthday. I think it's a wonderful idea."

"You'll do it?"

"Don't sound so surprised. Isn't that what you wanted?" asked William.

"Yes it is, but I never expected."

"Don't be negative, young man. Positive thinking has brought you this far. I presume you know my address, particularly as you know my ex-directory telephone number."

"As a matter of fact I do."

"Good, then put a contract in the post to arrive no later than two days time. I shall sign and insert the price at the same time."

"But that's just it, the price. I'm not sure we can afford you."

"The price sir, will not be negotiable. If you want the best then you have to be prepared to pay for it. However, my quote will not disappoint. Thank you and goodbye."

Martin was listening to a dialling tone again. He was amazed, not only to find he had booked a man whose work he admired, but the fact that the conversation had ended so abruptly.

Martin wasted no time in making the next call.

"Hello?" answered Laura.

"Laura? It's Martin, from the University."

"Hi, Martin, how are you?"

"Just great. Have I got an assignment for you."

CHAPTER 18

"Are you sure Stewart's okay, now, Sean?" asked Laura.

Reilly allowed his fork to hover in mid air before answering the question. "Of course he's okay."

"Well you would say that, you're a man."

"And what's that supposed to mean?"

"Oh come on, darling," winked Laura. "It's a well known fact that men notice nothing. How many couples do you know who have split up and when we've spoken to them afterwards, the husband claims it was such a surprise, that he thought everything was fine?"

"That doesn't mean to say we don't notice anything, so it doesn't. You women are so complex, even *Poirot* would have a problem proving something's wrong."

Reilly chose now to eat his curry before the onslaught came. He wasn't sure when he'd have the chance to reply again after that one.

The intimate surroundings of the restaurant with its dim lighting and background music created the romantic ambience he'd been hoping for. Of the dozen or so tables only half of them were occupied. Each of the couples was so quiet and intimate they may as well have had the place to themselves.

Laura's dark brown hair shone. She'd recently had it cut shorter than normal, allowing it to rest on the base of her neck. Her eyes glistened and her soft Irish accent added to her mystique.

"We're not complicated at all, it's you lot: you can't read the signs."

"Only 'cause they're in Braille."

"Quite the comedian tonight, we are. Anyway, back to Stewart, do you think he's over the incident with Jacqueline?"

Reilly put down his fork, sipping his Guinness. "It was a hell of a shock, finding someone you're close to murdering people with such precision. But I don't think he wanted her as much as she wanted him. He didn't say anything. He handled it in his usual way, bottled it up, threw himself into the job, wouldn't allow anyone to see his emotions."

Laura took a sip of wine. "Well, he's no different to any other man, is he, then? I sometimes think if you would allow your emotions to come out instead of seeing it as a sign of weakness there may be more marriages saved."

"I suppose you're right."

"I worry about Stewart," said Laura. "He's such a nice man, so particular about his health and cleanliness but he doesn't have much luck with women."

"I wouldn't say that, he was married to Sarah for over twenty years."

"I'm sorry, darling," replied Laura. "I didn't mean it that way. If you look back he's always blamed himself for the death of his mother despite the fact that he was twelve years old and couldn't do anything about it. Then came the tragic consequences surrounding Sarah's death. He's never going to forgive himself for that one as long as he lives."

"Which wasn't his fault either," said Reilly.

"No, not at all, but he doesn't see it like that, nor will he ever. As far as he's concerned he made the wrong decision trying to break up the brawl. He was in the wrong place at the wrong time."

"Sarah was the one in the wrong place. A little more to the left or the right and the bullet would have missed her completely."

Laura realised they had arrived at a point in the conversation when it would neither help nor solve anything. A little thought was what counted, for the people they held in high esteem.

She put down her glass. "And then Jacqueline. Do you think he loved her?"

"From the things he was saying, no. But from the look in his eyes I'd say he had some feelings for her."

"Oh my God! Sean Reilly, king of the leprechauns, one man combat zone, actually noticing someone's eyes."

"Just listen to yourself, would you, woman," said Reilly, holding off another fork full of food. "You underestimate me. In fact I notice your eyes a lot."

"Is that so?" challenged Laura.

"I certainly do, in fact, I'm just wondering which one I'm going to poke out first."

Laura laughed. She loved her husband so much. He was so unpredictable, so funny, always threatening to sort her out. She knew deep down that despite his hard man image – and he *was* hard, had to be in his job – he would never hurt her. He had never raised a finger to her in all the years they had been married. Yes, they had had disagreements, and surprisingly, it was Sean who had always made up first: despite the many times she had wanted to make the first move. He was a family man at heart. He loved them – would do anything for them.

"Big mistake, Sean Reilly. If you leave me with an eye I'll scratch both of yours out."

"Is that so. Do you know who you're dealing with here?"

"I most certainly do. Why else do you think I'm threatening?"

They giggled and touched hands and their laughter reminded Laura of the first time they met. It was a balmy July night. They were teenagers. Sean was sitting with her grandfather on the coastline known as The Giants Causeway. Sean spent hours with old Seamus. She tried to sneak up on them both. The old man had heard her and chosen to ignore it. But at the last moment he turned, frightened the life out of her. She fell, sprained her ankle. Then dropped her camera in the water. Her grandfather howled with laughter. The teenager standing next to him was shocked, judging by the expression on his face. Despite her grandfather's protests to leave her, Sean helped her up, took her home. She cursed all the way but he took no notice. Laura instinctively knew that she had met her future husband that day.

"I love you, Sean."

"I know you do," he replied.

"Aren't you supposed to say something here?"

"Like what?" Sean asked.

"I think you're supposed to return the compliment."

"Well now, I don't think I can be doing that. You see, we men are not supposed to notice anything and we're not supposed to show our emotions, so you shouldn't be expecting a reply."

"You're a first class pig, Sean Reilly. I think you need to be reminding me why I married you."

"I'll do no such thing. If you don't know your own mind I don't see why I should help you find it."

"Oh I know my own mind, right enough, you'll see."

Sean laughed and finished the last of his Guinness. He signalled the waiter, ordered another, asking Laura if she wanted more wine. She said she was quite happy with what she had at the moment.

"You seem in a good mood tonight, Laura."

"I am." She helped herself to another mouthful of pasta.

"Is it the university job?"

"Yes, but I can't think why. I mean, I've never even heard of this guy. When Martin rang me he was so excited that he'd managed to book some obscure actor called William Henry Corndell for the Uni. Like I said, I've never heard of him."

"Have you checked him out?"

"I have. Can't find any reference to him."

Laura had recently changed direction with her career. For many years she had been a freelance photographer. Examples of her work were framed around their two-storey house in Yeadon. More recently she had gone back to the second love of her life, entertainment journalist. Most magazines carried her reviews of the local and regional plays. Every three months she travelled down to London to keep her eye on what was up and coming and would eventually be touring.

"Wallace Henry Corndell, yes, but not William."

"Who was Wallace?"

"A big film director back in the sixties, worked for Ealing, turned out a string of comedies. Judging by the reports I've read he was very good at his job."

"Is William a relative in the same line of business?" suggested Reilly.

"Perhaps, but not as successful, otherwise I would have heard of him. Anyway, mine is not to reason why. Martin absolutely raves over the man. Said he saw him down in London when William was rehearsing for *Phantom of the Opera*."

"Well there you are then, he must have a talent."

"But that's just it, I can't find a reference for that either. We all know Michael Crawford was the star of that show, and there have been various leading men since, but I'm sure that William Henry Corndell wasn't one of them."

Reilly finished his food, sat back in his chair. As Laura had already finished hers he signalled the waiter once more for the desert menu.

"It must be costing the university a small fortune if they're shipping him all the way from London for one night."

"That's just it, they're not. Apparently, he lives locally."

"Where?"

"About five or six miles from us, in Horsforth."

"Does he now? Well I never knew that."

"See! It's like I told you earlier, you men never pay attention."

Laura leaned forward and whispered very discreetly in order to catch her husband's attention.

"I'll bet you haven't even noticed I'm not wearing any underwear tonight."

CHAPTER 19

Gardener glanced at the clock: 7:30.

He was feeling guilty for spending the last two hours at home, leading something close to a normal life. Before leaving the station he'd phoned ahead and Malcolm had made an early dinner of char grilled chicken breasts and salad, with granary baguettes. All three ate together before Malcolm had taken off for a night at the small private cinema in Headingley. They were showing a Terry Thomas black and white comedy double bill. Gardener hoped it would lift Malcolm's spirits.

He'd cleared the pots, grabbed a shower, thought some more about the case. Most of the team had spent the day trawling through the huge pile of witness statements, consulting HOLMES. A number of cases came to light regarding blood being drained but none of them bore any of the hallmarks of the Leonard White murder.

Despite being frustrating it was challenging. There was nothing Gardener loved more. The main things on his mind were the watch committee and the puzzles, the connection being Harry Fletcher. Gardener could not figure out why Fletcher would wait until now if there had been a conflict within the group. In spite of the fact that he kept fading in and out of life over the last twenty years he had always been local. Why not take his revenge before now?

In the kitchen, Gardener placed a cup of herbal tea on the tray before him, and a can of coke for Chris, as well as a number of chocolate bars.

He continued to think about the murder. The most unsettling aspect was the disguise. How were they ever going to catch someone if he was that good with a brush and a bit of greasepaint? As Reilly pointed out, they would have to wait for a mistake. But would the public? There was no telling how many people the killer would take out before he made that fatal error.

Gardener picked up the tray, heading for the garage with one further thought in his mind. No matter how hard it proved to be, he would find an answer. He was *not* going to have some maniac running riot through his city.

The connecting door was open. Gardener pushed it wider with one foot, comforted by the scene before him. Chris was dressed in an oil-stained boiler suit that was at least two sizes too big. A rock anthem CD was playing. The smell of oil and petrol suffused the air. Nuts and bolts clanked as they landed in glass jars. Gardener smiled. His job was very demanding. If all he could grab were a couple of hours now and again he'd settle for that.

Chris glanced at his father before immediately clearing a place to put the tray.

"Thanks, Dad." He grabbed his coke and a chocolate bar.

As Gardener took stock he couldn't believe how clean and tidy the place was. Chris had put everything in boxes, which he'd carefully labelled and placed in some sort of order. Nuts, bolts, screws and washers of all descriptions had been segregated into different glass jars and the garage was beginning to feel more like home than a workshop, especially as Spook was stretched out on a cushion on one of the shelves, casually washing herself, totally unconcerned at what was happening around her.

"You've done a terrific job, Chris."

"I've been at it for a couple of days."

"How come?"

"Last time I saw you in here you were searching all over for a few nuts and bolts, losing your patience."

Gardener laughed. "That's par for the course. It's part of the restoration process. You lose things and you're allowed to swear a bit while you find them."

"Do you want me to chuck these all over the floor again?"

"Yeah, right."

The music on the CD changed to Jim Steinman's *Rock and Roll Dreams Come Through*.

"We don't get enough family time like this together, Chris. The way things are at the moment I have to grab it while I can."

"It's okay," said Chris, taking a slurp of coke. "I wouldn't want your job. I don't care how good the money is."

"It's not as good as you think."

"Why do you do it, then?"

That was a good question, thought Gardener. Working all the hours God sends, chasing perverts and criminals and murderers with no thanks and no patience and no help from the public, isn't be ideal from anyone's point of view.

"It's all I know. And it's personal."

"What do you mean?"

Gardener pointed to his chest. "It's in here. I suppose it's a bit like a priest. You might wonder why he does his job and he'd probably tell you it's not a job but a calling. That's how I feel. It's more than a job, and it has been ever since I first started. And to be honest it goes back to what happened to your grandmother."

Chris seemed deep in thought about the answer before asking. "Do you think you'll ever catch all the criminals?"

His son was full of good questions tonight. "I doubt it. And in a way, I hope not."

"Why?"

"Because then I'll be out of a job."

The track on the CD changed to ELO's *Hold On Tight*.

They both laughed.

"At least then you can do something you really want, like fixing bikes."

Gardener finished his chocolate bar and sipped his herbal tea. "I doubt I'll ever be good enough for that. Your grandfather might be."

"Is he good?"

Gardener nodded. "He's the real brains behind this restoration. I've spent a long time tinkering with bikes because I love it, but I'm not in his league."

"I thought he was a gardener," said Chris.

"He was, but that's what he did for a living. His passion on a weekend was his motorbikes. I know he used to love his job but there was a time when he totally refused to work weekends. He spent it with his family and his bikes."

"Did he have many?"

"Not really, no. I can only remember him having about six in life, and never usually more than one at a time. He almost gave up after he nearly got arrested."

"Granddad did?"

"Yes. God that was funny."

"What happened?"

"He had a Triumph Speed Twin. It was his pride and joy. It was the business. I think it was a bloke called Edward Turner who was responsible for it. It had everything a bike could want.

"I can't remember what year your Granddad's was but he looked after it better than he looked after me I think. Always polishing it: stripped and rebuilt it every year. It looked like it had come out the showroom every time you saw it. Anyway, this one time, he'd finished his annual strip and rebuild, polished it like a new pin and took it out for a test drive. Police stopped him near Rothwell. They'd had a report that one had been stolen from a showroom in Leeds. The description matched your Granddad's."

Gardener was laughing now as he remembered. "He had no identification on him whatsoever. The police impounded the bike and took him in. Me and your Gran had to go down there with all the documents and sort the whole mess out. It took us an hour to get him out of there and when we all got home, bike included, there was a letter waiting for us to say he'd forgotten to pay the television licence and if he didn't he was going to get a visit from the police."

The pair of them erupted into raucous laughter, startling Spook, who glared at them as if they had completely lost their minds.

CHAPTER 20

Janine Harper's mood was nuclear. She couldn't believe that old bastard, Cuthbertson. He'd tricked her into doing the final stock take for the auditors on her own.

It won't take long, he'd said, and it is an emergency. A couple of hours and you'll be done, and you can still go out and enjoy yourself afterwards.

He had to be fucking joking: the mood she was in?

She'd suspected all day that he'd been leading up to something. He'd been too nice: offering her a longer lunch than normal: making afternoon tea, *and buying the cakes!* He was normally as tight as a duck's arse. The only way to force a warm drink out of him was to stick your fingers down his throat.

And then came the crunch phone call, a little after four o' clock. His sister had been taken ill, rushed into a hospital somewhere – although where, he'd failed to mention. Janine didn't think he had a sister; she'd thought his only family was a test tube.

She checked her watch: a little after nine-thirty. She should have been with her friends now. The four of them had made plans to go out for drinks and then on to the Italian on New Briggate. They didn't treat themselves very often. The recession had tightened their pockets.

Janine sighed loudly. She really couldn't believe she was doing it. Well ... she would show Cuthbertson. Boy would he receive a major shock when he opened the door tomorrow morning. Give him a fucking heart attack if she had her way.

She put the clipboard down and picked up her mobile phone, calling her friend, Angie. No one answered. She called Sarah next but her phone was switched off. They were obviously having a good time.

She threw the mobile down on the shelf. It bounced on to the floor, where the battery disconnected and the phone slid under the Dexion shelving.

"Fucking wonderful," cried Janine. Could things be any worse?

In the haunting silence that followed, she suspected that perhaps things could, because the door to the shop had actually opened.

Who the hell could that be? Surely to God it wasn't a punter who thought it was late night opening: or worse ... a gang of drunken idiots?

It could be anybody – maybe a tramp, they wandered all over Leeds, day and night. Perhaps he had popped in to keep warm. She'd never shift him. He might be plastered on Meths. He could do anything to her. And there was no one around because no one else worked so late. All the other shopkeepers had gone home by now and none of them lived above the premises.

Janine's nerve ends tingled. She thought she had locked the shop. Her legs grew heavier and the space inside her head started to close in. Palpitations were squeezing her chest and she honestly thought she was going to stop breathing.

Oh Jesus, what was she going to do?

She glanced around for a possible weapon. The shop was full

of dangerous things she could use: liquids or powders she could throw into someone's face. She'd open a bottle of Acetone. Chuck that in his face and his eyes will end up in his arse. She'd teach him to mess with her.

Janine slowly reached for the bottle.

Wait a minute. What was she thinking of? Who else could it be at nine thirty on a Friday evening? It was very obviously Cuthbertson, coming back to see if she was doing the job properly. Checking up on her.

Maybe his story had been genuine. Perhaps he did have a sister who had taken ill. He had been to see her and on his way home had felt guilty enough to see if Janine was still here and needed a hand.

Well, whether he had or not, she would give him a piece of her mind. By the time she was finished he would be in the next bed to his sister.

Janine marched straight through into the shop.

She nearly puked when her eyes focused and fed the message to her brain.

"Oh ... my ... fucking ... God..."

CHAPTER 21

Wednesday morning in the centre of Leeds and Alan Cuthbertson was enjoying yet another early spring day. Despite being a little overcast the temperature was quite high. He was strolling to work, observing the masses doing the same.

The amount of people walking and eating never failed to amaze him. Everywhere he turned someone had food in their hands: he passed a bunch of youths who – judging by their appearance – had been out all night; cigarette in one hand, McDonald's in the other. A middle aged couple on other side of the road were trying to have a conversation whilst devouring one of those submarine sandwiches that shops specialise in now: breakfast in a bun. Don't these people ever rise early and sort out their own breakfasts? Are they really that lazy? Staying in bed till the last minute before rolling out and into a suit and straight out of the door.

It wouldn't have happened in his day: discipline was paramount.

Cuthbertson turned into the arcade, toward the shop. He almost collided with a tramp: one of many in the city centre these days, asking for handouts, leading you to believe they weren't eating.

And what happened when you gave them the money? Straight down the chemist for a bottle of Meths.

"Could you spare some change, mate?"

"No!" shouted Cuthbert son. "Piss off and get a job like I have."

The tramp turned on him. A wave of fear surged through Cuthbertson's aged body. He'd heard how nasty they could be. He wished he hadn't said it now. Apart from the two of them the arcade was empty.

"It could be you one day, son. You could be homeless, just like me."

Cuthbertson chose to ignore him, scurrying away to his shop.

At the entrance he reached into his pocket for the keys. He tried the correct one but it wouldn't turn the lock.

Strange! Surely Janine had locked up last night? Then again, the mood she'd been in … she could be a right little madam when she wanted.

He tried the Yale key. When that didn't work he reached and turned the handle and pushed open the door.

He would have to have words with her. She was becoming very lackadaisical of late. Forgetting to lock up was the last straw. And he wasn't happy with the way she addressed customers. He would definitely nip it in the bud.

The shop was unnaturally dark as he entered. He pinched his nose, wondering what in God's name the smell was.

Cuthbertson reached out, switched on the light, turned a little too fast. He lost his footing and hit the floor like a sack of potatoes.

He was still on the ground when he glanced upwards.

The sight that greeted him saved him from falling again when he fainted.

CHAPTER 22

An ambulance with flashing blue lights parked in front of the arcade. Alongside that were three more squad cars and a van with dark tinted windows. Uniformed constables were standing in front of scene tape. Gardener and Reilly jumped out of their car, flashed warrant cards, walked down to the shop. At either end of the arcade, morning shoppers gathered, craning their necks to see what had happened.

The entrance to the shop was sealed with reflective scene tape. Inside, Gardener heard the voices of both Fitz and Briggs.

Sitting outside on a chair, wrapped in a blanket was a man. Gardener estimated his age around sixty. The small amount of grey hair he had left on the sides of his head above his ears was close cropped. The man wore round, wire-rimmed spectacles. He had a bulbous nose and his lips were thick and protruding. His complexion was the colour of flour. His teeth were chattering so hard, Gardener didn't think he would have any left in another hour.

The rest of his team was dotted around the arcade. Most of them were talking to what he suspected were the other shopkeepers.

A constable in front of the shop handed the two officers their white contamination suits. Gardener dressed. He was about to enter when Briggs stepped out.

"Bit nasty in there, Stewart." He nodded towards the man on the chair. "That's Alan Cuthbertson."

"Did he find the body?" asked Gardener.

"Afraid so."

"Not touched anything, has he?"

"I doubt it. He hasn't spoken since I got here. In fact, I don't think he's spoken since he found her."

"Who found him, then?" asked Reilly.

"Bloke next door in the camera shop: name's, Battersby. He heard an almighty crash and came running to see what was up. Cuthbertson had passed out. Battersby left him to it while he rang us."

"Where is he now?"

"Back in his own shop."

"Anybody questioned him?"

"Just doing it. You'd better take a look, Stewart. I've told Scenes of Crime to hang fire until you've been in. I'm warning you now, it's much worse than the last one."

"How do you know it's the same killer?"

"There's a quote on the wall," said Briggs.

"And it's *worse* than the last one?" questioned Reilly.

"Well you two go and have a look, I'm having a fag."

"I thought you'd given up," said Gardener.

"When you've seen what's in there you might join me." Briggs nodded to Cuthbertson again. "No wonder that poor bastard's lost his marbles."

Gardener pushed past Briggs. Reilly followed.

Inside the shop, Gardener pinched his nose. The coppery odour of blood was ever present, along with the putrid aroma of urine and excrement.

The room wasn't particularly big but an awful lot had been crammed into the space for display purposes: tailors dummies dressed in various costumes with a variety of different hairstyles. Two of the walls had shelves with latex masks and wigs and a whole range of chemicals and powders for stage use. The only bare wall in the shop was to the left of the counter.

That wall contained the message.

Which was partially hidden by the body.

The girl was naked, hanging upside down. Her legs were open, held that way by two ropes attached to ceiling beams, knotted tightly around her ankles, which – Gardener realised – bore no chafing. As his gaze wandered further down her colourless body he didn't notice any signs of sexual abuse, but he realised a closer inspection may reveal otherwise.

Her arms had also been tied and held outwards by ropes, intricately wound around the mannequins, connected to the counter at one side, and the window ledge at the other. Her throat had been slit, allowing the blood to drain into a large bucket beneath her head.

Had she been dead at that point? He'd figured she must have been, otherwise there would be blood-spatter.

That's something Fitz would eventually be able to tell him. The pathologist was standing quietly behind him, arranging the tools he would need.

"Notice something, Sean?"

"He's getting more adventurous," said Reilly. "But I'm noticing a lot of things, which one are you thinking of?"

"The wall behind her has no blood-spatter. Why?"

"He's done her somewhere else?"

"Possible. But how could you get a body into the arcade and into the shop without anyone seeing you?"

"He managed it in the theatre."

Gardener conceded. His partner had a point – a theory that once again supported the art of disguise. He wondered what the latest creation had been.

The SIO glanced around the shop in disgust.

Steve Fenton nodded. "I'll be outside, give us a shout when you need me."

Gardener blew out a sigh, nodded at Fitz: "Okay."

He stopped Steve Fenton leaving the shop. "Any sign of her clothes?

"Not so far."

Gardener turned his attention to the quote:

"THE NIGHT PASSED – A NIGHT OF VAGUE HORRORS

– TORTURED DREAMS."

What the hell was that supposed to mean? And where had it come from? Another film they would probably never trace?

He suspected her blood had been used to write it. That was something else which threw up a number of questions: was all the blood in the bucket hers? Was any of it missing? Was it mixed with someone else's?

In spite of the fact that he knew beyond any doubt she was dead, he still had to check. He felt for a pulse. No one questioned him. It was the duty of every officer – where possible – to preserve or save life.

Briggs came back into the shop, muttering about the mess and the bastard who'd created it.

"Does she have a name?" asked Gardener.

"Janine Harper. Bloke next door identified her. She's worked here for years. He thinks she's about twenty-five. He's not sure where she lives."

"Any idea what time it happened, Fitz?"

Fitz sighed, removing a thermometer from her rectum. "Judging by the results I'd say he started last night, reasonably late, so as not to be disturbed."

The pathologist leaned forward and pointed. "Look at the bruising to the face. I think she resisted him. He probably punched her a few times, eventually overpowered her and then most likely drugged her to be able to get her into that position."

"Why was she in the shop late at night by herself?" Gardener asked. "It wasn't her business."

"Ask him," said Briggs, pointing outside.

"I intend to, if he ever decides to speak."

Gardener didn't say anything else but walked around the counter and through to the back of the shop.

Reilly followed.

"There are signs of a struggle," suggested Gardener.

His partner nodded.

A small number of bottles and boxes were scattered around the floor. The SIO glanced closely at the shelving and then down at the floor.

"The nearest one's been moved, probably by force."

"Maybe she ran into here to try and escape."

"Where to?"

Reilly had no answer. "He obviously followed her."

"There's still no trace of blood-spatter. So she couldn't have been killed in here."

"That suggests she was still alive when he came into the shop," offered Reilly.

"So what the hell did he do with her?"

"More to the point, where?" added Reilly.

Gardener turned back into the main shop, read the quote: "What's that supposed to mean?" He stood contemplating. "I suppose it blows the theory of the watch committee." He nodded towards Janine Harper. "She certainly wasn't on it."

"Maybe not," said Reilly. "But her father might have been."

"Her father?"

"Val White gave us the names of the committee members. If my memory's right, there was a bloke called Jack Harper. If there's a connection, it doesn't blow your theory entirely."

Gardener glanced at the floor. "If that's the case, we definitely need to find Harry Fletcher now."

"What about him out there, Cuthbertson?" said Reilly. "Do you reckon he's capable of murder?"

"Could be," said Briggs.

"I'm not so sure," replied Fitz. "His shock looks pretty genuine to me. I realise you can't rule him out, but he's a bloody good actor if it is him."

"Isn't that what we're looking for, an actor?" said Gardener. "Someone with the ability to disguise himself, someone who has the means?"

"What's his motive?" asked Briggs.

"Let's find out."

Gardener walked over to the front door. He spoke to the constable. "Clean him up and take him back to the station for questioning."

He turned back and addressed Fitz. "Meanwhile, can you sort out the post mortem as soon as possible? I'm particularly interested in the fact that there's no blood-spatter but there are indications of a struggle in the back room. He must have killed her in the shop. Question is, what's he used in order eliminate her heartbeat? You know as well as I do if he'd done that while she was still alive, this place would be one God awful mess."

Fitz nodded. "Okay, we'll remove the body and let the SOCO's do their job."

Gardener shouted for Steve Fenton. "You know the drill: sweep for prints. I'd like another ESLA. Be careful with the ropes. The knots look different to the last one."

He turned to Briggs. "I'll have to speak to the team. We'll need to find out where she lives and speak to her parents.

"If they haven't already been on the phone to report her missing," Briggs replied.

"I assume she's not married, there's no wedding band, nor a line to suggest there was one," said Gardener. "We need a written report of his information next door. And all the CCTV evidence we can lay our hands on."

"What a mess," said Briggs. "The shit's going to hit the fan with this one."

"Can you put a call into the FSS for this one?"

Briggs nodded. "How the hell does he manage to do all this without someone seeing him?"

"He doesn't," said Gardener.

"Come again," said Briggs.

"Plenty of people see him. He isn't worried about people seeing him because nobody knows what he really looks like. Take a look at that crowd out there." Gardener pointed through the window. "He could be in that lot, somewhere. The front row, maybe. We'd have no idea because we don't know him. He knows that, he's playing on it. He can commit atrocities like this every day. He knows we're never going to catch him."

Gardener wanted out. He'd been here long enough. The smell had coated the insides of his nostrils.

"There's something else, boss," said Reilly. "If Jack Harper's dead and this was his daughter, that means *your* father is on the list as well."

"I know. I've thought of that already."

Another young constable appeared in the shop doorway. He waved to Gardener but kept his eyes on the floor.

"What is it?"

"The press, sir, they'd like a comment."

"I'm sure they would. I suppose we'd better tell them something. If we don't they'll only make it up."

Gardener walked out of the shop, stripped off his paper suit and deposited it in a bin. Briggs and Reilly followed. He spotted a team of Operational Support Officers heading in his direction.

"I'd like you lot to split up and question every shopkeeper in the arcade. Find out what they know about Alan Cuthbertson and Janine Harper and the customers who come in here on a regular basis. I'd also like a couple of you out front on the streets today, question everyone you see. Find out if they were in the town last night. Did they see anyone they considered eccentric?"

He turned to Briggs. Despite his loathing of the press, he knew he would have to use them.

"I think we'd better ask the press to appeal for witnesses."

CHAPTER 23

"**W**hat do you think, Sean?"

"About Cuthbertson? I'll know better when we've spoken to him, boss."

They were sitting in Gardener's office ahead of the interview. As usual, Reilly was dressed in a brown leather bomber jacket and jeans. He emptied the contents of a coffee cup and then threw it into the bin at the side of the desk.

Gardener was sitting with his hands bridged and his chin resting on them. He'd been reading the scribbled notes submitted by the officers who had interviewed the other shopkeepers in the arcade.

"The comments from his colleagues are not very favourable."

"Go on," said Reilly.

"The guy who runs the camera shop next door reckons he's a loner, keeps odd hours, a little strange with his behaviour, rarely socialises. I have the impression he doesn't like Cuthbertson."

"We both know there's nothing wrong with that description, boss. He could be talking about you. But you're no killer."

"How do you know?" laughed Gardener. He really appreciated the working relationship he had with the Irishman. Had it not been for Sean Reilly, he doubted very much he would have overcome the effect of Sarah's death quite so readily.

"It's not that so much, Sean. Battersby reckons he's quiet and subdued a lot of the time, as if he has things on his mind. Never discusses his private life, leaves the shop at all hours."

"Did he know why Janine Harper was working late at night on her own?" asked Reilly.

"No. Battersby noticed the lights were on but he had no idea who was there, though he doubted it would be Cuthbertson. Something about his manner doesn't add up," said Gardener. "I appreciate the death of his assistant would have an effect, but I thought he was too preoccupied."

"Perhaps he did it, boss. Maybe the silent treatment was a good piece of acting while he thought up an alibi for where he was yesterday."

"Maybe. According to Battersby he left the shop around four o' clock."

"Okay, so there's his opportunity. It must take a good three or four hours to apply make up to the quality that this man needs. But we still need a motive, and he could have an alibi."

"Battersby left at six-thirty."

"Did he see Cuthbertson come back?"

"No, and he didn't see Janine Harper leaving either," replied Gardener.

"Did he say anything about their relationship?"

Gardener rifled through the notes in front of him. "No, except that they were total opposites. At times, she could be quite lively. They did have their differences, which appears to have been the usual thing, young versus old. Fresh ideas coming up against aged resistance."

A knock on the door interrupted their conversation. Colin

Sharp's head appeared around the side of the door. "He's cleaned up and ready to talk now, sir."

"Thanks. We'll be there in five minutes."

"There's something else – something you ought to know."

"Go on," said Gardener.

"There's a lot of marks on his body."

"What kind of marks?" Reilly asked.

"Scratches, bites. Bruises."

"Has he now?" said Gardener. "Are they fresh?"

"They're recent, but I wouldn't like to say when."

Gardener gathered up the notes and returned them to the folder. "Time to go and find out what they're all about."

CHAPTER 24

"Is it the work of the same killer?"

The question was from Johnny Stevens, an experienced journalist with *The Yorkshire Post*. Alan Briggs knew he had served his time on some of the worst cases in the county. The Yorkshire Ripper to name but one. He was a bloodhound, well paid. Delivered results.

A meeting with the press was the last thing Alan Briggs wanted right now. The day started terribly with the discovery of Janine Harper's body: became worse because he was summoned to a meeting with his superior – who shouted loud enough to wake the dead. Now it hit an all time low because Gardener was otherwise engaged.

Not that Gardener would have cared. Offering him a press meeting was like serving up garlic bread to Dracula. As much as he admired Gardener's dedication to the job and the reason for his hatred of the press, he would have much preferred to interview Alan Cuthbertson.

"There are similarities between the two murders. We are taking into consideration the theatrical and geographical links."

"Oh, come on, Briggs."

"Hey!" The DCI raised his hand, stopped him there. "Mister Briggs to you, if you don't mind."

"Okay, Mr Briggs," Stevens repeated the name with distaste. "Who has he killed this time?"

"You know very well I'm not at liberty to say."

"Is it a child?" shouted another reporter.

"No, it is not a child."

"Has he killed another thespian, Mr Briggs?"

Briggs took his time in answering because he knew what would come next. But he couldn't hold out forever.

"No."

Johnny Stevens was on his feet again. "The public have a right to know what's going on, Mr. Briggs. *We* have a duty to tell them, and *you* have one to tell us."

"I agree that the public have a right to know, son, and as soon as we have something concrete to tell them, we will. But this meeting is about utilising the newspapers to appeal for witnesses. We want the public of Leeds to keep their eyes open, report anything unusual."

"Well if he hasn't killed an actor it must be one of the general public," shouted another reporter. Briggs had never seen him before.

"How do you feel about him changing his approach? If he is picking on members of the public, then there should be no shortage of information."

"There won't *be* a shortage of information, son, but we have to carefully consider what's relevant."

"What if we consider it relevant?"

Before Briggs could answer that question, another reporter jumped down his throat. The questions were coming thick and fast.

"Do you have any leads?"

"We have discovered one or two points worthy of further investigation." Briggs was pleased with himself for that one.

"Have you identified the man?"

"We are at present interviewing someone." Briggs held up his hand. "But let me make it absolutely clear, he is only helping us with our inquiries, he is not a suspect."

Another reporter stood up. He was about to throw a question when Briggs himself rose from his chair.

"I'm afraid I'll have to stop you there, gentlemen, we do have a very important investigation on our hands. Thank you for your time."

Briggs left the room, closed the door behind him, relieved that it was over. He was still furious by the fact that they were no further on: two murders within a week, both in the same part of town. There were similarities, neither of which had turned up any evidence. The next meeting in the incident room would be one to remember.

CHAPTER 25

Gardener studied Alan Cuthbertson.

The expression of fear on the shop owner's face had Gardener concerned. Was he frightened about the situation he was in; felt he was being fitted up for something he hadn't done? Or was it guilt? Because he *had* committed murder and the police had figured him out a lot sooner than he'd anticipated.

They had taken his clothes and supplied him with a plain black tee shirt, dark blue jogging bottoms and black plimsoles – standard issue custody clothing. Cuthbertson's pallor was deathly white. He constantly twitched. He also rubbed his hands together a lot whilst inspecting his fingernails every few seconds.

"Am I under arrest?" he asked.

"Not yet," replied Gardener. "You're helping with our enquiries."

"Do I need a solicitor?"

"Do *you* think you need one?"

"I haven't done anything wrong!" he shouted.

"Bit of a shock for you, seeing that" said Reilly.

"Shock!" repeated Cuthbertson. "I was bloody traumatised. It's not every day you open your shop and find your assistant hanging upside down with her insides in a bucket."

"Not so shocked that you didn't take everything in by the sound of it," said Reilly.

Cuthbertson fixed Reilly with a stare. "What are you suggesting?"

"How would you describe your relationship?" asked Gardener.

"What's that supposed to mean?" retorted Cuthbertson. His eyes were like slits and his expression had hardened. "I've heard about you lot and your strong arm tactics, well you won't get me to admit to something I haven't done."

"We don't want you to. But we would like an answer to the question I've just asked."

"Oh, God." He placed his arms on the desk and supported his head with his hands. "What a bloody mess."

Gardener didn't feel the need to repeat the question. He chose instead to simply stare at the suspect.

Cuthbertson glanced upwards. "Do you mind if I smoke?"

"Actually, we do," replied Gardener. "Neither us smoke, we don't see why we should breathe in yours."

Cuthbertson sighed. "My relationship." He lifted his head and rubbed his hands together.

"Well. It was pretty much like any other. She was a good worker. Usually on time: never really took time off sick."

"Had she caused you any problems recently?" asked Gardener.

"I think she's had something on her mind. Last couple of days she'd been late and her attitude with customers wasn't what I would have expected of her. More than once I had to smile and make an apology."

"Did she say what it was?"

"No, but she was certainly withdrawn. I did ask of course, but she just blamed it on women's problems. Maybe it was boyfriend trouble."

"Do you know the boyfriend?" asked Reilly.

"Yes, met him a couple of times. He'd picked her up from the shop. He seemed all right, but then don't they all when you only see them for a couple of minutes?"

"Do you know anything else about him? His name? Where he lives? His job?"

"Carl Simpson, lives over Esholt way, don't know where exactly. Plays in a band as far as I know. He's a drummer, likes to make a bit of noise. Not the sort of band I'd want to see, nor you two by the look of you."

"Were there any other problems?" asked Gardener.

"Nothing she let on about."

"So you worked well together?"

"Yes, I just said so, didn't I?"

"How long had she worked for you?"

"About five years. The shop had been growing steadily busier and I advertised for an assistant. She was the best of the bunch."

"Did she ever talk about her home life? About her relationship with her parents?" asked Gardener.

"A little. She had a younger sister who was still at college. Her father's dead. Her mother takes in ironing."

News of her father's death struck a raw nerve with Gardener. *Was* it Jack Harper of the watch committee? If it was then they needed to find Fletcher for all sorts of reasons.

"Did you know her father?"

"No. He died before Janine came to work for me."

"She ever mention his name?" Gardener was fishing.

"I can't remember. Look, where the hell are you going with all this? It's not helping find the killer is it?" asked Cuthbertson, his tone suggesting his nerves were taut.

"We have to build a picture of what Janine was like," said

Gardener. "You've already told us she wasn't herself of late, we need to know why. Was it family problems? Boyfriend trouble? Had someone threatened her? Did she have money problems? Any debt? Do you know anything about her social life?"

"I'm her employer. The kind of questions you're asking me should be directed at her mother. She knows her better than I do."

"In that case," said Reilly, "Let's talk about you."

"Me!"

"Aye, you. Tell us something about yourself?"

"There's not much to tell."

"I wish I had a pound for every time I'd heard that, don't you, boss? I'll tell you what: we'll make this easy for you. We'll ask questions, you answer. How long have you had your business?"

"Thirty years. I haven't been in the arcade for thirty years because it wasn't there then. I started off in a little village, Burley in Wharfedale back in the eighties. That's where I live you see."

"Business was good then?"

"Not to start with. But I've always been interested in theatre and stage and I had a lucky break thirty years ago. I won twenty five thousand pounds on the football pools. It was a lot of money back then. So I decided to pack in work and open the shop."

"I see," said Gardener. "So because you'd won all that money it didn't really matter whether or not the business got off to a slow start, you had enough capital to see you through."

"That's about the size of it. Look, are you sure I can't smoke? I thought I had rights."

"You have," replied Gardener. "To a telephone and a solicitor and any other reasonable requests. But we don't like smoke: we consider it unreasonable. Would you like a coffee?"

"I'd love one, please."

Gardener left the table. Outside the interview room door he

asked for two coffees – fresh ones, not the crap from the machine, and a bottle of water.

He came back to the table and sat down.

"Okay, so you had the shop at Burley. When did you decide to move to Leeds?"

"Ten years ago. Business was expanding and I was beginning to attract lucrative custom from London. A lot of my business is mail order."

"I'm pleased you mentioned that. We would like to see records, everything you've sold, both over the counter and mail order for at least the last five years."

"That isn't a problem. Anyway, I moved into Leeds, on Briggate. Five years ago I decided to take one of the arcade shops because it was considered a more prime position. And I took Janine on."

A uniformed officer returned with the drinks. He left them on the table and walked out.

"What about your customers? How well do you know them?"

"I know a few, repeat business from people who are touring."

"What about new customers? Have you had any in the shop recently that you haven't seen before?"

"Quite a few."

"Any strange ones?" asked Reilly. "An eccentric? Someone who stands out a little more than usual?"

"Can't say that I've noticed. Most of the people who come in are pleasant. You get the odd few that think they're above everyone else, people who think that just because they're in a local production, they're film stars."

"Anyone come to mind."

"Not off the top of my head, no." He sipped his coffee.

"I'd like a list of all your clients, Mr Cuthbertson: names and addresses."

"I don't know if I have the addresses of all of them."

"We'll settle for everyone that you do have," replied Gardener. "Now, let's come back to something you said earlier. You'd always been interested in theatre and stage. Films as well?"

"Yes, films as well."

"What's your favourite?" asked Gardener.

"Pardon?"

"Your favourite film, what is it?"

"I ... er ... I'm not sure. Something black and white I imagine, an Ealing comedy."

"Why?"

"What do you mean, why?"

"Simple enough question, Mr Cuthbertson. Why do you like films from that era, Ealing comedies in particular?"

"Because they knew how to make films then. Good wholesome films with people who could act. Not just the comedies, but the kitchen-sink drama as well: films that dealt with real people in real situations. Not the garbage you get now, science fiction, horror: sex. There's enough horror in the real world without having TV and cinema ram it down your throat. You only have to look at my shop to see that. And here you are accusing me when I haven't done anything."

"No one is accusing you. If anything, we're trying to eliminate you from our enquiries and the only way we can do that is to be very thorough. Wouldn't you agree?" asked Gardener.

"Absolutely."

"Wouldn't want to go to prison for something you haven't done, would you, now?" said Reilly. "Especially for a crime like this. You know what they do to people in prison who have killed women?"

"Look if you're trying to frighten me..."

"We're not," replied Gardener. "We're trying to find out why a young girl has been butchered on your premises, and there are times when our job is not very nice but we still have to do it. If you're innocent, you have nothing to worry about. Now can we please get back to the matter in hand?"

Cuthbertson took another sip of coffee.

"Ealing comedies," said Reilly.

A silence descended upon the room. When it was obvious that Reilly wasn't going to elaborate on them, Cuthbertson spoke up. "What about them?"

"Does the name Wallace Henry Corndell mean anything to you?"

Cuthbertson took his time before answering. "No, should it?"

"William, maybe?"

"No. I've never heard of him, either."

"What about Inspector Burke?" Gardener asked.

"Who the bloody hell's he?" asked Cuthbertson, and then added. "Another one of your lot?"

"For a man who likes his films you don't know much about them," said Reilly.

"I never said I was into films, not in the way you mean. Theatre and stage is more my thing."

"I see, " said Reilly. "Well that figures, type of shop you run. Like dressing up, do you? Putting on the make up, that kind of thing?"

Cuthberston narrowed his eyes. "I've done a bit, why do you ask?"

"What other interests do you have?" asked Gardener.

Cuthbertson stalled before answering, as if he was trying to work out where they were heading. "I like to read."

"What sort of books?"

"Biographical. Mostly non fiction."

Reilly leaned forward and folded his arms across the top of the table. "For long weary months I have awaited this hour."

"Pardon?" asked Cuthbertson. Turning to Gardener, he asked, "Is he all right?"

"Do you not recognise it? And you being a thespian, shame on you."

"I never said I was a thespian. Look, is it me, or is it hot in here?" Cuthbertson loosened his shirt collar and ran his hands around his neck.

Gardener wondered why he done that now. He'd seemed okay until Reilly had mentioned the quote. Why had that unbalanced him?

Gardener leaned forward. "The night passed – a night of vague horrors. Tortured dreams."

"Look, what the hell are you two talking about? Is there something in the coffee? If I'm not under arrest why am I still here?"

"I've told you already, you're helping with our enquiries. We just wondered how well you knew your films, and whether or not you recognised the two quotes."

"Oh I see." Cuthbertson folded his arms. "You think I did it, and now you're using the quote on the wall next to Janine's body. Trying to catch me out." He leaned forward himself now, a smug smile crossing his features. "I'm afraid you'll have to do better than that, gentleman. I've already told you, I have nothing to hide."

"I wouldn't say that judging by the state of your body," said Reilly.

"What?"

"How did you come by the marks?" asked Gardener.

"I don't know what you're talking about."

"Take your shirt off," demanded Reilly. "Maybe that will refresh your memory."

"Look, okay, I admit to having one or two bruises, but they're not what you think."

"How do you know what we're thinking?" asked Gardener.

"You two think I killed Janine, and the bruises on my body are proof. That's what you're thinking."

"Wouldn't you?" said Reilly. "On the night a young girl was butchered in your shop, you'd left at four o'clock and was not seen again until the next morning. But when you do make an appearance, your skin looks like you've survived a terrorist attack."

"It's not as bad as you're making out."

"Show us," said Reilly.

"Gentlemen..."

"Show us now!" Gardener demanded.

Although Cuthbertson appeared unwilling, he did finally peel off his shirt.

Gardener grimaced. His back bore the marks of a cat of nine tails: long, stripe shaped cuts. Most of the bruising was purple, yellow in the middle. What Gardener couldn't understand was why Cuthbertson had not shown any outward signs of discomfort. But having said that, the man had not sat back in his seat.

"So where you were last night and how did you get those?" asked Reilly.

Cuthbertson replaced his shirt and returned to his seat.

"Well?" persisted Reilly.

"It's not what you think."

"You keep trying to tell us what *we're* thinking, instead of what's going through *your* head," pressed Gardener.

Cuthbertson rubbed his hands down his face and sighed heavily. "I never killed Janine Harper. She was my assistant, my friend."

"Last night!" Reilly reminded him. "Where were you?"

Cuthbertson remained tight-lipped for some time. He had certainly done something wrong but for the record, Gardener still didn't think he *had* killed his assistant.

"Ruffin Street," he replied, quietly.

"Say again," said Reilly.

Cuthbertson brought his head up a little fast, his manner aggressive. "You're enjoying this, aren't you? I said, Ruffin Street."

"I thought you did."

Gardener tried to picture the area. He knew where the street was but he wasn't quite sure what Cuthbertson was trying to say.

"What's on Ruffin Street, Mr Cuthbertson?"

"I'd have thought you'd known, being a policeman."

"I'm aware that it's an area of ill repute but I don't frequent the place myself. So you'll have to do a little better than that. We need your alibi."

Cuthbertson sighed, reached into his pocket, brought out his cigarettes.

"Oh, no," said Gardener. "You've been told."

"For Christ's sake, just one?"

"Not until the interview is finished. Now are you going to tell us what you were up to last night?"

Cuthbertson threw the packet on the table.

"I ... I was..." He stopped talking, licked his lips.

Gardener waited.

"I was at Madam Two-swords. Happy now?"

Gardener turned to Reilly. "Where the hell is Madam Tussaude's in Ruffin Street?"

Reilly's smile widened. "Trust me, boss, you wouldn't want to know. But I'll tell you this and I'll tell you no more, it's not a waxwork museum."

"What is it?"

"Madam Two-swords – and the spelling is two as in the number, and swords as in the sharp bladed implements that knights used to use – is a house of ill repute for people who like to be fulfilled sexually in a very strange way."

Gardener glanced at Cuthbertson who was staring at the floor.

"Go on," said Gardener.

"Madam Two-swords has not been blessed with beauty: face like a blind cobbler's thumb. Rumour has it she was born a she-male, had both sets of tackle. Apparently, a few years back she had another male member grafted on to her body, enabling her – with the use of modern technology – to be able to satisfy females in both entrances at once. Though God knows what she does for male clients ... maybe you can tell us, Mr Cuthbertson."

"Don't bother," replied Gardener. "Are you a regular?"

"Yes."

Gardener passed over pen and paper. "Write the number down. We'll check. Were you there the night Leonard White was murdered?"

"Yes, I was."

Gardener couldn't believe what he was hearing. "What? Do you go for that kind of punishment every night?"

"No."

"How often?"

"I'm there most nights, but not for anything physical. A lot of them like to dress up and wear make up. I can supply all their needs. Sometimes I help them put it on."

Gardener shook his head.

Cuthbertson continued. "But I can promise you, I never murdered Janine and I didn't do Leonard White, either."

Gardener realised there was little more he could ask Cuthbertson at the moment until he could confirm his alibis.

He informed the man he was free to go for the time being.

CHAPTER 26

"We need to nail this bloke, and fast! Otherwise we're all going down." Briggs was agitated.

The incident room was full but you could have heard a fly fart in the next world.

"I've had the press and the Commissioner on my back, and neither of them are in the mood for negative answers."

"It isn't our fault," said Reilly, glancing at the stranger sitting quietly in the corner of the room.

"Well everybody seems to think it is," retorted Briggs. "We're paid to protect the public and we're failing. We've had two murders on our patch and the press have already made the connection. In fact, they know as much as we do because we can't do our jobs properly."

Briggs threw his folder on the desk and studied the photographs on the easel.

"So, can anyone tell me anything new?"

Sharp inched forward. "I've spoken to the taxi driver who picked up Leonard White on the night he was killed, or should I say, the man impersonating Leonard White."

"And what did he have to say?" asked Briggs.

"Very little. He wasn't called in advance, he simply happened to be driving by the theatre at the time and was flagged down."

"Where did he take him?"

"The station."

"The station?" questioned Briggs. "It's only a five minute walk for Christ's sakes."

"He was an actor," said Gardener. "Would you walk in his position?"

"Okay," said Briggs. "Fair point. What happened when he dropped him off? Did he see where he went?"

"No. White shoved a ten pound note in his hand and then walked into the station without waiting for change."

"Don't suppose he's still got the note, has he?"

"He didn't say."

"Well check it out for God's sake! People keep souvenirs for all sorts of reasons."

Gardener interrupted. "What good would it do us? We wouldn't be able to lift any prints worth having."

"We don't know that," said Briggs.

Briggs addressed Colin Sharp again. "Did White say anything while he was in the taxi?"

"Apparently not. He got in, told him to go to the station and then got out after paying. The driver tried to engage him in conversation because he recognised him, but White wasn't having any of it. He simply ignored him."

"Brilliant. Did you question anyone at the station? Ticket booth operators, railway porters, cleaners, tramps?"

"I did, but no one saw anything unusual."

"They must have done for Christ's sakes, he wasn't exactly dressed for travelling on trains. Didn't White buy a ticket to anywhere?" demanded Briggs

"I did talk to the person who was selling tickets all night. I showed him a photo because he didn't know who Leonard White was, but no one of that description bought a ticket."

"Well he can't have just disappeared in the middle of a fucking station! He was a well known actor."

"He may not have left the station as Leonard White," said Gardener.

Briggs hadn't thought of that and quickly moved on. "Anything on CCTV?"

"We're still checking," said Sharp.

"Keep at it. And while we're on the subject of transport, what about white vans?"

Anderson spoke up: "We've drawn a blank so far. Not many companies hire out seven and a half ton trucks, those that have can account for them, and the customers."

"How does he do it?" shouted Briggs. "Not only does he *walk* around Leeds but he drives around in big white vans that no one remembers seeing, both of which finally disappear into thin air. Well thank Christ somebody has their eyes open. Eyewitness reports indicate a very strange person seen in Leeds on the night Janine was murdered. We've interviewed a couple of them and managed to sort out an artist impression."

Briggs passed around the sketches from his folder.

"You'd have to be blind not to notice *him* walking round. It looks like Dracula," said Anderson.

"You may be right, Anderson. It's certainly someone. I want everyone with a copy of this to start rifling through film and theatre magazines, see if we can get a positive identity on the character. I'll admit he looks like a vampire so it might narrow the field. Check out the horror films, God knows there's enough of them about."

"This is precisely why we can't catch him," said Gardener. "The first murder saw him impersonating Leonard White. His second sees him as someone totally different. He can commit as many as he likes if we don't know what *he* looks like."

"I agree, but there might be a link between the people he's impersonating. It might be something to do with films, maybe they're all from the same film, or a series of films made by the same director: or the same actor. Have we got a list of the films White made? Did he star in anything with a vampire that looks like the impression?"

"I've made a start on that one," said Dave Rawson. "I called his agents and they've agreed to draw up a list."

"How did you get on with Cuthbertson?" Briggs asked Gardener.

"It's not him," said Gardener. "He's very strange but he has a cast iron alibi."

Gardener briefed them about the interview and the things he'd uncovered.

"We still have no idea if there's a link between Cuthbertson and White?" said Briggs. "Was Janine killed when it should have been Cuthbertson?"

"It's a possibility," said Gardener. "Which could rule out the watch committee connection. I think there's a real urgency now to find Harry Fletcher.

"The CCTV from the arcade is interesting enough but it doesn't show us anything more than we already know."

Reilly switched on the recording and they all watched as a vampire character – one matching witness statements – entered the shop at nine forty-two and left well after midnight. No one else was in the arcade so he was allowed to come and go unchallenged.

"Two murders carried out with relative ease," said Briggs. "We're struggling because we don't know what he looks like.

Look around the room. You're all out there doing your job but not one of you has come up with anything concrete. I'm not knocking any of you, I know how hard it is, but if he murders someone else – and the chances are he will – we're all going to be back out there, *looking* for another job. It's not funny, we need a positive lead."

Briggs rubbed his forehead. "What about Scenes of Crime?"

"We found Janine Harper's mobile phone in the back of the shop, under the Dexion shelving. No idea why it was there. Maybe she was trying to call us, and in the struggle it was knocked under there. Anyway, we've checked it for prints and can only find hers. We've also gone through the contacts and all the messages so we have a lead on the boyfriend."

"Good work," said Briggs.

"And we found a list," offered Fenton. "It looks like an order for make up but it's not easy to make out. It was screwed up in a bin and it looks like it's had coffee on it. The only thing I can really see is the name, Corndell."

"Anyone know that name?" asked Briggs.

"I do," said Reilly.

Before the Irishman had a chance to elaborate, Thornton came through the door and apologised for his lateness. He was also out of breath

"Everything okay, Frank?" asked Briggs.

"Yes." He turned in Gardener's direction and had the common courtesy to offer his apologies to his superior officer. "Anyway, I've uncovered something interesting. The knots used to hold Janine's legs were different to the first murder. He used a double loop bowline."

"Which is what?" asked Gardener.

Thornton explained the technicalities of the knot. "Apparently, it was used at sea for lowering injured men from boats, one leg through each loop."

Thornton sat down, sipping the coffee he'd brought in with him, staring at the stranger in their midst.

Gardener took over. "So once again we have a link to the Navy, or the fishing industry. The first time, he used a sailor's eye splice. This time he's used a double loop bowline. So someone needs to check these out. Is our killer a fisherman? Or does he simply have a good knowledge of knots and he's using that fact to throw us?"

Gardener glanced at Thornton. "Well done, Frank, can you keep going with that one? Find out as much as you can about the rope itself."

"Right, Reilly..." said Briggs.

"Excuse me, sir?"

The voice belonged to the youngest member of the team, Patrick Edwards. He was fresh-faced, nineteen years old, and had an earring in one ear that no one was pleased about, but in today's modern society they weren't allowed to discriminate against him.

Briggs glanced at him but didn't offer a question.

Edwards took it as his cue. "I've got something on a missing limo. Took a call about ten minutes ago from a company in Bradford who hire them out for all sorts of reasons: parties, weddings. Anyway, one of them has gone missing. It was hired out for the whole of last week and should have been returned on Monday. It hasn't."

"What? And it's taken them till now to report it missing? Okay, as soon as we're out of here get yourself over there lad and get every scrap of information you can."

Briggs turned his attention to the Irishman.

Reilly stood up. "The list that scenes of crime found ties in with what the boss and I have in mind. We have a lead on Corndell and we're going to see him this afternoon."

Briggs was quick to notice a confused expression on Gardener's face. "Does your partner know about it, Reilly?"

"Of course he does. William Henry Corndell is his name."

"And where does he fit in?"

"He's an actor. Lives in a big house near Horsforth."

"What makes you think he has anything to do with it?"

"I'm not saying he has, but something Laura said tells me he might be able to help, if nothing else. Apparently, there's a bloke out at the University who books all the entertainment. He reckons this William Henry Corndell is the best there is. Worked the stage in the West End – films as well. Anyway, he's playing a one man show at the Uni and Laura's covering it."

"Fair enough, it's a lead."

Gardener asked a question of the CSM, Steve Fenton. "Any luck with that piece of film starring the infamous Inspector Burke?"

"Yes and no. The tech lads have finished with it. They tell me it's not an old piece of film. It was made to look that way with modern technology. It was filmed recently but that's all they can tell us."

"What brand of video tape?"

"TDK."

"Can you get anything from the batch number?" Gardener figured he was searching for a needle in a haystack. No one used VCR these days. But he had to try.

"Not the kind of info you wanted. I spoke to TDK this afternoon. The only thing they can tell us from the batch number is that it was manufactured about fifteen years ago and not necessarily in the UK."

Gardener sighed, disappointed. "What about the tape you took from the theatre."

"Same with that, it was also TDK," said Fenton. "We're pretty sure the words shouted are 'look out', but no idea if it's been recorded live or comes from a film."

Gardener updated the ANACAPA chart even though there was little new evidence.

Briggs addressed them all. "I think its time to introduce you to the new man in the corner, I've noticed the looks you're all giving him."

The man stood up and offered a smile.

"Trevor Thorpe," said Briggs. "The profiler."

CHAPTER 27

As the officer in charge, Gardener walked over and shook hands with the man, introducing himself and using the opportunity for a quick but close inspection. He was slightly shorter than Gardener and similar in weight. His rugged exterior conveyed a tough life. The left eye was a little bigger than the right, and he was quite clearly blind in it. A scar on his forehead ran down past the eyebrow, below the eye. His brown hair was closely cropped with flecks of grey running through it. The texture of his face resembled a piece of old leather. Gardener wondered what the gay receptionist in Skipton would have thought of him. Thorpe was dressed in a well-worn tweed jacket and a pair of brown corduroy's and brown, casual slip-on shoes.

Gardener returned to his seat. As he did so he asked the question. "So, Mr Thorpe, I'm sure DCI Briggs has briefed you about everything that's happened, do you have anything to add to what you've seen so far?"

"Can I thank you all first for ... er ... inviting me."

Thorpe walked around the room with his hands behind his back, like a schoolmaster. When he spoke he stared at the ceiling.

"There was a lot of ... er ... work accomplished here: a lot of ... articulate planning. Couple it with the ... clues ... and you can see straight away that this man is ... very intelligent. He cares about what he does. It's an ... art form. He plans everything ... down to the last detail. He has medical knowledge."

Gardener thought Thorpe sounded like a politician. "Why, in your opinion, is he doing it?"

Thorpe went back to his seat and sat his legs astride, rested his arms on the back, choosing to face his audience rather than the ceiling. "Because he can."

He lifted one hand matter-of-factly. "I think he likes playing ... sadistic games. He'll have played them all his life. When he was younger it would have been ... animals, children younger than himself, in fact ... anything that was defenceless."

Gardener was beginning to feel irritated by the way the man started a sentence and let the words hang in the air before completing it, as if he had a stammer. Perhaps that was his manner. He had to accept that the man was here of his own free will. He was not being paid. Maybe Gardener simply didn't like what he saw.

Thorpe stood up, started to pace, staring at the ceiling again. Gardener felt like he was being lectured.

"Murder usually stems from a ... deadly fantasy, a need to ... exert power over the victim, to ... inflict pain ... and fear, which can then be played for real. He almost certainly has ... a grudge, and he is ... exerting his power. I think you'll find that's because he was ... repressed when he was younger. He had a ... domineering mother who ... allowed him no freedom. No chance to ... express his emotions.

"And that is what we are seeing here. He's er ... no different to most serial killers. Because they kill so ... casually, without emotion, they're ... almost impossible to catch ... just as difficult to understand. As far as ... he's concerned, killing is an art form ... no different to eating a meal."

He returned to his seat and pulled a handkerchief from his jacket pocket and mopped his brow.

"Everything all right, Trevor?" asked Briggs.

"Er ... yes ... may I have a drink of water, please? I ... er ... need to take a tablet."

Briggs asked Patrick Edwards to do the honours. After the tablet, Thorpe continued: "Now, where was I? Oh ... yes ... most of them live ... er ... outwardly normal lives and have a very ... high I.Q. We can see that by the ... games he's playing, and the ... puzzles he's leaving."

"Why does he drain the blood?" asked Reilly.

Thorpe took to his feet again. "Well, you see, there's another ... interesting point. Blood ... may be ... very sacred to him. Have you checked to see ... if either of these ... people ... who have been killed ... have any blood related diseases? Particularly in the case ... of the girl. Was she promiscuous ... was she HIV positive? Maybe he thinks that blood is ... very precious ... and these people..." Thorpe turned and reached out with his arms. "...are not treating their bodies like a temple, as he does."

"What makes you say that?" asked Gardener.

"Everything we've seen so far. The man is ... articulate. He's ... careful, precise. You have no leads ... because he leaves you no clues ... with which to catch him. Here ... is a man who takes life ... very seriously."

Thorpe cast Gardener a glance that made his skin crawl. His eyes were almost closed, forcing his mouth to rise upwards in a leer. "So should you!"

Gardener's mobile interrupted their meeting. After a concerned conversation, he flipped it off and glanced at Briggs. "It's Fitz, he wants us over at the morgue straight away."

"Why? What's wrong?" asked Briggs.

"He wouldn't tell us over the phone," replied Gardener. "But he said we're not going to like it."

CHAPTER 28

The three of them made it to the morgue in record time. Fitz was in his office. The desk was impeccably tidy, as if all the paperwork had been positioned using a setsquare. The files on the shelf behind him were arranged neatly in alphabetical order with the writing facing the same way. Gardener couldn't identify the piece of classical music that Fitz was listening to but assumed it to be an opera.

"You didn't waste much time," said Fitz, glancing at Gardener.

"It sounded urgent."

Fitz rose from his chair, adjusted his glasses. "There's never an urgency when you're dealing with the dead."

"Well there is in our case," said Briggs.

"Follow me."

Fitz left the office, collecting a green gown and a fresh pair of gloves from a cupboard. He walked over to Janine Harper's corpse and removed the cover. Her fragile body lacked colour, emphasising the severity of the bruising on her face. Only now, she had a Y-shaped incision where Fitz had done his job.

"What have you found?" asked Briggs.

"Something that needs further investigation," replied Fitz. "There are traces of a drug called Ephedrine in her bloodstream."

"What's that?" asked Gardener.

"It's an alkaloid drug normally used to relieve the symptoms of asthma."

"Did she have a history of asthma?" asked Briggs.

"Yes, according to her records. I also found alcohol in her system, sherry to be precise, along with traces of nuts."

"What type of nuts?"

"Nothing specific, a bit of a mixture."

"Which leads us where?" asked Gardener.

"I think, and I stress, think, that what he's done is ground the nuts into a fine powder and mixed them with the sherry, which, when using the correct quantities creates a venomous cocktail of the drug Ephedrine. I'll come back to that in a second, but just take a look at this."

Fitz lifted the head. "De-epithelialisation."

"What the hell is that?" asked Reilly.

Fitz drew out Janine's tongue. It was red raw, inflamed.

"He's very carefully removed the top layer of skin from her tongue."

Briggs stared at the ceiling and sighed. "Did he do that when she was alive?"

"There wouldn't be much point when she was dead," replied Fitz.

"Oh Jesus," said Briggs.

"Someone must have heard the screams," said Reilly.

"How?" Gardener asked. "It's not as if someone's going to stand around while you pull out their tongue and then slice off the top layer of skin, is it?"

"I wondered about that," said Fitz.

"Is that what the Ephedrine was all about? He's drugged her so he can perform delicate surgery?" asked Gardener.

"I don't think so. There are traces of a very mild sedative in her bloodstream as well. For what it's worth I think he entered the shop and used the element of surprise to take advantage. They've had a bit of a fight, which he won by exerting his strength – you can see that by the bruising."

Fitz pointed to the top of her left arm. "If you focus just here, there's a pin prick where he's injected the sedative. That made her drowsy, more co-operative.

"I suspect he's then taken his time to set up precisely how he wants her, and waited for the sedative to wear off before carrying out the second part of his plan.

"He's removed the top layer of skin from her tongue. And he also appears to have scraped her fingernails clean. In fact, they're immaculate. I'd say that's because he doesn't want what's underneath being used against him."

"Like Trevor Thorpe said, he's very precise," commented Briggs.

"So where does this drug come in?" said Gardener. "The one that's made from sherry and nuts?"

Fitz sighed. "He had another purpose in mind. You see, Ephedrine is a relief for asthma sufferers but it can have diabolical side effects if you raise someone's sense of fear to the limit and then administer lethal doses of the cocktail he's mixed up. Combined with adrenaline it eventually causes a stroke. But before you die, the agony would be immeasurable."

"Is that what she died of?" asked Briggs. "A stroke?"

"In the end, yes, but one drawn on through careful calculation."

"Why is he going to such lengths?" asked Briggs.

"Because he can," replied Gardener. "It's like your profiler said, he's exerting his power. But I think it's more than that, I think he's making a point. We just don't know what it is."

"Any recorded case, Fitz?" asked Reilly.

"Not that I'm aware of. But better use of the police computers and the Internet may provide us with clues. It's a very clinical and precise way of killing someone. It's almost as if he's perfected the technique."

"You think he's used the method before?" asked Gardener.

"It's worth keeping an open mind," said Fitz.

"Stewart, Sean," said Briggs. "Pull out all the stops and find this bloke!"

"We'll have one of the lads draw up a list off all thespians living in the area while Sean and I go and interview the one living in Horsforth."

"Before you go rushing anywhere," said Fitz. "I haven't finished."

"What else has he done?" asked Briggs, as if he couldn't believe there would be anything else.

Fitz walked over to the stainless steel counter at the back of the room.

"I found this inserted in her anus."

"What is it?" asked Gardener.

"It's a glass tube," said Fitz. "There are no signs of sexual abuse. And the tube inserted into her anus was not done so for sexual reasons."

Fitz picked up the glass vial, held it out in front of him. "The next puzzle is in here."

Seeing as the pathologist was the only one wearing gloves, no one else volunteered.

After Fitz had removed the paper and unrolled it, they could see another verse had been printed on the same style paper as before.

Another one gone ... how many more?

Pity you couldn't save this little whore

I've left puzzles and clues, but you haven't got very far

Here's another: follow The Scarlet Car

I implore you again, to study your needs

Another is all set to fall, down and out, in Leeds.

CHAPTER 29

As Reilly pulled the car to a halt outside the wrought iron gates, Gardener jumped out and surveyed what could only be described as a kingdom.

He gazed upwards wondering whether or not Corndell was simply security conscious or totally paranoid. The gates were electronically controlled, which opened out on to a gravel drive surrounded by pine trees, all under the watchful eye of CCTV cameras. He couldn't see the house but he could guess its size.

Reilly stepped up beside Gardener.

"Remind you of anyone?"

Gardener glanced at his partner. "Derek Summers?"

"One and the same. Let's hope these entertainment types are not all tarred with the same brush."

Gardener shuddered as he recalled the havoc a group of paedophiles had caused him and his partner three months previously: he'd been beaten within an inch of his life, his son had been kidnapped, his father had gone through hell, and he'd lost the only woman who'd meant anything to him after his late wife, Sarah. But through it all, his friend and partner, Sean Reilly had stood by his side, fighting all the way.

"God forbid, Sean. I don't think I could deal with another one."

"I'm not sure which is worse. Summers was bad enough I'll grant you, but whoever is torturing and killing people the way this bloke does is on another level."

Gardener stood with his hands in his pockets. The bright, Thursday March morning with its clear blue sky added to the postcard view before him.

"This is one hell of a place, I can't wait for a proper look."

"You'd better press the intercom, then."

Gardener did as advised ... and waited, but no one answered.

"Do you think he's out?"

"I doubt it, boss, it probably takes him a week to get round it all."

Gardener laughed as the intercom buzzed.

"Yes?" asked the voice.

"Mr. Corndell?" questioned Gardener.

"May I inquire who's asking?"

Gardener glanced at Reilly, and then at the intercom. "Major Crime Team, Mr. Corndell. Detective Inspector Gardener and Detective Sergeant Reilly, we'd like to ask you a few questions."

"But you have no appointment, I don't see people without appointments."

Gardener enforced his authority. "We don't need one, we are the police."

The reply – when it came – sounded forced. "You'd better come in, then."

The gates opened. Both detectives returned to the car and drove into the grounds.

When the house into view it was something else: a three-storey, Victorian mansion with gothic turrets on either side. Built with grey Yorkshire stone and a grey slate roof, the building had dark oak frames and leaded windows, with two black, arched front doors. The gardens were well landscaped: the perimeter covered in poplar trees. As they drew closer, the poplars were replaced by bay trees. To the right of the building was a double garage. Opposite the front door was a large fountain.

Reilly pulled the car to a halt and switched off the engine.

"Even Derek Summers would have had trouble keeping up with this one."

"It's not bad for someone we've never heard of," said Gardener. "How does he manage to make such a good living if he's not in the limelight?"

"Perhaps it's time we went and found out."

Both men left the car and approached the house. Gardener rang the bell.

Eventually, the door opened.

CHAPTER 30

An agitated William glanced at the detectives. They were peering back with confused expressions.

He didn't like the one on the right, wearing the brown bomber jacket and jeans. He was hard and William suspected there would be trouble, most likely a personality clash. The other one was well groomed, smartly dressed in a blue shirt, black slacks and a grey striped suit jacket. William warmed to him, especially the grey leather hat.

"Come in," said William, invitingly.

The two men stepped over the threshold. William shut the door and leaned against the wall, returning to a conversation on his mobile.

"I'm sorry?" He paused before resuming. "Perhaps you'd be kind enough to tell Rupert Julian that if he's not happy with my script we can always bring in Wallace Worsley to direct."

He rolled his eyes, covering the phone with his hand.

"Please excuse me. Problems with Hollywood."

When he returned to his phone he noticed that the taller and more well dressed of the two detectives was studying the film posters decorating most of his dark oak, panelled hall.

"I can promise you, George, we shall not be having this conversation again," said William. "Either Rupert Julian stands down or I take my script elsewhere."

Having said his piece, he cut the connection, gripped his walking stick and shuffled towards them.

"I do apologise, gentlemen."

"Not at all, Mr. Corndell. I was admiring your posters."

"Wonderful. Are you into films, Mr..?"

"Gardener," he replied. "And my partner, D. S. Sean Reilly. I'm afraid I don't get the time, but my father does, he's the biggest film buff I know."

"Really," replied William, wondering where he was heading.

"Oh yes, never away from the cinema."

"Any particular era, Mr. Gardener?"

"He likes pretty much anything, the older films in particular, black and white, something with a story. I'm sure he'd like a look at these."

"A man after my own heart. It's taken years, Mr. Gardener, and a lot of patience," replied William, before adding. "You see that poster there."

William pointed and Gardener followed the line of his cane.

"That's an original for Boris Karloff's *Frankenstein*, made in 1931. There are only four left in the world and one recently sold for a hundred and ninety eight thousand dollars."

"Jesus Christ!" said Reilly, "For a poster?"

William laughed. "Language, Mr Reilly." He glanced back at Gardener. "Do you know something? Karloff was still an unknown at 44 when he made that film, and it was his eighty-first. What do you think to that?"

The detective called Gardener glanced at him with a strange expression.

"The things I could tell you about the film world, Mr Gardener, but I'm sure that isn't why you came here."

"On the contrary," said Gardener. "It is *one* of the reasons."

"Dear me," said William. "Where are my manners? I haven't offered you a drink. Please come through."

He led them into the kitchen where he made drinks and small talk before finally taking them through to the conservatory. He asked Gardener if he would be kind enough to carry the tray. William had always liked the pleasant ambience the room created with its tiled floor and cane furniture. Everything was clean and precise and smelled fresh, the way *he* liked it.

They all sat down. William picked up the conversation. "Films play a big part in my life, Mr Gardener, so how can I help you?"

"Have you starred in many?" asked Gardener.

"None," replied William.

"Oh," said Gardener. "I thought you were an actor."

"I am," replied William, sipping his tea. "But I prefer to act on a stage rather than behind a camera. Not that there's anything wrong with acting for a camera, but I think there's more skill involved in theatre. I'm also a script writer and I regularly have my work accepted in Hollywood."

"That must be rewarding," said Gardener. "Are you responsible for any of the modern day material gracing our screens at the moment?"

"Not at all, Mr. Gardener, my work is deeper and more meaningful than the stuff you see in the cinema today. There is more emotion to my material, more acting skill required. I write with the old masters in mind, those that didn't have the privilege of working with sound. Now that ... was acting."

"So, if you don't write film-scripts for Hollywood, what do you write?"

"I do write film scripts, as you call it," replied William, sipping his tea and becoming more unsettled. He didn't like being questioned.

"But I also supply the Hollywood agencies with a lot of theatrical material, regularly seen all over America, most of which is governed in California."

"Have you starred in any of your own material," asked Gardener.

"Only once, in London. It was a play shown at Her Majesty's Theatre before *The Phantom of the Opera*."

"Was it a success?"

William smiled, tolerating the intrusion into his private domain. Didn't mean to say he had to like it.

"Mr. Gardener, all my work is successful. I also took the leading role in *The Phantom*,"

"I thought Michael Crawford was in that," said Reilly.

"He came after me, Mr Reilly." William smiled. "Unfortunately I broke my leg and was unable to continue ... hence the cane. I don't have to use it all the time, but I have my off-days when the stiffness is a little too much."

"Apart from your love of theatre and your script-writing, I can see you also collect film memorabilia," said Gardener.

"Oh, yes, all the time. It's a life's work trying to track down the lost films of the silent era. I have my own cinema."

"Really?" he asked William. "Where?"

"Here ... in the house."

"Your knowledge of films might just come in useful," said Reilly.

William wished they would come to the point.

"You'll forgive me for asking," he said. "But I find it strange that you two gentlemen should come out here to my house and talk to me about films, I'm sure that there's something else on your minds."

"There is," said Gardener. "We're investigating a couple of extremely unpleasant deaths in Leeds recently."

"Are you talking about the young girl who was killed in the shop in the arcade?"

"Did you know her?" asked Gardener.

"No, but I read about it in the papers ... well ... didn't everyone?" He leaned even further forward. "You don't think it was me, do you?"

"Was it?" asked Reilly.

William stood up, his left eye twitching rapidly. "Am I under arrest?" His clever answer had backfired.

Gardener left his seat as well. "Not at all. We've come to you because we believe you may be able to help us. With your knowledge of film and theatre you might be a real asset."

"Of course," said William, sitting back down, using the arms of the chair as a guide.

"Would you take a look at these, see if you recognise them?" asked Gardener, passing over a piece of paper containing the quotes they had found next to the bodies.

William studied the paper before passing it back to Gardener. "I can't say I do, but they're very dated."

"Why do you say that?"

"Read the phrasing, Mr. Gardener, people don't talk like that now."

"So they're not from anything you've seen?" asked Gardener.

"I wouldn't say that," replied William, sipping more tea. "I have seen literally thousands of films, and not just the well known ones. My collection goes as far back as 1900. And in my experience that could well be the era from which they originate, the golden age of Hollywood, the silent films. If you study what's being said there, that was how they spoke when they didn't have the advantage of sound. I really do think you're a long way back."

"So the person we're looking for may be old, or he might live his life in that time period?" asked Gardener.

"Possibly both, maybe neither," replied William. "May I ask why you think he's an actor?"

"It's speculation at the moment, but the people he's killed so far have both been connected to the entertainment world."

"So you think he might be a failed actor? Someone with a grudge?"

"Not entirely, but we have reason to believe that he's very good at disguising himself. The eyewitness reports we've collated describe him as looking like two completely different people."

"Maybe it *was* two different people."

"Unlikely, the modus operandi was very similar, and then we have the quotes, quite apart from the fact that he was actually the spitting image of one of the people he killed."

William was about to take a drink but decided to hold his cup before it reached his lips. "You don't mean that nice Leonard White?"

"You knew Leonard White?" asked Gardener.

"Yes, I did. Not that I worked with him but he actually starred in one of my father's films many years ago, just as he was starting out."

"Which one?" Reilly asked.

"*Tales From A Village Pub*, 1957, it was a compendium of short stories. I saw him on and off over the years."

"But you hadn't seen him recently?" asked Gardener.

"No. But I must say I rather wanted to go and see him at the Grand Theatre the night he was killed. He was only there for the one night and I would have loved to have heard him talk, perhaps even had the chance to talk to him myself."

"Where were you that night?" asked Reilly.

"I was here, at home."

"Alone?" questioned Reilly.

William knew that one was coming. "I'm always on my own, Mr Reilly. I am in constant demand with my work and I rarely, if ever, get the chance to leave the house these days."

"Didn't you buy the house from Leonard White?" asked Gardener.

"My father did, many years ago."

"How well did you know him?"

"My father?" grinned William. "Sorry ... just my little joke. Well ... I wouldn't say I knew him all that well. I have seen most, if not all, of the films he made at Hammer. You have to remember we travelled in different circles. When my father bought this house I was still in London and remained there until after he'd retired. It was quite sad really because he never had the chance to appreciate it, he died four months after buying it. I came up to Leeds after his death and stayed to look after my mother."

"Is your mother still alive?" asked Gardener.

"I'm afraid not, she died of cancer many years ago."

On that note, William finished his tea and continued with another question.

"If he's that good with his disguise, how will you catch him? You won't know what he looks like."

"Very true," replied Gardener. "That's something else we wanted to ask you about, make-up techniques."

"That's an art in itself, Mr. Gardener."

"Are you involved much with make-up?"

"Very little. Over the years of course, with my theatre work, I have applied my own. As I said, my life is script-writing these days."

"Not completely," said Reilly.

"Sorry," challenged William.

He knew he would have problems with the Irishman. Where the hell was he going now?

"It's not all writing, is it, Mr. Corndell?" retorted Gardener. "I believe you've recently accepted a live performance at the University of Leeds."

"You're very well informed."

"It pays to be," replied Gardener.

"It's true, then?" asked Reilly.

"Yes, it is. The gentleman who books the entertainment called me a few days previously. May I ask how you knew?"

"My wife's a theatre critic. She'll be there, I'm sure she'll give you a good review."

"She won't need to, Mr. Reilly, my work speaks for itself."

"Will it involve make-up?" continued Reilly.

"It most certainly will."

"Where do you buy it?"

"Quite a few places, The Internet mostly. But unfortunately for me, I have visited the shop in Leeds where the young girl was killed," replied William.

"Why unfortunate?" asked Reilly.

"Because despite what you and Mr. Gardener say, Mr. Reilly, I still feel as if I'm a suspect."

"Quite the opposite," replied Gardener. "If you were a suspect we'd have had you at the station by now. No, my colleague wants to know more about make-up. For our man to be so practised in the art of disguise, he would need quite a lot of different products. We wondered if you'd know what they were and whether or not the shop in Leeds would sell them. Or would you need to be somewhere far more specialised?"

"Oh I see." William nodded. "Well, without knowing the extent to which your man is disguising himself it's difficult to say. However, if he can pass closely for Leonard White he must be good."

"Why would someone use Aluminium Powder?" inquired Gardener.

"Colouring his hair, particularly white or grey. What about the second murder, did he look like Leonard White then?"

He noticed Gardener glance at Reilly before replying.

The detective reached into his pocket and produced an artist impression of the vampire. "From the eyewitness reports we have we think his disguise was this one."

"Oh my good God!" shouted William.

"Do you recognise the character?"

"No, but to create an effect like that you'd need quite a few things. I would imagine flexible collodion for one, which is a plastic skin adhesive. It provides a coating for make up construction. And then there's rigid collodion, a liquid used to make scars and pock marks. When you put that stuff on, it draws and puckers the skin. For something like this he obviously used a wig, and then there's the costume..."

"All of which you can buy at the shop in Leeds?"

William did not like the line of questioning and, despite remarks to the contrary, still felt like a suspect.

"I would imagine so," he replied. "As I mentioned I have used the place on occasion, but I don't think I've spent a lot of money there, or taken too much notice of their costumes. You really do have your work cut out, gentlemen."

A silence followed before Reilly spoke.

"Is it true that all you thespians are a tad superstitious?"

"I'm sorry?" replied William.

The Irishman really was a strange one. He did like changing the subject.

"Superstitious," repeated Reilly. "I've heard a lot of strange stories about actors, particularly those in the theatre."

"Well, of course there are a number of superstitions connected with the theatre."

"And what are yours?"

"Since you ask, I don't particularly like live flowers being delivered before a performance. They have a very short life and I believe it reflects the life of the play. I'm not particularly keen about whistling on stage, it's bad luck and can lead to accidents. And under no circumstances do I like someone wishing me good luck."

"And away from the stage?" Reilly persisted.

"I'm not sure I follow you." William's patience was wearing thin.

"I couldn't help noticing when we drove up to the house that it's surrounded by poplar trees. As you draw closer you have bay trees, or laurels, if you like. And then as sure as God's my witness if you haven't got houseleek placed in the roof."

"You're ... very observant, Mr Reilly."

"It's my job."

"To answer your question, you're quite correct about the trees. If you're that knowledgeable, perhaps you know that laurel trees guard the doors of great men's houses."

"I certainly do, but I also know that the bay tree is said to keep away witches, devils and bad luck, and that a house guarded by such a tree should never be struck by lightning."

"I can't say I know anything about that, Mr Reilly," replied William. "And I'm certainly not aware of houseleek, as you call it."

"Are you not? So you haven't placed it there as a protection against lightning?"

William's stomach lurched. "I can't have done, can I? Which begs the question, which one of us is really superstitious?"

Reilly made no reply.

William was feeling really unsettled. He found the talk of thunder and lightning disconcerting. He was desperate to move the conversation away from himself.

"And tell me, Mr Reilly, where did you learn about myths and superstitions?"

"I'm Irish, Mr. Corndell, we invented most of them."

"Oh, does that mean they're not true, then?"

"You tell me," retorted Reilly. "You're the superstitious one. There's no shortage of the colour red around here. Your hall has a tiled floor which contains red, and then there are red velvet drapes leading into each of the rooms and *they* all seem to have something red in them."

"Red is my favourite colour, Mr. Reilly, mostly because it's the colour of Aries, but also because it's associated with good luck, health and joy, and hence of the living body as opposed to the corpse."

"And you're not superstitious? I'll bet you know as well as I do about the references in folklore to the use of threads, ribbons, wool, or pieces of flannel which prevent a variety of ailments," continued Reilly. "And isn't red thread used as a protection against witchcraft?"

"Is there anything else I can help you gentlemen with?"

"And it has nothing to do with it being the colour of blood?" asked Reilly.

"Why would it?" replied William.

"Just curious, Mr Corndell, it *was* you who made the comment about the living body and not the corpse, was it not? I thought maybe you had a kind of superstition about blood being pure and all that."

"I really haven't the faintest idea what you're talking about."

At that precise moment, Gardener's mobile chimed. He reached into his jacket pocket and then excused himself into the kitchen where he took the call.

Reilly asked William if he could use the bathroom.

After the phone call and the toilet break the two detectives returned to the conservatory.

"I'm afraid we'll have to leave you, Mr. Corndell." Gardener turned to Reilly. "That was the station, apparently Albert Fettle wants to see us, urgently."

"It's no problem, Mr Gardener, I'll show you both out."

As Gardener reached the door he turned to face William. "Just one more question."

"Which is?" asked William, having grown tired of them both.

"What's your favourite film?"

"Excuse me?"

"Your favourite film. You must have one, a film buff of your calibre."

"I certainly do, *A Blind Bargain*," replied William, still wondering why the question had been asked in the first place.

"Can't say as I know that one," replied the detective.

"You won't, Mr. Gardener, before your time."

"I'll have to look out for it. What about *The Scarlet Car*?"

"I'm afraid you have me there, Mr Gardener. But if you have the time I'd be more than happy to look it up for you," replied William, knowing they hadn't.

"Another time, maybe. Anyway, thank you, you've been most helpful. I'll leave you a card and perhaps we could call back if we need you again."

Gardener tipped his hat.

"Don't hesitate," said William.

CHAPTER 31

The atmosphere at the theatre was still grave when Paul Price met them at the stage door.

"Do you have any idea when I can reopen?" he asked, testily.

"Shouldn't be too long, Mr. Price," replied Gardener. "We do have a few more people to interview."

Price's expression showed his irritation. "So you're not here to tell me its business as usual?"

"No, we're here at Mr. Fettle's insistence."

"You do realise how much this is costing me, don't you?"

"Not as much as Leonard White," replied Gardener.

"Have you made any headway catching the lunatic responsible?"

"It is a murder investigation." Gardener turned to glance down the street. "And I would rather not discuss it on the doorstep, if you don't mind."

Paul Price stepped to one side, allowing them down the stairs to where Fettle kept himself hidden.

"Two policemen to see you, Fettle. Though I can't think why."

"I asked 'em," replied Fettle, still invisible to the naked eye.

When it became obvious that no one was going to speak until

Price left, he grunted and did so, adding that he could be found in his office if needed.

"He's like a bear wi' a sore head, you've really upset him," said Fettle, when he finally appeared.

"He's the least of our worries," replied Reilly.

"You've not found him, yet, then? Anyway, best come in and have a pot o' tea."

"Tea is the last thing we need, Mr. Fettle," replied Gardener.

"I'm sure it is, but it'll do for starters."

Fettle drew them in and poured the tea from a recently boiled kettle. He then threw a book on the table, opened to a page which contained the photograph of a man Gardener had asked him about on a previous visit.

"Inspector Burke of Scotland Yard." Fettle proudly announced. "You asked me if I knew him last time you were here."

When Gardener realised he had been holding his breath he still didn't speak but turned to the front cover of the book. It was an old issue of *Film Review*.

"Where did you get this?" he asked Fettle.

"I've had 'em years. Been in that cupboard over yonder." Fettle pointed but neither man bothered to see where.

"So which film does the photograph come from?" asked Gardener.

"London After Midnight," replied Fettle.

"And what do you know about the film other than Inspector Burke?"

Fettle sat down and sipped his tea. "It's a bit of a classic, maybe the most famous of all the lost films."

Gardener suddenly thought back to what William had told him about collecting lost films, wondering if he had it. More to the point, what hadn't William told them? Had it been a cryptic clue

... like those found with the bodies?

Gardener realised he was ahead of himself. Perhaps a lack of evidence on the case had forced him into thinking irrationally.

"Go on," he said to Fettle.

"It's commonly known as the Holy Grail of archivists and film collectors throughout the world." Fettle picked up a scrap of paper. "Last known record of the film existing were in the 1950's. According to what I've found out, an MGM vault inventory from 1955 shows the print being stored in Vault 7. In the 1960's there were a fire in Vault 7, destroying the last surviving print."

Reilly whistled through his teeth.

"What makes it so rare and collectible?" asked Gardener, intrigued.

"Not sure, I never saw it. Quite a lot of things I should imagine, it were at the top of MGM's hit parade for 1927-28."

"Twenty-seven?" interrupted Gardener.

"Oh aye, it's going back a bit."

"It was a silent film, then?" asked Reilly.

"Aye," replied Fettle. "I mean, it were one o' them films that broke records: eerie sets, and Chaney's vampire make up were incredible."

"Who's?" asked Gardener.

"Lon Chaney."

"Vampire make up?"

"Aye." Fettle flicked over a couple of pages and Gardener grew intensely cold. He pulled out the picture he had of the eyewitness reports of someone dressed like a vampire in Leeds on the night Janine was killed. They were alike to the last detail.

"Who is Lon Chaney?" asked Gardener.

"You're kidding me," replied Fettle. "Only the greatest actor that ever lived."

"Well I've never heard of him."

"You won't have, will you? He were well before your time."

That was another comment William had made to Gardener when questioned about his favourite film, it being well before his time. He tried to recall more of the conversation. The only thing that came to mind was the developing argument between William and Reilly over superstitions.

"Can you recall any of his other films?"

"The two most well known were *Phantom of the Opera* and *The Hunchback of Notre Dame*."

"Did he star in something called *A Blind Bargain*?"

"I think he did," replied Fettle.

Gardener realised he was still standing. He sat down, grabbed his mug and took a mouthful of tea.

"So, what do you know about Lon Chaney?"

"He were a genius. In the early 1920's there were a well-known saying around Hollywood, 'Don't step on that spider, it might be Lon Chaney'. His make up were that good he were known as 'The Man of a Thousand faces'. Both his parents were deaf so the only way he could talk to 'em were through mime, which is where he picked up his ability to act. He were brilliant, man. His make up … well, you've never seen nowt like it. He did it all himself."

Fettle pointed to the page. "That film were just the business and he did all his own make up. In fact, I remember reading somewhere that the film were so chilling it inspired a murder. Some bloke in London claimed, after seeing it, he had visions of Chaney's vampire character. It terrified him so much that he went into an epileptic fit and killed an Irish housemaid."

"I thought you said he played Inspector Burke."

"He did," replied Fettle. "He also played the vampire. Two parts – just look at the make up involved."

Gardener turned to Reilly. "Well even if we don't know who's doing it, we know who he's emulating."

"I wouldn't say that entirely," replied Reilly. "Remembering where we've just been."

"What do you remember about *A Blind Bargain*?" he asked Fettle.

"Not much, I never saw that one, either."

Fettle left the table and lunged over to the cupboard in the corner. He tossed a few books around, created a fair amount of dust, before returning with another dog-eared copy of *Film Review*.

"Here we are. Another lost film, second only to *London After Midnight*. In fact, he played two parts again, the mad scientist and the ape man."

"What was the film about?" asked Gardener.

"Summat about a doctor who's experimenting on people and apparently, the half man half ape is the result of one of his earlier experiments."

"I take it all his films were silent films."

"All except one, I think," replied Fettle.

"In which case, the words came up on the screen if the actors spoke to each other."

"Aye," replied Fettle.

"You've no idea if a film script for these films still exists, have you?"

"You must be kidding," said Fettle, finishing his tea. "Although I did hear talk once that there were a book about the reconstruction of the film."

"*A Blind Bargain*?" asked Gardener.

"Aye," said Fettle.

"Any idea who wrote it?"

"Haven't a clue, sunshine."

Gardener turned to Reilly. "Sean, make a note, see if we can find the book."

"You reckon he's using quotes from Chaney's films?" asked Reilly.

"It's looking that way," replied Gardener.

"What quotes?" asked Fettle.

"I'm sorry, Mr Fettle, we've kept them from the public. You remember that day you took us into the cellars and we found a puzzle?"

"Oh aye."

"They're not the only ones he's been leaving. We've found 'one line' quotes next to the bodies."

"And you think they're from the films?"

"Possibly," replied Gardener.

"And if you could get film scripts you'd know for sure."

"Maybe."

"Do you have a copy of the quotes?"

Gardener passed over the evidence bag with the paper he'd shown to William.

After a couple of minutes, Fettle shook his head. "No, can't help you there."

"Do you know anyone who can?"

"No, afraid not. You see most of Chaney's films are missing and I doubt there's any records of the scripts lying around, they're just too old."

"Do you know if any of the films are available today?"

"Only way to find out is to use that net thing. I dare say you might pick up *The Phantom of the Opera*, or *The Hunchback of Notre Dame*."

"I'll check that out," said Reilly. "I'll also ask Laura what she knows, or maybe who she knows. Her friend at the University might help."

"Maybe Corndell could," suggested Gardener.

"Who's Corndell?" asked Fettle.

"William Henry Corndell. Do you know him?"

"Should I?" asked Fettle.

"I would have thought so," replied Gardener. "Given his pedigree."

"Pedigree? What pedigree?" asked Fettle, taking a mouthful of fresh tea.

Gardener and Reilly told Fettle what they knew about William, which, to be honest, when they thought about it, wasn't very much.

Fettle consulted all his *Film Review's* but nothing materialised.

"There's plenty about Wallace Henry Corndell. He were a pretty prominent director."

"Did he ever make a film called *Tales From a Village Pub*, starring Leonard White?" asked Gardener.

"Aye, he did, but Leonard White weren't the star of the film."

"But he was in it?" asked Reilly.

"Aye. But there's no mention of a William."

Gardener stared at Fettle. "Got a question for you. Do you know anyone connected to the London theatre scene?"

"What do you want to know?" asked Fettle.

"I want to know about William Henry Corndell. He came up here from London. Apparently he's big in the world of theatre, writes a lot of material, and he once played the role of *The Phantom* before Michael Crawford."

"I didn't know there were anyone before Crawford," said Fettle.

"Corndell seems to think there was," said Reilly.

"Can you find out for me?" asked Gardener.

"Aye, I can. In fact, a mate o' mine used to work backstage at *Her Majesty's*, I'll see if I can track him down, he'll know."

"Thanks. And while we're on the subject of people, do you know anyone called Harry Fletcher?"

Fettle grew silent before answering. "The name rings a bell. I think he were a writer, worked for *The Playhouse.*"

"Do you know where he is now?"

"Can't say as I do, I haven't seen or heard from him in ages."

"When did you last see him?" asked Gardener.

"Oh, Christ, must have been ten, fifteen years ago, when he were at *The Playhouse.*"

"Any idea where he lived, back then?" asked Gardener.

With his eyes screwed shut and his mouth agape, Fettle resembled a frog. "Sorry, Mr Gardener, I didn't know him that well."

"Do you know anybody who does?"

"You could talk to the people at *The Playhouse,* but I don't think he's still there."

"He isn't, and the people who are don't know him, either."

"They've probably changed staff since then."

Gardener was still frustrated despite having acquired more information about the case. Someone would have to check out Lon Chaney, and William, all of which would take time, and there was still no real evidence to the murderer's identity. Which meant he could strike again and the press really would have a field day.

He had another thought. "Did Lon Chaney make a film called *The Scarlet Car?*"

Fettle consulted more of the *Film Review* books. Time passed before he eventually spoke. "Aye, he did."

"When was that?" asked Gardener.

"1917."

"Christ," replied Reilly. "What was that about?"

"Doesn't say," replied Fettle. "But you've gotta remember,

Chaney made bloody hundreds of films. Most of 'em were little shorts, three or four reels, they weren't all feature films, so there isn't much information about 'em."

"Whispering creek?"

Fettle seemed pleased to be useful. "*The Tragedy of Whispering Creek*, that's even further back, 1914."

"What's that about?" Reilly asked Gardener.

"That was the name of Corndell's house, Whispering Creek."

"Seems to me that this Corndell bloke has a bit of an obsession wi' Chaney," said Fettle.

"That's what worries me. On the face of it, so does the killer. He's very good with make up. He leaves clues, which may or may not be from the films but I suspect they are. Even in the clues, there's a reference to one of Chaney's films," said Gardener.

He rose to leave. "Okay, Mr Fettle, thanks for the information, you've been a great help. If you could look into what we've asked I'd appreciate it."

"No problem. I'll give you a ring when I've done."

Gardener and Reilly climbed the stairs to the stage door. Before leaving, Gardener stopped, turned, and walked back down to Fettle.

"What you forgotten now?"

"I don't suppose the names, Rupert Julian or Wallace Worsley mean anything to you, do they?"

Fettle consulted books again.

"I don't think you'll find them in there," said Gardener.

"I think I will," said Fettle. "They don't sound like actors with modern names, do they?"

"Directors, from what I can gather."

"Aye, you're right there," said Fettle, eventually. "What do you want to know?"

"The kind of stuff they're directing at the moment?"

Fettle glanced up from the book and laughed. "You're joking, aren't you? They're both dead, man. Years ago."

CHAPTER 32

Despite having mixed feelings about the information they had so far received, Gardener sensed an air of trepidation descending upon the incident room. His colleagues were beginning to show signs of wear, as they always did when an investigation yielded nothing but dead ends – as though you were pointlessly pursuing every avenue for no good reason.

On the face of it, the meeting with William Henry Corndell had proved intriguing to say the least. His knowledge of his trade may well prove valuable. He knew enough about the films and the theatre to provide a smattering of information, although Gardener had been far from satisfied and would like to have heard more.

However, he had provided a link worth pursuing. A connection between silent films and the man they were trying to find. But was the killer really emulating a film star? If that was the case, had Fettle provided the answer in Lon Chaney? Was William himself obsessed with Lon Chaney, and had simply chosen not to mention it? What about his lost film collection? What did he have in there, and did he have all of Chaney's?

Gardener also suspected that there was a lot more to the house than met the eye and Sean Reilly had already revealed to him that each and every one of the rooms upstairs were locked. Why was that? Surely there was little need to lock any door in your house if lived on your own – and never left. Did he have a house full of valuable items, or was he hiding something?

Was he mad? Had the whole interview been an act? His secretive behaviour from the start had set Gardener on edge. The security surrounding the house and the way he had peered at them when answering the door after he had finally shown himself. Once inside, Gardener overheard the conversation on the mobile, which left him doubting its authenticity. Was he really speaking to himself, especially considering what Fettle had told them about the director's that William had mentioned?

Though the meeting with Fettle had confirmed the link to Lon Chaney, it revealed nothing further about Corndell. Gardener was satisfied that they *were* searching for a man with an incredible knowledge of the film world, and very likely the actor, Lon Chaney, for whatever reason. But the fact that Fettle had never heard of William Henry Corndell – given his pedigree – was interesting.

Gardener was also concerned about William's superstitions. He knew from past experience his partner's knowledge of fables. Sean Reilly – despite his hard man image – was the king of the leprechauns. He had told Gardener countless stories of his time back in Ireland when he was growing up. Reilly knew them all. So he'd found it very interesting when William was being challenged, and how defensive he had grown regarding his beliefs. As though he was superstitious but at the same time embarrassed at having been found out.

So was Corndell who he said he was? Who he led people to believe he was? Based on a first meeting with little evidence, had they actually been talking to the maniac responsible for the two most violent murders they had ever seen? Or was Gardener on the wrong track? They had so far drawn a blank with every lead. Had he allowed himself to concentrate on someone who was perhaps, simply mad but harmless?

One way or another, he would have to incite his team into producing results before another murder was committed.

Briggs opened the door and entered the room, breaking Gardener's train of thought. He threw a folder down on the table and immediately launched into the meeting.

"Right. Let's recap on what we already know. I'll go first. I've had a lengthy meeting with Janine Harper's mother and the Commissioner. Neither one is pleased about what's happened but we have discovered that Jack Harper was her father. The same Jack Harper that served on the watch committee with Leonard White and Harry Fletcher."

Briggs paused. "Which leaves us with one link. Your father, Stewart. So, if it's okay with you, I'd like to have a word with him. While you might know him better than I do, I'm concerned about your involvement becoming personal."

"It isn't personal," replied Gardener.

"Maybe not," said Briggs. "But I warn you, Stewart, if the killer finds Harry Fletcher before we do, then you know as well as I do where this is going. What we need to know is why. Perhaps the only people who can tell us are your father, or Harry Fletcher."

Gardener took over, glancing at Dave Rawson. "You spoke to Val White, Dave, did she give you a list of her late husband's films? Does she have an alibi for the night Janine was murdered?"

"Yes, on both accounts. The list of White's films is pretty long and I've used a couple of the support officers to try and track them down, or at least people who knew White, to see if we can find any further connection."

"Okay, and what about Val White?"

"She'd been to his funeral that day and was at a bereavement held in his honour on the night time."

"So that rules her out."

"What about Janine's boyfriend?" Gardener asked. "Did anyone speak to him about his movements?"

Thornton raised his hand. "I did, sir, with Anderson. Apparently they'd had a row and he hadn't seen or heard from her."

"What was the row about?"

"He said it was personal," replied Anderson.

"How personal?"

Anderson shifted about uncomfortably. "It was something to do with sex. I don't particularly want to go any further."

"I don't want you to, either," replied Gardener. "Okay, so they had a row. When *was* that exactly?"

"About a week before," said Thornton.

"And they never saw each other after?"

"No. He wanted to give her some time to cool off. That and the fact that he wasn't sure whether or not he actually wanted to see her again."

"Anything strike you about his nature that may lead you to think he had homicidal tendencies?" asked Gardener.

"No," replied Anderson. "If he has, his sexual tendencies are outweighing them at the moment."

"He was out shagging another bird that night," said Thornton.

"And she's confirmed, I suppose," said Gardener.

"Oh, definitely, three times, apparently."

"Which rules *him* out and leaves *us* where?" asked Briggs. "I'll tell you where, back to square one. Two murders, no witnesses, no killer, no clues."

"Steve?" said Gardener. "Any luck with forensics? Any prints from anywhere?"

"Not yet."

"In that case, check this out." Gardener produced a polythene bag containing the paper with the quotations, which only he and William had handled.

"What's that?" asked Briggs.

"It's a piece of paper with the quotes on. When Sean and I went to see William Henry Corndell today I let him handle it. I'm the only other person who has."

"Well done," said Briggs. "How did you get on with him?"

"He's intelligent, and he knows a lot about his trade. But I think he has a secretive side." said Gardener.

"Don't we all?" asked Briggs.

"I'm still not sure whether or not the whole interview was an act."

"What are you trying to say?" asked Briggs.

"We need to take a closer look. He's locked up inside a huge mansion that looks like a shrine to the film world. It's full of posters and very probably props."

"And locked rooms," added Reilly.

"What do you mean, locked rooms? Have you been searching his house without a warrant, Reilly?"

"It wasn't my fault I couldn't find the toilet."

"Oh, Jesus," said Briggs, running his hands down his face. "Why is it everything he does has disaster written all over it?"

"With all due respect, sir," said Gardener. "You'd have to see him to know what we're talking about. He's superstitious, although he denies it. Eccentric. He hates being challenged. Self-conscious. He was dressed all in black with a red tie. Not that that's a problem, but you'd think he could match a few more colours together."

"None of which proves he's mad," retorted Briggs.

"Maybe you're right. When all said and done, he did provide what I think will be a valuable clue."

"Go on," said Briggs.

"He suspected the quotes came from the silent film era, the golden age of Hollywood as he calls it. He thinks that's how people spoke in those days, without the use of sound."

"Did he recognise them?"

"He said he didn't."

"But you think otherwise?" Briggs asked.

Gardener nodded. "We went to see Fettle afterwards, the old guy who looks after The Grand in Leeds. He told us about Lon Chaney, an actor in the silent films who was a master of disguise. He played the part of Inspector Burke of Scotland Yard, and the part of the vampire here." Gardener held up the artist impression. "In a film entitled, *London After Midnight*."

"I remember him," said Briggs. "He also made that film about the Hunchback."

"And *The Phantom of the Opera*. Fettle also mentioned a film called *A Blind Bargain* – another of Chaney's about a mad scientist – both of which are what you call 'lost films'. William told us he collects lost films, and that his favourite was *A Blind Bargain*, and he provided us with a lot of information about make up. What bothers me most is a conversation he was having on his mobile phone – supposedly with Hollywood – when we arrived. He was discussing the choice of director for his work. He wasn't happy about it and said he would make changes if they didn't like his script."

"The problem is?" asked Briggs.

"When I asked Fettle to verify these directors, both of them had been dead for years."

The silence that followed was claustrophobic.

Gardener sensed the clocks ticking and the wheels turning. Had they found their man?

Gardener faced Trevor Thorpe, the profiler. "Trevor ... any thoughts?"

Thorpe was dressed as they'd seen him previously, in a tweed jacket and brown cords. Once again, he left his chair and glanced at the ceiling as he walked.

"Well ... Mr Gardener ... a very interesting ... character. Someone I would ... perhaps like to meet. Did he appear ... very confident ... when challenged?"

Reilly nodded. "Pretty much."

"What was his house like? Clean and tidy?"

"Yes," replied Gardener.

Thorpe returned to his chair and sat down, exactly as he had last time, legs straddling the chair and arms across the back. "Did he have a display of ... curtains ... in the house?"

"As far as I remember," replied Gardener, confused.

"Did you check the knots in the cords?"

"No, why?" asked Reilly.

"Just curious," replied Thorpe. "Our man ... likes to tie knots ... does he not? And the colour red ... was prominent, you say?"

"A little more than usual, yes," replied Reilly.

"And he appeared ... confident, you say?" Thorpe asked, spreading his arms out in front of him.

"Most of the time," replied Gardener.

Thorpe stood up and stared Gardener in the eye. "They're all coincidences ... Mr Gardener. We need to ... find out more. Is he married? Was he married? I think the man we're looking for ... is not a ... loner."

He now chose to stare at Reilly. "Security conscious ... I doubt very much ... he will be. He's spent so long being ... repressed ...

that he now wants to be ... free! He will not lock himself away. He'll be out ... most nights, mixing ... and ... mingling, because he craves ... company. He wants to express those ... locked in ... emotions. He wants to feel ... wanted! Loved!"

He sat back down on his chair. "No ... Mr Gardener ... I don't think Corndell ... is your man. You're seeing what you want to see ... because it fits in with what you ... think. You need to widen your ... thought patterns."

Thorpe said nothing else, and when it was obvious he'd finished, Briggs took over.

"Okay, how do you want to proceed, Stewart?"

Gardener turned to face the team. "Colin, I'd still like William Henry Corndell checked out. See what you can find. Where did he live in London and what was he up to? Find out everything you can about him after he moved here. Check his credit and his bills. Fettle has a contact who worked for *Her Majesty's Theatre* for years. According to Corndell, he played the part of The Phantom before Michael Crawford, so Fettle's checking that for us.

"Thornton, Anderson, you two check out Lon Chaney. Find out every film he's been in and what they're about. I also want you to see if you can locate anything on a film called *The Scarlet Car* which was one of the clues left on the last puzzle."

Gardener pointed to the copy on the board.

"Look at the last two lines. He's telling us he's about to kill another in Leeds. What does he mean by down and out? Is it an area none of us frequent? A seedy part perhaps, which puts Alan Cuthbertson back in the picture. He regularly visits places of ill repute. Or does he mean something entirely different? A tramp maybe?"

Gardener thought back to Derek Summers and the Christmas murders. At the time he met someone called Bob Crisp, a disbarred lawyer who'd turned tramp and lived underground in fear of his life. Since that investigation had been closed he hadn't seen the man. But he'd had no reason to. A pet hate of Gardener's was anything unclean. He shuddered as he thought of the time he'd been beaten senseless because he'd dressed like a tramp. Only to regain consciousness in their company and the man he had been searching for. But at the same time, he also realised what a friend Bob Crisp had turned out to be.

Question is, where is he now?

"I want the rest of you to continue trying to find Harry Fletcher, chase up the leads we already have. Explore new avenues."

Gardener faced his partner. "Sean, can I have a word?"

He and Reilly returned to their office.

"What's up, boss?"

"I'm not happy. What Trevor Thorpe said puts Cuthbertson back in the picture."

"Fair comment. But what's your problem?"

"You will tell me if you think I'm cracking up. I know you will, so I'm not going to ask. But did I – at any point – describe Corndell's house in any real detail?"

Reilly blew up his cheeks and puffed out the spent air. "I'm not really sure, boss."

"I am," said Gardener, walking towards the door. Before opening it, he glanced back towards Reilly. "I did not go into great detail about the house, but Thorpe seemed to know all about it."

CHAPTER 33

The following morning, Gardener showed Alan Briggs through to the kitchen. Malcolm was sitting at the table drinking his second cup of tea. The meeting was meant to be informal. Despite Briggs' reservations, Gardener thought it best if they spoke to his father at home and with him present.

"Now then, Malcolm," said Briggs. "How are you keeping?"

"I'm fine, Alan. You?"

"Can't complain. Is there any more tea in that pot, Stewart?"

"Coming up, sir."

Briggs pulled out a chair and sat opposite Malcolm. "I'm only here to ask you a few questions about Leonard White and the watch committee, if you don't mind? It's a sensitive issue and by rights, Stewart shouldn't be with us, but he thought you might feel a bit better if he was."

Gardener placed a cup of tea in front of Briggs and took a seat at the table. He noticed the strain in his father's eyes, the drawn expression on his face. Since White's death he hadn't been sleeping well. The fact that Jack Harper's daughter had also been killed had brought the whole issue closer to home.

"What can you tell us about the watch committee?" asked Briggs.

"There isn't much to tell, Alan. We used to vet the films when they came to Leeds. We had the power to censor what we felt was unacceptable."

"And did you?"

"In a few cases."

"Any in particular you can remember?"

"Not off the top of my head. I remember we considered a couple that were soft porn gone a little too far. We suggested cuts and the directors agreed."

"So you had to get the director's permission?"

"Not really, no. We just thought it polite to involve him."

"Did the directors approve without opposition?"

"Mostly. They knew we had the power to ban the film, if they hadn't," replied Malcolm, sipping his tea.

"Where did you do all this, Dad?"

"The Town Hall in the early days. Then, as time moved on, so did we." Malcolm paused. "I think we moved over to a warehouse, near The Playhouse."

"Can you remember where?"

"Not the exact address, but it was at the back of The Playhouse."

Gardener nodded. "I know where you mean, don't think it's in use now."

Briggs nodded, resumed his questioning. "You knew Leonard White pretty well, didn't you?"

"There were people who knew him better."

"The day he was murdered at The Grand, you went to see him. Is there anything you can think of now that was unusual about his behaviour?"

"Only the tea. I told Stewart he was legendary for halting productions because he wanted a regular supply of tea. When a tray of tea came for us both at The Grand, he never touched a drop."

"Did he pass you yours?"

"No."

"Did he move the tray?"

"Not that I can recall. In fact, to be honest, he was applying the finishing touches of his make up but he was wearing those surgical gloves."

"Finishing touches? What time were you with him?" asked Briggs.

"About two o' clock, as I remember."

"And you didn't find it strange that he was applying the finishing touches of his make up at two o' clock in the afternoon when he wasn't due on stage until seven thirty in the evening?"

The expression on Malcolm's face changed. "Now you mention it, it did seem a little odd, but I didn't think anything about it at the time."

"What about his voice? Can you remember if it sounded any different?" asked Briggs.

"It was a little higher. But voices change."

"The colour of his eyes?"

"Can't say as I noticed," said Malcolm. "But you have to remember it was a good twenty plus years since I'd seen him and I had no reason to believe it was someone else."

"Fair point," said Briggs."

Gardener interrupted. "Dad, can you think of anything that brought the committee into disrepute? Were there any arguments about anything in particular? Were any of the members ever threatened?"

Malcolm sat back in the chair. "I've had a lot of time to think about it, Stewart, and I have remembered something, way back."

"Go on."

"I'm trying to think. It's such a long time ago but I'm pretty sure that one film did have to be banned."

"Why?" Briggs asked.

"I can't remember," said Malcolm.

"Was it pornographic?"

"I don't think so, I'd have remembered that," laughed Malcolm. "Harry Fletcher would know. He used a to keep a diary, with him being a writer. If there were any films he particularly liked, he made a note of the closing credits. He also kept meticulous notes of the films where we had recommended cuts."

"How well did you know Harry Fletcher?" asked Briggs.

"About as well as I knew the rest of them. We socialised quite often, went out for meals as a group and discussed the films."

"Had you ever met him, or heard from him before the watch committee formed?"

"A couple of times, mostly at the cinema. I'd read a couple of his books."

"Did you meet up with Harry Fletcher more than the others?" pursued Briggs.

"Not particularly."

"What was he like?"

Malcolm paused. "When I think about it, typical writer, a bit strange."

"In what way?" Briggs asked.

"What I mean by strange is, he was very quiet, a bit of a loner. You wouldn't see him for weeks. There were occasions when he missed the watch committee meetings and then offered little explanation as to where he'd been. He'd just tell us he was working on a new book and had to meet deadlines. He was very inquisitive, obsessive. He was always asking questions without ever really telling you why."

"What kind of questions?" Gardener asked.

"I really can't remember, Stewart, it was too long ago. I suppose he'd ask us questions when he was writing a new book, to help with his research. He was a people watcher as well, but most writers are."

"What were his books about?" asked Briggs.

"As far as I can remember, thrillers, murder mysteries. One of the two I read was similar to Agatha Christie, only not as good."

Malcolm took a sip of tea and then asked: "Why are you asking me all these questions about Fletcher?"

"We can't find him," said Briggs. "We've checked the electoral register and he's not on that. We can't find any bank records apart from a couple that were closed down years ago. We've even spoken to the people at The Playhouse and the only address they had for him was a flat, somewhere in Leeds. But he's moved on since then."

"He didn't live in a flat when I knew him."

"Where did he live?" asked Gardener.

Malcolm cupped his hands under his chin. "Burley in Wharfedale. I remember it well, he had a little cottage, set back from the main street. It had a conservatory and a small study where he used to write. I can't quite remember the address but I could take you there."

"We need to check it out," said Gardener. "What about a telephone number?"

"I might be able to help." Malcolm stood up and left the room.

Briggs turned to Gardener. "He's doing well. I can see it's taken its toll but he's handling it great."

"Yes," replied Gardener. "I'm pleased, he's been so down of late."

"He must have a lot on his mind, Stewart. He knows as well as we do that the connection is most likely the watch committee and if we find Harry Fletcher dead, then he's next. The only thing he's come up with so far is a banned film and he can't even tell us what that was about."

"I'm sure if we give him enough time he'll remember. He's brilliant with films."

"Okay," said Briggs. "We'll change the subject and then come back to it."

Malcolm returned to the room with a phone number. Gardener left the table and rang it. The line was dead so he called the station, asking them to follow up, supply an address.

Gardener sat back down. "No luck. I've asked the station to check it out."

"Stewart was just saying how much you enjoy films, Malcolm. Do you go and see many?"

"I love films, Alan. Always have. I go a couple of times a week. Chris joins me at least once."

"What sort of films?"

"Something with a bit of a story, like the old black and white's years ago. They knew how to make them, then."

"Are you into horror?" asked Briggs.

"I've seen a few," replied Malcolm.

"Remember an actor called Lon Chaney?"

"Who doesn't?"

Gardener was especially grateful to Alan Briggs for the way he was handling the interview.

"What was so good about Chaney, Malcolm?"

"He was the best – pure magic to watch. They called him 'The Man of a Thousand Faces."

"Why was that?"

"Make up expert. There wasn't anything he couldn't do. He did it all himself and he used to carry a little black bag around. I did hear that the make up case is in the Natural History Museum in

Los Angeles. But the thing is, nobody knew how he did things. He used to endure such pain and torment just to get the part right. He wore a seventy pound hump for *The Hunchback of Notre Dame*, and for *The Phantom of the Opera* he was said to have pushed discs up under his cheekbones to create the effect."

Briggs' expression grew distasteful. "Going a bit far, isn't it?"

"That was Chaney for you," replied Malcolm. "He was a perfectionist. That's probably why he was the highest paid actor in Hollywood."

Briggs then slid the quotes towards Malcolm. "Do you recognise these?"

Malcolm studied them but shook his head. "No, but if you don't mind I'll write them down and check it out. Do you think they're from Chaney's films?"

"Possibly," replied Gardener.

"Even if they are, son, and even if the killer is an expert with make up, just like Chaney was, it still doesn't tell you why he's doing it, or who he is."

"True," offered Briggs. "But if we know that's where he's heading, we may find something in Chaney's past that will give us a clue. Was Fletcher ever into that kind of thing? You know, make up and acting?"

"No. Not in the time that I knew him. He was a bookworm. Why? You don't think he's your man, do you?"

"That's why we need to find him, Malcolm. If he isn't the killer, he could be the next victim. If he is..."

Briggs left the sentence unfinished, leaving Gardener aware of the implications. He knew his father well enough to know that he, too, would have worked out the answer.

"Have you heard of a director called Wallace Henry Corndell?" asked Briggs.

"Yes. That's who Leonard White bought his house from."

"What about William?"

Malcolm paused before answering. "There's no director of that name."

"Not a director, dad, an actor," said Gardener.

"I don't recognise him as an actor, either. What's he been in?"

"Mostly theatre work," replied Gardener. "But I get the feeling he's living off his dad's reputation and I can't find reference to anything he's been in. He reckons he was in *Phantom* in the West End before Michael Crawford."

"I thought Crawford was the first," replied Malcolm.

"So did I."

"And you suspect he's lying? Do you think *he's* the killer?"

"Well if he is, it'll take some proving," replied Gardener. "We have very little evidence against him."

Malcolm snapped his fingers loudly. "That film that was banned by the watch committee. I know why I can't remember much about it, I wasn't there."

"Why?" asked Gardener, feeling awkward, as if he should know.

"I was in hospital, don't you remember. I was landscaping for Leonard White at the time, the property in Horsforth, Corndell's huge place. I landscaped the grounds for him when the drains gave way and collapsed. I fell in and broke both my legs."

Gardener did remember. His application for the police force had been accepted but his start date was delayed so as he could help his father to recuperate.

"Can you remember why the ground gave way?"

"From what I heard the house had a series of tunnels running underneath it."

"Anything confirmed about the tunnels, why they were there?" asked Briggs.

"I've no idea," said Malcolm. "Harry Fletcher came to see me in hospital. He had his book with him and he told me about a film they'd had to ban. Apparently it was the most horrific thing they had ever seen."

"Can you remember anything else about it?" asked Briggs.

"No. It was such a long time ago. But I'm sure the records will be kept somewhere."

"Even from thirty years ago?" asked Briggs.

"It's a long shot, but it's worth a try."

"Makes sense," said Gardener. "If the director had his film banned. But surely it wouldn't have caused that much trouble. Wouldn't he have simply edited it?"

"I don't think he did," said Malcolm. "There was more to it than that. I'm sure Harry said there was bad blood."

"Maybe we're on to something, Stewart," said Briggs. "See if you can trace the records, and while we're at it let's tighten up our search for Fletcher. If he still has the diary that may be one reason why we can't find him, it might hold the biggest clue we have."

"Let me trace the records," offered Malcolm. "I'd have a better idea where to look than you. Besides, my name may still carry a little bit of weight."

"If you're sure?" asked Gardener.

"I'd like to do it. Who knows, it may help to catch the lunatic before he does any more damage."

Malcolm rose from the table and left the kitchen, in search of a notebook and pen.

"Are you okay with that, sir?"

"If we could spare someone to shadow him, it might serve two purposes."

"Protect him and at the same time lead us to the killer."

"Works on TV, doesn't it?"

Gardener laughed.

Malcolm returned to the kitchen. "There's someone outside waiting to see you."

"Me?" said Gardener. "Who is it?"

"You'd best go and see."

Gardener was puzzled. He wasn't expecting anyone. However he was delighted that Jeff Harrison had finally returned with his Bonneville chassis frame.

CHAPTER 34

Martin Brown had tried to call William three times already, and it wasn't even eleven o' clock. Each call had remained unanswered. In fact, he'd been unable to reach William since his first and only call.

He was concerned, and had been since the return of the contract, which had been promptly signed, sealed and delivered the day after he'd sent it. William had made clear his conditions. Under no circumstances should any of his demands be disobeyed, or he would refuse to perform.

Martin sighed and sat back in his seat, perusing the paperwork. He studied the contract, hoping to Christ the University could maintain the standards required.

In the hall a bunch of noisy students had gathered outside his door.

He returned his attention to William's first demand – the election of a supervisor to oversee the whole project from the beginning. The man would arrive on March 31st and set up the stage.

Martin hadn't yet seen him, but to be honest he'd hardly had chance to leave the office.

William's man would hand pick his own crew to help with whatever construction was required. Once the stage and the sound system had been designed to William's satisfaction, the hall had to be closed and locked and no one allowed access except William's supervisor: and only *he* would be present to greet William when he arrived – around noon on the day of performance.

Anyone found whistling on the set will be fired; particularly if the tune was Three Blind Mice. No live flowers should be present, or delivered before hand. No interviews will be granted either before or after the performance. The first customer to buy a ticket and enter the hall should not be a woman.

William had requested that the dressing room walls be painted with pastel colours and furnished with a dressing table, a mirror, adequate lighting, and a comfortable stool. A meal consisting of a green, crisp salad, accompanied by Chinese green tea should be delivered to the room no later than four o' clock. William would dine alone.

The biggest surprise – and only bonus – was that William had agreed to put on the show for free.

Martin couldn't work that one out. But then again, he couldn't really work any of it out.

He sighed loudly, wondering if anyone in the world would even see William, including himself. He still couldn't help feeling that the person who said he was William, wasn't, that it was some two-bit actor masquerading as a more superior one.

He threw the signed contract back on the desk and left his office, in search of said supervisor.

When Martin entered the theatre hall he was taken aback. The Gothic stage set was magnificent, with red velvet drapes and impressive backdrops containing huge still-frame photographs from very early Universal horror films. There was no doubt that one of them was the Notre Dame cathedral. A round platform – similar to the one where The Hunchback had been tied and whipped in the village square – had been erected centre stage. In Martin's opinion, there were heavy overtones of Lon Chaney here.

Four strobe lights were equally positioned around the base of the podium and the fog machines were currently being tested. Between all the photos, the design of the crumbling brickwork with its arched windows and gothic turrets impressed Martin. All of them had been coated with cobweb spray and enhanced by carefully concealed lighting.

A mixture of smells assaulted Martin's nostrils: some he could place; mint – and possibly avocado, which reminded Martin of a shampoo his wife had recently bought. There were others but he had no idea what.

The effect was sensational. The students were going to love it. Perhaps William really did know what he was doing. Judging by the set, the show would be nothing short of spectacular.

Martin suddenly jumped as the haunting sound of Mike Oldfield's *Tubular Bells* reverberated through the sound system. Although he couldn't see the speakers, they had a sound quality to die for. He wondered if the music had been chosen for the show. He couldn't see how it fitted in.

Martin breathed a sigh of relief when, at last, he saw someone on the stage, who may or may not be William's electorate.

The music stopped before the man made his approach. Martin was surprised by his appearance. The man was seventy if he was a day. He wore a grey boiler suit and carried a small bag of tools in his left hand. He had a flat cap and a pair of pince-nez perched over the bridge of his nose and a thick grey moustache. His eyes were a little watery, and so black and so deep they resembled two olives on a bed of cream. His skin and neck supported the fact that he was mature in years and Martin struggled to believe that the old man was William's supervisor.

"Can I help you, son?" asked the old man, with a bow bells accent. His voice was a choking rasp, as if he smoked sixty cigarettes a day.

"I was looking for William Henry Corndell, I don't suppose he's here?" asked Martin.

"Cor blimey, mate, you ain't asking much, are you? He's a very busy man, our William."

"You know him, then?" questioned Martin.

The old man jumped back and nearly dropped the bag of tools.

"Know him? Know him, well o' course I know him. What do you think I am, a doughnut?"

Martin was beginning to wonder. No one still talked like that down in London, did they: unless they lived in Albert Square?

"Are you his stage supervisor?"

"I am." The old man jumped down off the stage – pretty sprightly for his age – and extended his right hand. "Jake Bollard."

Martin was about to shake when he noticed the old guy wearing surgeon's gloves. But that wasn't what stopped him. It was the name.

"Pardon?"

"Bollard, Jake Bollard."

He did shake, so as not to cause offence. "Nice to meet you, Mr Bollard." Martin struggled to remain straight faced.

"And you are?"

"Martin Brown, I'm in charge of entertainment. I wanted to see how things were going and if the team were looking after you."

"Champion, mate." Bollard turned and admired his handiwork. "Where are they?"

"Gone for a tea break, they've worked like ten men. I thought they deserved it."

"Fair enough. It's looking good." Martin didn't know what else to say.

"It has to, he's a bit of a stickler is old William." Bollard turned and let out a rasping laugh, slapping Martin on the shoulder. "He'll bloody well have me if he hears me calling him old."

Martin laughed as well, despite not finding the comment – or the slap – very funny. "Where is he, then?"

Bollard's expression switched as quickly as his manner. "Don't you read contracts, son? You won't see him today."

"Why not?" Martin asked.

"He's never in the theatre the day before. Never has been, it's one of his little quirks."

"I see. How long have you worked for him?"

"As long as he's been doing it," replied Bollard, dropping the bag of tools and sitting on the edge of the stage.

"He's reliable, then?" asked Martin. "It's just that I find it a little strange that he isn't here, overlooking everything ... a man of his calibre."

"He doesn't need to be, does he? That's why I'm here. I know exactly what he wants and where he wants it. Things have to be done in a certain order and William will not enter the building until they have."

Martin was becoming more concerned. "What kind of things?"

Bollard stood up and waved Martin towards him. "Come with me, son."

Martin accepted a helping hand on to the stage. The smell caught his nostrils first and as he glanced upwards he saw the garlic bulbs. They were mostly hanging by threads but from the floor you couldn't see them.

"What are those for?" asked Martin.

"To keep the spirits at bay," replied Bollard. His wild-eyed expression conveyed his belief in the statement he had made.

"Spirits?"

"Oh, yes, my son." Before Martin knew what was happening, Bollard had climbed up on to the podium and positioned himself as if *he* was going to do the show. His arms were open and his gaze high. Tubular Bells regurgitated its way around the sound system again. Quite how, Martin had no idea, he hadn't seen anyone operate anything.

"You see," shouted Bollard, glancing back down towards Martin. "There are those that believe the nature of William's plays invoke spirits from beyond. He uses well known quotes from some of the old masters which have the power to summon."

Martin stepped back as Bollard's voice suddenly boomed out through the sound system. He must have had a hidden microphone.

"O' winged serpent, I summon thee to me
Come forth through the clouds for all to see."

The music reached a crescendo, the density of the fog deepened and Martin started to cough but Bollard continued unabated, his timing perfect.

"Seek out the sinners and toll the bell
Boil them alive in the fires of Hell."

The stage grew silent but not before a huge crashing sound: the strobe lights were extinguished, the smoke machines stopped and the darkness became so total that Martin started to wonder what had really happened, and which side of the dividing line between good and evil he was now on.

"Mr Bollard?" said Martin. "I really think you ought to climb down, it's not safe for a man of your age."

The lights came back on and Bollard was directly in front of Martin, startling him.

"What do you mean, my age?"

"How did you do that?" Martin glanced around. Nothing on the stage was out of place and whatever had caused the crash must have come from the sound system.

"It's in my blood, my son. Been doing it all me life, so don't you worry about me."

Jake Bollard reached down into his bag of tools and brought out a small bottle. He opened the top and took a quick swig of the not quite clear liquid.

"I don't think you should be drinking when you're in charge of such expensive equipment, Mr Bollard."

"Drinking!" said Bollard. "Drinking. What do you think this is?"

"Well ... I'm not sure but it looks like alcohol."

"Give over, son. Try it." He passed the bottle over.

Martin sniffed up. Whatever it was immediately coated the inside of his nostrils and he sneezed violently. His eyes stung and he could hardly see for the excessive water.

"Jesus Christ! What is that?"

"Garlic vinegar, mate. Me and William, see, we swear by it. Protection, my old son. The protective qualities of garlic were valued during the plague epidemics in the seventeenth century. Thieves who plundered the homes of the sick drank this to safeguard them from infection. Sure you don't want a drink?" He offered the bottle again.

"No thank you, Mr Bollard, I'd really like to make tomorrow night's performance."

Bollard put the top back on and placed it in the bag of tools. "Yes, I know what you mean. Anyway, I've loads to do, so if you don't mind I'll let you get back to your work."

He walked away without saying another word.

CHAPTER 35

The ultimate scene of the film listed by most historians as one of the ten greatest of all time was finally approaching, and his state of pleasure was beginning to reach a crescendo.

Mary Philbin – played by Christine Daae – had left the Paris Opera House via the mirror in her dressing room, had then been led by horse through the catacombs and eventually by boat across an underground lake to the Phantom's lair. Once Mary had realised it was The Phantom she had fainted. She had now woken up and, hearing music, had wandered through to the main room where she saw Lon Chaney aka The Phantom, playing the organ.

Boy was Mary about to receive a shock.

William had drawn his knees up underneath his chin, allowing his dressing gown to fall either side of his legs – but it didn't matter because he was wearing his jim-jams.

He was busy, preening every fingernail he had with his teeth, placing the nail on top of the tooth and rubbing it backwards and forwards. He removed his hand from his mouth and giggled silently to himself, stamping his feet on the edge of the chair, wondering where on Earth Mary had found the courage to do what she was about to.

"She's going to do it, Erik. She's going to get you," he mouthed, quietly, to the Phantom, as if the people on the screen could actually hear him.

"Watch out, Erik. She's coming." His voice grew a little louder.

He felt his erection build, but knew he wasn't allowed to touch himself. His mother had always told him it was dirty to do such things: and that men who did should be locked up. It was usually that thing between their legs that caused most – if not all – of the trouble in the world. He'd never really understood what that was all about. You only went to toilet with it.

However ... he had heard about other things.

Anyway, no time for that.

Mary had sneaked up behind The Phantom now. All music had stopped because he had realised she was there. The tension onscreen was electric, so much so that he felt the hairs on the back of his neck rise.

"Oh, God, Mary. You shouldn't do this, Erik will be so annoyed."

She reached her hand forward and the overwhelming silence made him fidget so much that he flipped back into the chair so hard it nearly overturned. His heart jumped into his mouth, his erection died and his legs weakened.

"Fuck!" he shouted.

He could have spoiled the best moment of the film. It's a good job he was alone. If he'd been in a public cinema, someone behind him chewing popcorn would have had the fright of their life if he'd landed in their lap.

People were such heathens! How dare they go to cinemas to watch a masterpiece and sit there chewing popcorn and hot dogs and crisps and spilling coke down their throats, burping, shouting, farting and annoying other people because they had no manners?

Well, he'd been brought up differently. The cinema was no place to conduct a gourmet delight, nor was it any place to mess around with girls on back rows, and he'd seen and heard plenty of that going on in his time.

That's why he had his own private screenings.

Mary's hand travelled towards Chaney's head.

He jumped out of the chair and approached the screen. Running on the spot, stamping his feet and clenching his fists, he giggled hysterically because he knew what was about to happen.

"You'll be in so much trouble, Mary," he shouted, pointing his finger at her.

Her hand was on the mask and he found it hard to contain himself any longer. He sunk to his knees and raised his arms in the air, as if paying homage.

"Go on, Mary, go on. Fuck the trouble, just get on with it."

He brought his hands back down and tugged the sides of his dressing gown, which had now opened completely.

At last, Mary pulled off the mask, revealing the horribly disfigured face in full close up.

"Yes!" he shouted, back up on his feet. "Yes, yes, yes."

He jumped up and down on the spot but was still unable to take his eyes from the screen and the sheer magic that Chaney had created.

"Lon the master!" He fell on to his back and stared up at the picture.

Throughout the film, Lon's haunting appearance had moved him. He was little more than a skeletal frame with a coat on, and his eyes were so deep that you could hardly see the pupils. The face had two big black holes delicately placed as if in a dead man's skull. Lon's skin was stretched across his bones like a drum. William knew from his research that it wasn't white, more a pasty yellow.

Although he had a nose there was little worth talking about.

The reel came to an end and the hideous face had been replaced with a bright white screen. The projector continued to turn the reel so that the only sounds were the motor and fan, and the celluloid as it continually tapped against the projector frame.

William stood up and switched on the light. Stepping into the booth he turned off the projector. He had to sit down for a moment because his breathing had grown erratic.

Whilst resting, he reminisced about the rumours circulating Hollywood on the use of the make up and how Chaney had managed to do it. Most of the stories were complete and utter garbage: propagated myths, in which the actor was said to have placed discs in his cheekbones and wire pins in his nose to distend his nostrils. Those same people had also said he wore a seventy pound rubber hump on his back while filming *The Hunchback of Notre Dame*.

Did these people actually know anything?

The answer was, no, they didn't. But he did. And he was going to recreate the face of the Phantom, the finest piece of make up he had ever seen ... and it wasn't for his little piece at the university. Oh, no, it was so he could frighten the fucking life out of Harry Fletcher: another one of those bastards that had tried to ruin him many years ago.

And he hadn't forgotten.

Leonard White had paid the price, as Jack Harper would have done had he still been alive. But no matter, his daughter had helped him more than she would ever know.

And the police still didn't have a clue. Nor would they ever find out. And even if they did, what could they prove? No one could ever identify him. All anyone ever saw was what he'd created. How can you accuse what you can't see?

He removed the reel from the projector and placed it back in the canister. He glanced around the room and located its place in the rack.

His cinema was a long room, which took up the entire top floor of his house: situated above his bedroom, a storage room, and his make up room. It had spiral staircases at either end that led down into the bedroom and make up room. The projection room was at the back while the screen covered the opposite wall. He had built storage frames for his films on both the left and right hand walls and in between those were a variety of film posters and a selection of original reviews. His eyes came to rest on one such article as he was putting the film away:

"Universal has turned out another horror. This newest of specials is probably the greatest inducement to nightmare that has yet been screened ... Lon Chaney is again the "goat" in the matter, no matter, if it is another tribute to his character acting. His make up as the hunchback within the Notre Dame cathedral was morbid enough, but this is infinitely worse, as in this instance his body is normal with a horrible face solely relied upon for the effect ... It's impossible to believe there are a majority of picturegoers who prefer this revolting sort of a tale on the screen."
Variety.

"Obviously written by a tit!" he remarked, screeching loudly at his use of such profanities.

He also had the original reviews carried by *The New York Times* and *Moving Picture World*, both of which were far superior pieces and gave Chaney the credit that he deserved.

He had no idea who had reviewed the film for Variety, but he'd loved to have met and had a few minutes with him. The man wouldn't have written anything else like that, certainly not for Chaney anyway.

Who did he think he was? You couldn't say things like that about a movie icon. Chaney was the greatest actor that had ever lived.

And I'm the second, he thought.

Martin Brown had already found out but he hadn't been aware. William was tickled pink with his performance at the university earlier today. The goons helping had erected the stage in record time, leaving him to entertain Mr Brown. He'd have loved to have seen him taken a swig of the garlic vinegar. It would have blown his balls across the stage.

That thought alone nearly made him piss his pants as he broke out into huge belly laughs. He ended up on his knees, holding his stomach, rocking backwards and forwards at the thought of Martin Brown coughing up his entire insides, imagining a lung landing at his feet.

He calmed down and then thought back to the two outings he'd already made. Posing as a chauffeur was a good idea but the shock on Leonard White's face was the icing on the cake as he'd woken up to find he was face to face with himself. That had almost finished Leonard White there and then; dignity, composure, piece of mind, the whole fucking lot had gone out of the window as he'd soiled himself: then stuttered so much that he sounded like a pneumatic drill.

That had creased William.

As for Janine Harper. Well that little piece of work had had it coming right from the beginning. She'd had no idea how to treat customers, so when he knew for certain whom she was, boy did he have a field day. Her face had been a picture the night he had entered the shop dressed as the vampire. Her jaw had dropped so far she could quite easily have licked her own arse.

He stood up and placed the film in its correct location on the shelf, glancing upwards as he heard the rain bouncing off the roof. He switched out the lights in the cinema, descending the staircase into his make up room, taking a few minutes out to study the two creations he had lined up for his next performances: one for the university and the other for Harry Fletcher. He was growing quite excited about both.

He fastened his dressing gown, turned out the lights in the make up room before heading for the kitchen.

As William entered, he heard another sound: one that made him freeze!

The house felt like it had shuddered, but not as much as his insides. The growl wasn't simply a rattle it was a real royal rumble in the fucking jungle. The glass in the frames trembled and it sounded to him like one had cracked.

He immediately ran from the kitchen to the living room and then out into the conservatory, before deciding that was not the safest room in the house either.

Another peel of thunder reverberated overhead and the night sky lit up as a sheet of lightning raced over the top of the glass-domed roof. He ducked and clenched his buttocks as the rain blasted the windows.

"Shit, fart, piss, bollocks," he shouted. He had to find somewhere else to hide.

He ran out of the conservatory, into the hall, glancing into a gilt edged mirror, watching his little chest rise and fall.

He often found solace by talking to himself.

"Don't worry, you're quite safe. You're okay. You have plenty of protection outside the door. No lightning will strike the house."

Thunder roared overhead as if to contradict.

"Fucking hell!" he shouted, leaving the hall and running up the stairs.

"Blankets, sheets," he mouthed, running into a spare bedroom: his heart felt as if it was on fire.

He pulled open cupboard doors and drawers and threw everything he didn't want into the middle of the room. After grabbing as many blankets and sheets as he could carry he saw another flash of lightning illuminate the grounds of his house through the bedroom window.

"Oh My God ... she's here."

He lunged forward, dropped a couple of the blankets, tripping and falling out of the door. He managed to pick them up despite his blind panic before racing down the stairs two at a time. The last four he took in one big leap and nearly broke his fucking legs.

He ran to the front door and opened it, checking the grounds. He knew he'd seen her. She was out here somewhere, waiting for him. The bitch: callous, old, bastard bitch from hell.

He left the front door open and ran straight to the back door. Bouncing into a kitchen cupboard he knocked a set of steel finish pans across the floor. He opened the door and once again checked everywhere he could see.

A peel of thunder and a flash of lightning sent him back into the house at double speed, his dressing gown hanging from his shoulders. His pyjamas were wet through and his hair was stuck up in places and clinging to his face in others. His feet were dripping wet because he'd run outside without his slippers.

"Fucking Bitch!" he shouted, incensed. She'd made it thunder.

He left the doors open so that any lightning or thunderbolts would pass straight through. He picked up the pans and rammed them into the cupboards: couldn't have those hanging around.

In the hallway he covered up the mirror, muttering to himself.

"All shiny objects and mirrors should be covered, lest they attract lightning bolts."

He raised his arm and pointed upwards. "You won't g ... g ... get me."

Oh Jesus, stuttering now ... must calm down.

He ran into the conservatory, covering everything he deemed dangerous. From there he shot into the living room to do the same. When he was satisfied he ran into the hall and headed for the kitchen.

The problem came when he tried to put the brakes on. Wet feet and tiled floors don't mix well. As he slid along the floor he came to land near the back door ... and there she was ... glaring at him.

"Oh, Jesus."

"Don't you blaspheme at me, young man! Maybe it's time I taught you some manners."

"You keep away from me."

The old woman continued to glare with a gaze that was probably capable of stopping the lightning, never mind creating it. Her silver hair was pinned into place with such severity that it stretched her eyes higher into her head, forced her nose into a point and drew her lips back over plaque-coated teeth. She wore a black dressing gown tied tightly in the middle. Her chest was so flat that it made no difference which way she faced. Her hands were clenching and unclenching and the ends of her fingers were stained with nicotine, or was it French polish from the broomstick she'd used to fly in on, from fuck-knows where.

"Keep away from you?" she repeated. "That's the trouble with you boy, no discipline. I think it's high time you and I took a walk."

You can fuck that right off.

He was in no mood for another of Nanny Cranshaw's beatings. He was sure she'd left for good. How come she kept turning up whenever there was a storm outside? And why was she never wet? He'd seen her on the outside to start with. She should be sodden by now.

Nanny Cranshaw leaned in quick and close. "Come on, boy! Get up!"

He slid back along the floor, remembering all too well the storm that had started it all those years ago. And if she had her way she would leave him out there again, but that wasn't going to happen. Not now. Not tonight.

There were three things he hated in life.

Spiders: because they made his flesh creep.

Storms: because they simply frightened the fucking life out of him.

And Nanny Cranshaw; boy was she the worst.

"Come on, you stupid, disobedient boy," shouted the old woman, but from somewhere behind him.

His head spun round so fast it resembled a Catherine Wheel on bonfire night.

"Oh, God." He felt urine spurt into his jim-jams and then the floodgates opened, leaving a puddle around his feet in no time.

She had blocked the doorway and any entry into the safety of his house, which left only one direction for him ... the garden ... and the storm ... and God knows what else.

"Well!" she demanded.

CHAPTER 36

Friday April 1st

Gardener was sitting on the office, reflecting. He had spent most of the previous day with his father, trying to trace any records the local watch committee may have left behind: and a banned film would surely leave a stain. They were still operating but out of a government office in the centre of Leeds with private screenings at various places. None of the current members recognised Malcolm although one of them remembered hearing his name mentioned more than once.

After a lengthy conversation they had discovered that no records older than ten years were available. They were also told that they might have better luck with one of the local historians or maybe the film museum in Bradford.

Having driven over there, Gardener had treated his father to a pub lunch and, afterwards, had tried the museum. All records had been stored on discs and could be accessed by computer but they, too, proved fruitless. There was no mention of a banned film, despite Malcolm's persistence that it had caused a stir at the time.

What little time they had left before people were starting to wind down for the evening was spent trying to trace Harry

Fletcher. Two people had remembered him though they had no idea of his whereabouts now: one of them however, had seen him recently, he simply couldn't remember where. Frustrated and tired they drove home.

Gardener had spent the evening trawling the Net in an effort to shed further light on the banned film. Malcolm had no details and no title so he'd given up a little after ten o' clock.

On a more positive note he had downloaded a short history of Lon Chaney and a bibliography, neither of which proved useful. One site had contained an appraisal of Chaney by none other than, William Henry Corndell. But try as he might, no further information about Corndell himself was forthcoming. Nor could he find anything that connected the quotes at the scenes of the murders, or even the quotes themselves.

Gardener was left with questions and no answers. Why was there no reference to Corndell in the West End musical, *Phantom*? Or Hollywood? More importantly, who really *was* the man who lived in a world full of dead people but thought they were still alive? Maybe he would find out when he joined Laura and Sean for Corndell's university performance tonight.

Sean Reilly came into the office and placed a coffee and a cup of tea on the desk; he was carrying a packet of Bourbon Creams in his mouth, which he also dropped on to the desk.

"Is that from the machine?" asked Gardener.

"It's free," replied Reilly.

"But it's from the machine," insisted Gardener.

Reilly passed over the biscuits. "Have one of those, it'll take the taste away."

"It's not the taste I'm worried about, it's the after effects. Colin Sharp claimed this stuff has turned his water green."

"He's only saying that to get attention. He thinks we might

actually treat him as an equal."

Gardener laughed, taking a biscuit. "So, how did you get on yesterday?"

"Some pretty interesting stuff," said Reilly. "Initially, the planning department knew nothing about any tunnels under the house or the grounds. But one of their senior guys who's been there years had a story to tell: apparently, the house had originally been built in 1840 by a man called Jacob Wilson, a pretty wealthy industrialist by all accounts, into everything. Anyway, he owned a mine and he had the house built near it. One of the problems he had was transporting the coal so he devised a network of tunnels under the ground which led to the railway station."

"Which one?" Gardener asked.

"Horsforth."

Gardener leaned forward on his desk. "We had a witness who said that Leonard White had entered the station in Leeds. No one has a record of him buying a ticket. No one saw him leave and no one knew where he went to."

"Sounds about right."

"Do you think there's a tunnel under the station in Leeds which goes to Horsforth?"

"Still looking into that one, but I did find out about one of those nature walk things that goes from the station and eventually finishes up there. Which would be a hell of a walk to do at night. We're appealing for witnesses."

"Okay. It may not be much of a lead, but it's something. Let's see if Briggs will put a couple of the junior officers on to it. In the meantime you and I should go and see Corndell again, see if we can have a better look around the house.

"I'm all for that," replied Reilly.

A knock on the door diverted Gardener's attention. Steve

Fenton opened it and walked in, immediately helping himself to a biscuit. Before the door actually closed, Frank Thornton and Bob Anderson entered, each carrying a folder in one hand and a coffee in the other. They, too, helped themselves to biscuits.

"What the feck's going on here, then, open biscuit day?"

"Give it a rest, Reilly, you probably pinched them anyway," said Thornton.

"That's hardly the point now, is it?" replied the Irishman.

"Depends whose office you raided," said Anderson.

"Yours."

Gardener was amused by the banter of his colleagues, the first since the investigation had started, as far as he could remember. "Okay Steve, what do you have for us on the prints?"

Fenton reached out for another biscuit but Reilly was quicker and held them close to his chest. "Information first, son."

"What's up, found all your spuds but lost your biscuits in Ireland now, have we?"

"Cheeky bastard."

Fenton turned to Gardener. "Nothing, sir. Yours are on there. And Corndell's I assume, because his are not on file."

"Okay, it was worth a try. Give him a biscuit, Sean."

"Feck off! That's no good to us."

"Frank? Bob? What have you got?"

"There's a lot of information about Chaney but I don't suppose any of it's new," said Thornton. "I've copied some stuff and put it in the folder. Basically it's a rag's to riches story about a bloke who was born to deaf and dumb parents. His ability to act came from miming for his parents. He went to Hollywood but it was quite a few years before he made it big.

"He did make a film called *The Scarlet Car* but I think the killer has used it purely as a red herring, but it *was* filmed in 1917 and information is a bit bloody thin on the ground. I think the film rhymed with what he wanted to say and the only reason was to point us in Chaney's direction."

Thornton seemed embarrassed by the fact that he'd found very little.

"Despite being an icon, very little was known about Chaney," said Anderson. "Apparently, it's believed he once gave an interview and the only thing he said was, 'My whole career has been devoted to keeping people from knowing me', and with that he got up and left."

"You're joking," said Gardener.

"Apparently not. He was very secretive. As I said, there was no bigger film star but very little was known about him."

"A bit like our friend, Willy," said Reilly.

"At least Chaney had a traceable career," replied Gardener. "Anything on Harry Fletcher?"

"I spoke to a bloke who used to work with him at *The Playhouse.* Apparently he left there and went to work in one of the Broadway theatres in New York. Anyway, he didn't stay too long and the last time the man saw him was a couple of years ago. He was back living in Leeds but didn't say where and he was quite excited about a new project but didn't say what."

"What is it with these thespian types?" said Gardener. "They're always shrouded in bloody mystery. Keep trying. He must be somewhere. If you've found one person who knows and remembers him there may be others, we need to find them."

"Before it's too late," said Reilly.

"Assuming he isn't the killer," replied Gardener. "Trace the flights, there must be records."

"But it's two years ago," said Thornton.

"I know that, but we need a break before someone else gets

murdered. Trace the flights, talk to the taxi drivers, someone must have picked him up: maybe recognized and remembered where he took him. If it was a hotel they'll have records. There will be a trail: it's a matter of finding it. We can't leave any stones unturned."

Colin Sharp interrupted the conversation as he knocked and walked in. He also had a coffee in his hand and managed to spot the biscuits straight away. "Hey, my favourites."

"And everybody else's by the look of it," moaned Reilly.

Gardener glanced at Sharp. "Okay, what do you have?"

"Not a lot."

"If one more person says that today," said Gardener.

Sharp sat down in the only available chair and opened his folder.

"I checked out with BT first. You might find this interesting. In the last ten years, Corndell's only had one phone call to his landline and hasn't made any."

"What?"

"He's made no calls and received only one."

"Who was that from?"

"Martin Brown," said Sharp.

Gardener glanced at his partner, Reilly. "Isn't that Laura's friend at the university?"

Reilly nodded. "What about his mobile?"

"He doesn't have one," said Sharp.

"He does," said Gardener. "He was using it when we visited."

"Sorry, sir, according to my records, he doesn't have one."

Gardener was confused but didn't see the sense in arguing. Sharp was a very dedicated member of staff who chased up leads with a determination he'd never seen before.

"Okay, patronize me: check a little deeper, will you? How does he pay for his BT line?"

"All his transactions are done electronically. He never goes into the bank or pays a bill in person."

"Which bank is he with?" asked Gardener.

"An independent in London."

"Why London?" asked Gardener, astonished.

"I assume it's because he came from London originally."

"But surely you would change banks if you moved so far away," pressed Gardener.

"Unless you wanted to hide something," said Reilly.

"What about an income?"

"He doesn't have one," replied Sharp. "But then again, he doesn't need one. His parents left him over three million pounds, and the house."

"How did his parents die?" asked Gardener.

Colin Sharp sorted through his notes. "His father had a heart attack."

"Brought on by what, I wonder," said Gardener.

"Who, more like," said Reilly.

"I don't think it was anything to do with William. He was still down in London when it all happened."

"Doesn't mean much," said Reilly. "He could still have had a hand in it."

"Well ... he could, but it doesn't seem feasible at the moment."

"What about his mother?" Gardener asked.

"Died in 1985: cancer."

"Okay," said Gardener. That tied in with what William had told them. "Anything else?"

"The only thing left for me to do is follow up the London lead, find out everything I can about his life down there. If anything's going to give, that's where it will come from."

"In that case go down tomorrow. That privately owned bank must have a previous address. His father was famous enough, try the film studios, the West End – and that reminds me, Sean, check with Fettle and see whether or not his mate has any information."

"Do you two really think Corndell is our man?" Thornton asked Gardener.

"He's at the top of the list for now."

"Then why don't we bring him in?" asked Anderson.

"No evidence," said Reilly.

An air of defeat circulated the room.

"Another murder should do that," said Anderson.

"Only if we can tie him in," said Gardener.

"Does he have alibi's for the previous two?" asked Steve Fenton.

"No, but you can't prove or disprove what he's said because he was home alone. And let's face it, even if he wasn't, who's to know with the two disguises he's used? Quite frankly, another murder would put us bottom of the popularity stakes and Briggs would come down so heavy on us we'd have to reach up to tie our shoelaces."

Gardener sighed as another knock on the door came and Patrick Edwards poked his head around the frame.

"Anything on that missing limo, Patrick?"

"Not a lot," replied Edwards. "Still hasn't turned up. It was paid for in cash by a man called Robert Sandell, and we've now found out all the documents produced were false."

"Wonderful," replied Gardener. "Okay, I have something else for you. I want you to check all the rental companies and find out whether or not a William Henry Corndell has hired any vehicles recently using electronic transfers from a London bank as payment? Colin will give you the name of the bank."

"Okay, sir," replied Edwards, still standing his ground. "Sir, that number you wanted us to check ... Burley in Wharfedale?"

"Oh, yes."

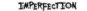

"It's not in service any more, when the owner sold the property and moved on the new owner had it changed."

Gardener glanced at the sheet of paper that Edwards had passed over. The address – a side street off the main street – seemed familiar.

"Who lives there now?"

"Someone called Cuthbertson ... Alan Cuthbertson."

CHAPTER 37

Mid-day had come and gone and with early afternoon approaching, Harry Fletcher had to try to organise tomorrow's supplies for the soup kitchen. He'd been at work since six o' clock and he was bushed, having prepared and served all the breakfasts, and afterwards, helping to rearrange the furniture in the room of the big house for tonight's local Council meeting.

But five minutes with a cup of tea and his diary wouldn't hurt.

Mary Phillips – one of three volunteers was cleaning the kitchen. She'd said it was fine by her if he took a break, seeing as he started two hours before anyone else. Kathy and Sarah (the other volunteers) had left early due to doctor's appointments.

Harry took a sip of the now lukewarm tea. He dipped a custard cream and popped it into his mouth, savouring the taste because it was the only thing he had eaten today.

Since leaving New York, Harry had changed his life completely, starting with his name. Here, he was known as Henry Fowkes, the name he was known by on Broadway. He had a very strict diet, eating virtually nothing during the day but finishing the evening with a decent meal.

Two hours prior to supper he used his time wisely, writing in the study, another room within the house, where he also lived. After his meal, he would then spend a further two hours writing, before retiring to bed early with either a good book or his portable television.

Since returning to Britain he had enjoyed himself but his current project was coming to an end and he felt that he should speak to his friend, Stan, very soon about the whole thing. He had hoped he'd see Stan today but he hadn't yet shown his face.

Harry liked Stan.

The first time the man had walked into the homeless shelter – which quite frankly had only been three months ago – Harry had known he was the one. Stan was perfect for the part without a word being spoken. For all Harry had known, Stan could have been a deaf mute. But he wasn't and they had started speaking and the more they had talked the more he'd seen his project opening up into a bestseller. Americans loved stories about eccentric Englishmen.

Stan's first appearance had been towards the back end of January when the weather had turned bitter. Hunched into a topcoat with the flaps of his deerstalker down he'd crept quietly through the door, glancing everywhere, as if he was searching for someone but he wasn't sure who.

He wore woollen mittens with his fingers poking through, reminding Harry of the old rag and bone collector, Albert Steptoe, who regularly appeared on TV throughout the sixties and seventies, but that's where the similarity ended. He always had a pipe clamped firmly between his teeth, perfecting a Sherlock Holmes exterior that Conan Doyle would have been proud of. There was no tobacco in the pipe: whether it was because he was trying to give up or he couldn't afford it, Harry had never determined, and it didn't seem that important anyway.

Stan had chosen a quiet corner in which to sit and as Harry approached, he'd tipped his cap and then hesitated, as if he shouldn't really be there. Harry had laid a hand on his shoulder because he felt sure that Stan *would* have left the table *and* the shelter had he not made the gesture.

Harry had made tea and sandwiches and sat with his newfound friend while he had consumed them. Stan's mannerisms had reminded Harry of a typical, old English gentleman, as though he had suddenly materialised out of nowhere from that Victorian era.

H. G. Wells came to mind. Harry had a vivid image of the film *Time After Time*, where Wells' famous time machine had transported Jack The Ripper to modern day San Francisco. The butcher of prostitutes had quickly adapted and after a change of clothes had blended perfectly into the seedy side of the town. Wells on the other hand had stuck out like a sore thumb. His old-fashioned values and manners had forced him into many bewildering predicaments.

To Harry, Stan was a mixture of so many different people from films he'd seen and that was why he was perfect for Harry's new project. He wanted to take the play – and Stan – back to the New York theatre district because he knew it would be well received.

For the last two months, all Harry had done was churn out Stan's life story, using their conversations to fill his blank pages. He knew he had a guaranteed success. Erica Barry, played by Diane Keaton had done exactly the same thing in the film, *Something's Gotta Give*, with Jack Nicholson.

Stan's strange phobias and superstitions also suited the part. Harry would never forget the day Stan had encountered a spider underneath the table where he was eating. Well, actually it had climbed up the leg and ran across the top. Stan had almost turned the place upside down in an effort to leave.

Stan didn't like storms either. That had proved another interesting day. Harry had closed all the doors and windows and had insisted that Stan stay at the table and finish his meal. He would never forget the fear in the man's eyes and *his* insistence that all doors and windows should be opened at once to allow any lightning bolts to pass straight through. With white knuckles he had gripped the table, refusing to eat. When the storm had finally passed, Harry had paid a taxi driver to take Stan to wherever he felt he needed to be.

But for all that, he enjoyed Stan's company. All he had to do now was persuade him to give up his life here. What life? Harry knew he was homeless, but homeless people lived somewhere, even if it *was* only a makeshift shelter at the back of the shops on Albion Street. Harry had toured the city in search of Stan and none of the vagrants had had any information. No one knew him: neither had they heard of him. He'd checked the other shelters but Stan had not frequented those either. Having finally found the taxi driver and asked him where he had taken the man who resembled Sherlock Holmes, the answer had been, somewhere in Horsforth, one of the parks, he suspected.

Harry was puzzled by that one: and that was another thing about Stan, he loved his puzzles.

"Hello Henry," said a voice behind him.

Harry turned and saw the man he had been thinking about. Stan was staring down at him, dressed in his usual garb.

Poor Stan must have had a tough life. Harry estimated his age as mid sixties, and because he had odd eyes his expression was one of constant torture. Not only were they different colours, one was lower than the other and bore the marks of a nasty scar. Harry had brought it up in an earlier conversation but Stan had refused to talk about it. His skin was extremely wrinkled and leathery to touch, like the hide of a bull. But for all that, he was well nourished. Although he ate little at the shelter, the man had to be eating somewhere.

"Stan, my man, how's it hanging?"

"Oh, Henry, I'm not at all sure I shall ever catch on to your use of language."

"You should've have done by now, what with living on the streets."

Stan removed his pipe from his lips before speaking. "One cannot change one's upbringing, Henry. A terrible place the streets may be, but because one lives there doesn't mean one should lower one's standards and adopt the ways of those who do."

"I've not seen you for days, where have you been?"

"Keeping low, Henry, pondering over the rising violence within the city and wondering where a man's to go for safety in times of crisis."

Harry wasn't keen on the tone of conversation today. But Stan could be like that. One time he would be all cheerful and full of himself, talking of a life that Harry wasn't sure he had actually lived, but simply wanted to. It was saddening to hear. Other times he was very philosophical, taking the world's problems to heart. Today was going to be one of those days. Perhaps it really would be best for him to tackle Stan about a change.

"Come and sit down, Stan. I'll make a fresh cuppa and then I'd like us to talk."

Stan did as he was asked and then returned the pipe to his mouth.

When the tea was made, Harry placed a cup in front of his friend.

"I've brought your favourites as well, fig rolls."

"Praise the Lord that I should ever have found a friend like you, Henry."

"What's troubling you, Stan?"

"Is this to be the subject of our conversation, what is bothering me?"

"Amongst other things, yes."

Stan placed his pipe on the table and sighed and rolled his eyes upwards, the way Alastair Sim used to in those Ealing comedies of the fifties.

Harry thought again that he was so perfect for his play. It was simply a question of whether or not he could adapt to another life and utilise what was very obviously a natural talent. It was one thing to convey expressions and mannerisms in everyday life, but to display them on a stage in front of a crowd of people was another matter entirely.

"I know things, Henry."

"What kind of things, Stan? Come on, drink your tea and have a fig roll."

"You don't understand, Henry. Tea and fig rolls will not help alleviate the problems of the world."

Stan's tone worried Harry. Despite knowing what he could be like he had never seen him acting as weird as today: another indication that he should make his move.

"Has something happened?"

The old man gripped Harry's hands with a speed that startled him. "Do you not read the newspapers, Henry?"

"Which papers, Stan? What are you talking about?"

"There's a murderer on the loose. He has to be stopped."

"You don't want to worry yourself about that. I'm sure the police will catch him before long."

"I hear things on the street. The police have no idea who they're looking for. They have no idea where he'll strike next. The city of Leeds is no safe place."

"When you say you know things," said Harry. "Do you mean you know things about the killer which could put you in danger?"

Stan remained silent for so long it really unnerved Harry. During the ensuing silence his thoughts were sporadic. Was Stan's life in danger? Did he know the killer, or something about him?

And then he had the worst thought of all. Was Stan the killer?

"Where exactly do you stay at night, Stan?"

Stan's glare created a feeling of depression within Harry. Their conversation was not going to plan.

"The streets are unsafe."

"Would you like to stay here tonight?"

"Is it any safer here than anywhere else?"

"Well, I'm here. There'll be plenty of other people here tonight, we have a council meeting."

"I'm not sure, Henry, you are too good a friend to me, I have no desire to place you in the danger I myself may be facing."

"Nonsense, you're worried and I'd like to help. And there's something else we can talk about tonight."

Stan picked up the empty pipe and puffed on it, as if it contained tobacco. "What?"

"My work here is nearly done, Stan."

"Are you leaving?" Stan's eyes widened and his grip grew tighter and it was only then that Harry had realised his hands were still coupled to those of his friend. "You can't leave! Where will I go, who will I talk to?"

"Well that's just it, Stan. Where I'm going, you can come, too."

"What?"

His friend seemed horrified by the suggestion. Yet only seconds ago he had feared for his life on the streets.

"I'm going back to New York. I want you to come with me."

"To New York? Are you out of your mind? I can't go to New York, it's less safe than here."

Stan stood up and abruptly let go of Harry's hands.

"Besides, I don't know anyone in New York. What if they don't like me? Or I can't make friends? What shall I do, then?"

"Stan, stop worrying and calm down. You'll be with me."

"Doing what, for heaven's sake?"

"That's what I want to talk to you about," replied Harry.

Stan made for the door, knocking over a chair in the process. "I can't. I just can't." He turned to Harry. "Don't you realise, Henry, here is all I know? I may not have much of a life, I may be in danger, but I know here. We drive on the right side of the road. We don't eat pancakes smothered in syrup for breakfast. We drink Earl Gray tea, not coffee in Styrofoam cups..."

Harry thought he had stopped but the barrage continued. "We are civilised human beings." He pointed a crooked finger at Harry. "We don't carry guns."

Harry sensed the man was physically distraught and suspected the situation was about to spiral out of control when Mary Phillips came into the room. Her appearance momentarily calmed Stan down.

"Is everything all right, Mr Fowkes?" asked Mary, a strawberry blonde that carried a little too much weight, wore a little too much make up but for all that, her heart was in the right place.

"It's fine, Mary, Stan's just a little worried about something. But I've asked him to come and stay here tonight, haven't I, Stan?"

His friend hesitated before replying. "If you're sure I'm not intruding."

"Don't be soft, man." Harry turned to Mary. "Can you make up a spare bed for me?"

"Of course I can." She turned to Stan. "You'll be more than welcome, love."

He tipped his deerstalker. "If you're sure it's no bother."

"None at all," said Harry.

He tipped his hat once again and bowed. "I must be on my way."

"Where are you going?" asked Harry.

"There are things I need to attend to but I shall return. And only if you are sure." It was a point he kept making.

"I've said so. You stay here tonight, we'll have a meal and a talk and I'm sure everything will seem much better in the morning."

"You're very kind." He stepped back into the hallway. "Till tonight, Harry."

His friend was gone in an instant.

"That's odd, Mr Fowkes," said Mary.

"What is?" asked Harry, clearing away the pots into the kitchen.

"He just called you, Harry."

CHAPTER 38

Gardener glanced around. The university theatre wasn't particularly big, which made it more intimate.

The building was bursting with students whose dress sense was more suited to the *Hitchhiker's Guide to the Galaxy*. There were colours of every description and garments that were so loose, at least three of them could have fitted comfortably into one item and shared the cost.

Despite Reilly having made a little more effort with his attire he was still dressed in denims. Laura wore an expensive two-piece suit in emerald green with matching jewellery. Gardener however, had once again used his son as a guide. He was wearing a plain black jacket tailored by *Pinstripe*: a midnight blue Lee Cooper shirt and a pair of bleached black *Koman* original vintage jeans – imported from the United States. He wasn't convinced but Chris told him they were in. More than half the students must have thought so because they had glanced in his direction as if he played a part in the events about to unfold.

The stage had been prepared to create the perfect ambience to an evening which he suspected would be full of surprises;

the fact that William could actually act for one. Two blackout curtains had been used to maintain the secrecy of what lay behind. There were speakers either side, positioned top to bottom. A fog machine belched out a fine mist at carefully timed intervals, and the lighting created an eerie silhouette of a sinister figure, rising up and down on the surface of the curtain, reminding Gardener of the very early vampire film, *Nosferatu*. Background music was Mike Oldfield's *Tubular Bells*. The idea was clever but he was unable to concentrate fully because of what had been said at the meeting earlier in the day.

The uppermost thought in his mind was whether or not he was obsessed by the fact that he thought William was the killer when there were quite clearly other links and further evidence pointing to two additional people: namely, Alan Cuthbertson, despite the alibi's: and the mysterious Harry Fletcher, whom no one could find.

He turned to Sean, noticing that Laura was deep in conversation with the person next to her.

"Did you manage to find Cuthbertson, Sean?"

"No: called him three or four times and then took a car round his place. Neighbour said she hadn't seen him for a couple of days, which was unusual because if he ever went anywhere he normally left her a key to look after the place."

"Has she gone round to see if he's okay, or still there?"

"Only once. She was out in the garden and heard his phone ringing. If he *was* in he never answered. After that I drove round to Ruffin Street to see that freak, Two Swords. They haven't seen him for a couple of days either."

"I don't like the sound of this. You don't think he's done anything stupid?"

"Like topping himself and leaving a suicide note to say that we're responsible because we wouldn't leave him alone? It's a possibility."

"I wasn't actually thinking of that: more along the lines of fleeing the country. Have you tried the shop?"

The music changed. Gardener didn't recognise it except to say that it was probably from a horror film.

"Yes, still closed. I don't think he's left the country, boss. I'm sure the neighbour would have seen him bundling a suitcase into a taxi. She didn't strike me as the type to miss anything. We should probably check the airports anyway."

"Like we really need this right now," said Gardener. He changed the subject. "Anything on the rental companies?"

"Not yet, but that's a big job, so it is."

Gardener leaned further forward, noting that Laura was still talking.

"Do you think she'll miss us for a few minutes?"

"What do you have in mind?"

"I thought we might pay a visit to our friend's dressing room, seeing as we're all in the same building at the same time. We may not get another chance."

"It's a good idea but I think you'd achieve more if you went alone," said Reilly. "I don't think he'll talk anyway, but if he sees both of us we'll have no chance. What do you think he'll say now that he didn't before?"

"Nothing, but I'd just like him to know we're here. And while I'm at it I'd like a word with Martin Brown. I want to know what time William arrived, and how."

"I'll talk to Martin," said Reilly.

"Okay."

He noticed Sean lean towards Laura and have a quick word in her ear. She glanced around and then pointed to a man on the far side of the stage, talking to one of the students, which he took to be Martin Brown.

Gardener and Reilly left their seats, shuffled to the end of the row and finally down to the stage where they figured Martin Brown's conversation was coming to an end. He smiled and politely nodded as the student walked off.

Down here, as close to the stage as he was going to be, Gardener sensed it was much warmer and wondered whether or not it was an effect of the lights.

"Can I help you gentlemen?" asked Martin.

"Maybe," said Gardener, flashing his warrant card. "We'd just like to ask you a few questions."

"Has something happened?"

"We're interested in Corndell."

Martin Brown wasn't at all what Gardener had expected. Standing a little over six feet he had mousy coloured hair in a style more erratic than most of his students. Perhaps he hadn't combed it today. He wore a beige shirt, left hanging out of his denim jeans and a pair of loosely fastened, brown loafers. Despite being born and bred in London there was only a trace of an accent. He was slim and had one of those postures that could easily be mistaken for a man who preferred other men. The receptionist at Skipton would have been in his element.

"You could have picked a better time, he's on stage," he replied, glancing at his watch. "He is due on in ten minutes and I have to announce him."

"It won't take long. How and when did he arrive here today?"

"I really haven't the faintest idea."

"I thought you ran the entertainment around here," said Reilly.

"I do."

"So how come you don't know what's going on?"

"Because I have a lot more to do than keep my eye on who comes and goes and at what time."

"You must have some idea," said Gardener, eager to return to the point.

"I believe it was around four o' clock. I wasn't here myself. Naturally, I would assume he arrived by taxi."

"I wouldn't assume anything with this man," said Reilly.

"What are you trying to imply?" asked Martin Brown.

"Nothing," said Gardener. "We're just making sure you answer the questions correctly and to the best of your knowledge, not with what you think you know."

Martin Brown glanced at his watch again, seemingly more agitated.

"So, did he arrive by taxi, or didn't he?" pressed Gardener.

"Just a minute." He walked over and consulted another colleague. On his return he had better news.

"Yes he did arrive by taxi, just after four o' clock."

"From where? And do you know which taxi firm?" asked Gardener.

"Look, is this really necessary? I do have a show to present."

"We wouldn't be asking if it wasn't," said Reilly.

"Aren't you Laura's husband?"

"Now that *is* an unnecessary question," replied Reilly. "But for the record, yes. So, can you tell us where he was brought from?"

"No I can't. I assume, rightly or wrongly and quite frankly I don't care, his home in Horsforth."

"I'd like to go backstage and have a word with him," said Gardener.

That statement took Martin Brown one step closer to madness, or so his expression conveyed.

"Are you kidding me? The man is about to go on stage and present a show. Have you any idea of the kind of pressure he will be under?"

"Not as much as me," replied Gardener.

"I don't think it would be wise."

"I'm not really interested in your opinion, Mr Brown. And whether or not you like it, I *am* going behind that curtain and I *am* going to have a word with your client."

"Are you here on official business?"

"In what capacity?" Gardener asked.

"Police capacity. Has Mr Corndell done anything wrong?"

"Not to my knowledge."

"Then I don't see any reason why it can't wait until after his show. And before you ask, I have to tell you his contract specifically states that no one will be granted interviews either before or after the show."

"I don't want an interview, I simply want to wish him all the best," Gardener answered.

"Haven't quite gone the correct way about it, then, have we? As I mentioned, his contract stated no interviews, no guests. He was very particular about the contract being followed to the letter."

Gardener noticed the crowd growing restless. The background music changed again, to another heavily orchestrated piece he didn't recognise.

"Do you have that contract to hand?" asked Gardener.

"It's in my office."

"I want a copy before I leave. And now, I'm going backstage for a quick word, after which, you can introduce him." Gardener turned to his partner. "Sean, you stay here and see that Mr Brown is kept amused."

Gardener tipped his hat and walked off.

He entered the stage through the side curtain, suddenly caught off balance by the atmosphere.

The set was incredible, with red velvet drapes and huge

backdrops and images from horror films: as was the cathedral. In between the photos, the crumbling brickwork had arched windows and turrets, bearing the hallmark of a million spiders spinning their webs. And he could smell garlic.

But none of what he saw had prepared him for the centrepiece. In the middle of the stage stood a huge podium surrounded by strobe lights, which were currently being switched on and off one by one. A fog machine added to the effect. A number of stage hands were asking the person on the podium if everything was okay, and he knew from the replies that it could only be one person behind the breathtaking make up.

Even Gardener – who was by no means a film buff – knew that William had recreated the character Quasimodo from the film, *The Hunchback of Notre Dame.*

The attention to detail was fascinating, hypnotic. His nose was shaped like a tetrahedron, a sort of four sided, triangular pyramid, with a mouth arched like a horseshoe. William's left eye was pushed upwards and his eyebrow had bristles like those of a carrot. The right eye was buried behind a tumour. He had irregular teeth like the battlements of a fortress and a horny lip over which the teeth protruded, like a walrus tusk. His head was covered with red bristles and between his shoulders he had a hell of a hump. How he had balanced it, Gardener had no idea. His legs were so strangely positioned that they only touched at the knees, as if they had been broken in order to achieve the effect.

He wore a dark grey, three quarter smock that must have been laid on a warehouse floor for the last ten years, and a tight pair of black leggings, for which, Gardener was sure William had used padding. No one on Earth could have legs like that. The whole effect was neatly finished with William trussed up and held firm to the podium by chains that appeared to be real but were surely not.

Suddenly, as if in slow motion, William turned his head, spotting Gardener.

Despite the intense amount of make up, Gardener detected an expression of pure rage on William's face. His remaining eye widened and nearly popped out of its socket.

"Would you please remove that man from this stage ... now!" he whispered, but still managed to make it sound like he was shouting.

"Now, now, Mr Corndell, that's no way to treat an old friend."

"If you were my friend Mr. Gardener, you wouldn't be here. I will not give you any further instructions other than ... either leave the stage now or the whole show is cancelled."

"If that's what you want," replied Gardener.

Martin Brown appeared at Gardener's side. "Can I ask you what the hell you think you're doing?"

"I told you. I came to see an old friend."

"You don't look like a friend from where I'm standing. Now you either leave or I'll call the police and have you removed ... officially!"

"Okay." Gardener raised his hands.

As he was about to leave he turned. "Oh, William, by the way..."

The hunchback glanced in his direction but didn't speak.

"Good luck," shouted Gardener. He didn't wait for a reply.

As he passed the curtain in front of the stage he could hear the commotion he had caused. William was quite clearly distressed and Martin Brown was doing his best to reassure him that everything was fine and that they really had to continue with tonight's performance. Gardener doubted very much that it would be cancelled now, what with William already chained up, but it may well be delayed.

One thing was certain. William's excellent use of make up had only confirmed his suspicions about who their killer could be.

Gardener joined Reilly back in his seat, removing his hat.

"How did it go?" asked the Irishman.

"Let's see, shall we."

"You didn't upset him, did you?" asked Reilly, smirking.

"Would I?"

The main hall lights dimmed and the background music died. The lighting creating the eerie vampire effect on the black curtains diminished and, eventually they were lifted, leaving the red velvet drapes and a silhouette of The Hunchback. Finally, the entire stage lighting petered out, leaving the whole place in darkness.

The tension was electric. People spoke in hushed whispers and he could see that most of them struggled to contain their excitement. Three girls sitting in front of them giggled and pushed each other.

The drapes opened, followed by the hiss of fog machines and a blast of the white mist. The speakers roared into life and despite the fact that he'd been ready for something happening the sound still startled him and half the audience. He did not recognise the piece of music but figured it would feature in one of the film versions of the character William was playing.

At that moment, Gardener was beginning to believe there was a possibility that William really could act; perhaps he had been a big name in the theatre, had done all the things he'd professed. The effect was certainly dazzling.

All four strobe lights lit up, each one of the beams directed at William. Even with his head bowed and the chains in place, he still managed to send a ripple of fear around the audience.

The music grew in volume and intensity and as it reached a crescendo, died instantly. In that moment, William raised his head and screamed, breaking the chains, launching them across the stage. He raised his hands, which were now free, and glared directly into the audience. More so towards Gardener: or so it felt.

Until that point, the show was as professional as any he'd seen.

What came next blew those thoughts completely.

Whether it was William's fault, or the podium on which he was standing, Gardener didn't know, but the whole thing completely overbalanced and William fell forwards.

He hit the stage with a thud and rolled over, crashing into one of the monitors at the front. Despite the sound created by the pandemonium, the word 'bollocks' was very prominent.

But for that, no one would really have known whether the slip was part of the show or not.

William was quickly on his feet and the whole audience erupted into raucous laughter. Students rolled about in the aisles and laughed and pointed at the pathetic figure on the stage.

Gardener stifled a smile but that was wiped from his face when William pointed outwards and shouted:

"Fucking police!"

He stormed off the stage to his right.

The laughter died, replaced by questions.

Gardener and Reilly were quickly out of their seats, heading towards the front, leaving Laura open mouthed.

They reached the front row. Martin Brown was already on the stage, glancing around.

As they stepped up, he turned on them. "Are you satisfied?"

"About what?" Gardener asked.

"That you've managed to ruin the whole evening."

"How do make that out, Mr. Brown?" asked Gardener.

"You upset him. He was all for cancelling the show but it was me who persuaded him otherwise. I could see he wasn't happy. But I'll tell you this much." He pointed a finger in Gardener's direction. "I will be placing a formal complaint about your behaviour here this evening."

"We're just doing our job," said Reilly.

"You told me you were not on official business. As far as I'm concerned you came here deliberately to upset him, for what reason I have no idea. What the hell has that man done to warrant you hounding him?"

"Where is he now?" asked Gardener.

"I have no idea, but wherever it is I don't suppose he'll want to see you."

"That's irrelevant."

Gardener pushed past Martin Brown but was unsure in which direction to go. He turned back again.

"Where are the dressing rooms?"

"That way."

"Don't point," said Gardener. "Show me!"

Martin Brown reluctantly did so, glancing back at the students who had paid good money for the show and were now lost as to what was going on.

At the end of the corridor they found the door to William's dressing room open ... and empty.

To the side, the door that led out on to the street was also open, the cold night air creeping in.

Gardener stepped outside but he couldn't see anyone.

Martin Brown was in the dressing room when he came back.

"He must have gone. Are you satisfied?"

"Not really." He turned to his partner. "Sean, let's take your car."

"Where are you going?" asked Martin Brown.

Gardener didn't answer but simply left the building. When they reached his sergeant's car and jumped in, Reilly turned and asked:

"Horsforth?"

"I don't think he could have got that far just yet. Drive around the streets: see if we can see anything of him. After all, the way he looks he won't be hard to spot, will he?"

Fifteen minutes of driving in all the directions they could think of yielded nothing. Gardener was mystified. William couldn't possibly have disappeared so quickly, unless of course he'd managed to flag down a taxi immediately.

Or he had his own transport.

They eventually pulled up outside the house at Horsforth. Gardener jumped out of the car and in the background, through the trees, he noticed lights burning at downstairs level. Then a bedroom light went on.

"He must be here, Sean."

Reilly stood close to the gate and the intercom. He reached into his inside jacket pocket and drew out the small mini cassette recorder and then pressed the button on the wall.

The intercom flicked into life with William's unmistakable voice:

"I do not wish to talk to anyone."

The intercom cut off and the bedroom light went out.

Reilly pressed the intercom once more but nothing happened.

CHAPTER 39

Saturday April 2nd.

Gardener was in the office for eight o' clock. The heating hadn't yet kicked in and the room was chilly. Reilly hadn't arrived and the overpowering silence was something he could do without. He crossed the room, switched on the small radio perched on the window ledge and immediately re-tuned to Radio 2, listening briefly to a news broadcast about the economy. As he turned towards his desk, Maurice Roberts, the night shift duty sergeant tapped on his door and entered. He was holding a clipboard.

"Morning, sir."

"Morning," replied Gardener, about to take a seat.

"A message came in for you last night, about nine o' clock."

Gardener remained standing. "Who from?"

Roberts consulted his notes. "A man called Henry Fowkes."

"Can't say as I know him. What did he want?"

Gardener's emotions started to race. Although Roberts hadn't said as much, his manner and his posture were associated with bad news. He wasn't his normal cheerful self and the expression in his eyes was not simple fatigue.

"He runs the St. John's Hospice."

"Where's that?" asked Gardener.

"In the town, sir, a couple of streets from Mark Lane. You know, where the St. John's church is."

Gardener slumped in his chair with an exasperated sigh. The mere mention of the building immediately brought to mind the name Bernard Thornwell, a victim of the Christmas murders, a case that seemed a lifetime ago but wasn't: more vividly, the grotesque condition in which they had found his corpse within the grounds.

"What did he want?" asked Gardener, preferring to leave his thoughts for another time.

"He was a bit concerned about one of his ... clients, is how he put it."

Gardener wondered where the conversation was going. "Concerned, how?"

Reilly's presence in the office lifted Gardener's tension a little.

"He didn't go into details, sir," replied Roberts. "But a man he's come to regard as a friend was acting very strangely yesterday: worried about the state of the city and the violence. He was particularly concerned about a killer whom we can't catch. According to his friend, we had no idea who we're looking for and he feared for his own safety."

"Did he give any names?"

"No, sir. I had the impression that Fowkes thought he was a doctor – patient confidentiality and all that. Anyway, he left a contact number."

Gardener glanced at his partner and then to Roberts. "Did he say anything else?"

"No, but the way he was talking, I think he had a lot more on his mind. He wants to speak to you."

Roberts placed the number on the desk and then left the office.

"Any chance we have a lead on Harry Fletcher there, boss?" asked Reilly.

"It's possible. Shall we ring the number or drive straight over there?"

"We may as well drive..."

Reilly's answer was cut short as duty sergeant Roberts launched himself back into the room.

"Sir?"

"What is it?"

"We've just taken a call from the St. John's Hospice, there's another body, I think the killer may have struck again, only this time, it's much worse."

"Worse! What could be worse than last time?" asked Gardener, moving around the desk.

"The woman's hysterical but she did manage to blurt out the name Henry Fowkes. She kept saying 'poor Henry'"

"Let's move." Gardener said to Reilly.

CHAPTER 40

Everyone arrived simultaneously: Gardener and Reilly, forensics, Fitz, and even Briggs. Gardener jumped out of the car and immediately started barking orders, which included sealing off the building with scene tape, constables to be placed front and rear and no one allowed in or out until he said so.

He glanced around. It was surprisingly quiet. Considering it was a homeless shelter he would have expected to see more people. The building was Victorian, three-storey, in a good state of repair with guttering, window frames and front door, all new.

Entering the building, Gardener heard hushed female voices in another room. To his left, a group of vagrants made him shudder. A lifelong hatred of anything unclean – particularly tramps – did little to abate his mood.

He turned around. Glancing down the path he shouted to one of the officers. "Come in here."

He faced the tramps. "I'm afraid you gentlemen will have to leave."

"What about our breakfast?"

The two policemen entered the building.

Gardener gave them their instruction before walking away.

In the kitchen he found the three women, each in tears, comforting each other. A strawberry blonde was leaning over a draining board, repeating the phrase, 'poor Henry'. A large pot stood on the cooker and, above that, the one thing he could have done without.

Scrawled on the wall ... written in blood, was the new message.

Gardener's whole world closed in around him. The kitchen was suddenly reduced to the size of a shoebox; sounds were blocked out, people disappeared, and he sensed a rush of adrenaline like he'd never before experienced. His whole body felt like it had pins and needles. He was cold, but at the same time he was sweating.

Briggs' loud voice brought him out of his momentary stupor.

"I don't suppose anybody recognises *that*?"

Gardener finally read the message:

So far so good, for a house with a curse on it.

Drawn on the wall underneath the message was an arrow, pointing to the cooking pot.

Gardener dreaded to think what was inside.

He turned to the three women. "Has anyone touched the pot?"

The strawberry blonde nodded. "I did."

He realised the stress she was under but he needed to know the answers to his questions. "What exactly did you do?"

She took her time in replying. "I lifted the lid."

"Other than the pot, have you touched anything else?" he asked her.

She shook her head, as if to confirm she hadn't.

"Can you tell me your exact movements from the time you came through the door?"

She was obviously very upset and Gardener sensed she was perhaps closer to the man they called Henry Fowkes than the others. He waited patiently while she described her movements. She'd been the first to arrive. Let herself in, hung up her coat and came straight through to the kitchen, where she'd remained, joined by the other two as they arrived.

Fitz came into the room. Gardener produced a pair of gloves. After slipping into them he approached the cooking pot and lifted the lid.

The strawberry blonde turned her head and let out a stifled sob.

The pan was three quarters full with warm, clear water. A severed head stared back at him. There was no blood and Gardener wondered if it had been drained prior to death – and where.

Because the water wasn't boiling the skin had not blistered and the face would be recognisable to anyone who knew him. The eyes were open and the depth of shock disturbed Gardener: if they could speak he was quite certain he would not want to hear what they had to say.

"Is this the head of Henry Fowkes?" he asked the strawberry blonde.

Although she didn't answer, one of the others confirmed it.

"Has either of you been anywhere else in the house?"

They said they hadn't.

"So none of you have any idea where his body is?" Gardener asked.

Once again, they confirmed they did not.

Frank Thornton and Bob Anderson were also in the room. Gardener addressed them. "Can one of you take these ladies out of here and see if you can arrange for a strong drink? Meanwhile, call the station and have them send round a couple of female councillors."

Gardener wasn't very pleased that they had probably contaminated the crime scene but there was little he could do about it now.

Briggs had moved a little closer. "What's that in the bottom of the pan?"

Gardener followed his line of vision and only then did he notice what Briggs was talking about.

He glanced around the kitchen and found a pair of tongs and lifted out the object: a sealed test tube with a note inside.

Briggs turned away in frustration. "This bastard's been busy." He threw his arms in the air. "And I suppose no one saw him again. And even if they did we're not likely to know who the fuck he was this time."

"We don't know that, yet," said Gardener, removing the stopper and the note from the tube.

The silence in the room became intolerable as each man patiently waited for Gardener to unfold what would more than likely be another puzzle, which would send them off to God knew where in order to find God knows what: but hopefully, the remainder of the corpse.

He read the message out aloud:

Here's the man you've been looking for,

So continue your search, out through the door.

Poor old Henry has met his doom,

If you want the rest, it's in his room.

"Does this mean we've found Harry Fletcher, who might be called Henry Fowkes?" Briggs asked.

"Possibly," said Gardener, passing the note to Briggs. "At least it would explain why we couldn't find him."

Before leaving the kitchen, a uniformed officer deposited a bin of scene suits and each officer donned one. They walked slowly through the house to find the three women whom Thornton had taken away. They were all sitting in a lounge.

"Which one is Henry's room?"

One of them women stood up. "I'll show you."

"It's okay," said Gardener. "Just tell us."

After the information, Gardener, Reilly and Briggs traipsed up the stairs to a second storey landing.

Briggs glared in Gardener's direction. "Before we go in here and see what he's left for us, I want it made abundantly clear right now that I don't care if we have to turn the entire city upside down or how many men it takes, I want this lunatic caught."

Gardener glanced at Reilly and then to Briggs. He understood his superior officer's frustration, for he felt it himself. Choosing not to reply, he turned and opened the door.

Nothing on Earth could have prepared them for the carnage.

The smell hit them first and each man took an involuntary step back, assaulted by a vile, cloying odour, which immediately coated the insides of their nostrils. Gardener doubted that the remains of a skip full of tightly packed corpses sealed up for the entire summer period would have topped it.

His cast iron reserve almost slipped and forced him to show his emotions. He had seen what The Roundhay Ripper had left behind, had attended all manner of suicides, observed the victims of car crashes, lived through the experience of the Christmas murders; and he was pretty confident that his partner had seen his fair share of atrocities during his time in the Royal Ulster Constabulary. But, here, in a Charnel House in a Yorkshire city, in a man's private study, they were now observing perhaps the most inhuman degradation that any of them had ever witnessed.

Briggs remained speechless, as did, Fitz, Anderson and the SOCO's – who by now had joined them.

Even Reilly inhaled a sharp breath.

In the middle of the room, was the naked corpse of Henry Fowkes. To all intents, he was levitating. In a spectacular illusion, his whole body had been suspended in mock crucifixion, but there was nothing holding him in place: at least, nothing they could see.

The entire room was awash with blood. By far the biggest and most disturbing stain was on the ceiling. He had obviously been decapitated here, in his study. Large globules that had been ready to fall to the floor had finally given up and congealed. Splash patterns doused the walls and the carpet and his PC.

"Jesus Christ!" said Briggs, peering a little closer. "What's holding him up?"

Gardener glanced to the sides of the room and immediately understood. A series of pulleys were screwed to the walls and as he strained his eyes he could make out the tines of catgut, or fishing wire. It had been would so tight that the limbs it held were bulging and must have been close to being severed.

In his right hand, a sheet of A4 paper had been fastened. It had the same scroll pattern as the ones they had seen at each crime scene, and no doubt contained another cryptic message.

On the floor, directly below Henry's body were a pile of discarded clothes, amongst them, a deerstalker and a pipe.

However, despite everything, the killer had really played an ace, because the most disturbing scene was that the corpse was not headless, raising the question of all questions.

Whose head was on top of Henry Fowkes' neck?

And how was it held in place?

"I really don't believe this fella anymore," said Briggs. "If Henry Fowkes' head is in a cooking pot in the middle of the kitchen who does that belong to: and where is he?"

Gardener scene suit rustled as he brought his hands to his head and ran them down his face, exhaling a loud sigh.

"We need to see what's on that paper."

Briggs turned to Fenton. "You lads seal the room off and do what you have to do, as quickly as you can. He's right, we need to see what's on the paper."

He turned to Gardner. "We have to do something, Stewart. The press get wind of this and we'll all be out of a job. And quite frankly, I can't see any way of preventing them from hearing about it."

"Well let's start by going downstairs and interviewing."

CHAPTER 41

The blonde appeared more composed. She took a sip of tea and then introduced herself as Mary Phillips.

"How long have you worked here, Mary?" asked Gardener.

"Four years," she replied.

"What do you do?"

"A dog's body really." Her gaze was devoid of emotion. "I suppose that's a bit harsh, I help out with a bit of cooking and bit of cleaning, nothing special."

"How long have you known Henry Fowkes?"

"He started work here two year ago." She took another sip of tea and Gardener suspected he was going to glean little more information from her than standard replies to his questions. But he'd settle for that ... for now.

"Did he live here?"

"Yes, his room were up the stairs, and he pretty much had the run of the house in return for all he did for us."

"Which was what?"

"He ran the place, Mr. Gardener. He were up early in the mornings, cooking all the breakfasts. Once that were over, we'd all have a cup of tea and then we'd straighten the place round. He used to see to all the deliveries."

"Did he have any family that you know of?"

"No."

"Any idea how he spent his spare time?"

It was a while before she answered and Gardener wondered whether or not she'd actually heard him or had simply forgotten the question.

"Come to think of it, no."

"When did you last see him?"

"Yesterday teatime, about five o' clock. We'd set out the room out for the council meeting."

"Do you know what that was about?" asked Gardener.

"Henry wanted to try to raise extra funding to keep the place open. We rely on charity, you see. He thought if he could get the council involved we might be able to keep going indefinitely. Anyway, they came for an inspection."

"They? Do you know how many?"

"Afraid not."

Gardener stood and left the room. When he found Bob Anderson he asked him to contact the council for a list of all the names of the people who had attended last night's meeting.

When he returned he continued to question Mary Phillips. "You don't happen to know where he worked before here?"

"I've no idea, but I did hear him mention America once or twice. But he were a very private man, never said much about his personal life."

Gardener's heart was beginning to sink slowly towards his shoes.

"Did he say where in America?"

"If he did I never caught it."

"What's America got to do with anything, Stewart?" asked Briggs.

"Something Thornton and Anderson had found out. A number of years ago, Harry Fletcher left Leeds to go and work on Broadway. He came back a couple of years ago but no one's seen him since."

"Who's Harry Fletcher?" asked Mary Phillips.

"That's what we'd like to know. Tell me, Mary, do you happen to know if Henry was his real name? I don't suppose he was ever called by any other name, was he?"

Mary's expression darkened. "Now you mention it, yes. Only yesterday."

"Go on," said Gardener, growing concerned when she had stopped.

"Well I found it a bit strange. We had a bloke came into the shelter a few weeks back. Started to talking to Henry and they were getting on right well. Anyway, yesterday, Stan – that were his name, Stan. Anyway, he were in yesterday and he were in a right state with himself and Henry asked me to make a bed up for him. He wanted Stan to stay the night."

"And did he?" asked Gardener.

"I don't think so."

"You don't know?" asked Reilly.

"Well I've not checked his bed." She rose to her feet.

"It's okay, Mary, love, you stay where you are," said Briggs. "You tell us the room and I'll check."

She did as she was asked and then sat back down.

"Carry on, Mary," prompted Gardener. "A strange incident."

"Oh, yes. When Stan were leaving he called Henry by the name of Harry. I just thought it were a mistake ... but maybe it wasn't."

Tears welled in her eyes and she brought a handkerchief to her face.

Briggs returned. "The bed hasn't been slept in."

"I know this is hard for you, Mary, but we have to carry on. You said that Stan left, have you any idea where he went?"

"No, he just said he had business to see to and that he would come back later."

"But you never saw him come back?"

"No."

"How well did you know Stan?"

"I didn't. In fact, until yesterday, we'd never really spoken. I'd only nodded to him. He seemed pleasant enough."

"Any idea where he came from?"

"No. He were a down and out, but I've no idea which places he went to, and Henry never said."

"Couldn't give us a description, could you, love?" asked Reilly.

"Shouldn't be a problem. He'd certainly stand out in a crowd. I'd say he were in his sixties, and he had odd eyes, they were different colours and one were lower than the other. He had an awful scar as well, just under the right eye. He'd not looked after his skin, poor love, but then who could? When you're living rough, moisturiser's not top of your list, is it? Lots of wrinkles, and it looked leathery. But for all that, he didn't look hungry."

Gardener really didn't like where the description was heading. "How did he dress?"

"Well, there's another funny thing: he reminded me and Henry of Sherlock Holmes. He had a deerstalker, and he used to smoke a pipe, well, not smoke it exactly, just stick it in his mouth, as if he used to smoke and give up."

She gave out another sob. "Do you know, I can't believe anyone would do something so awful." Her voice rose an octave. "He had his head cut off, and where's the body for God's sake? Who would cut off a head and take the body?"

Gardener hadn't the heart tell her what they'd found upstairs but he figured she'd find out soon enough.

"I appreciate you didn't know Stan very well, but in the time you did see him, was there anything unusual about his behaviour?" asked Gardener.

"How do you mean, like?"

"Any phobias, superstitions, tendencies to act abnormally?"

"There was one thing, he were frightened to death of spiders. He nearly turned the kitchen upside down one day when a spider ran across the table where he were eating. His dish flew in the air, food went all over the wall, his table fell over and he nearly trampled it to pieces in an effort to get out."

"At least that's something," said Gardener. "Anything else?"

"To be honest, Mr Gardener, I didn't really know him, and Henry didn't talk about him that much, either."

Gardener sighed inwardly. For someone who could cause so much damage, information was pretty thin on the ground.

"Can you think of any strange things happening over the past week or so?"

Mary Phillips paused and then said. "Nothing that I know of." And then she cried into her handkerchief again.

Gardener thought it best to terminate the interview. She was stressed enough as it was.

"Okay, Mary. You've been a great help. I'll leave you a card, if you remember anything, no matter how trivial you think it is, ring me. Day or night, I'll get the message."

Mary took the card and he told her she was allowed to leave.

Before she actually left the room, Gardener called over. "Miss Phillips?"

Mary turned. "Yes?"

"Just one more question if you don't mind. I know you've worked with Henry for two years, and you've said he was a private man. But, can I ask, did you spend any time alone with him? In his quarters ... or anywhere else for that matter?"

"What are you suggesting Mr. Gardener?"

"Nothing. I simply want to ascertain how well you got on. At some point I'm going to have to go over his room and collect all his personal belongings. I'd like you to try to remember and make an inventory. I need to know if there's anything missing, anything personal."

As quick as a flash her eyes widened. "Do you think there is?"

"I really don't know. I wondered if you knew him well enough to do that for us." Gardener smiled.

Mary Phillips paused before answering. "I'll try Mr Gardener."

After she had closed the door, Briggs glanced at Gardener. "What was all that about?"

"Just a hunch," said Gardener.

He turned his back and paced the room. "So there we are. Once again we've been given a perfect description of someone who doesn't exist: someone who doesn't look like that everyday."

A knock on the door interrupted Gardener's chain of thought. He answered and Steve Fenton passed over the note they'd found upstairs.

Gardener read it and then passed it to Briggs:

Three dead, and I bet you're vexed.

I'm sure by now you'll know who's next.

But how will you stop what you can't see?

Let's face it Gardener, you'll never catch me.

A penetrating silence had enveloped the room, allowing Gardener his personal thoughts.

He turned, resting his back against the door, struggling to come to terms with everything. The killer's intelligence took him well beyond the norm. He was quite right in what he was saying, how could he catch a man he couldn't see? Any eyewitness reports were useless, which was why the killer had been allowed to come and go as he pleased. It didn't matter if he was seen or not, no one could possibly identify him.

So who was it?

There were two possibilities but no way of proving either. Cuthbertson could well be their man. He had the ability to disguise himself and regularly applied make up for the freaks over at Madame Two Swords. His only saving grace was his alibis and the fact that he was genuinely shocked by the death of his assistant, Janine Harper.

Which left William Henry Corndell, a man they knew little or nothing about: a mystery man. And Gardener was willing to bet he could disguise himself a whole lot better than Cuthbertson ever could. However, he was a suspect without a motive; but he had no alibi they could confirm; aside from last night. If anyone could give him an alibi for last night, it was Gardener himself.

Where did that leave him?

Technically speaking the note was incorrect: it said three dead; but there were in fact now four. So who was he and how did he tie in to everything? Were the murders still tied to the watch committee? Did that mean there was a fifth member that no one had so far talked about? There couldn't be, his father would have known.

And what of his father's safety? There was no question now that his father would be next: that the murders were revenge for something that happened years ago with the committee and, quite clearly, had to involve the banned film ... the one that no one could remember – the one that had no traceable records. Did the killer have anything to do with that? Was he so computer literate that he could hack into the necessary archives and wipe clean any information that could lead them to his door?

Gardener turned to Briggs. "The more I think about it, sir, the more convinced I am that William Henry Corndell has something to do with it. I know it's not much but I've never come across anyone who can create a disguise like the man we're looking for. And if you'd seen Corndell last night, you'd realise it puts him well in the frame."

"But that's the problem, isn't it, Stewart, last night. He has an alibi, you saw him at the theatre."

"He wasn't there all night. We know that for a fact."

"Didn't you turn up and find him at home?" asked Briggs.

"We turned up at his house," replied Reilly. "Doesn't mean he was there."

"I thought you spoke to him on the intercom," persisted Briggs.

"Not really," said Gardener. "He said he didn't want to talk to anyone and refused to answer any further calls. We need to talk to him again, even search the property if we have to."

"On what grounds?" Briggs asked.

"On a number of grounds," replied Gardener. "His home is littered with references to the film world, the Golden era as he puts it. He has a cinema in the house. The day we called to see him he was talking on a mobile phone, there are no records of him having one. To say that he's a great actor seems to be a serious over statement. If he's so in touch with Hollywood, why is that he's only taken one phone call to his landline in the last ten to fifteen years? Why is it I can't find any reference to any of his material?"

"None of these things make him a killer: eccentric, maybe, but not a killer," retorted Briggs.

"So why keep all the rooms in your house locked if you're the only one that lives there?" Reilly asked. "What is he hiding?"

Gardener continued. "He's a master of disguise, last night was all the proof I needed. He lives in the past. We know for a fact that we're looking for someone who has an obsession with an old film star by the name of Lon Chaney. Last night's performance was a homage to Chaney. He's already admitted to me that his favourite film was one called, *A Blind Bargain*, that's a Lon Chaney film."

"What about the other film, the one the watch committee banned? Can we tie him to that?" asked Briggs.

"Not at the moment, we don't even know what it is," replied Gardener. "I'm sure it's only a matter of time. And last time we spoke to him, his conversation on the mobile referred to two Hollywood directors, both of whom have been dead for years. Sir, we really do have to interview this man a second time. However circumstantial it all looks, we need to speak to him again. He's unbalanced."

Briggs sighed and glanced at the note he held in his hand. "You do realise I'm in an awkward position, Stewart."

"In what way?" Gardener asked.

"Whoever the killer is, whether it be Corndell or someone else, he's made it personal. You and I both know that your father is next and last on the list. Which means, I might have to remove you from the case."

Gardener raised his hands to the ceiling. "Why does this always happen to me?"

CHAPTER 42

Sunday April 3rd.

Gardener and Reilly were on their way to see William. To his way of thinking if he kept out of Briggs' way then the DCI couldn't order him off the case. At the moment that was unthinkable: there were too many unanswered questions for his liking and he and Reilly had worked the case from the start, so he wasn't going to give it up easily. He wanted to see Corndell again: flush him out.

He contemplated what little he knew. The banned film must surely hold the key to everything, but why could he find no records? Did William's ability and intelligence stretch to such levels that he was able to hack into the security systems and wipe all traces of himself?

There were also other factors leading them to his door. He was a master of disguise. Despite showing signs of mental incompetence, he appeared incredibly intelligent. Wasn't there a thin line separating genius from madness? He supposedly wrote scripts. Couldn't he therefore be the author of the verses and puzzles? Corndell lived in an old fashioned world and had an obsession with Lon Chaney. The man they wanted fitted that description.

Or did he? Was Gardener thinking straight? Or was he simply contriving the evidence to fit the crime because he disliked Corndell so much?

He needed to speak to so many people. Fitz to see if any of the current cases matched previous murders. Fettle to see if he could enhance their knowledge of Corndell any further than the bottom rung of the ladder. Colin Sharp, had he uncovered anything from Corndell's past that would satisfy their desire for an arrest?

Or was he barking up the wrong tree? Was Corndell guilty because Gardener wanted him to be?

He hoped not, because that would seriously question his ability to do the job. Perhaps today's visit would put an end to it once and for all.

Reilly brought the car to a halt outside the gates. Gardener jumped out and pressed the intercom. He glanced at the cloudless blue sky and wondered why they were having such reasonable weather for the beginning of April. Maybe global warming was to blame.

After a healthy wait, a terse voice replied to the intrusion. "Yes?"

"Mr. Corndell? D.I Gardener and D. S. Reilly, we'd like to talk to you."

"I told you last night that I didn't want to speak to anyone and my views have not changed."

Another little point that irked Gardener: Corndell's perfect alibi for last night's murder was none other than himself.

How *could* he have murdered Harry Fletcher?

"I don't care what you want! *I* want to speak to *you*."

Their conversation continued over the intercom. "Mr. Gardener, you're not listening to me. This is police harassment and if you continue I shall be forced to call my solicitor."

"Maybe he should use his mobile," suggested Reilly.

"It's you who's not listening," replied Gardener. "Now we can do this the easy way or the hard way, it's entirely up to you. The easy way is to let me in and answer my questions. The hard way is for me to go away and return with a warrant, arrest you on suspicion of murder and then turn your entire house upside down. Am I making myself clear?"

During the time he spent waiting for the reply, Gardener wondered if William really *had* decided upon the second option.

Eventually, the intercom buzzed and the gates opened. Both detectives jumped into the car, cruising slowly down the drive. The door opened as they came to a stop.

Gardener stepped inside to find William still in his dressing gown. Underneath the gown he wore a pair of blue and white striped pyjamas, decorated with *Winnie The Pooh* logos. He knew better than to ask, deciding it was further confirmation of the man's lunacy.

"Do you realise what time it is?" asked Corndell, pointing his mobile phone at them.

"Of course I do. I've been up since five o' clock this morning."

"I'm not surprised," replied William, closing the door after Reilly had entered. "I do hope you've come to apologise for last night."

William held his head high and his nose in the air as he glanced down at the pair of them. He placed the mobile in the pocket of his dressing gown.

"I have nothing to apologise for."

"How dare you?" he shouted, jumping back, clenching and unclenching his hands. "You people have persecuted me..."

"I wouldn't say persecuted!" shouted Gardener, cutting him short. He did not want the situation escalating beyond his control.

He was here for a reason and he was going to make sure they stuck to the point. With his temper close to boiling point he chose his words carefully and spoke slowly.

"We're investigating crimes of a very serious nature. We will conduct ourselves in a manner to which we see fit. Now if you have a problem with that, then you contact the police complaints commission, but quite frankly your case will not hold water."

"I do apologise, Mr. Gardener, and please forgive my lack of manners. If you would like to come through to the conservatory I shall make fresh tea for us all."

Gardener suspected he was being manipulated because of the sudden change in William's manner.

He told Reilly to go with William whilst the tea was made, not to let him out of his sight. Gardener stayed in the conservatory. Eventually, both returned.

"Now then, gentlemen, I'll pour the tea and you feel free to ask me anything you like."

All three sat down and Gardener removed his hat.

"Where were you last night?"

"You know very well where I was," replied William, sliding their tea across the table.

"After the show."

"You turned up here wanting to speak to me but I wouldn't let you in."

"I *know* where I was. I'm asking *you* where you were – answer the question!"

"Of course. I was here, Mr. Gardener, where else would I be?"

William's smug smile was irritating Gardener.

"Has something happened?" William banged the teapot on the table and stood up. "Has someone else been murdered, and you want me for a scapegoat?"

"Such a vivid imagination, Willie boy," said Reilly. "No wonder you write scripts."

Gardener ignored William's question.

"Perhaps your CCTV will show us what time you arrived back at the house, Mr. Corndell?"

"It would if it was working"

"Oh, well now, isn't that convenient?" said Reilly. "Your closed circuit TV system is on the blink the night you need to prove your innocence."

William took a sip of his tea. "I beg to differ, Mr. Reilly. It is you who has something to prove ... not me."

Another condescending reply that made Gardener's skin crawl. As far as he was concerned, the man had guilt written all over his face but what they lacked was concrete evidence. And at the rate they were going they would never find it.

"What's wrong with your CCTV?" asked Gardener.

"That's a silly question, Mr. Gardener. If I knew that I wouldn't have called them out."

"Name of the company, please."

William left the room but returned quickly, with a card.

Gardener read it, put it in his pocket and then continued. "I'd like to ask you a few questions about our previous meeting ... in particular, your phones."

"What about them?" replied Corndell

"According to the information we have, you don't have a registered mobile number, and you've only received one call to your landline in the last ten years."

"Am I under arrest?" asked Corndell.

"No."

"Suspicion, then?"

"The very nature of your business means we have to carry out a detailed investigation," replied Gardener, before adding. "If for no other reason than to eliminate you from our enquiries."

"Perhaps it would be better if I phoned my solicitor, Mr. Gardener."

"Something to hide, Willie? Use your mobile, why don't you?" suggested Reilly.

To Gardener's astonishment that's exactly what William did. He picked up his mobile and placed a call through to his solicitor and asked him to return the call when it was convenient.

"Give me that number." Gardener demanded.

William did as he was asked and wrote the number down. He passed it to Reilly who placed the slip of paper into his pocket.

With a smug expression, William continued the conversation. "You see, Mr. Gardener, your records must be incorrect. Most of my business is either conducted on line or through my mobile."

"Our evidence doesn't support your statement," replied Gardener, making a mental note of the fact that William used a computer regularly.

"Then I suggest you retrace your steps." William took another sip of tea. "Now we've cleared that one up, what else would you like to ask me?"

Gardener was unwilling to show his annoyance but he realised he was treading water. Without a warrant, he couldn't force the issue.

"Let's talk about films, in particular, your cinema..."

William stood up, beckoned them, cutting Gardener dead. "Say no more, Mr. Gardener. I shall take you."

He set off and then turned back to face them. "I do realise that under normal circumstances you would have to obtain a warrant to do this, and we all know that if I push you hard enough, you will. I have nothing to hide so I am now inviting you of my own free will into my cinema."

Gardener wondered if William was recording the meeting. No one spoke like he did. They followed him up the stairs. He made a point of showing them his favourite film posters, informing them of their value and rarity. At no stage was his attitude or his expressions those of a guilty man. Before continuing up to the top landing, he turned and spoke to them.

"I think I should take you in here first, Mr. Gardener, it's my make up room."

William opened the door and switched on a light. The whole room was an archive to the past. Along the back wall stood a range of mannequins dressed in a variety of guises. Gardener immediately recognised the costume from last night's performance of The Hunchback; The Phantom was also there, and others of which he had no idea.

"I don't recognise all of them: enlighten me."

"Over there," pointed William "Is the ape man from the film, *A Blind Bargain*. And there you can see the clown from the 1924 film, *He Who Gets Slapped*."

"Who starred in those films?" asked Gardener.

"Lon Chaney, of course."

William had made the statement so boldly that Gardener was convinced he was trying to rile him.

"I thought Lon Chaney only made horror films, so what was the clown film about?"

"It shows how little you know about him, Mr. Gardener. He was the greatest actor the world has ever seen. The film was based on a play by the Russian writer, Loenid Andreyev. It had a successful run on Broadway in the 1920's. Chaney plays a struggling scientist in Paris who is betrayed by his wife and his benefactor, Baron Regnard. The Baron stole his essays: took the credit, and his wife. Disillusioned, Chaney eventually runs away and becomes a clown in a circus, changing his name to 'He Who Gets Slapped' because his role lets his fellow clowns slap him no matter what he does."

William had thrown in details that very few people left alive would know. Maybe that's what Gardener needed, Corndell knocking nails into his own coffin. Perhaps now he could alter the course of the interview by turning up the heat and giving him the opportunity to hang himself.

"Fascinating," said Gardener. "Are they all Chaney outfits?"

"Not at all. That one there which – to you – probably looks like a bunch of rags is in fact from the first short movie adaptation of a United States version of the film, *Frankenstein*, made in 1910, in which the monster is played by Charles Stanton Ogle. A very prolific film, Mr. Gardener for which I probably have the only remaining copy; and that, may I add, cost me a fortune."

The atmosphere in the room was intense. The walls were dark. The floor was natural wood, stained and polished. Opposite the mannequins was a tile topped table running the length of the wall and above that a huge, dusty mirror. The tabletop was crammed full of paraphernalia: wigs, creams, face powders, jars of chemicals. The whole space had a distinctly unsavoury odour that he couldn't place, a sort of sour, spicy smell.

William leaned forward and reached under the table. Producing a bin bag he removed the clothes from the dummy wearing The Hunchback outfit.

"What are you doing?" asked Gardener.

"You'll want these for forensic testing Mr. Gardener. You have my permission to take them."

Gardener glanced at Reilly and then to Corndell.

"Do you require any samples of my make up?" he asked.

Reilly answered the question. "What would be the point?"

"Evidence, Mr. Reilly. After all, you are trying to eliminate me."

"Come on now, Willie, old son. You're only offering this lot to us because you know damn well that you've been careful and we can't prove a thing. On top of that there's no evidence that the costume you've given us was the one you were wearing last night."

William turned. "That remark Mr. Reilly, implies that I am your killer. If my solicitor were here, you'd have to retract that."

"But he isn't, is he, Willie?"

William glared at Reilly. "If you would be so kind, Mr. Reilly, as to please use the name my mother gave me. Now, gentlemen, is there anything else you require from this room?"

"No," replied Gardener, a little curious as to why a man accused of such horrific crimes was choosing to throw evidence their way if he *was* guilty?

"Then shall we move on to the cinema?"

Gardener followed William up the staircase, into the room. He glanced around, impressed. It was long and angular and stretched across the top floor of the house. The projection booth was at the other end while a screen covered the wall nearest to them. The films were placed in racks on the left and right hand walls. There was yet another odour in the room that Gardener also failed to place.

"What's that smell?"

After a pause, Reilly replied, "Mothballs."

"Not quite, Mr. Reilly," said William. "What you can smell is celluloid, a plastic made from camphor and cellulose nitrate. But ... as you so rightly point out, it does smell like mothballs, which were actually made from camphor many years ago."

William smiled and Gardener was growing ever confident that the man's pomposity would be his undoing.

But had *he* realised it? Was he now playing games?

Gardener surveyed the room before finally resting – ironically enough – on a framed review of the film, *He Who Gets Slapped*.

"Lon Chaney as 'HE' stands out as possibly the greatest character actor of the screen. In this role, he displays an understanding of character beyond anything that he has done heretofore. Those who have seen him in The Hunchback *will want to see him in this, and they are going to be agreeably surprised by his work"*

Variety.

Gardener strolled slowly around the room studying each and every one of the films on display. They were contained in a number of silver canisters banded together. He glanced at the titles, recognising some but not all, wondering how many of those featured Chaney. *The Hunchback* and *The Phantom* were obvious, as were *A Blind Bargain* and *London After Midnight*. But *The Dark Eyes of London* didn't ring any bells, nor did *The Invisible Ghost*, *The Black Castle* or *Imperfection*.

Gardener wondered what the value of the whole collection was.

"The last time we were here, you said it had been a life's work trying to track down lost films from the silent era. I can see what you mean, now. It must have taken you years. How did you manage to find them?"

"It's my life, Mr. Gardener. If it's something you're interested in, you'll pull out all the stops. They've cost me a fortune but they're worth it. Take this one for instance." William pulled the reels forward. *"London After Midnight..."*

Gardener cut him off. "Interesting you should start with that. Isn't it commonly known among film collectors as the Holy Grail of archivists?"

"That's one way of describing it."

"I was reliably informed that the film was destroyed by a fire in the 1960's. So how did you come by it?"

"You're talking about the fire in vault 7 at MGM. That very well may have been the last surviving copy that anyone knew of but my father passed this copy on to me. He had been the proud owner since the thirties."

"Know the film well, do you?" asked Gardener.

"Like the back of my hand." William's answer was sharp and his expression stern, as if his intelligence had been insulted.

From his inside pocket, Gardener produced the artist impression of the vampire: the one drawn from the eyewitness account on the night Janine Harper was killed.

"Then how come you didn't know who this was the last time we visited?"

"Oh come now, Mr. Gardener, it's hardly a likeness is it?"

Gardener had to allow the man credit for not hesitating.

"We have a witness who'd disagree with you. In fact, when we showed it to him, he knew who it was straight away."

"What are you trying to say?"

Reilly answered. "That either you don't know your films as well as you think..."

"I am the last word on Lon Chaney, young man," shouted William, indignantly.

"Or ... I *was* going to say before you opened your trap ... that you're leading us up the garden path."

"I am leading you nowhere. I am simply answering your questions to the best of my knowledge, as I have always done."

"If you're such an authority on Chaney," challenged Reilly, "Why didn't you know who that was?"

"Because it looks nothing like the character from the film."

"There is a resemblance, you could have guessed," suggested Gardener.

"Guess, Mr. Gardener? Guess? Where would we be if I were to guess all of my answers? Some innocent person would have been locked up by now, that's where."

Gardener ignored William's outburst, trying to recollect the other connection to the film, Inspector Burke, and the video they had first watched at the hotel in Skipton. So far he had not recognised anything that led him to believe that it had been filmed here. But then again, he hadn't seen the whole house yet.

He walked up and down each side of the room, checking all the films. "Any of these yours, Mr Corndell?"

"They're all mine," replied William.

Gardener sighed. "I meant, did you write any of them?"

"How could I have, Mr. Gardener? As you can see from the titles and the dates, most, if not all, were written before I was born."

Gardener turned to face William, leaving Reilly to continue writing the titles in his book. "Tell me again what it is that you write."

William sighed, as if tired. "Stage plays. I told you last time, my work is regularly shown in America."

"Is it fair to assume that you would know other writers who have their material accepted in America? On Broadway for instance?"

"Very possibly, it never hurts to be aware of the competition," replied William, choosing to move away from the films and nearer the staircase that led down into the make up room.

"Does the name Harry Fletcher ring any bells?"

"Can't say it does. Just starting, is he?"

"Couldn't really say. It's just that you seem to know all of the big names: Lon Chaney, Boris Karloff..."

"I actually met Karloff, many years back, just before he died, on the set of a film called *Targets*."

Gardener continued: "Wallace Worsley, Rupert Julian..."

"Don't talk to me about, Julian," scoffed William.

"Funny that. He *is* the one I wanted to talk about. Last time we were here you were having a conversation with George about a director called Rupert Julian. If I remember correctly, you said 'either Rupert Julian stands down or I'll take my script elsewhere'. Do you remember that?"

"Well I would, wouldn't I?" replied William. "It was me who said it."

"I checked out that name, Rupert Julian: he died years ago. Why are you writing scripts for a dead man?"

William suddenly burst out laughing, a high pitched screech in which he rocked so much he held his stomach and almost lost his balance and fell down the spiral staircase.

After he had regained his composure he answered. "Mr. Gardener, you're so funny. I'm not writing for *the* Rupert Julian who directed Chaney, I write scripts for his son."

Gardener laughed with William. "Yes, you're right, I am a little odd. Must be the policeman in me. Where do you write your material?"

"In the study, downstairs."

"Do you have a computer?"

"Who doesn't, these days?"

William frowned. Gardener took it as a good sign. Time to capitalise.

"Good, because you're going to take me down there now and you're going to show me some of the scripts you've had accepted. You're going to give me the titles of your most successful American plays and then you're going to tell me where I can reach Rupert Julian junior and your friend George, so they can verify your story. I also want to see bills from your Internet service provider and your mobile."

William's mood changed. Maybe the added pressure was paying off. Gardener noticed that Reilly had finished writing and was standing beside him.

"Why should I do that?"

"Because I'm a policeman and I want to check everything you've told me in order to eliminate you from our inquiries. If I find any differences I'm coming back. And I'll bring a warrant and a team of forensic officers and one by one, bit by bit we are going to turn this whole house upside down, with or without the presence of your solicitor." Gardened paused and moved closer. "And should I find just one small spec of evidence which connects you and your guilt to my investigation, Mr. Corndell I am going to wipe the floor with you. Am I making myself clear?"

Without warning, William stormed off down the spiral staircase, through the make up room and down the stairs and into the hall, which was where he stopped, glaring at the front door.

As Gardener and Reilly arrived at the bottom of the stairs, Corndell made as if to open it.

"I think you'll find your study is that way." Gardener pointed.

"I know exactly where it is, thank you very much, but as far as I'm concerned your interview ends here. I have co-operated of my own free will, Mr. Gardener. I have provided you with evidence to clear my name, yet you continue to persecute me. From here on in, any interviews with you *will* be conducted in the presence of my solicitor, and if you want personal details from me, you can damn well provide that warrant you're talking about."

Gardener had physically rattled William: his left eye twitched and his top lip trembled.

"I want you out of my house, now!" shouted William.

"So soon, Willie boy," said Reilly. "Why the change of mood? A little too close to the truth, are we? Guilty after all, maybe?"

William pointed his finger in their direction. As he started to speak he stuttered. "I ... I am no ... no more guilty than you, Mr. Reilly." The last part of his sentence was said so fast that Gardener barely heard his reply.

Reilly stepped in closer. "I'm struggling with that one, Willie boy. I don't believe you."

William's breathing grew irregular.

"I'm surprised at you, so I am, you being a superstitious young man as well."

William's eyes widened and the remark jolted him into speech.

"Superstition!" shouted William, his legs quivering and his arms shaking. "What does that have to do with anything?"

"Oh, come on, Willie boy, you're playing games with me, so you are. I thought you knew everything there was to know about folklore. If you do you should know about the 'Murder in the Red Barn', the Maria Marten case."

William started pacing the hall, mumbling, talking to himself as if they weren't there.

"Think they've got me ... trying to fool me."

He stopped abruptly and stared at Reilly. "Who's Maria Marten?"

"You don't remember the play that was based on the tragedy: and you a playwright? Mind you, was a bit before your time, so it was. 1828, I think, the year after Maria's death. She was a simple village girl betrayed by a member of the gentry.

"Maria was the daughter of a mole catcher who met a well to do farmer at Polstead, near Ipswich. He was called William as well, William Corder. She became pregnant and urged William to marry her. But he didn't want to because he loved Mary Moore, who lived near London and was more his type. Anyway, to cut a long story short, he persuaded her to meet him at the Red Barn near the family farm. She did, and was never seen again.

"Corder went to London and married Mary Moore. Eventually he came back to Polstead and assured Maria's parents they were married and now lived in London."

Reilly moved as close to William as he could. "But, Mrs. Marten suddenly had three successive dreams in which her daughter lay murdered. She persuaded the authorities to carry out a search. Maria's body was found in the Red Barn. After his arrest, William Corder was pronounced guilty and hanged at Bury St. Edmunds. His skin was removed and cured and then used to bind a copy of the proceedings of the trial."

Reilly continued to stare at William. "And I'll tell you something else, Willie boy."

"What?" William demanded.

"The book can still be seen today at Moyses Hall, the Bury St. Edmunds' museum."

William coughed and a bead of snot dropped and hung from his nose.

"What does this have to do with me?"

"Funny you should ask. Mrs. Harper, Janine's mother, isn't happy. Can't rest. But then, why should she? Her daughter was horribly mutilated. So much so that she had to have a closed casket funeral. And now, she's having nightmares, and she's convinced that Janine was killed by a thespian, not only an actor but a writer as well."

Gardener watched as the information sunk in but William didn't show any emotion.

"Not only that, but he lives in a big house by himself."

William wiped his nose on his sleeve and sniffed loudly. He stood upright to his full height and laughed.

"You're bluffing, Mr. Reilly."

Reilly stepped back.

Gardener noted the change, unsure whether or not it was planned.

"Question is Willie boy, are you going to call it?"

William confidently strolled towards the door, grinning, reaching for the handle, all the while staring at Reilly.

He turned quickly, and in doing so, disturbed the curtain a little to the right of the frame.

A spider surged forward, heading straight for him.

Gardener noticed the colour drained from William's face and his body stiffen with pure fear.

William's dressing gown had fallen open and as the spider reached his feet a faint whining sound emitted and a wet patch darkened the crotch of his Winnie The Pooh PJ's.

William struggled but uttered a few words. "Get that thing ... away from me."

Reilly leaned forward and put the spider in the palm of his hand.

"What's wrong Willie boy, do you not like the little wee fellas?"

William's breathing quickened and his eyes widened as Reilly inched the spider closer to his face, and then blew it the rest of the way.

William screamed and raised his arms in the air and took off in the opposite direction, still shouting as he continued down the hall and into the kitchen.

Gardener watched in horrified fascination as a series of curses and shouts followed his disappearance. Utensils and pots and pans and cups and saucers were launched across the room, each one landing in an ever-growing heap at the wall: one actually smashed a pain of glass.

Gardener turned to Reilly. "Was any of that true?"

"What?" Reilly asked.

"That stuff about Maria Marten and the Red Barn."

"Of course it was."

Back in the kitchen, William was sliding a huge Welsh Dresser in front of the doorframe.

Eventually, the whole building grew quiet.

As Gardener closed in on the kitchen he could hear William muttering to himself.

He turned to Reilly. "I think we've seen all we need, Sean. It's time we closed the net on him."

"Well, I've seen enough to know he's as mad as they come. Have you any idea the strength it took to move that feckin' thing?"

CHAPTER 43

Gardener pushed open the stage door. Reilly followed him down the steps towards Albert Fettle's office. Nothing had changed. The little spot of cleaning that Fettle had claimed he was doing last time was still unfinished. Next to his tea making facilities was a small radio. Gardener didn't recognise the tune but he knew it was from the big dance band era.

He heard Fettle's voice before he saw him. The door leading into the theatre opened and he appeared, with Paul Price close behind: the latter bearing a distinctively unhappy expression as he saw the two detectives.

"Hey up, how are you doing?" shouted Fettle. He continued without waiting for an answer. "You two know how to time things right, don't you? I've just brewed a pot o' tea and I've some of me favourites to go wi' it. Nice packet of fig rolls."

"Can I reopen my theatre, yet?" asked Paul Price.

"Answer another couple of questions for me, Mr Price and I don't see why not," replied Gardener.

"So it's not me you want, then?" asked Fettle.

"All in good time, shorty," said Reilly.

"Come on, get yourselves in here, this tea's nearly mashed."

While Fettle continued with the tea, Gardener addressed Price. "How long have you worked here, Mr. Price?"

"I'm sure I've answered that question, on your first visit."

"Then refresh my memory."

"Thirty years."

"Does the name, William Henry Corndell ring any bells?"

Price hesitated. "As a matter of fact it does, just can't think why."

"Has he ever worked here?"

"Not to my knowledge."

"Is it likely that he has but under a different name?"

"That's always possible. I can check the files if you could give me more details."

Gardener turned to his partner. "Sean, will you go and check the files with Mr Price, see what you can come up with?" He then added. "Leave me your notebook before you go."

"Here," said Fettle. "Best take your tea."

"You said I might be able to reopen, when will that be?" asked Price.

"As soon as you find out what we need to know."

Price gestured for Reilly to follow him. Gardener entered Fettle's room and took a sip of tea.

"You still chasing this Corndell bloke, then?"

"Any news from your friend at *Her Majesty's*?"

Both men sat down. "Aye, there is. He never played the part of *The Phantom*."

"He didn't?" questioned Gardener, curious.

"Not in so many words, no. He were given a trial run in the West End, more or less as the show were starting. He were Michael Crawford's understudy, and he only got that 'cause of his father, Wallace.

"Anyway, he were promising, knew almost everybody's lines. Apparently, he's got a good memory, remembers facts and figures like there's no tomorrow. He turned up to every performance and in rehearsals he were brilliant. Problems started when he were faced wi' an audience."

"In what way?" Gardener asked.

"He panics. He were given his chance in the main role one Saturday matinee. Apparently Crawford's car had broken down and he weren't gonna make it until the evening performance, so they gave Corndell the green light. Apparently, he were useless, fluffed his lines and wrecked half the scenery. Worst bit were when he were doing the scene in the graveyard on top of the big cross. He fell off and broke his leg."

Gardener thought back to the university performance. That had also ended in disaster, resulting in Corndell blaming the police.

Fettle slurped his tea and bit into a fig roll.

"Anyway, it finished his career. But even if he hadn't fell off and broke his leg he'd never have got another chance."

"And that was his one and only time playing the main part?"

"As far as I know. After that, no one else in the West End touched him."

"Any idea what he did after that?"

"No."

"Okay, well that's something. He's reliable, this friend of yours?"

"Oh aye, he worked there for over thirty years."

Gardener took another sip of his tea. "Have you still got those film books?"

"Aye." Fettle left the table and reached into the cupboard. "What do you want to know?"

Gardener produced Reilly's notebook with the titles of the films in Corndell's library.

"Do you remember any of these?" He passed the list to Fettle.

"I know them two. *The Dark Eyes of London*, that's pretty old. It were written by Edgar Wallace. It's about a bloke who runs a home for the blind and he uses a giant to drown the insured victims."

"Another Lon Chaney film?"

"No, that were Bela Lugosi. And so were that one, *The Invisible Ghost*. That's about a bloke who murdered his wife and she comes back to haunt him, he keeps seeing her all over the place, before he goes mad."

"*The Black Castle*?" asked Gardener.

"Not sure about that."

Fettle flicked through his copies of the *Film Review* before finally consulting the *Halliwell's* Film Guide.

"Here it is, an 18th century knight avenges the death of two friends who have attended a hunting party at the castle of a sadistic Viennese count. I certainly haven't seen that one."

"Are any of these real collectors pieces?"

"Doubt it: *The Dark Eyes of London*, maybe. Can't say I've ever seen a copy of that."

Gardener sighed and sat back. None of the films that Fettle had talked about bore any similarity to the murders that had been committed, so it seemed unlikely that the killer was copying an obscure film in particular.

"Who was in *The Black Castle*?"

"Boris Karloff and Lon Chaney junior."

"Karloff played *Frankenstein*, yes?"

"Aye, in 1931."

"Apparently, Corndell has a US copy of the film made in 1910 starring a bloke called, Ogle."

"Fucking hell," whistled Fettle. "That'd be worth a fortune."

"What about that one, *Imperfection*?"

"Never heard of it."

After consulting all the books, Fettle drew a blank. "I can't find any reference to a film of that name. Do you know 'owt about it?"

"No, other than the fact that it's in Corndell's library."

"Well it's not one I know."

"What about banned films, anything spring to mind?"

"There's been plenty of 'em over the years. *Freaks*, in 1932. MGM made it but disowned it. A lot of people said it were tasteless. I think it were cause they used real freaks: a bit like that other film, *The Sentinel*, in 76, they used proper freaks and *that* got banned."

"Do you know of a film that was banned by the local watch committee in Leeds in the late seventies or early eighties?"

Fettle thought long and hard. Gardener could almost hear the cogs turning inside his head.

"No."

Gardener started to wonder about the title of the film, *Imperfection*, and how well it defined William. He needed to find out more about it. Was that the title of the banned film they were looking for? What was it about? Why had it been banned? And if that *was* the film, what connection did it have with William and how had he managed to obtain a copy?

"Last time we spoke I mentioned a director by the name of Rupert Julian. You said he was dead."

"Aye, he is," replied Fettle.

"Did he have a son?"

Fettle finished his tea and another biscuit. "I've no idea. I've never heard one mentioned but I'm not as well up on directors as I am the films: you could soon find out."

"The Internet?" suggested Gardener.

"Aye. Maybe you could check up on that film ... what were it? *Imperfection*?"

"I might just do that."

Reilly and Price entered the room. Paul Price had a copy of a letter, which he passed to Gardener.

"I thought I recognised the name, Corndell. He sent me a letter a few months back."

Gardener took it but didn't read it. "What about?"

"He wrote and asked if he could have a tour of the place, quite some time ago now."

"Why?"

"He said he was an author and he was writing something new which he wanted to set in the Grand Theatre: asked if I would mind showing him round so as he could get the feel for the place."

Gardener glanced at Reilly. "Why would he do that? According to him he's spent his life in theatres up and down the country, writes regularly for Broadway."

Price continued. "He mentioned his success in America. I asked him if he had a website but he said he didn't. I was hoping to do a little checking myself. He also said he wrote his material under different names."

"Can you remember any of them?"

"I'm sorry, no."

"Yet you still met him and showed him round?" questioned Gardener.

"Oh yes. I didn't mind. I had some free time on my hands. The only thing I stipulated was that he should write nothing that would bring the theatre into disrepute. I also asked him of the success he'd had in America and he mentioned one or two titles, which I later wrote down on the back."

Gardener turned the paper over and studied the titles. He didn't recognise either. He then passed the paper to Fettle.

Gardener was about to ask Price another question when Fettle jumped out of his chair. "Hey, I know that one, and it's not one of his."

"Which one?" Gardener asked.

"*Blood's Thicker Than Water*."

"Who wrote it?" asked Gardener.

"Yon lad as worked for *Playhouse*."

"Harry Fletcher?"

"Aye, that's him. He wrote *Blood's Thicker Than Water*. I remember reading about it somewhere."

"Any idea what it's about?" asked Gardener.

"Not really, no. Summat about a feud between two brothers, which goes on for years, until one of 'em's dying. I just remember reading a review and it were taking The States by storm."

"That's one of them," said Paul Price. "That's one of the names he said he used. Harry Fletcher. I remember it now."

Another nail in Corndell's coffin: he said he didn't know Harry Fletcher.

Gardener's mobile chimed. He fished it out of his pocket and answered. After listening to the caller he glanced at Reilly.

"We'll be there in five minutes."

CHAPTER 44

"Who found him?" Gardener asked the officer guarding the door.

"The prospective new owners, over there," he nodded.

The couple's appearance spoke of wealth: camel hair coats, jewellery; finest Italian leather shoes. The woman was blonde, slim, mid forties with a long, deeply lined face. The man was stocky, perhaps early fifties with a good head of hair, tightly curled and grey. He was smoking a cigar: to calm his nerves, maybe. His wife cast glances which indicated she'd rather be anywhere than a shopping arcade in Leeds that harboured a dead body, particularly a shop they were going to buy. And from her expression, the purchase was not her idea.

Gardener and Reilly suited up and entered. The interior of the shop was still gloomy and despite the cleaning service having done their best they had been unable to eradicate the smell of death. That had nothing to do with Alan Cuthbertson's corpse: more the legacy of Janine Harper.

Cuthbertson was laid on the floor behind the counter. He had been no oil painting in life, but death had decided he would be remembered with an expression that welcomed his fate.

"What time?" Gardener asked.

"About ten minutes before I phoned you."

"Who else have you told?"

"I phoned the station and they said someone was on their way. They told me to phone you."

Gardener turned his attention to the matter in hand. The shop had been stripped bare. Everything that had been on display on the night of Janine Harper's demise had been removed for forensic testing. Once the police had finished with it, Alan Cuthbertson had told them to burn it. Gardener had wondered about Cuthbertson's state of mind during that time period, his personal feelings at having seen his life's work tainted – if not destroyed – by the actions of a lunatic: and to add insult to injury, a suspect in a murder case. The idea of returning to a building responsible for so much trauma was obviously too much.

The empty pill bottle stood on the counter, as did the half finished bottle of whiskey: and what he surmised was a suicide note.

"I wonder what made him do it?" asked Reilly.

"I hope it wasn't us," replied Gardener.

"We didn't do anything wrong, boss. We were doing our job."

Gardener glanced at his partner. "Maybe *he* didn't see it like that."

Briggs arrived, suited and booted, and then made his way into the shop, glancing behind the counter.

"What have we got?"

"Suicide," replied Gardener.

"Anyone read the note?"

"Not yet."

Briggs tore open the envelope. With a confused expression he glanced at Gardener.

"It's addressed to you, Stewart."

He handed over the letter and continued to study the corpse.

"Why has he written a letter to you?"

"I've no idea."

Gardener read it:

Dear Mr Gardener.

I appreciate you had a job to do and I want you to know that in no way do I hold you responsible for my suicide. It is fair to say that I have lost everything: the business I had spent years building, my assistant, who meant more to me than you'll ever know, and the lifestyle I tried so hard to keep secret, becoming public knowledge. It's that lifestyle more than anything that has brought about my final agonising decision, to take my own life. I have been diagnosed H.I.V. positive and as far as I can ascertain, there would be little time left anyway. There are two things you need to know: Firstly, I am not your killer and have no idea who is. All I do know is, you must catch the man. Secondly, proof which backs up the first statement, I could never have killed my own daughter. Janine was my flesh and blood, born from an illicit affair. Though why the secret had been kept after Jack Harper's death I shall never know.

Gardener sighed and passed the letter over to Briggs. He read it:

"Do you think she knew?" he asked.

"I've no idea," replied Gardener.

"I still can't understand why he'd write a letter to you," said Briggs.

"Maybe he didn't," suggested Reilly.

"Meaning what?" asked Briggs.

"I'll grant you it's not the killer's style, but maybe he staged all of this and then wrote the note to throw us of the scent."

"If that's the case, how did he know Janine Harper was Alan Cuthbertson's daughter?" asked Briggs.

"He knew enough about Janine Harper to kill her for the reasons he did," added Reilly.

"I appreciate your point, Sean," said Gardener. "But Alan Cuthbertson wasn't a member of the watch committee and that's what this seems to be about. The watch committee and the banned film."

"Unless it isn't," said Briggs. "Do you know anything about this banned film, yet?"

"I think I'm on to something, but nothing concrete."

"Then how do you know the murders are connected to a banned film?" asked Briggs. "I'm sorry, Stewart, but we're no nearer to solving the case now than we were at the beginning. So for all we know, Alan Cuthbertson's death might well be tied into it. For God's sake, this bloke moves around like a fucking spectre. No one ever sees him and he's managed to commit the most brutal killings, and have time to write notes."

"It still looks like suicide to me, nothing more," said Gardener.

"Maybe Fitz can tell us," replied Briggs. "Which reminds me, where the bloody hell is he?"

Before Gardener had time to answer, his mobile rang.

Briggs and Reilly turned their attention to the corpse while Gardener took the conversation.

"We're on our way," said Gardener. "That *was* Fitz, apparently he's found something unusual connected to Janine Harper's death. He wants us over there now."

CHAPTER 45

Fitz threw a folder on to his desk and ran his hands down his tired face. His expression was a mixture of fatigue (evidence of the long hours he had worked the case), and elation at having possibly found a piece of the puzzle.

"Would you gentlemen like coffee?"

Gardener and Reilly nodded and Fitz turned around from his desk. He reached for the percolator, a new addition to his office, and a much-needed one from what Gardener could see.

"Smells good, whatever it is," said Reilly.

"Some friends of mine have recently returned from Canada, brought back these butter toffee coffee beans. I wrecked my wife's cheese grater trying to grind them."

"And your fingers I shouldn't wonder," said Gardener.

"It's not one of those. It has a little compartment. Put the cheese in, press a lever with one hand and turn a roller with the other. Quite good, really."

"But not on coffee beans," said Reilly.

"Afraid not. Had to use a blender in the end."

Fitz placed their coffees in front of them.

IMPERFECTION

"So, what have you got for us?" asked Gardener.

Fitz sat back in his chair. "Janine Harper: you remember that she had a lethal cocktail of Ephedrine in her system. I suggested that the killer may have perfected the technique."

Both men nodded, sipping their coffee.

"I've found some new evidence. I consulted Mathew Stapleton about it: he's one of the country's leading toxicologists up in Edinburgh. When I spoke to him he was in London. The method unsettled him for a week. He'd heard of a similar case.

"He used the computers at the University College Hospital. Surprisingly enough there were no records, nothing in the archives: nothing on paper. Having said that, the paper files only date back to the eighties. Anything further back had been stored electronically."

"Had the files been erased?" said Gardener.

"They think so but they're still checking. You see, all other records of suspicious deaths around that time were still on file."

"Murder isn't the only technique he's perfected," said Gardener.

"Mathew spoke to his father: turns out that one of his colleagues had performed the autopsy on the lady in question."

Fitz opened his folder, removed the notes.

"Her name was Elizabeth Cranshaw. She was 61 years of age and worked as a nanny for a well to do family who lived in Weybridge in Surrey."

Gardener's heart sunk a little when he thought of how far back the incident may have occurred.

Fitz continued. "It was the next morning before the old lady had been found dead in her room: still sitting in her favourite chair with her novel resting on her lap. According to the report she looked quite peaceful, despite what she must have gone through."

"So we're not talking exactly the same M.O. here?" asked Gardener.

"She hadn't been hung and brutalised, if that's what you mean," replied Fitz.

"So the link is the Ephedrine?"

Fitz nodded. "Elizabeth Cranshaw had suffered from asthma all her life. The results of the autopsy discovered sherry in her system, believed to be her favourite tipple while she was reading. Mixed in with the alcohol was a pretty hefty dosage of nuts that had been ground into a fine powder. A massive heart attack caused her death. In fact, the report confirms that her heart had been so overworked that it had literally exploded."

"Were the family interviewed?" asked Gardener.

"Yes, they were cleared. Apparently, Elizabeth Cranshaw had been to London on a shopping expedition. She'd been out of the house all day. The parents – who were normally at work – had remained home for the day to supervise their son. When the nanny returned they went back to the studio."

"Studio?" Gardener asked.

"Pinewood, in Buckinghamshire. The boy's father was a film director."

Gardener's heart sunk. In his confusion his earlier calculation suggested that the killer should be in his sixties, which suspended belief. However, the other option was equally unthinkable. Could he possibly have started something so gruesome at such an early age?

"Who was the boy?"

"William Henry Corndell."

CHAPTER 46

Monday April 4th.

William was mad.

In fact, he was absolutely fuming!

Who the hell did she think she was, writing garbage about him? A two-bit journalist cum theatre critic who thought she knew it all, and had the audacity to write such a damning article about his performance: like those tits at *Variety* who had pulled down Chaney.

Was she there? Didn't she realise that none of it had been his fault? He'd been persecuted by the police from the time they had entered the building.

But he had her number all right: and theirs. Both detectives had been round here yesterday, trying to catch him out. See if he'd crack under the pressure of their schoolboy tactics. But William was better than that.

He screwed up part of the paper in his hands, slamming it down on the kitchen table.

He knew what their game was. And he also knew how desperate they were. They had no evidence. They were fishing, laying bait and hoping he would fall into the trap. Well he wouldn't ... because he was clever and they were not. He'd given them enough clues and they still hadn't been able to piece it all together. And even if they had, how could they arrest him unless they caught him? Which wasn't about to happen because he was too good.

He had only one person left upon which to exact his revenge.

William chuckled to himself. Boy did he have something special planned for Malcolm Gardener. If only they had seen the film, the one that Malcolm Gardener's watch committee had so self righteously banned: they would know what was coming, and to who, and how public it would be.

He grabbed the paper, raising it enough to see the headline and the damning review that followed. He forced himself to read it again, knowing he would need to be in the worst, most foul mood ever, to be able to see his plan through to the end.

Local actor's fall from grace.

Local thespian, William Henry Corndell had chosen not only the University Theatre in Leeds, but also his birthday of April 1st, for what should have been his most triumphant performance; instead, it will long be remembered as his most dramatic exit, aside from breaking his leg in London's West End on the set of **The Phantom of the Opera.**

After almost a twenty year absence from the stage, Mr Corndell had been hired by the entertainment manager, Martin Brown to share with the audience a rendition of some of Hollywood's darkest character's, created by the legendary Lon Chaney.

Despite a dramatic stage setting and a superb entrance, the whole show came to an abrupt end in less than a minute as Corndell fell from the podium. What followed was a vile string of abuse from Corndell, aimed at the audience and blaming them for his obvious lack of talent.

William is the son of the much loved and best-remembered film director, Wallace Henry Corndell.

William slammed the paper on to the tabletop once again.

How dare she say I have a lack of talent? I am the greatest screen idol since Lon Chaney ... may even be better than him.

No, William, don't be stupid: no one is in Lon's class. You're a close second, but you're not as good as the master.

What had happened at the university was not his fault.

And all through the years, his untimely mishaps had never been down to him.

Someone else had always been to blame: because they didn't understand him. He was an artist, couldn't they see that?

Nanny Cranshaw couldn't, the old buzzard.

William giggled hysterically. He'd taken care of that old bat, big style. She wouldn't be bothering him again.

God she was a bastard!

William laughed so hard and rocked so much that he almost overturned his chair and fell on to the floor.

The day she had tried to inflict her discipline upon him was one she had finally rued: he could see her now, telling him that children should know their place; be given a time for meals and eat what they were told to, whether they liked it or not. They should go to bed when told; only offer an opinion when asked.

He cringed when he thought of how loud she could shout, glancing over his shoulder to see if she was behind him now. But there was nothing for him to worry about: he'd seen her off. At least he thought he had, but she had a knack of turning up. He really must have a word with his father about her. If she had left and stopped caring for him, why did she keep coming back?

William screamed and kicked the paper on to the kitchen floor:

thinking back to the day she had put his first make up kit in the dustbin, the same day the refuse collectors were coming, so he would never have the chance to retrieve it. The one his father had bought for him.

But that was the problem, you see, no one had ever taken the time to appreciate him.

Like those two bullies at the private boarding school he'd had to attend after Nanny Cranshaw's untimely death. They had taken William for an idiot as well. They had played pranks on him, like dragging him into the school showers and ramming a hose-pipe up his backside and turning on the water; stringing him up naked and using him as a punch bag before shaving off all his pubic hair ... burning it off more like.

But when he'd decided to turn the tables and play his own tricks on them it was different, wasn't it? No, they didn't like that one bit.

The police had never been able to pin that one on him either, and his use of make up had been tested to the absolute limit that weekend.

William needed to change and go to the warehouse. He needed time to think: needed his computer, because with the help of technology he had successfully been able to eradicate all his tracks. No records of Nanny Cranshaw's death, the public school incident, the banned film...

No ... he was fireproof.

CHAPTER 47

Colin Sharp had returned from London during the early hours of the morning. It was early afternoon before he'd found his way to Gardener's house for a meeting. Malcolm had gone to the cinema to see an old fashioned black and white double bill that was right up his street. Gardener had asked his father to take a mobile with him: despite knowing he was under surveillance.

Gardener placed coffees on the table, the scene reminiscent of the time he'd asked Sharp to prepare a file on Derek Summers, the entertainment agent cum paedophile cum porn king.

Those thoughts led him into thinking of Jacqueline and his feelings from that afternoon were still quite clear in his mind: the day he had found out that his new girlfriend, the female minister of his parish, was a murderer. She had only been killing the perverts who had raped her as a child. Despite the fact that he was an officer of the law, and she had done wrong, part of him couldn't help but think they had all received their just deserts.

Gardener sat down and cleared a space at the table. The files had all been neatly laid out.

Sharp took a sip of his drink. "That tastes good. You don't know what a relief it is to be back."

"Not keen on The Smoke, then?" asked Reilly.

"They do things differently down there. I'm not saying it's right or wrong, it's just different."

"What do you have for us?" Gardener asked.

"He's definitely an odd-ball, but there's nothing concrete here. Having said that, what I've found out might be enough to hold him for a while."

"Go on," said Gardener. He had a gut feeling that it was going to be one of those cases. William Henry Corndell was probably guilty, but lucky enough to walk free because what little evidence they did have wouldn't stand up in court.

"Nothing odd about his early life unless you count the fact that he didn't go to school."

"He must have been educated somewhere," replied Gardener. "From what we've seen he's intelligent."

"If not a little loopy," said Reilly.

"Oh, he was educated," said Sharp, "Just not in school. His mother and father paid for a private education at home. He had two different teachers and they looked after him until he was about fourteen."

"Did you speak to them?" asked Gardener.

"Only one of them: the other one died in a traffic accident a few years ago. Anyway, she said the same as you, he was intelligent, but he didn't always use it, or show an interest. His pet subject was English. He used to love writing stories. They were always gruesome but she blames his father for that: he used to take him to the film studio a lot, even bought him a make up kit when he was eight.

"Eventually, William spent most of his time at the studio. He worked with his dad on the films, and with the professionals in the make up department by the time he was ten.

"And it was about that time William discovered Lon Chaney, and how good *he* was. He was never away from the library, or the film studio's archives, reading everything he could lay his hands on. By the time he was twelve, he'd honed his skill so much that most of the professional actors preferred him to any of the regular crew.

"The private tutors eventually left and his mother and father hired a new nanny by the name of Elizabeth Cranshaw."

"We already know what happened to her," said Reilly.

"The people I spoke to said she had a stroke," said Colin Sharp. "She was old."

"Age had nothing to do with it," said Gardener. "We've since learned from Fitz that Elizabeth Cranshaw was an asthmatic. She'd had a heart attack, which probably led to a stroke, brought on by a lethal dose of sherry, mixed with nuts that had been ground into a fine powder, creating the drug, Ephedrine."

"What does this have to do with William?"

"Janine Harper was killed the same way."

"Interesting," said Sharp.

"Did you speak to anyone that knew both William and the nanny? Someone who could verify what kind of a relationship they had?"

"Briefly: the old lady had a daughter. They were together on the day of her death, shopping in London. She said her mother never stopped complaining about William. He was highly strung, bad tempered, would go out of his way to play tricks on her. She did say her mother could be quite hard to get on with, and she was a bit strict: maybe the lad was just rebelling against a disciplinarian."

"Not worth killing for," said Reilly.

"Well, after what you've told me, maybe there was more to it. Elizabeth Cranshaw told her daughter about William's strange behaviour, and the fact that he hated authority, and she figured the only way to get her message across was through his make up kit."

"What did she do with it?" asked Gardener.

"That much I don't know, the daughter never told me."

"She probably got rid of it," said Reilly. "That would send him up the wall, so it would. Especially if he was using it at the studio."

"I'm sure it would be reason enough for William to kill her ... in his eyes," said Gardener.

"But he can't have been much more than ten or twelve," said Sharp. "Surely he wouldn't have had the know how at that age."

"I wouldn't count on it," replied Gardener. "And that's something we're all guilty of, underestimating him."

Colin Sharp finished his coffee.

"In that case, the next bit of information is going to kill *you*."

"Why doesn't that surprise me?" asked Reilly.

"After the nanny's death," continued Sharp. "His parents were so worried that they booked private counselling sessions for him. They figured he was traumatised. The psychiatrist's report suggested that William was withdrawn but it wasn't just down to the death of the nanny. It was a mixture of things, like William never having gone to an ordinary school where he was allowed to mix with other children his own age."

"Oh that old chestnut," offered Reilly.

"The other problem was spending too much time at the studio where his only company were adults. He felt that William was trapped in a world of make believe and displayed an unhealthy interest in horror, particularly Lon Chaney.

"A private boarding school was suggested. His parents settled on Thatcher's, it's about ten or twelve miles from Eton but rarely gets mentioned and lives in Eton's shadow. He stayed there almost constantly, only ever had a couple of weekends at home.

"According to his teachers, he was bright, could handle the discipline but often questioned his superiors about their brand of punishment and their reasons for it. He never complained about the food and he even had his own room, pretty much home from home."

"So what was the problem?" asked Reilly.

"There must have been one," added Gardener.

"Oh, there was, big style," said Sharp.

Gardener didn't like the sound of that.

"Two students." Colin Sharp consulted his notes. "Nick Craven and Peter Holliwell. According to sources they used to play tricks on him."

"Didn't you speak to them?" asked Gardener.

"No, and I'll tell you why soon. One time, they attacked him in the showers, shoved a hosepipe up his arse and turned the water on. William spent a few days in hospital but wouldn't tell anyone what had happened, just complained of stomach pains. Another time they strung him up naked and used him as a punch bag before taking matches to his pubic hairs."

"Couldn't have happened to a better person," said Reilly.

"Any idea why?" asked Gardener.

"Nothing I could find. You know what it's like, kids pick on other kids for no reason, particularly at boarding schools."

"Probably more so."

"Anyway, it all kicked off one weekend when all the students bar three were going home, those being William, Craven and Holliwell. Two of the masters stayed back, the rest were on leave. From what I've picked up, Craven and Holliwell were going to play a prank to end all pranks on William.

"But it didn't work out. No one can tell me what really happened that weekend but the end result was something out of your wildest nightmares.

"It was due to kick off in the laundry room where they were going to strip William naked and stick him in an industrial washing machine. Nothing went to plan and even to this day the police are convinced the lunatic responsible for what happened to all three is still walking free."

"They don't think William had anything to do with it?"

"That's the impression I got."

"Go on," said Gardener.

"Nick Craven sustained a massive head injury, it looked like he'd been hit with a shovel. Police reports confirm that when he woke up he found a note – or should I say – a puzzle, a clue, which led him to the headmaster's office, where he found Peter Holliwell's left leg. The shoe, sock and big toe were all missing, and the other toes were broken. Craven realised it wasn't a fake and threw up."

"Have you seen any of the puzzles?" asked Gardener.

"Yes, got a copy here." Sharp passed them over.

"The second clue was on the floor outside the headmaster's study. Craven was led to the games room where he found a severed arm gripping a pool cue, as though it was still playing the game.

"The rest of the body had been placed all over the school and Craven ended up back where he had started, in the laundry room. And that was where he found Holliwell's head, inside the washing machine, a finger stuck up one nostril and the severed big toe inside its mouth.

"When the authorities turned up, Craven was totally deranged: couldn't tell them anything. He was taken to a local hospital and then admitted to a mental asylum. He's been there ever since.

"Holliwell's body was eventually sewn back together so his family could bury him. There were no prints on any of the limbs and, in fact, no prints anywhere."

"And William?" Gardener asked casually.

"Well, there's the mystery. He was found in a cupboard. Locked on the outside and no way in other than the door. He looked as if he had been beaten pretty badly and both his arms had been broken, or it seemed that way. Eventually, the doctors examined him and found that despite his beating, his limbs had not been broken. They were just severely bruised."

"If it looked that way, then he meant it to look that way," said Reilly.

"I don't see how," replied Sharp. "How the hell could you break your own limbs – or make it look like you have – and then lock yourself inside a cupboard that has the bolt on the outside with no way in other than the door?"

"I know it sounds far fetched," said Gardener, studying the puzzles that Sharp had passed over. He knew they were not film quotes but he recognized the style in which they had been written: similar to those they had found in their own murder case. "But if you knew how good this guy was with make up, you'd see what we're saying."

"He can't be that good, sir."

Gardener crossed the kitchen and picked up the phone. He put a call through to The Grand Theatre and asked for Fettle and waited.

After a couple of minutes the familiar voice came through the speaker.

"Now then, what do you want?"

"You're pretty good on Lon Chaney films. Did he ever make one that featured a cripple? Particularly where he was the cripple."

"I think he did. Give us a minute."

Gardener heard Fettle leafing through his film magazines before returning to the phone.

"Aye, it were a film called, *The Miracle Man* made in 1919. I'll read what it says: 'four crooks try to take financial advantage of miracles performed by a blind faith healer. One o' the crooks, called *Frog*, played by Chaney is able to contort his body to appear crippled. The plan is for the *Frog* to crawl up to the Miracle Man and pretend to be healed in front of a large group of spectators.'"

"And Chaney played the part?" asked Gardener.

"Aye, nobody's really sure how he did it. The director wanted a real contortionist for the role, but none o' the one's he saw could act, so Chaney did it himself. Managed to make it look like he'd broken most on his bones."

"Thank you."

Gardener replaced the receiver and joined his colleagues at the table. He told them what Fettle had told him.

"Do you really think William did all that himself?" asked Sharp.

"I do, yes," replied Gardener. His only problem was proving it. Once again, they had everything they needed, albeit contrived, but no proof.

"Did William ever return to the college?" asked Gardener.

"No."

"No surprise there," said Reilly.

"What are you going to do?" asked Sharp.

"I think we'll have to show Briggs your evidence and then see if he'll get us a warrant for his arrest. Did you delve into his bank accounts?"

"I did. We need to take a closer look. His father left him about three million pounds all told, if you take the property into account. All the cash was deposited into an account at a private bank in London. What with client confidentiality and the fact that I didn't have a warrant they wouldn't tell me too much. What I did find out was that he has taken out large sums of money and the bank is either not sure what he's done with them, or won't tell me."

"Most likely the latter," said Reilly.

"In that case, use the computers and the banks up here to find out what you can. My guess is, he's set up accounts in different names and he's used them to finance his little ventures, perhaps maybe to hire transport. How else would he get around and do the things he's done?"

"Makes sense, boss," said Reilly. "We need somebody to help Colin. The quicker we get this bastard out of normal life, the better."

"I agree," said Gardener.

He turned to Colin Sharp. "While you were down there did you go over to Pinewood?"

"Briefly."

"Did you get a list of his father's films?"

"Yes," said Sharp, leafing through his files. He handed over the relevant paperwork.

Gardener studied it but couldn't find what he wanted.

"You ever heard of the film, *Imperfection*?"

"Can't say I have," replied Sharp. "Why?"

"No reason," said Gardener, disappointed. The phone rang. He picked it up hoping it wasn't Briggs.

"Sir, It's Frank."

"Hello, Frank, what can I do for you."

"We've just had a call from Mary Phillips. She wants to speak to you urgently."

"She leave a number?" asked Gardener.

Frank Thornton gave him the number and then mentioned that Briggs had been asking after him.

Gardener called Mary Phillips.

"Oh, Mr Gardener, I'm so pleased you've called."

"Is there a problem?" he asked.

"A little one. You asked me if I'd look and see if there were anything missing from Henry's room, after you'd finished with it, like."

"Is there?"

"Yes, love. It's his mobile phone, I can't find it anywhere."

CHAPTER 48

Gardener realised he still needed more evidence if he was ever going to bring William Henry Corndell before a jury.

Despite having gained further knowledge he had no proof that William had actually killed the nanny, or the two students – one of whose mutilation had sent the other round the twist.

However, in his favour, were the murders with the puzzles, the use of a lethal cocktail as a weapon of disposal, and Corndell's genuine obsession with Lon Chaney.

Was that enough?

And where did the film, *Imperfection* enter into the equation? He was convinced that it did ... somehow. But even Malcolm had no recollection of such a film, and he must have been one of the world's leading authorities.

That created another problem. Malcolm had been at the cinema all afternoon and Gardener had heard nothing from the officer trailing him so everything must have been fine. Still, he hadn't been able to settle.

When Chris had arrived home from school the pair of them had spent an hour in the garage, sorting through the Bonneville engine components, checking what could be re-used and what couldn't. But even then, his concentration was lacking. Eventually, Chris had finished up and gone to his room.

Gardener heard the front door open. He glanced at the kitchen clock. It was a little after six. He realised that he hadn't yet prepared anything to eat. But it wasn't the end of the world: worst-case scenario, they could all go out for a meal or phone for a take-away.

As Malcolm entered the kitchen he heard voices.

"Stewart, I'd like you to meet someone."

Gardener glanced over his father's shoulder and noticed Martin Brown standing in the doorway.

"Mr. Gardener," said Brown, nodding. "I didn't think I'd be seeing you again so soon."

"The feeling's mutual."

"May I come in, there's something I need to tell you?"

"Of course, come and sit down."

"I'll make us a cup of tea," offered Malcolm.

Gardener was confused, concerned. His dad had gone to the cinema for an afternoon matinee: having returned with Martin Brown, he suspected that something was wrong; but the old man appeared to be fine.

Gardener stood up. "Is everything okay?"

"Depends what you mean by okay, son."

"Has something happened? Are *you* okay?"

Gardener wasn't happy with his father's evasive answer.

"I'm fine. We're here, or should I say, Martin's here, because he thinks he may owe you an apology and he may also have disturbing news for you."

Gardener sat back down and glanced at Martin Brown. If the man was here to speak, then he would let him.

"It's about, Corndell," said Brown.

"Everything about him disturbs me. What's he done now?"

"I'm not sure that he has. I met your father this afternoon for the first time. I had no idea who he was."

Martin Brown stopped talking while Malcolm put the tea on the table.

"We ended up in the cinema foyer during the interval," said Malcolm.

"What did you go and see, anyway? You never said."

"A Lon Chaney double bill as it happens."

Gardener grew cold at the mere mention of Chaney. "Which ones?"

"*The Phantom of the Opera* and *The Hunchback of Notre Dame*," said Martin.

"The Hunchback was first," said Malcolm. "At the interval I went out for a coffee and a chocolate bar, felt a little peckish. As I turned around, Martin here knocked into me and I spilt my coffee. He ordered fresh drinks and we started talking. It turns out that he was sitting directly in front of me."

"We talked about films in general, and Chaney, and how good he was," continued Martin Brown. "And then Corndell slipped into the conversation. I told your father that I was in charge of the entertainment at the University and about the fiasco earlier in the week. Your father then told me who *he* was and who *you* were and what you were involved in."

Gardener wondered how much his father had told Martin Brown.

"Dad you're not really supposed to discuss police cases. In fact, *I'm* not supposed to discuss them with *you*."

"Under normal circumstances I would agree, but these are not normal, and I *am* involved," replied Malcolm. "I haven't given away any secrets but what we've stumbled across could prove useful."

"Go on," said Gardener.

Martin Brown sighed. "I booked William Henry Corndell because of what I'd thought had been a glittering career. Everything I'd heard – and seen for that matter – was nothing short of stunning. The man is an absolute genius with make up. He can do anything. I've seen him on the London stage for *The Phantom*..."

"You actually saw him play the part?" interrupted Gardener.

"No. I had a friend who worked for the theatre and I was given back stage passes to one of the performances. I was there on the morning William was given his big break and his rehearsal was nothing short of a revelation. He put so much emotion into the part that the stage hands reckoned he was better than Crawford."

"Did you use the tickets for the performance?"

"No, My wife – girlfriend at the time – took ill, and we couldn't make it. But I later heard he had an accident."

"It was a little more than that," said Gardener. "I found out that he's brilliant in rehearsals but no good in front of a crowd. During the matinee he fluffed his lines, wrecked the scenery, and eventually broke his own leg, blaming everyone but himself."

"I never heard that."

"Take it from me, it's true."

"That puts the night at the university theatre into perspective a little bit. If he is frightened of crowds that's probably why he fell off the podium."

"Exactly. And he used the fact that we were there – putting pressure on him – as an excuse for his own incompetence."

"That's where the apology comes in, I think."

"Don't worry about that. What else have you got to tell me?"

Martin Brown appeared hesitant, as if he didn't want to speak.

"Martin, you're not under arrest, anything you tell me will be in the strictest confidence."

"Malcolm told me about Leonard White's death, and the quote on the dressing room wall. 'For long weary months I have awaited this hour.'"

Gardener's stomach tensed. "And?"

"I know which film that comes from; or should I say which two films. It's a quote from *The Phantom of the Opera*, the Lon Chaney version, released in 1925."

"Two films?" pressed Gardener.

"Before we go any further, Mr. Gardener, I need you to tell me if there were other quotes at the scenes of the other murders, and what they were."

"You do know I'm not obliged to tell you anything," replied Gardener.

"I'm only trying to help. Maybe it's my turn to inform you that anything you tell me will be in the strictest confidence. Do you want to catch your killer?"

Gardener struggled with his conscience.

"Your first murder was Leonard White," continued Martin Brown. "He was found hanging in a theatre."

Martin Brown stopped talking but Gardener realised he knew more. His glare forced the man to continue.

"At the autopsy you found a puzzle carved into the man's chest."

Gardener left the table without saying anything and collected the file from a cupboard in the living room.

Although the central heating was on, he felt a chill. Martin Brown had told him something that only the police knew.

Back at the table he sat down and studied the file and then asked Martin Brown for the second quote:

"The night passed – a night of vague horrors – tortured dreams. The second murder," said Martin Brown. "You found the second body hanging upside down in a kind of reverse crucifixion.

Furthermore, at that autopsy you found another puzzle about the case, in a test tube, inserted into the victim's anus."

The blood in Gardener's veins had turned to ice. Either Martin Brown knew more than was good for him because of inside information ... or he was their killer. And in all honesty, Gardener wouldn't know: he wasn't sure anyone else would either. He couldn't believe the tension in the room. It felt like time had stood still. No one was drinking. In fact, it didn't sound like they were even breathing.

"The third quote?" asked Martin. "Would it be, 'so far so good, for a house with a curse on it'?"

Gardener nodded.

"Your third victim was found in a locked room, suspended in the crucifixion position once again. However, this time the body was the right way up, naked, and his real head was missing, but he had someone else's in its place. Along with a puzzle in his right hand."

Gardener was mortified. His stomach ached, his legs felt weak. "How do you know all these things?"

"Each of the people killed was a member of the local watch committee and had been killed by an independent film producer because they had banned his film for being too horrific. The man was totally incensed because he was unbalanced. But the police couldn't catch him in the film because he was a master of disguise."

"What film are we talking about?" asked Gardener, as if he didn't know.

"A film called *Imperfection*, written by William Henry Corndell, and produced by his father, Wallace."

"Have you seen the film?"

"Yes?"

"Where?" Gardener asked.

"An underground copy. The film never made it to the big screen. The one the censors issued an 'X' certificate for was not the film distributed around Leeds. Therefore, the local watch committee that your father sat on banned the film immediately, told him in no uncertain terms he had to make cuts: it was too violent, too graphic; he had to cut it and then re-present it."

Gardener glanced at his father. "But you weren't there that night: you didn't see the film."

"Corndell obviously doesn't know that," replied Martin Brown.

"So Corndell made a film back in the seventies and has basically lived it out since then?"

"Sounds like it. He's killed everyone the same way as he did in the film and used quotes from Chaney's films because he's obsessed with the man. Three down, one to go, and we all know who that is."

Martin Brown stared at Malcolm.

"Do you mean to say I've been going out, unaware that my life was at stake?" asked Malcolm.

"Actually, no," replied Gardener.

"What do you mean?" asked Malcolm.

"You've been under twenty-four-hour surveillance for some time. Every move you've made has been watched and monitored."

Malcolm's bottom jaw fell open and nearly hit the table. After he'd regained his composure he asked: "Why didn't you tell me?"

"I couldn't, Dad. Firstly, we've never been sure of our facts from the beginning, and secondly, because of that we didn't want you worrying unnecessarily. Thirdly, we had to make sure everything you did was natural, so we could lull the killer into making an attempt and therefore expose himself."

"But I could have been killed."

"No you couldn't, we know what we're doing."

"I've never seen anyone following me," said Malcolm. "Corndell could have taken me anytime he wanted."

"He couldn't," argued Gardener. "You were being watched, and the reason you didn't know was because you weren't meant to; and the reason you didn't see him was also because you weren't meant to. That's how good a job we've been doing?"

Malcolm didn't reply.

Gardener grabbed his mobile and scrolled his way through the phone-book menu.

"What are you doing?" asked Martin Brown.

"I think it's time I spoke to our friend, William."

"I have his landline number," said Martin.

"It's okay," smiled Gardener. "We'll ring his mobile."

"But he doesn't have one," argued Martin Brown.

"Yes he does," said Gardener.

"I can assure you that William Henry Corndell does not have a mobile phone, and never has."

Gardener continued to dial the number and then passed his mobile over to Martin Brown as it started to ring.

He glanced at his father. The old man had not spoken since he'd found out that the threat on his life had been serious enough to have him placed under police protection. And who could blame him? Gardener felt as if he had let him down: all he'd wanted was to protect a parent, as he would his children. As the years passed, Malcolm was growing frailer: which hurt him, because he could do nothing to stop nature's intentions.

Martin Brown placed the mobile on the table with an expression of defeat. Gardener had not heard much of the conversation, short as it was, but he was curious now.

"Why were you convinced he didn't have a mobile phone?"

At first, Gardener didn't think Martin Brown was going to

answer: the man continued to stare into his empty cup.

"I have a friend who works for BT. He told me that Corndell had no listed mobile number and had had only one call to his landline in ten to fifteen years. But the bill was paid regularly and on time."

Gardener passed his mobile over to Martin Brown once again. "Ring him."

"Pardon?"

"Ring your friend. Ask him again about the mobile."

"I can't do that."

"Why not?"

"His method ... his programme for finding out the information isn't legal."

"You let me worry about that," replied Gardener. "Right now, I want you to ask him again."

Martin Brown did as he was asked and dialled Dave Pearson's number.

He answered on the first ring.

"Dave? It's Martin."

"Okay, Martin, what can I do for you?"

"It's about Corndell, and his mobile phone?"

"Oh not that again. I thought we'd been through all that," replied Dave, tersely. "He doesn't have one."

"Yes he does. I've just spoken to him."

"Well he's obviously bought one since you last spoke. Let's face it, if he's in the demand you seem to think he is, then he'll need one."

"Will you check the number for me?"

"What's the point?" asked Dave Pearson.

"Just do it, will you?"

After another sigh and another moan, Dave Pearson checked the number Martin Brown had given him.

He then grew silent, and stayed that way for some time.

"Dave? What's going on?" asked Martin.

"There's something amiss with the account."

"What is it?"

"I don't know, yet."

Martin Brown used his hand to cover the phone while he explained to Gardener what was happening.

Eventually, Dave Pearson started to chuckle. "Well, well, well. Our friend Corndell *has* been busy. Is he a bit of a buff with computers?"

"Could be. Why do you ask?"

"The software has uncovered something."

"Your illegal software, you mean."

"Steady on, Martin, don't shout too loudly."

"If you knew what I knew it wouldn't matter any more."

"Okay, to cut a long story short, his phone used to belong to someone called Henry Fowkes."

Martin Brown broke the connection and placed the phone on the table. He told Gardener what Dave Pearson had told him.

CHAPTER 49

Tuesday April 5th (a.m.)

L aura had left the house early in the morning, spending the best part of the day in the centre of Leeds, shopping for clothes. She had returned to Yeadon about an hour previously, depositing her carrier bags before popping back out again to pick up a parcel at the airport. Her intention had then been to drive back home but the car had other ideas.

All morning her engine management light had been on, indicating a problem that the garage had been unable to find two days previously when it had been booked in for that reason. The excuse the garage had given was that their computers had been attacked with a virus which had somehow been passed on to the Tech Check unit they were using. She now wondered if it had transferred the virus to her car. She supposed it was possible but would readily admit she knew nothing about computers or cars: so if you mixed the two together she was doubly lost.

What she did know was that the car was not running properly.

Overhead, the rich blue skies were cloudless, creating yet another warm day for the time of year.

Laura had her driver's door window open and was currently

listening to a classical piece on the radio. As she drove down Rawdon road heading towards Horsforth the car misfired.

"Oh, Christ, don't do this to me."

Suddenly, the dashboard illuminated and the vehicle rolled to a halt at the side of the road. Despite having lost her power steering she managed to guide it into a drive fronted by a pair of magnificent wrought iron gates.

She tried in vain to start the engine but it simply turned over without firing.

Laura jumped out of the car and reached back in for her handbag. She took out her mobile phone and glanced around in order to ascertain where she was. Phoning the breakdown service would be something akin to passing an X-Factor audition and then she would probably have to wait about four hours before the tow truck arrived, which they would promise within the hour.

Laura took a peek inside the grounds of the house beyond the gates.

"Someone's tight on security," she said to herself.

After phoning the breakdown service, she also left Sean a voicemail message.

Laura pressed the intercom button and waited for an answer, which came quite quickly.

"Hello?"

"I'm sorry to bother you but I've broken down outside your gates. I thought it only polite to let you know."

"How unfortunate. Are you all right?" came the reply.

Laura recognised the voice but she couldn't place it.

"Yes, I'm fine. I've phoned the breakdown service and they've promised to be here within the hour. Is that a problem?"

"Not at all. But we can't have you waiting out there by yourself in this day and age, you never know who's around. I'm going to open the gates to allow you a little more room for the breakdown service. And if you'd like to take a walk down I'll make you a nice cup of tea, er ... I'm sorry ... you never told me your name."

That's rather nice of him, thought Laura.

"I don't want to put you to any trouble," she answered.

"Goodness me, that is rather an unusual name." She heard him laugh before he said. "It's no trouble."

With that said, the gates silently opened.

She spoke back into the intercom. "Thank you. My name's Laura ... Laura Reilly. I'll see you in a couple of minutes, mister, er?"

The intercom clicked off but the man on the other end never gave his name.

The walk to the mansion wasn't as long as she'd imagined. When she arrived, the front door was open, which led her into a panelled hallway framed by film posters.

She then turned and saw her host.

CHAPTER 50

April 5th (a.m.)

Briggs stared at the file on his desk. It included everything Gardener could muster: along with the folder Colin Sharp had prepared, and details of the information everyone else had supplied. It had taken Briggs an hour to sort through it all, with the help of Gardener and Reilly who were now sitting opposite.

"Well done, Stewart, Sean. There's a lot of information here."

"Enough to gain a warrant for his arrest?" asked Gardener.

"I don't see why not," replied Briggs, sitting back and folding his arms across his chest.

Outside the office window the view was once again one of blue cloudless skies: perhaps the only consolation to what they were all going through.

"Can I ask you a question, Stewart? And I'd like *your* opinion on this one as well, Sean," said Briggs.

"Go on."

"From everything we've seen, you're absolutely sure it's Corndell?"

The question knocked Gardener off balance a little. "As sure as I can be, why?"

"What about Martin Brown?"

"The thought did cross my mind, particularly when he came out with the information that no one else knew."

"You're barking up the wrong tree, sir," said Reilly. "If Martin Brown was our killer then why didn't he abduct Malcolm at the cinema? There was nothing to stop him."

"Maybe he wanted to rub Stewart's nose in it," offered Briggs. "You know what these people are like. Brown takes the opportunity to befriend Malcolm at the cinema. They get talking, Malcolm takes him home to meet his son and therefore gain some more inside knowledge. You said yourself he gave you information that only we knew."

"From a film written by Corndell, one that he'd seen," protested Gardener.

"How long ago, Stewart? A bit of a good memory, wouldn't you say? Can you remember quotes from films over twenty years ago?"

"I can't, but I bet my dad can. Point I'm making is if you're a film buff, then maybe you would remember these things."

"And another thing, sir..." Reilly pointed out. "Laura knows Martin Brown. She's worked with him, so she has: she hasn't given me any reason to suspect him."

"And you still haven't seen this film anywhere, or come across anyone but Brown who knows anything about it?" Briggs asked.

"Actually we do know who has a copy," said Gardener.

"Who?"

"Corndell," replied Gardener. "He has a canister in his cinema with that title on."

Briggs sat back and stayed quiet for a moment or two.

"Okay Stewart. I'll go with it. I'll get the warrant, you get him off the streets."

"How long will it take?" Gardener asked.

"Not long," replied Briggs. "But there is a problem."

Gardener's stomach lurched. "Go on."

"I'm afraid I can't let you handle the case."

Gardener knew it had been coming "Why?"

"Because whoever it is, whether it's Corndell or Martin Brown or someone we haven't yet come across, they've made it personal. Your father is next in line. How would you feel if I allowed you to drag Corndell in, spend all day interviewing him, only to find when you got home your Dad was missing, or worse, strung up?"

"That won't happen if we get Corndell off the streets," said Gardener.

"I'm not taking that chance, Stewart. I appreciate all the work you've done on the case, but I still have to ask, are you one hundred percent certain? And the answer is no. Even now, your judgement may be clouded..."

Gardener was about to say something but Briggs put his hand out to stop him.

"What I want you to do is go home and spend time with your Dad. *You* keep him under twenty-four-hour protection ... at least until this thing blows over. Reilly and I will handle Corndell's arrest."

Briggs stood up and nodded to Reilly. "Come on, let's go."

Gardener had no chance to reply.

CHAPTER 51

April 5th (mid-morning)

Gardener pulled his car to a halt opposite the stage door and switched off the engine. As he glanced at the poster on the wall, the show advertised Dr. Hook on the *Hits & History Tour*. He vaguely remembered a couple of their songs.

He glanced further down the street to where the road crew were unloading the trailer. It never failed to amaze him how much gear these bands carried around. He wondered if they really needed it all.

Through the stage door and down the steps he heard Fettle humming to himself. When he came into view he realised why, the man was making tea.

"Just in time," said Fettle. "Fancy a brew?"

"Do you ever do anything else apart from drink tea all day?" replied Gardener. "I'm afraid I don't have time this morning."

"Why's that then?"

Gardener felt heavy and hollow, if that made any sense. He really wanted to be there to see Corndell's reaction when they arrested him, but he understood the reasons behind it.

He told Fettle about what they'd found: Harry Fletcher's body; the link Fitz had discovered to Corndell and the nanny; Martin

Brown's story about the film, and very possibly the fact that they may have a copy of it; and albeit reluctantly, the reason he'd been removed from the case.

"I'm sure your mate can handle it," said Fettle.

"I know he can," replied Gardener. "Anyway, that's what I wanted to say, if you come across any more information to seal Corndell's fate, you only have to ring Sean and let him know."

Fettle nodded as Gardener turned and mounted the steps to the stage door. Before he reached the top, Fettle called him. Gardener came back down and Fettle was standing with two dog-eared copies of *Film Review* in his hands.

"Thought you might like to show these to your dad. Might take his mind off things and cheer him up a bit."

"Thank you, I'm sure he'll love it. I'll get them back as soon as possible."

"There's no rush," said Fettle, returning to his tea and biscuits.

Outside, Gardener settled himself in the car and threw the books on the passenger seat. But before starting the car he changed his mind and picked one up, leafing through.

He was about to put it back on the passenger seat when he came across a photo that made his blood curdle. His knees weakened, his fingers tingled and he felt numb.

It couldn't be!

Gardener fumbled for his mobile phone.

CHAPTER 52

April 5th (mid-day)

Briggs launched himself towards the door but it took another two attempts before it caved in.

When it did he jumped back into the hallway and held his nose. "Jesus Christ!"

Reilly covered his nose and walked into the room. The place was a tomb. As he'd suspected by the view from the outside, the window had been covered with newspaper. The floor had no carpet, only bare boards. The walls were back to brick. An old fashioned range adorned one wall: frames – which had probably hung for years – had been removed, exposing clean wallpaper. For what purpose he had no idea.

In the middle of the room, tied to a rocking chair was the naked, headless corpse of the man they suspected was Trevor Thorpe.

Briggs sighed. He'd taken a harried call from Gardener who had spotted the image of Trevor Thorpe in one of Fettle's *Film Review's*. The photo was in fact Lon Chaney in the lead role of a film called *The Road To Mandalay*.

It had taken them almost an hour to find Thorpe's address and drive to the remote farmhouse.

Briggs stared at the emaciated body, bound tightly with cheese-wire: having been there some considerable time. He'd struggled to free himself, the congealed rivers of blood trailing down his chest attested to that fact.

The area around the chair was heavily soiled. Whoever had killed him had – at first – been feeding him, otherwise where had the excrement come from? The killer had then changed tactics and starved his victim to death.

Briggs glanced around the room for any notes with verses but there were none.

"What are we dealing with here?" Briggs asked.

"One sick individual."

"How long do you reckon he's been here, Sean?"

"Hard to say ... I reckon at least a month."

Briggs clenched his teeth. "If this is Thorpe, and I'm sure it will be, then the killer has been disguised as our profiler and he's listened to everything we've had to say. What's more, he's took us all for idiots, by throwing us duff information, about the kind of person we should be looking for."

"He's a clever man, so he is."

"Either that, or he's lucky," said Briggs.

"No, sir, he's clever. And he's been allowed to get away with it because he's so damn good with a brush and paint."

"Corndell it is, then?"

"Too feckin' right."

Briggs walked outside for a breath of fresh air and checked the signal on his mobile, glancing up at the three-storey farmhouse. It was old and in need of repair, resembled every other farmhouse he'd ever seen: missing roof tiles, damaged render, leaking gutters, and rotting window frames. It was hardly befitting an ex-police profiler. He noticed the barns and outbuildings were no better.

The place was so remote.

"It's the middle of nowhere for Christ's sakes, Sean. Why the hell does he want to live here?"

"Who's to say he does?"

"What do you mean?" asked Briggs.

"The only letter we have is the one you received. We don't know anything about him, only his reputation. Who's to say he actually wrote the letter? Who's to say that's him in there?"

Briggs sighed loudly and called the station.

CHAPTER 53

April 5th (early afternoon)

"There's something wrong," said Reilly. He pulled the car to a halt outside the wrought iron gates.

"Why?" Briggs asked.

"Because the gates are open."

"Drive on, Sean, I'd like to have a look at this place, and the maniac that lives here."

Reilly put the car in gear and drove down the gravel drive, parking outside the front door.

Briggs opened the car door and heaved himself out, glancing around.

"I can see why you'd want to protect the place." He turned to Reilly. "Have the gates always been closed?"

"Yes, you have to ring the intercom if you want to talk to him."

Briggs knocked on the door, retrieving the warrant for Corndell's arrest from his inside pocket.

When there was no answer he knocked again, before eventually trying it. Stretching his legs he walked around the perimeter. When he reached the back door he knocked once more.

When Reilly tried the handle, the door opened.

He glanced at Briggs. "I'm not happy."

"Okay. At least let's take a look around while we're here."

Briggs shouted Corndell's name but there was no answer.

He noticed that the kitchen was spotless and strolled through, glancing into each of the other rooms, which were equally as clean. There was no sign of life downstairs.

Briggs admired the film posters. Reilly pointed out the original Frankenstein poster with Boris Karloff and told his superior officer how much it had sold for recently.

"What? For a fucking poster?"

"That's what I said."

"And that's what he paid for it?"

"No, he didn't say he'd paid that much, just that's what it went for when it sold recently."

Briggs sighed heavily. "Some people have more money than sense."

They covered the rest of the house and Reilly showed Briggs the make up room and the cinema. But the whole building was like a mortuary: no sign of life.

Reilly fished a piece of paper out of his pocket and then reached for his cell phone. "Shit, I must have left mine in the car, have you got yours?"

"Who are you calling?" Briggs asked.

"William ... who else?"

Briggs dialled.

The phone continued to ring but no one answered.

CHAPTER 54

April 5th (mid-afternoon)

Back at the house, Gardener parked the car on the drive and let himself in through the front door. He went straight to the kitchen and switched the kettle on, placing the two *Film Review's* on the table. He pulled two cups from the rack and started to make tea, wondering if his father was in the shed, his usual place of rest.

From a feeling of dejection at having been removed from the case, he was now elated at having found what he considered to be another nail in Corndell's coffin. The photo of Chaney in the *Road To Mandalay* had sent a chill right through him but the sense of satisfaction that followed was immeasurable. He was pretty sure he'd receive a phone call soon to tell him Corndell was safely tucked away in an interview room, and that the next couple of days spent with his father would simply be a paid holiday, and not a case of total protection where Gardener would be unable to let his father out of his sight.

Gardener checked his mobile but there were no text messages or missed calls.

He tried the handle of the back door and found it unlocked, which meant his father should be down the garden in the potting shed. The kettle boiled so he poured the tea into the pot before going to find him.

Gardener was surprised that his father wasn't in the shed when he arrived. He tried the garage and he wasn't there either. A wave of sadness passed him as he glanced at the Bonneville, which had been abandoned. He really wanted to finish the project.

Gardener checked every room in the house before running back out to the potting shed. He now had his mobile in hand, already ringing his father's number.

A feeling of trepidation hung in the air.

Where was he?

The phone shrilled.

Gardener heard it!

His guts turned to ice.

The ring tone was coming from the shed. Gardener peeked in and the phone was on the bench, his number lighting up the display panel.

What did that mean? Had he wasted too much time between the station and coming home? Shouldn't he have come straight home and not bothered to take a detour to see Fettle? Why had he done that? What had gone through his mind? Surely his father was more important than Fettle.

Had Corndell slipped the net? Had the call to Briggs and Reilly to inform them about Trevor Thorpe actually been the final nail in his father's coffin? Had they gone to check out that lead instead of arresting Corndell first?

Back in the house, Gardener was about to call the station when the doorbell chimed.

In frustration he threw his mobile on the nearest chair and ran into the hall.

Opening the door he was confronted by a UPS van and the driver, dressed in the standard brown uniform. A parcel delivery was not high on his list of priorities and only served to irritate him further.

"Mr Gardener?" asked the driver.

"Yes."

"Parcel for you."

Gardener thanked the driver, took the package, and walked back into the living room before a thought suddenly hit him.

The man had not asked for a signature. Gardener picked up the parcel. It was rectangular shaped, about twelve inches by eight. There were no stamps, no UPS logos and no writing other than his name.

He ripped the package open and quickly scanned the contents: a photo and a newspaper clipping.

Dropping them on the floor he ran outside where he found the driver in the process of starting the van. The fact that it was a pleasant day meant he hadn't shut the door, which gave Gardener the opportunity he needed to pull the driver from the seat, drag him out of the cab and throw him heavily against the side of the vehicle, so much so that he dented one of the panels.

"What the fuck..."

He gave the driver no chance to say anything else. Instead he banged his head against the panel in an effort to subdue him.

Only now did the driver's features register in his mind. He was a similar height to Gardener but much thinner. His complexion was tanned and he had a beard and moustache, which Gardener was trying to pry from his face in an effort to see whether or not it was real.

"What the fuck are you doing, man? You're ripping my face apart..."

"Who are you?" Gardener shouted, breathless, grabbing his shirt and shoving him back towards the van again.

The driver was on the ground in a sitting position with his legs underneath him. He wasn't going anywhere.

"I'm a UPS driver for God's sake." He tried to push Gardener out of the way. "This is assault, I can have you arrested for this."

"We both know you won't. What's your name?" asked Gardener, his heart pounding.

"You tell me who you are first."

Gardener used one hand to release and flip open his badge without bothering to explain further.

"Oh, shit."

"Let's try again, shall we? Name?"

"Gary Barlow ... and don't bother, I've heard all the jokes."

Gardener had no idea what he was talking about. "Show me some identification ... now!"

"It's in the cab, any chance you can let go?"

Gardener did so. The driver wasn't a threat, and he'd established that it wasn't William.

He handed over his ID for inspection.

"Tell me about the parcel."

"Nothing to tell," said the driver.

"Don't mess me about, otherwise I'll arrest you for conspiracy to murder and have you inside so fast you'll break the four-minute-mile by at least half. Now start talking."

"Look. I haven't killed anyone, and I don't know what you're talking about. Anyone in my position on my shitty salary would have done exactly the same."

Barlow pulled his shirt back into place – as if it suddenly mattered – and sat on the step of his van.

"Done what?"

"I just did what he told me to. A couple of hours ago, a bloke asked me if I wanted to earn a few quid. I asked how much, he said five hundred pounds, in cash, and he had it in his hand. I asked him who he wanted me to kill, and all he said was he wanted a parcel delivering to this address, and asked if it was on my rounds. I said, for five hundred quid I didn't care if it was on the moon: for five hundred quid I'd take it."

"Where were you when he asked?"

"Horsforth."

CHAPTER 55

April 5th (late afternoon)

Briggs had called Gardener five times while Reilly drove through the centre of Leeds and finally out on to the road that led them to Churchaven.

The phone remained unanswered.

Reilly eventually brought the car to a halt on Gardener's drive, noticing there were no other vehicles.

Having the advantage of being a very close friend, Reilly knocked on the front door and walked in. Briggs followed Reilly into the kitchen where they found a puzzled Malcolm staring at two teacups and a pot of cold tea, in the classic 'scratching the head' pose.

Startled, Malcolm nodded and greeted both men.

"Have you seen, Stewart?" Reilly asked.

"No, but he must have been here at some point. Look at this lot."

"Where have you been?"

"Only next door. I was in the potting shed when Harry popped round and said he'd just brewed up, so I went for a cup."

"And you haven't seen or heard from him?" asked Briggs.

"No. Is something wrong?"

"We're not sure," replied Briggs. They all sat at the kitchen table and Briggs briefly told them that he'd removed Gardener from the case and that shortly afterwards they had taken a call from him with some important information, which led to another corpse.

"Maybe we should ring him," suggested Reilly, fishing in his pocket for his mobile. "Shit, I've done it again, the bloody thing's still in the car."

"It's okay, Sean, I'll ring," said Briggs.

"You ring: I'll get *my* phone."

As Reilly came back in he saw Briggs and Malcolm rushing round the living room trying to locate the ring tone from Gardener's mobile. They eventually found it down the side of a chair.

"Something's wrong," said Reilly. "Cold tea on a kitchen worktop and his phone stuffed down the side of a chair. He left here in a hurry."

"So where's he gone, and why?" asked Briggs. "And why was it so important that he had to leave without calling us?"

"Christ! Would you look at that? My phone's not even switched on, so it isn't."

As soon as it was, Reilly had a voicemail message.

He listened intently.

"Is it your boss?" Briggs asked.

"No, Laura, her car's broken down. But she hasn't said where, just that she's phoned the recovery people."

"Is she okay?" asked Malcolm.

"I'll give her a ring at home, she should be there by now."

Briggs' concerned expression did little to abate a feeling in Reilly's mind.

The Irishman disconnected after ten rings.

"No answer?" asked Briggs.

"No."

He called her mobile.

On the third ring a male voice answered. "Erik speaking."

"Erik!" repeated Reilly. "Who the feck is Erik?"

"Oh, Mr. Reilly ... I'm sure you know the answer to that by now." The connection died.

Reilly tried again but the phone had been switched off.

"Erik?" Briggs asked.

"Corndell!"

Reilly threw the phone on the chair as if he was bowling a maiden over: it landed next to Gardener's.

"That bastard has Laura somewhere."

"Why Erik?" asked Briggs. "Who does he think he is now?"

"I suspect he thinks he's The Phantom," said Malcolm. "From the film."

"Oh Jesus!" replied Briggs.

"Who he is or who he thinks he is, doesn't matter," said Reilly. "*Where* he is, that's what I want to know. When I find out I'm going to kill him."

Reilly's temper had scaled new heights, his fists clenching and unclenching. As far as he was concerned, Corndell had signed his own death warrant.

"Calm down, Sean," said Briggs. "Losing your temper won't help Laura."

"Won't help Corndell either, when I find him. So where the hell is Stewart?" asked Reilly. "He must know something, which is why he's left here without telling anyone. He hasn't even left a note. That means he was in a hurry."

Reilly hoped so, because the only thing that would stop him wiping Corndell from the face of the Earth was if his partner found him first.

Briggs phoned and informed the station before putting his mobile in his pocket. "I think I know where they might be."

CHAPTER 56

April 5th (early-evening)

Gardener parked the car and switched off the engine. He remained in the vehicle, studying the warehouse opposite: what was thought to be a disused warehouse, for which he now knew better. In the sodium glow of the streetlamps it resembled the mausoleum he imagined it would be inside. The sky was clear and he noticed the start of a slight ground frost.

After the disagreement with the UPS driver, Gardener had gone back inside the house and forced himself to remain calm. It was the only way he was going to think rationally.

It was obvious who had paid the driver five hundred pounds to deliver the package containing a clue as to whom he held hostage.

But it didn't tell him where.

For that he had to rely on his police instinct and his memory, and a conversation with his father and his superior officer, Alan Briggs. The warehouse behind The Playhouse was where the watch committee had held their screenings: the very same group of people that had banned William Henry Corndell's film, *Imperfection*.

To Gardener's way of thinking, that's where he had to be.

He had then made a few phone calls and used his influence to obtain answers: the warehouse belonged to a film production company called *After Midnight Promotions*: which in turn belonged a man called Roger Balfour. It didn't take a genius to work out where that had come from. Two minutes studying the *Film Review's* revealed that Roger Balfour was in fact found murdered in his London home and the investigation led by Inspector Burke of Scotland Yard, all of which came from the film *London After Midnight* starring Lon Chaney.

Gardener phoned Martin Brown, who in turn called his friend at BT. *After Midnight* was a very active company with an Internet service provider: they had regularly made and received calls and the bill was paid on time. And Roger Balfour did in fact own the company; at least, that was the name provided.

Gardener also remembered it had been the name used to hire the missing limo that had picked up Leonard White from the hotel in Skipton.

All that evidence could only point to one man.

William Henry Corndell.

He'd then phoned the station to find out that Reilly and Briggs had gone to see Trevor Thorpe, after which, they were going to Corndell's with an arrest warrant.

Gardener figured they would have been far too late.

In the car, he glanced at the parcel he'd received and removed the photo and the newspaper clipping: the photo was of Laura. The clipping was the damning review she had written about Corndell's performance at the University theatre. So it was pretty obvious that he had Laura in there. And during the time that Gardener had spent with Fettle, William had probably taken his father.

So God knows what he was going to walk into.

Glancing at the dashboard clock it was six-fifteen. He knew

that he shouldn't walk in there alone, but calling for backup could waste vital time.

Nevertheless, he owed Sean that much.

Reaching into his jacket pocket revealed he did not have his mobile. In that instinctive moment of panic he tried every pocket he had, before reaching into the glove compartment, even though he knew it wouldn't be there.

A picture suddenly came to mind: the realisation that he had thrown the phone on to an armchair before he'd gone to see who was at the door: he obviously hadn't retrieved it.

So now he had no choice but to walk blindly into the situation alone – seeing as public phone boxes were a thing of the past.

Annoyed with himself, Gardener stepped out of the car, locked the door. He saw little point in scurrying over to the warehouse. Knowing what he knew about Corndell and how security conscious he was, there would most definitely be CCTV watching his every move.

He confidently strolled to the building and opened the side door next to a roller shutter door.

It was unlocked. As he thought: he was expected.

The first thing he noticed about the inside of the warehouse was the clinical silence. Standing still, he could hear absolutely nothing. That made things worse, because if he couldn't hear them he would almost certainly telegraph his own moves.

Glancing around, he saw what he presumed was the missing limo, and the large white truck: parked in front of a corridor with rooms either side. As he crept forward and glanced in, the first office had a computer terminal and monitor, which was on stand-by. There was also a variety of other electrical equipment including, as he'd suspected, CCTV. As the screens revealed, it was also linked to Corndell's house.

Opposite that office was another. Standing on a tripod was a movie camera. The room had plain, bland walls, with a chair in front of one of them. There was no carpet. Gardener suspected it was the room where William had donned his Inspector Burke make-up: filming the small video clue he had left them.

Further down the corridor Gardener sensed a strong odour of leather before he came to the last two rooms: on the left, a small kitchen: on the right, a complete replica of the room in Corndell's house, featuring mannequins and mirrors and benches: a number of shelves were crammed with tubes and bottles – make-up he would need to apply.

Gardener walked inside and inspected the costumes. The Hunchback from the night at the theatre was there, complete with blood spatter patterns. The vampire costume Chaney wore in *London After Midnight* was also present, and it too had blood spatter.

It was obvious now how William had managed to do all he had without being caught. The warehouse was his centre of operations, not his house.

Outside the room he glanced to his right. A curtain blocked entry into the main warehouse.

He waved it aside and stepped through, into another world. The view was magnificent, one to make Hollywood sit up and take notice.

Straight ahead was a French street scene reminiscent of yesteryear. The ground was covered in a fine layer of dust: two circular pavements around ten feet in diameter had been constructed on either side, each with old-fashioned gas lamps. The street continued toward a brick pavement, where he noticed more traditional lamps. A swirling mist hung around the lamps.

He realised that the warehouse roof had been raised in order to accommodate the showpiece, a huge gothic building that had been backlit very carefully in order to create an eerie ambience, particularly as the façade had been constructed with cylindrical columns and arches. A series of steps led up to a number of doors, each with a wire grille front save one: a glass dome sat on the roof of the building, and on either corner were a number of angels glancing in different directions.

To Gardener's left, he saw an open carriage, needing only a horse and passengers. He felt a small amount of empathy for William. He clearly could have been one of the world's greatest actors if only his obsession had not pushed him to the brink of lunacy. His eye for detail was unparalleled. How did he have the time and the patience to create such visually stunning effects?

Before he had any further chance to think about what to do, a spotlight lit up one of the arches. Approximately fifteen to twenty feet high, standing in one of them, was William, as far as Gardener could ascertain: no one else was that good with make-up.

"At last, Mr. Gardener."

The voice confirmed it all. He suspected a hidden microphone: even at that distance it was crisp and concise.

Gardener walked slowly forward as William launched into his running commentary.

"The Paris Opera House is one of the most beautiful buildings in the world, Mr. Gardener. It contains levels beyond levels of cellars, fountains, chandeliers – the history of which is very dark and very interesting; it even has it's own ghost!"

It's talking to me, thought Gardener, as he continued, with little idea what he was going to do, or in fact what he was going to say once he *was* up close. All he did know was that he was at an extreme disadvantage from the positions they were in.

William continued unabated: "Part of the mystique of the opera house Mr. Gardener, is the levels that it inhabits underground.

There are chorus rooms, green rooms, ball rooms, set rooms, cellars for waste props, closets, dressing rooms and many more kinds of rooms making up the building. The underground levels contain all sorts of gruesome objects from various operas that have been produced.

"Of course, Mr. Gardener, my replica is nowhere near as prolific, but it does contain a nasty surprise for you."

Gardener had reached the steps leading up to the only entrance door available. He had a much better view of William, and the character he was playing, *The Phantom*.

Even from where he was standing the attention to detail was so intricate that Gardener felt lost for words: all he could think was, what a waste.

William's head was little more than a skull with an up-tilted nose. The dark shading around his eyes gave them a hollow-eyed expression, emphasised even more by the line of colour under the lower eyelashes. And his ears seemed flattened against the sides of the skull, so much so that at first glance, he didn't appear to have any. His face was very pale and the head itself bore very little hair save a few fine strands.

Gardener was impressed and at the same time disturbed.

"How do you like what I've done, Mr. Gardener?"

"Where are they?" he asked.

"All in good time. Now, perhaps you can answer my question."

Gardener sighed, whether he liked it or not he would have to play the game.

"If you mean, do I actually enjoy watching lunatics mutilate people, leaving puzzles all around the city, I can't really say I am that impressed, Mr. Corndell. It's people like you who make my job extremely unpleasant."

"I'm not talking about that, you peasant!'

It was the first time Gardener had seen any real emotion from the man. And he realised he'd touched a raw nerve because Corndell's left eye had started to twitch, something he had noticed only once before when he thought he was being threatened.

William gripped the sides of the arch in which he was standing and Gardener found himself praying that he had not done too good a job with the exterior.

"But seeing as you brought up the subject, perhaps we can discuss what I've done ... why I've done it? Isn't that what you shrinks are all about?"

"I am not a psychiatrist, I'm a police officer."

Gardener was growing tired of the conversation and he certainly wasn't about to pander to the whims of an egomaniac, particularly when he was holding two people hostage who were not necessarily here.

William leaned forward. "You should be very interested in me..."

Gardener cut him dead. "That's where you're wrong. You're finished..."

William shouted and stopped *him* from continuing.

"How dare you insult a man of my ability? Can you imagine the impact that motion pictures had on the public of the 1920's?

"Long before cable networks, video tapes, DVD's and television, which brought movie stars right into your living room, the experience of a motion picture was magical, and going to a grand movie palace was a glamorous event."

He realised there was no stopping William now, even if he wanted to. He had the microphone, and there was probably very little he could do but let him have his finest hour. It would – after all – be his last, thought Gardener.

"A movie star set new fashion trends, for hair styles and clothes: many fans wanted to emulate their favourite actor or actress ... in his or her latest picture. Stars had loyal followers, none more so than Chaney. He was one of those performers that, despite a poor script and bad direction, managed to dominate his role.

"The man was a true legend, Mr. Gardener, and could only be admired. He was an inspiration and I have taken his place: I am the modern day master of the silver screen, the modern day 'man of a thousand faces.' Or at least I would have been if your father and his friends hadn't meddled. Who did they think they were? What right did they have to pass judgement on my masterpiece ... to ruin my career?

"Well let me tell you Mr. Gardener ... no right..."

Gardener cut him dead as he shouted.

"If you've quite finished, I have no wish to stand here all night while you give me what you think will amount to your finest hour. I want to know where my father and my friend's wife are. Now, if you don't tell me in precisely one minute, I'm going to forget that I'm a police officer and forget all about the law and if necessary I am going to chase you all around this fucking warehouse until I catch you: when I do I'm going to throttle you with my bare hands. Do you understand?"

William burst out laughing. "Such language, Mr. Gardener. I really don't think your superiors would take kindly to that. I do have rights, you know."

"His superior officer is having trouble with his eyes and ears at the moment," said Alan Briggs, standing in front of the curtain at the back of the warehouse. "And as for any rights, as far as I'm concerned, you gave up those when you started murdering people all over the city, and then decided to kidnap one of my officers' wives."

Briggs glanced at Gardener. "So you go right ahead, Stewart, do what you have to, so long as you get the information we need."

Briggs walked slowly towards Gardener, who had never been more pleased to see him than now.

But where was Sean?

Briggs whispered to him. "He doesn't have your Dad, Stewart. He's back at the station with a couple of junior officers. I left word with the desk sergeant to locate the rest of the squad and get them here, pronto."

Gardener turned and glanced at William. He wore a long dark cloak with one arm swept across his chest: even his clothes were covered in dust for emphasis. The other arm was reaching to something that Gardener could not see because of a low-slung velvet drape.

"Where is she?" asked Gardener. "Your time is up."

"How true that statement is, Mr. Gardener," said William.

Gardener realised how much confidence William had. You couldn't do what he'd done without self-assurance. That thought alone was worrying, because right now, he was holding all the cards.

"You'll find what you're looking for inside. And by the way ... best of luck."

William pulled the rope behind the low-slung drape.

Two things happened.

Firstly, he disappeared up behind the curtain to god knows where.

Secondly, the front doors of the opera house clicked open.

CHAPTER 57

The warehouse lights dimmed, leaving only those of the opera house for guidance.

"Right, forget that mad bastard for the moment," said Briggs. "Let's get inside and see what we have to do."

Both men took the steps two at a time and Gardener went through the door first.

The inside was as magnificent as the outside, only much more disturbing.

They were in a graveyard. An earthy smell and soft underfoot told him that the maniac had used soil – and not for appearance. Peering into the distance, Gardener could make out a series of randomly scattered tombstones and, what he suspected was mock trees. On the extreme right and left of the building were in fact two shrines: on either side of the headstones were two angels staring down at the names on those headstones. A small amount of green coloured lighting added to the emotional scene. Other than that there was very little light.

Gardener felt a breeze skate across the back of his neck, forcing him to shiver. He really didn't like it at all.

"Jesus Christ!" whispered Briggs. "How does he think of all this?"

"He's disturbed," replied Gardener. "He doesn't live in the same world we do. Everything about him tells you that."

Gardener moved forward and bumped into something solid, causing him to curse. Whatever it was must have grazed his shin.

"Steady, Stewart," said Briggs: he then shouted extremely loudly: "He could have given us some fucking lighting to work with!"

Which is precisely what their host did.

One by one, towards the back of the graveyard, four powerful halogen lamps lit the scene before them.

Gardener would have preferred the darkness

CHAPTER 58

William chuckled to himself as he surveyed his handiwork through the roof beams. Two police officers completely out of their depth, unaware of the situation they were caught up in, and therefore unable to help: something to which they were unaccustomed.

He reached forward and switched on the electric pump, which was connected to a water tank and a pipe. Slowly, the water started to pour out, in Laura's direction.

Laughing even more, William was thinking of how much he had enjoyed himself recently. He'd not had so much fun since disposing of Nick Craven and Peter Holliwell. He'd thought that was his finest performance to date.

But as Gardener had mentioned only minutes previously, his finest hour was yet to come.

He gripped the rope even tighter.

CHAPTER 59

Puzzled, Gardener noticed that he had bumped into a real tree stump. And that the headstones all around them contained names of all the people he knew: his father, the rest of the watch committee ... and even one for himself and Sean Reilly.

The shrines bore the names of William's parents: Wallace and Betty.

Corndell junior had a very sick mind.

His masterpiece confirmed it: the inside of the opera house was more unsettling than anything he'd ever seen.

Gardener and Briggs both ran forward at the same time, throwing up thick clods of earth and struggling to keep their balance.

Swearing and cursing, Briggs fell over, face-first.

Gardener stopped to help.

"No," shouted Briggs, his beard infested with soil. "Go and help Laura, she's more important."

He was soon on his feet and the pair of them reached a platform, breathless because of the energy it had taken.

The podium that William had used at the university theatre, the one featured in The Hunchback of Notre Dame had been illuminated by the four strobe lights. Chained to it – as Quasimodo had been – was Laura. Her hands and legs were tethered, connected to the base with rings, the type used on the nose of a bull. Four padlocks made sure she was not going anywhere. But more alarming was the crocodile clips gripping each chain, leading to somewhere inside or underneath the platform. Above her head, a constant stream of water poured on to her fragile body. That could only mean one thing. If they didn't release her, she was in for one hell of a shock.

If it had been anyone else, Gardener could have handled it, but Laura's terrified expression was crippling him, reminding him of the night Sarah had been shot, before dying in his arms on the streets of Leeds.

Laura's eyes were wide and dark, and the pupils so deep she resembled an owl. Her mouth had been sealed with tape. Her hair was clinging to her face, and Gardener suspected that the stream of water had only recently started, which meant that William was probably above them right now, still controlling everything.

The puddle of water around Laura's feet was spreading outwards, running off the podium.

"Quick, get the tape off her face," said Gardener.

"Don't touch her!"

Corndell's voice reverberated around the building.

So, the bastard was watching their every move. Gardener could not put into words how repulsed he felt. He hated being manipulated: knowing full well that he was now going to have to unravel a puzzle, and the maniac overseeing everything would do his best to hinder their progress.

"If you want to help her you'll have to listen very closely," said Corndell.

Gardener peered above, the only place he could be.

Briggs was also staring into the rafters.

Gardener's temper was shortening by the minute.

"Come on then, get it over with."

Corndell continued. "Everything you see is real: the chains, the padlocks, and the crocodile clips that lead inside the podium are all connected to a charger. The switch however is under my control not yours. There are four padlocks, which means there are four keys, and of course, they could be anywhere. And just to make things more interesting, the whole thing is set to a timer, and you don't have long. As I said before, Mr. Gardener, best of luck."

"Shit." Briggs ran forward and wrestled his way on to the platform, glancing at the timer. "Seven minutes left, Stewart."

Gardener had set off in search of the keys, but where the hell did you start? Four keys in seven minutes, and they could be anywhere.

CHAPTER 60

Briggs turned to Laura to remove the masking tape. "It'll hurt Laura, but if I do it fast you won't feel a thing."

Her whole body shook and she said something under the tape, but it was the expression in her eyes that warned Briggs he should contemplate a different action.

He took hold of the tape and very slowly peeled it back. Despite how much it must have been hurting, Laura was a little more relaxed about having it done that way. Finally, when it was all removed, she dipped her head forward and spat out one of the keys.

"Are you okay?"

"For now," replied Laura. "But I won't be in seven minutes."

"Sorry," said Briggs. "We'll get you out of here, don't worry."

He kneeled down and tried the key in one of the padlocks, instantly realising that it was too small. And all the locks were the same size. So if it didn't undo any of the locks, what the hell was it for?

He peered upwards.

Laura's expression darkened.

CHAPTER 61

Gardener reached the headstone bearing Laura's name, immediately raking his hands through the soil, scattering it much like a dog would. He felt so useless, but giving up was not an option. The keys had to be somewhere: pure logic persuaded him that one of them would be here.

In no time at all he struck lucky. The first key glinted from the reflection of one of the halogen lamps. He picked it up and shouted to Briggs, who was now in the graveyard.

Gardener ran towards Laura. "Keep searching, sir."

He jumped on to the podium and cradled Laura's head in his hands. He kissed her forehead. "You're going to be okay, I promise."

"Where the hell is Sean?" she asked.

"I don't know."

The key fitted the last padlock he tried but the sigh of relief from them both as it unlocked was like winning the lottery.

He glanced at the timer; five minutes: three keys to go. It was an impossible task. As he jumped off the platform he noticed Laura wipe her face with her free hand. He couldn't begin to imagine how she was feeling.

Briggs shouted and Gardener glanced in his direction. He'd found the second key in a tree.

The pair of them passed each other in the graveyard, Gardener aware of the futile task that lay ahead.

A thought suddenly struck him: what if all the keys were not inside the opera house? That frightened him even more but he knew it was a thought worth contemplating.

Where the hell *was* Sean? And the rest of the squad! Even though there was no guarantee, the more of them they had, the better off they would be.

As he turned and glanced back at the podium, Briggs had freed Laura's other arm and she was now desperately clawing at the chains.

Gardener ran outside and down the steps. It was a feeling that nagged him and he was stuck between a rock and a hard place. Should he continue inside, with Briggs? Or search outside, because he knew that William was insane enough to have pulled such a stunt?

As he glanced around the warehouse, he really didn't have a clue where to start. And another minute had passed: that left four; somehow, somewhere, they had to be lucky.

Another thought: was William telling the truth? *Had* everything been connected to an electrical charge? Or was he simply trying to frighten them witless? Whatever, he couldn't take the risk.

The silence increased the tension. Gardener glanced upwards to the arch that William had been in. Could the key be there? He stared at the warehouse floor, and to the gas lamps. Was it there? He glanced to his right and to the lone carriage, without a horse and passengers. Was it in there?

His watch told him he had three and a half minutes left.

It was so fucking useless, standing here with no idea. He wasn't playing a computer game. None of them had three lives.

IMPERFECTION

Where the hell was it?

Something about the lone carriage drew him. It bore a 'Keystone' logo on the side and that could simply be coincidence. And then again, maybe William didn't want to make it too difficult because he had a big finale in store. It may not be in the carriage but he had to start somewhere.

The smell of leather upholstery was pretty strong. Glancing around the floor of the vehicle he saw nothing he wanted. Leaping inside he checked all the seats, nothing there. He jumped back out and dropped to the ground on all fours, glancing underneath.

Bingo!

On a hook, screwed into the frame underneath, was a key.

At least he hoped it was the key they needed.

He ran into the opera house as fast as he could and struggled through the soil up to the podium. The third key released a leg, leaving only one.

With two minutes to go.

He turned his head from side to side and saw Briggs digging near the tombstones.

"Alan! Forget them, the last key won't be under any of those."

"Well it has to be somewhere ... we just can't stand around and do nothing."

Gardener glanced at Laura. "Any ideas?"

"No, I wasn't conscious, I woke up on here."

Briggs came back to the podium. "What about inside? The least we can do now is try and stop the bastard thing from going off and electrocuting her."

Gardener jumped off and faced the back of the podium.

There were two doors, held together by a padlock.

"Oh Christ." Gardener fell to his knees. "Not another."

He angled his head towards his superior officer, hoping and

praying he had an answer. He thought of Sarah, and wondered if history would repeat itself, only now, someone else's wife would die in his arms.

Briggs searched his pocket.

"Try this." He had produced another key.

It fitted.

And then the lights went out.

CHAPTER 62

William howled with laughter, his whole body shaking. He was having so much fun. And they hadn't seen the half of it yet.

He stopped laughing and kneeled down, peering into the darkness, tickled pink by the fact that they had been disabled once more. They must have thought they were doing so well, finding three of the keys: their idea of going into the podium and disconnecting the charger had been a great one, but he couldn't risk them doing that, because the other key was in there. So he had been left with no choice but to turn out the lights again.

William stood and gripped the rope in his right hand, chuckling again. Boy were they going to have some light in a minute, precisely all the time they had left.

He turned round, deciding to watch from the arch he had vacated when talking to Gardener.

"No you don't, sunshine," said Sean Reilly, punching William straight in the mouth: more than once.

William fell back and disappeared through the beams.

CHAPTER 63

Gardener heard the crash and glanced upwards, despite still being unable to see anything.

Suddenly the lights came back on.

Briggs was at the other side of the podium: he shouted, informing Gardener that he had thirty seconds.

Gardener saw William stuck upside down between the beams, precariously balancing, staring straight at them, his expression a mixture of fear and perverse delight.

He fumbled with the lock on the cupboard.

Briggs shouted that he had twenty seconds and to fucking well hurry-up.

The lock eventually opened and Gardener was faced with was a mass of wires, but the glint of a key underneath them all caught his eye.

He reached in and removed it.

Another crash from above and what he thought was his partner's voice diverted his attention for a split second as William fell a little further.

Briggs shouted. "For Christ's sake, Stewart, you've only got ten seconds!"

Laura was panicking, screaming for his help.

Gardener flipped the key into the lock. It clicked. Everything came loose and he scooped Laura up in his arms and they both fell away from the podium into the soil.

William hit the platform with a resounding crash. There had only been enough length on the rope – which had formed a tight noose around his wrist – for his feet to rest on the edge of the base.

"For God's sake do something!" he shouted, staring at Gardener.

That was all the time he had before the building turned negative.

The strobe lights went out and the electrical charge from the podium encircled William's body. His hair stood on end, his eyes bulged, and Gardener would swear that he created the vision the movies would have us all believe, that for a few seconds, they actually saw William's whole skeletal frame: the skull in particular, a row of wide, smiling teeth.

The electrical current had been so severe that it had straightened William's body into a standing position with his arms and legs spread wide

The charge suddenly stopped and the strobe lights came back on, as Reilly swung down a rope from the roof into the soil.

A whipping sound diverted everyone's attention as the rope around William's wrist suddenly caught fire: the flames shooting upwards into the rafters and setting the beams alight.

"Come on, get out!" shouted Briggs.

Reilly grabbed Laura and hugged her tightly. "Are you okay?"

She nodded.

More of the roof beams were aflame and in no time at all the building was set to become a raging inferno.

All four of them trampled like elephants through the thick earth below their feet, finally making it to the steps of the opera house. As they almost fell down them, a creak and a slam made

Gardener glance behind him. The only door that had ever been available for entry and exit had slammed shut.

William had planned everything down to the last detail.

Gardener bent forward with his hands on his knees, breathless, unable to believe how lucky they had been.

"Stewart, move yourself, for God's sake," shouted Briggs.

Like an alarm in his head, he realised something. If William had triggered that building to lock, he may well have triggered the main doors in the event that they had foiled him.

Gardener and the others bolted for the entrance. The doors were still open. Once on the street, they ran across to where all the cars had been parked and Briggs called the fire brigade on his mobile.

EPILOGUE

It was close to midnight when the fire chief pronounced the warehouse safe and secure: standing a little way from the two officers, Gardener heard the conversation between the chief and his colleagues. The building had been reduced to an outer shell. Everything inside must have been so old because the flames had caught extremely quickly.

All four of them had sat beside the car listening to the cracking and banging as the timber joists fell: and windows exploded as the fire raged out of control.

A crowd had gathered shortly before the fire services had arrived, some of them asking if they were okay. God knows the impression they must have given. One of the assembled onlookers had even gone to a burger bar around the corner and brought back tea and coffee and snacks for them.

Laura and Sean had stuck together like glue before he had finally taken her home around nine-thirty. The pair of them had enough.

"You never did tell me where Sean had got to," said Gardener to Briggs.

IMPERFECTION

His superior officer was a picture: the lenses of his glasses were so thickly coated with grime it must have been impossible to see through them; his face had been covered in soot and soil, and even a vagrant would have turned his nose up at the clothes he was wearing.

"I wasn't really sure myself," said Briggs, taking a sip of coffee. "When we got out of the car he told me to go inside. He said that if William saw all of us together he would have the advantage. And he would probably be cocky enough to think that we were stupid enough not to have split up."

Briggs paused, staring at the shell of the burnt out warehouse.

"He also said he would be much more use to Laura if he couldn't see the state she was in. At least he wouldn't be distracted."

Briggs glanced at Gardener.

"He was on a mission, Stewart. I've never seen determination like it. Even if I'd argued with him it wouldn't have mattered, he'd have done what he wanted anyway. As it was, I didn't get time, he was away around the building well before I had chance to think about what he'd said."

Gardener remained silent, thinking about what he'd heard before he'd managed to free Laura. He was pretty sure that Sean had manipulated William into that position, and very probably kicked him through the rafters on to the podium: though he seriously doubted there had been any intent to electrocute him because he couldn't have known.

Could he?

Briggs seemed to have read Gardener's mind.

"You don't think he killed him deliberately, do you, Stewart? It's just that, I thought I heard his voice before you unlocked Laura ... you know ... as if he was forcing him through the beams."

Gardener thought about his answer.

"I don't think any of us could be sure about anything we saw and heard at that moment, there was too much going on, sir."

Gardener stood up, desperately wanting to be away from the scene.

"Anyway, what does it matter now?"

The fire chief approached before Briggs made any reply.

"Which one of you is in charge?"

"I am," replied Briggs.

"Fire Officer Marshall." He shook hands with Briggs. "Everything's safe and sound for tonight. The council will be here in the morning and decide what further safety measures to take."

"Did you find the body?" asked Gardener.

"Body?" repeated Marshall.

"Yes, I'm afraid we couldn't save him," said Gardener, his heart in his mouth. He'd seen the bastard die: there couldn't possibly have been any escape.

The expression on Marshall's face was not a good one.

"We found three."

Briggs glanced at Gardener, horrified.

He waited while the chief was out of earshot. "Who else was in there?"

Gardener thought before replying. "Did you see the names on the two main shrines?"

"Can't say as I did," replied Briggs.

"They belonged to his parents ... but I didn't think the bodies would *be* there."

Briggs said nothing.

"I'm all in, sir. I'm going home."

Briggs nodded. "You take care, Stewart. You did a good job in there."

Briggs turned and walked in the direction of his car.

Gardener stood by his, glancing at the warehouse, thinking about everything that had happened. He realised how fitting the title of Corndell's film had been.

Imperfection.

It really did sum him up.

IMPERFECTION

ACKNOWLEDGEMENTS

The British Fantasy Society published the Ray Clark's first work in 1995, a 3,000 word essay on fellow writer, Graham Masterton. In 1996, a chance meeting in a London docklands hotel at a BFS Convention with Matt Williams (and Graham Masterton - himself later in the same evening) eventually led to Ray's first big break: the 1998 publication of Manitou Man: The World of Graham Masterton, nominated for both the World and British Fantasy Awards. Success followed with a number of short stories in various magazines between 1998 and 2003. 2007 saw the author's first collection of short stories under the title of The Lord of Misrule and Other Stories, released by an American publisher. The following year, the self-publication of a stand-alone horror novel, Calix, a terrifying psychological, rollercoaster ride into the unknown using the Salem Witch Trials as its backdrop. In 2009: Ray's short story, Promises To Keep made the final shortlist for the best short story award from The Tom Howard Foundation. The publication of Misrule 2: The Next Generation soon followed. In 2010: the short story, Purple Rain was published in the American quarterly publication, Carpe Articulum: A Twist in the Taste was also published in a collection by The English Heritage, entitled, Whitby Abbey: Pure Inspiration (available at Amazon and most leading retailers). 2012: The Priest's Hole, a horror novel published by Damnation Books in the U.S. Available as a paperback and a variety of electronic versions. In 2012: Canadian publisher, Double Dragon Press, re-released Calix with new artwork, both electronically and in paperback. In 2013: Canadian Publisher, Double Dragon published A Devil's Dozen, a collection of short horror stories. 2014: a new crossover novel entitled Seven Secrets from U.S. Publisher, Damnation Books. 2015: a second short story collection entitled, A Detective's Dozen, from Canadian publisher, Double Dragon. 2016: the first in the author's IMP crime series set in Leeds featuring Detectives Gardener and Reilly, entitled Impurity, from U.S. Publisher, Caliburn Press.